# Hailiorea

## Adam J. Austin

### Aswain Books

www.Aswainbooks.com

I dedicate this book to my daughter, Vivien Austin. Thank you for all the joy you've brought and for teaching me what's most important. Keep growing strong, but not too fast, please.

# Prologue

Andy, my brother told me several times that you're a writer with integrity so I'm going to go ahead and trust you. I don't usually trust anyone until I get to know them but I value his judgment. First, let's get started with some background info and a few rules I want you to follow. You can put this part in with the rest of the book if you want. Call it the "Intro" or something. You decide, you're the writer.

Rule number one is for you to write my story as I tell it. You should know, I'm not the most descriptive person. If I see a flower, I'll tell you if it's big or little or maybe what color it is but I don't generally go into detail on what type of plant it is, the curvature of its petals or how the effing light bounces off its surface. You can add in descriptions as you picture them in your head but keep from over embellishing things. No added characters or exaggerations. Believe me; this stuff is wild enough as is. Just make everything readable.

Next, no swearing. I curse, a lot. It's not something I'm proud of but it's who and how I am. Call it a pet peeve but young people might read this stuff and I HATE it when kids swear. I don't want my story to encourage them to be foul mouthed, disrespectful jerks. Cursing is for adults. It makes my skin crawl when kids do it. I've already swore a couple times so just replace those words with things like 'freak' and 'stuff.' I guess words like 'pissed,' 'hell' and 'damn' are ok. Christ, I bet they hear worse things on a daily basis anyways.

Third rule: Just write the damn story and share it with people. I rarely say please but I'm going ahead and saying it. Ok, so one more time, please. I can't make you do anything which means my story is at your mercy. You're recording my words right now. Just type them up and get it out there. This is my last shot at helping people.

I'm doing this on the fly so more stuff might come to me later. I know, I'm a pain in the ass but you'll just have to deal with it, sorry.

Now for some details about who I am and where I come from. Oh, I'm not going to get into how we've been able to talk just yet. That can come later. My story is full of stuff you'd consider supernatural so we'll take baby steps. Hell, I'm not even really sure how this all works but whatever, we're here together and that's what matters. I have no idea how much time I have, ten minutes or ten years, so it's best to get on with it.

My name is Jason Sworn and I'm talking to you from a not too distant future. I'm thirty-five years old and won't be born for several decades after the point in time you're in right now. From what I've learned I know a lot is going to happen between your time and mine. Our worlds are two entirely different places.

Every government, every nation, every person is going to change. The norms of old are now considered radical ideals; the fears and fantasies of your time are my reality. Jesus, even landmasses have changed. It's like the Earth itself was swayed by the upheaval.

In essence, the world became one giant contradiction. Some people foolishly dreamed of returning to the past while others strove for a new, impossibly unrealistic future. Security and stability were both prayed for and despised. Unbelievable goals of unity were achieved but corruption ran rampant. Sometimes the lying and cheating were so stupidly obvious it was almost comical. The damn shadows have been hidden right out in the open, in plain view for everyone to see and ignore. It's like seeing a full grown man literally steal candy from a child, the kid protests but everyone agrees the treat belonged to the man the whole time. The people gave up because they were beaten down to the point of feeling powerless and no longer caring. Any sense of justice had been nearly destroyed from most everyone.

I don't know how much better things were in your time but I know bad things have happened and we've all been damaged. It's like, shoot, I don't know, like everyone was tainted or corrupted somehow. A stain or stench we just couldn't ever wash off. I can't exactly pinpoint it but it's just a nagging feeling in my gut, a feeling I've learned to take note of over the last several years.

That being said, though, people are still people. Some are decent and others are pricks. I bet that's the way it always has and always will be. I chose to contact you at this particular time because I think it's far enough away to where you haven't been tainted yet. You're at a point where people can still change outcomes and can still make a difference.

Before I get into my account of world events, I'd like to address the whole 'don't mess with the past' thing. I've heard people with bigger heads than mine chatter on about how telling people their future will change the course of history. I've heard others babble on about multiple dimensions and how the past can't be changed. Instead, a new parallel universe would be created with different outcomes. All in all, I really don't care. I'm too tired and I've been through too much. Let's keep going.

I'd say I'm basically a warrior looking for purpose in life. I'm not a scientist or much of a philosopher. I've been selfish a good portion of my life and called a prick or worse on a near daily basis. That said, I know I'm a good man and I think this is my last chance to do some good for the world. I don't know if telling you all this will change anything or make your world turn out better than mine did but I feel like I need to give you a glimpse, a warning of how things can and probably will unfold.

I might as well describe what I look like. I can at least paint that picture for you a little bit. Modesty isn't my thing. I look effing great. I'm an inch over six feet tall and weigh a bit less than two hundred pounds with a muscular build. I have black hair, usually kept short, ice blue eyes, a healthy set of teeth and, on the rare occasion, a smile to die for. My only physical blemish is a good sized scar on the right side of my neck. I'd like to say the gash came as a result of some valiant effort on my part but no. I'll explain later, early in my story.

I remember being a kid and watching a show on TV called 'Order and Justice' or something... Cops were always catching rapists and sex offenders. Anyways, I sort of look like the main white guy on that show, if that helps at all. Whatever, I'm not doing this to make women swoon so I'll get back on track.

Over the next thirty odd years things are really going to change. You're going to see and hear about huge battles of ideals and treachery all over the world. On the surface, the root of the chaos is going to appear to come from powerful tyrants and dictators fighting against others who oppose them.

Outbreaks of violence will spring up all over the place, spreading like wildfire. Each instance will be contained but the embers will keep flowing and growing beneath the surface. The battles will be fought with bravery, fear, will power, cooperation and, sadly, the suspension of liberties. The last part is what really effed things up.

The powers that be said their goal was to defeat and protect us from evil but the laws and rules they passed caused more harm than actual help. The bad guys kept right along with their horrors and all the new regulations managed to do was turn many regular, peace loving people into radicals who were then, in turn, labeled terrorists themselves. I know now that these 'terrorists' or 'radical idealists,' as they were also called, were really just good people who didn't trust the government which was steadily growing more and more tyrannical. A lot of those 'radicals' who fought to bring things back to the way they were paid with their lives.

Like I said, this will go on for years, intensifying as time goes on. The Americans and most of Europe will struggle through massive political unrest, economic hardships and waning freedoms. Asia, India, the Middle East and Africa will become perpetual war zones. The fighting will be over several causes but in the end I suppose the true driving force will be greed. Greedy, murderous groups and governments lusting for more and more power. The entire globe will be engulfed in conflict and everyone will feel its sting.

The tricky part of it all will be that no one will know who their real enemies were. Neighbors will thrash out and hurt each other over differing ideals and suspicions. This will make the 'wars' impossible to win or lose, never ending. Think about it, with trust all but vanished, how is anyone supposed to fight an enemy you can't really see? The answer will be comically blunt; we'll look where we couldn't look before.

A man will enter into the world scene with an invention that will revolutionize everything. His name is August Cross, a relative recluse until his coming out who held so much wealth it'll be rumored he could buy his own continent. It won't be known by the public where or how he gained his fortune and it won't matter because he'll double it with the unveiling of his creation, the Cell Truth; a lie detection device so efficient not a single lie has beaten it.

The CT test, which causes violent, painful spasms to the user should he or she lie, arrived just in time. As the world continued to reel from the multiple, endless wars, several powerful world leaders will begin to outright rape citizens of whatever rights they had. This will, again, all be done in the name of restoring stability and most people will abide. It seemed so many years of pain, loss, death and fighting without any measure of success will be enough to break the collective will of the world. The CT test will finally offer a way of knowing who the real enemies were.

The common tagline for the Cell Truth will be, 'You can't hide when you can't lie.' Its administration will create a lot of opposition for its violation of privacy but the test's overall support will be greater. Most people will be so thankful to have the blindfold off they'll be more than willing to give up their deepest, darkest secrets just to confirm they weren't murderers or terrorists. Of course… oftentimes the judges on such cases were criminals themselves.

The test will require tremendous manpower to ensure it reaches all corners of the planet. The 'Truth Coalition,' made up of soldiers and citizens, will be the largest operation in terms of personnel under the flag of the United Nations. Most will cheer the actions, some will fear it and others will see it as the beginning of the death of sovereignty.

With the test in full force, the five years following will be known as the Truth Wars. The majority of fighting and bloodshed will occur over the 'terror zones' I mentioned before. At first, the introduction and implementation of the test will add fuel to fire, creating more fear, panic and fighting. Still, by knowing what people think and what their motives are, the armies of truth will be more united and powerful than ever.

Information will eventually get out, supposedly leaked by insiders, that several leaders and their armies were actually working in secret with many of the hostile groups. Not only that, many of the terrorist armies were actually pawns for select leaders, used to create fear and panic which would then allow the same leaders to consolidate further power in order to deal with the openly known evil regimes. Needless to say, even in their collectively shocked stupor, the populations of the world were outraged. As a result, the United Nations will be disbanded due to its utter inadequacy. Ironic that it was the UN's own zealous deployment of the CT test which led to its eventual downfall. It will, however, be replaced.

Around my twentieth birthday, nearly every nation in the world, bewildered by the outcomes of the Truth Wars, will sign into existence a new world government body. Commonly called the Global Union or 'GU,' the actual name will be Tehlasrin, a word from an extinct language we're told means unity. The Union will have resistance but it will endure. Its corruption and vile wickedness will only grow over time.

The governance of Tehlasrin will be absolute. Several countries will merge into various sub-states within the Union and the governments of all nations will answer to the GU's appointed leaders. By appointed, I mean men and women with the most money, power and political influence. Those with even half a functioning brain would doubt a single vote they'd ever cast mattered in the slightest.

The Global Union will: Offer security and order; diminish freedoms and nearly all personal privacy; prevent organizations from inciting any form of dissidence, most of all, rebellion; 'tolerate' the practice of various religions individually, any gatherings of more than two people for any faith based purpose will be banned; outlaw mass protests with severe punishment; demand any and all complaints be petitioned through local government military officials; remove any right for civilians to own or carry firearms; allow an independent press but only so long as it doesn't incite anger or excitement; supply a united world army comprised of soldiers from around the globe; require extensive permission to travel; disarm and abolish all nuclear weapons.

As I mentioned, at the same time all this was going on, odd geological occurrences were taking place. The most note-worthy of these were the formation of new, state sized, landmasses that will dot the world's oceans. Some scientists will try to give explanations on the phenomena but none of them will agree and really won't have the slightest clue.

All but a few of these new islands will be quickly gobbled up by the GU. Those exceptions will, of course, be claimed by a select group of the rich and powerful. The largest and most fertile of all will be taken by August Cross. By calling in on various favors from GU leaders and by donating a sizable amount if his fortune, Cross's island, which will be about the size of the old state of Michigan, will become a prosperous nation of its own. It will be officially named Aswain, but people will refer to it as 'Cross Isle' or, in a more comedic way, 'Pacificus.' Like the handful of others, the island nation will actually exist freely, outside the jurisdiction of the GU.

These independent states will be scrutinized, admired and jealously ridiculed by most people. Many will become suspicious and fearful of what activities transpire there but, nevertheless, August's nation will prosper and grow.

As for me, I'll live an unhappy life growing up, mostly due to self-imposed hardships thanks to my own stubbornness and stupidity. Leading up to the beginning of my story I'll have very few friends and a handful of brief, lousy flings with various women, all of which ended badly.

My strongest and only healthy relationship growing up will be with my older brother, Mark. When he dies, I'll believe I had nothing left. Like I said, he was, or will be a fan of your writing.

The only other area where I'll show success is in the military which I'll join at the age of twenty-two. That may seem odd at first, given my distaste for authority, but it'll make more sense later.

After an exceptional four year run, my military career will end, even worse, much, much worse than any of my romantic relationships. From there, things only get even more depressing. That's where I'll begin.

# Chapter 1

Tom, a man in his early sixties, smiled as he stirred the steaming, gray mess of goop sitting inside the flimsy, white, Styrofoam bowl in front of him. His snow white hair was disheveled and his wrinkled face showed signs of pain and wear behind his dark rimmed glasses. Despite all that, the smile on his face was genuine. Somehow, the old bastard was content.

I scoffed.

"What is this thing, this magic, this spark we call life?" He looked directly at me while he spoke. The thick lenses made his murky, gray eyes look a lot bigger than they actually were. "You shouldn't be so angry. Look," he paused, studying me, "life is a blessing, not a curse. Try to see some of the splendor in the world."

I glared back at him, wanting to rip his withered head clean off his neck. I hated the effer because he was so optimistic. The prick taunted me with it. How dare he even smile in this place? We were in hell and the son of a bitch was happy. I grunted, knowing full well the only thing keeping me from digging my fingers into his throat were the powerful meds flowing through my veins.

Turning from Tom's revoltingly kind face, I looked around at the sterile, bland, white room I'd come to despise. A dozen other men were crammed in the space with Tom and me, sitting shoulder to shoulder at long tables. It was the same group I ate every meal with. My pod.

There wasn't a decent man in the bunch and I didn't like any of them. To make things worse, space was extremely limited. Every second of meal was filled with bumping elbows and jerks breathing down my neck. Each contact set me on edge, sending waves of annoyance up and down my spine. I wanted to roar. Sure enough, another bump came from the man sitting to my right. I fumed.

We sat and ate our disgusting breakfast simply because starvation was only slightly worse. After more than a year, my body still wanted to expel each mouthful of the sludge.

The small mess hall was, for the most part, identical to the rest of the structure; sickly clean, white and plain. The walls, chairs and long rectangular table were also all white. Ventilation fans were constantly humming their monotonous, boring drum. Artificial lighting spat out a never ending glow of painful brightness that made everyone's skin look sickly and green in color.

The setting alone was enough to make my stomach turn but the keepers were the ones that truly made the Morbal Foundation for Rehabilitation a living nightmare. They tortured us regularly, seeming to savor every moment. Sure enough, several of the so called authority figures, who were jokingly there for our aid and protection, filled the crowded space with the rest of us.

I looked at Tom and felt my face fold into a dark scowl. The setting sucked, the food was repulsive, the guards were monsters and my fellow patients were pathetic, annoying slobs that took up space, crowding me into a near claustrophobic panic attack.

It wasn't clear how many inmates were kept within the facility's walls with me but I guessed the number was in the thousands. The keepers split everyone up pretty well, segregating us within our own pods of forty people.

The separation was fine with me. I hated just about everyone that crossed my path so it was just as well I saw fewer people than the place held. In over a year, I only bothered to learn the names of eight others. The rest were just blank, worthless faces I didn't give two damns about.

Another, ever so slight, bump on my right arm from my neighbor. I snapped without having time to think and reached over, grabbed the man's wrist with my left hand, pulled his body to me and then drove my right elbow hard into the side of his ribs. The moves were seamless and hardly anyone noticed. My neighbor only groaned, too drugged, weak or afraid to protest.

Tom noticed, of course. "Jason!" He said in an excited but low tone. "Control yourself. We're all packed in here like sardines and none of us like it. You can't let it get to you."

I snarled in defiance, angry at my ears for letting his stupid voice and stupid words into my brain.

At that moment, a different man sitting across from me began to sob. Sam, it was always Sam, a name I couldn't ignore no matter how hard I tried. "Lord…" He buried his face in his hands. "Help me, God. Please." The last word was nothing more than a whimper but it was still enough to set off others around the table. They barked at him to shut his yap.

Instead of joining them, I just shoveled another spoonful of slime into my mouth, trying to close out the world.

"There's so much more to your life than you know. You have no idea. Many of us are more than human." Tom spoke quietly, his eyes cut around the room as if making sure no one else was listening. He looked back at me and raised his large, white eyebrows. "You don't believe me but it's true."

Idiot. I dropped my spoon and curled my hands into fists.

"You're in pain." He continued. "We all are. This won't last forever. You need to have faith. Keep aware and listen to what God has set out for you."

A burning hot rush of blood flooded through my body. "SHUT THE HELL UP!" It was a roar, ferocious and wild, an animal warning. I couldn't help but enjoy the surge of power created from my anger "God? What God?"

"Calm down, Sworn!" One of the keepers ordered.

The command didn't register, I kept going. "Look around, moron. You think this is beautiful? Lovely? Magical? We're cursed, old man, doomed to spend the rest of our worthless lives in this asylum. We're tortured every day, fed vomit in a bowl and I want to rip my eyes out just to escape the whiteness. I HATE IT!"

"Sit down!" Another keeper commanded.

I didn't even realize I'd stood up while shouting down on Tom. I spared a quick glance at the guards who were all armed with powerful and painful shock gloves. With a snort, I sat back down and tried to eat a bit more.

My outburst seemed to have made the drum of the vents grow louder and I could feel slight vibrations under my bare feet. The same thing happened every time someone got excited and I guessed the keepers were pumping in additional chemicals into the air to drug and tranquilize any potential troublemakers.

Sparing a glance around the room, the clock showed it was eight a.m., nearly therapy time. Christ. I knew eating this slop was not only painful but also pointless. Therapy sessions usually ended with me throwing up everything I'd eaten in the past hour. My body started to shake at the thought of the impending daily ritual of torture. I cursed myself for being too weak, too cowardly to just end it all.

Across from me, Tom had the gall to keep going. He cleared his throat before continuing, "Yes, it's bright." His voice was cool and collected. "There aren't any shadows we can hide ourselves in but still, it's better than living in darkness."

My eyes slowly, grudgingly rolled up to take in the old, optimistic face. My teeth clamped onto my bottom lip. I could taste drops of my drug filled blood on my tongue. A sharp, icy claw dug into my chest and pierced my heart.

A nod then a slight smirk painted Tom's face. "I used to be like you." He licked his lips and pointed a bony finger at me. "No matter how bad things seem, I know my purpose and there's good in the world. You're part of the world and you should be happy to be so."

That did it. I lunged across the table, fueled by uncontrollable, long pent up rage that overcame the drugs coursing through me. Clearing the table, I grabbed the old man and pulled him down onto the cold, sterile, white, immaculate floor.

Some of the other patients dove out of the way while others were barreled over, falling to ground amidst knocked over chairs. Bowls of food splattered the floor and wall.

None of that mattered. I had him, had a firm grasp on his overalls and shook him violently, slamming his body again and again.

Tom's glasses were thrown from his face, revealing his eyes to be much smaller than they'd appeared seconds before. I looked directly into those eyes… wanting to see that spark of life he was rambling about to fade away forever.

"Happy?" I said with spite. "There's no good left in the world! All that's left is pain and suffering." I hissed through clenched teeth, still shaking him.

The old body helplessly flailed up and down. He tried to fight, desperately clamping his frail hands around my wrist, hoping to break my hold. There was no way. I was too powerful. His weak, pointless effort only managed to further feed my rage.

I wasn't sure what I was trying to accomplish but I didn't want to stop. It was impossible to think. The repeated blows to the back of his skull would eventually be the end of him.

Looking down on the man, I almost felt pity but not quite. I hated him because he mocked my misery. I wanted to shut him up. I wanted him to suffer. I wanted him to live and feel as miserable as I was.

"THAT'S ENOUGH!"

There was a tap on my back. I knew it was a keeper but I didn't relent. I started shaking the old man even more vigorously before releasing my right hand. I drew it back while balling it into a tight fist. My eyes locked onto Tom's face.

"I said ENOUGH!" The guard directly behind me said.

I knew what was next and heard the horrific buzz of the keeper's shock gloves charge up. I hesitated, frozen in a confused, unsure daze. Less than a second later, my vision was filled with a flash of light accompanied by a sharp, searing pain coming from my neck. I vaguely recall falling completely to the floor.

When I could finally see again, was it a minute or an hour later, I couldn't tell… I noticed I was on my back looking up at the ceiling. My body convulsed and writhed over and over in spasms of burning, electric agony.

"You finished?" I heard a man's cheerful voice ask. "Stop flopping around, three-nine-six-zero-four! It's time for your therapy."

A heartbeat later I was able to focus on the speaker's face. It was one of the keepers. He smiled like ghoul, hungrily leering over a plate of flesh. "Come." He went on. "We want you to get all better!"

A shiver ran through my entire body and my stomach clenched. I had to fight to keep from losing the entire contents of my breakfast right then and there.

"Get him up."

Several pairs of hands were on me, yanking me to my feet. As we marched out of the mess hall, down the blinding white corridor, I truly wished I actually believed in a god… maybe then I could pray for death.

-

"NO excuses! Shut up! I want everything perfect when he arrives. If anything is out of place, a spot on the floor, a patient out of place… anything! I promise you, you're finished. Understand?"

Bastard. The word rang through my throbbing head while I stared at the mother effer who took so much delight in my pain, the one who had already taken so much from me. *Doctor Maledro Morbal*, the sickest, sorriest and most cruel living thing I'd ever known. If I could be granted one wish, just one, it would be to see him suffer like no one ever had.

I watched the doctor punch the 'end call' button on the intercom before turning to me. He smiled after a brief look of surprise. The sets of hands that had forced me to the therapy room loosened their grip. I wasn't sure if my legs had regained enough strength to keep me standing on their own but they held.

We stood inside the room I'd grown to hate more than any other place in the entire forsaken asylum. Of course, the whole thing was blank and white, no decorations at all. Nothing but a restraining chair, a simple four legged table and a large, black view screen that covered the wall opposite the door I'd come in through. There was another door to my left that, as far as I knew, was forbidden for inmates to enter.

As always, resting on the table were several empty syringes with needles mockingly waiting to plunge into my arm. They sat by an assortment of crudely designed scraping tools and a set of hair trimmers. For whatever reason, each session ended with the freaks taking several vials of my blood, scraping my arms and legs and then buzzing my hair. I'm usually not much aware of anything at that point, though, but I do notice the scars, scrapes and bruises later on.

Here and now, I hardly noticed any of that. Instead I focused on the doctor's grinning face and started to shiver. Me, a grown man who'd fought wars and triumphed over enemies in countless life and death situations, terrified of an emaciated, weak looking, rat faced, egg head little man.

"Ah, Jason." Morbal purred. The anger that had been in his voice moments ago was long gone. "My favorite patient."

How had this monster managed to become the top authority in a place like this? Morbal was feared and hated by everyone, staff and patients alike. Still, it seemed neither he nor the whole place had any GU regulation. Get on his bad side, no matter who you were, and he'd destroy you. The doctor was free to do whatever he wanted within the white walls and he loved every minute of it.

In fact, the brief outrage during his call was the first time I'd seem him even the least bit rattled. Somehow, thinking about it, about the brief glimpse of a moment of weakness, strengthened me. I had no idea who was coming or why Morbal cared but the fact he was upset showed the demon-like man was still human. For a couple heartbeats, I felt like I was on equal footing with the tormentor. I decided, right there, I wasn't going to give him what he wanted so easily today. I was ready to fight.

The weasel of a man loved torturing me. He had learned to attack me where I was most vulnerable, mentally. I could withstand physical pain, sleep deprivation and starvation but my psyche was my Achilles heel and he knew it. The mental attacks began in earnest six months into my imprisonment here. Since then it's been the same… every single day.

He'd found out more about me than I thought possible. He knew what broke me, what pained me, what made me sick with guilt, despair and self-loathing. He'd learned that showing me the brutal torture of innocent people and animals was too much to handle. Seeing the imagery was worse than having a pound of salt poured into an open, gaping wound. I'd rather die than see or hear those things. The looks of delight on the faces of those doing the atrocities was always the final breaking point.

Every time, it felt like all the cells in my body erupted, bursting in agony. I wanted to help those being harmed so much but there was absolutely nothing I could do except watch. In time, I become overrun with sadness and blind rage, like an animal, unable to think or speak clearly. All I can do is hate. Hate the world and myself, including what I become during the sessions.

And *he* loves every second of it.

I usually collapse and throw up all over myself, screaming, struggling and crying like a helpless baby. If they didn't strap my arms and legs down I would've tried rip my skin off or run my head into the nearest wall. Anything would be better than seeing the evil injustices over and over again.

At that moment, though, I felt different. I was going to resist becoming the object of Morbal's amusement. My resolve started to build until the second another beast entered the room and stood shoulder to shoulder with the doctor. Forate Sevive, a burly, inhuman, wild creature who lusted and preyed upon the misery of others almost as much as his boss.

Forate licked his lips when he saw me. His dark, manic eyes blazed with madness. They were mostly hidden behind the mop of hair drooping down from the top of his head. Scars decorated nearly every inch of his thick face. His nostrils flared, sucking in air before blasting it back out again. He was a barrel of a man, unbelievably cruel and powerful. I'd more than held my own against a lot of men who were a good deal bigger than me, even bigger than Sevive, however, each time I managed to build the nerve and energy to fight him, it was like sparring with a full grown bull. He mopped the floor with me every time.

An icy wave of fright gripped my heart when I looked at him, standing side by side with Morbal. He'd long since forgotten his real name. A few others who'd been in the asylum much longer than me, mentioned a bit about the madman. Once a patient himself, his assigned number was four-eight-six-seven-five so now he proudly goes by the name Forate Si Sevive.

I trembled at the thought. To be driven so insane... I was afraid I'd be the same someday.

Forate took his gaze off me and looked at the men who'd escorted me. "Go." Despite his size, the big man's voice was high and nasally. The men quickly scampered away. Everyone except Morbal was terrified of the hulk.

"Sit." He ordered, motioning the god awful chair.

I couldn't move, frozen with fear. Forate had both his meaty hands on me in seconds before shoving me into the seat. A few moments later, my wrists and ankles were bound. The sick son of a bitch actually tried to tickle my right foot as he secured the last restraint. Vomit rose to the base of my throat.

This was it, here we go. Another torture session ridiculously labeled 'therapy.' I closed my eyes and reached deep down, far inside where that inkling of strength I felt earlier still lingered. Pulling it back up, when I opened my eyes they let out a cold, angry, powerful stare aimed right at the doctor's rat face.

Morbal raised his eyebrows and shot a quick glance at Forate. He nodded and smiled, saying, "Well, well, well," before turning back to me. "Feeling strong today, Mr. Sworn?" The doctor made an annoying clucking sound with his tongue. He did that whenever he became excited. "Feeling... hmm, what is it?" His beady eyes were partly closed as he smelled the air around him. "Defiance?"

I clenched my jaw. How could he read me so well?

"Oh, my poor, poor man." His sorry attempt at sympathy was as lame as could be. "You think I'm here to hurt you." He shook his head. "No. We love you. We need you. We're here to help. You'll see. In time, I believe we'll be friends."

I wanted to shout every obscenity in the book but I knew that was exactly what he wanted. He got off on upsetting me. NO. Instead, this time, I pushed him out of my head and only glared back at him. I knew better but couldn't keep from showing the slightest hint of a smile show on my face.

The doctor took a step back. He looked both surprised and angry. I started to feel proud I'd gotten to him, turned the tables a bit.

He soon composed himself, though, and clapped his hands. "Ok then, time for phase two." He lazily waved the first two fingers on his right hand at Forate.

The beast of a man didn't waste a second. As quickly as he'd fastened the straps around my wrists, they were removed. The tip of his nose brushed against mine. I could smell his rotting breath when he gave a wide smile. "Don't try to go anywhere."

In a flash, he was up and through the side door, leaving me alone with the doctor. My brain whirled. I was so shocked by the unexpected move I couldn't capitalize on the situation. If I was able to think, I'd have gotten out of my ankle restraints and rushed over to smash Morbal's face into the view screen or something, anything. Instead, I sat there, dumbfounded and stunned.

By the time I gathered my wits, Forate was bounding back into the room with two keepers, both armed with shock gloves. The orderlies marched over and stood at my sides. Oddly, they turned themselves around so they weren't facing Morbal.

My heart started to pound. The fear overcame me again. I cursed myself for being weak but this was all new. The unknown got the better of me. What were they going to do? My pathetic, pleading face looked up at Morbal.

He smiled in ecstasy after seeing my expression before giving Sevive a nod.

"HEY!" Forate shouted, making me jump like a startled little girl. He slapped me across my face and started breathing heavier than normal, sounding like a damn locomotive. "Look at me. It's time." He nodded his own head and smiled. "Are you ready for it, Thrine?"

He always call me that because he knew how much I hated it. My first two numbers were three-nine so he like to call me Thrine. My own inhuman, unnatural number name.

"Come on." Forate said softly as he bent down to bring his lips close to my left ear. "You're a murderer. You know it. You're a monster just like me. You know it."

I couldn't stop myself from looking at his face, feeling my eyes begin to well up with tears.

The behemoth looked disappointed, sad almost. "You pretend you're a better man. Better than me." He let out a quick, snide snicker. "You like to think you're actually a good man. That just makes you even more pathetic, more criminal because you can't face up to what you've done. You won't accept what you are." He paused a couple seconds, letting his words sink into my head. "You know it, yes? Yes."

I swallowed, shaking my head, trying to deny the wild man's words, fighting to block them out. It didn't work. Painful and twisted memories flooded my head bringing up so many ghosts from the past. They ripped my insides to shreds.

Forate's eyes dug into me. "That's right. You killed them. BUTCHERED THEM! And you loved it!" He swayed in delight.

"They deserved it!" I called in a begging tone. "They killed Mark!"

Both tormentors laughed at the same time. The big man continued. "You only pretended to care for your brother. He was just the excuse you'd been looking for. Mmm." He purred in delight. "Oh it must have felt so good ripping the life from their bodies. Destroying them and devastating others who loved them."

"Stop!" I pleaded. My head was filled with images of my brother's smashed body and his killers who ganged up on him. He didn't stand a chance. When he died I lost the only real friend I had, the only person I loved.

I sobbed at the thought then remembered how my rage and over inflated sense of justice took control. I executed those people even more viciously than what they'd done to Mark. I was a hypocrite, a monster, a killer. Forate was right.

"Well," Sevive started with a smile that showed nearly all the remaining dark, yellow teeth he had left in his head, "we've treated you with images you've loved long enough. Now it's time to move to the next level." He licked his dry, cracked lips and shot a quick look at Morbal.

The doctor grinned.

Forate stood up straight, quickly pulled a good sized, razor sharp looking knife out of his pocket and slammed it on the table in front of me. He jerked his face back to only an inch of mine and whispered, "Do with this as you will, brother." He smelled me. "Yes. You want to do it! But wait, not yet! I know you'll want to see this."

When he backed off I noticed I was trembling nearly as badly as when I'd been shocked by the keeper back in the cafeteria. My eyes focused on the blade while Forate's words rang through my dizzy head, preventing me from even wanting to escape. This was what I deserved. I was a guilty, defeated creature. Freedom was out of the question.

I studied the lethal, slick edge of the blade. The sick, soft, pale lighting in the hellish room shined off the metal. I could do it. Right now. I could end myself. A line of drool ran down from the corner of my gaping mouth. The ventilation started drumming stronger.

"Hey!" Forate shouted again followed by another sharp slap to my face. "Yes, you deserve to suffer. You know it. We can see."

I turned up to face him and we both nodded in unison. He was right about everything. I tried to speak the word 'yes' but only managed an animal like groan.

"Good!" Forate beamed with glee. "You're learning. As a reward, here's a sweet treat. BRING HER IN!" He shouted the last part toward the door for an instant then zeroed his smiling gaze back at me. "We're going to allow you to let it all out on this beautiful, little creature."

Two keepers entered the room, dragging a nearly completely naked, drugged up looking, ratty haired, dirt covered young woman. She barely put up a struggle. They dropped her on the floor in front of my feet.

"She's yours." The giant man blurted. "Take her, cut her, ravage her, violate her. Use her! DO IT!"

I broke. My brain actually felt like it split in half. I even swore I could hear a snapping crack come from my head. My body flushed, aroused and excited. Yes. To my own shock, I started to laugh, maniacally.

At that moment, I broke in half. There were two of me. The part that was good, just and rational separated from the lusty, psychotic animal that my body had become. Dazed, horrified and revolted, the kind part of me actually stood outside of and alongside the wicked, horrid man named Jason Sworn. I saw his face twitch and then twist into a terrifying blend of rage, disgust and fascination. The man, Jason, was evil… pure and simple. A monster.

I, that is the part of me outside myself, didn't see what Jason saw but I was aware he was watching Forate do some of the most horrible things imaginable to the young woman. Even as doped up as she was, the girl still screamed bloodcurdling wails of pain and terror.

All the while, Forate carried on, almost singing he was so jubilant. "You love this! Yes! It's so wonderful, it feels so right… SO GOOD!"

Jason continued to drool out of his open, smiling mouth. Sweat raced down from his forehead and tears streamed out of his eyes. He… I looked completely mad.

The humming from the vents grew even louder and seemed to vibrate the walls and floors. Forate's laughter echoed through the room while the tortured girl's vocal chords finally gave out. She could only whimper now.

"LOOK AT ME!" The Beast man demanded. "YES, YOU'VE MADE IT. YOU LOVE IT!"

A roar of celebration and victory filled the space. The exclamation didn't come from Morbal or Forate. To my shame, dread and utter despair, it came from me. I nearly gave up and died right there.

Forate hooted in joy. "We're bothers now! Join me! IT'S YOUR TURN. TAKE HER!" He stood up and motioned the wasted, broken, crumbled woman sprawled on the floor in a pool of blood and other fluids.

When I saw Jason smile and start to stand the last remaining semblance of humanity, of sanity erupted in me. I would NOT allow this to happen. Even though I was bodiless without a voice, I screamed. I screamed for the only things I had left; justice and control of my own actions.

With every ounce of energy I had left, I willed myself back into my own body. Back in control for the moment, I snatched the knife and rushed it toward my own throat. I'd rather die than be like *them*. This was it…

Quicker than I could finish the deed, though, Morbal happily hollered one word. "OUT!"

The knife started to dig into the right side of my neck when I heard the gloves on the two keepers charge up. My peripheral vision could see them reach for me as I cut deeper…

# Chapter 2

I woke up with a more miserable hangover than I ever imagined possible. The throbbing pain told me one thing right off the bat: I was still alive. Damn.

A little further thought told me that death was indeed freedom from this place but it also meant, death, which I realized I didn't want either. It seemed part of me still wanted to live after all.

Between the pounding waves of pain, my brain focused on one word, one feeling over and over: Failure. Morbal and Forate had won again and I'd been broken worse than ever before.

I cursed and looked down at my arms. There were new puncture marks up and down, all over them. They looked like a pack of vampires had gorged themselves on me. They were bruised, poked and scratched all to hell, covered with gross purple and red blotches. Whoever had molested me did so with absolute zero care. Why the eff did the sick bastards do that every time. I shivered.

Memories flooded back. I'd fallen further into madness than I ever thought possible. At the end, I really started to enjoy the mutilation on the young woman. I swallowed hard as a bead of sweat trickled down the side of my face. Another wave of nausea stirred in my gut accompanied by a horrible, stinging pain from the right side of my neck. I wanted to touch what I knew was a terrific gash but no such luck, my arms were strapped down to the bed.

The pain felt even sharper than the blade that had done the cutting. I thought about the gash, considering why it was there in the first place. Yes, I'd been weak. Yes, I was stupid for allowing the psychopathic predators to get the better of me but still, the very fact that the cut was there was proof that on some level, I'd beaten them. I truly was prepared to die rather than join them. I wasn't one of them.

I felt a bit of pride for the first time in what seemed an eternity. It was so strange feeling anything remotely positive about myself. I embraced the feeling as hard and long as I could, knowing it was fleeting and wouldn't last. The pain, shame and humiliation of what all happened were too strong.

I sunk further into my bed and finally became aware I was in the medical ward. I closed my eyes and let out a mocking laugh. It was funny how unfortunately stupid the whole situation was. They wanted me alive and healthy so they could torture me all over again another day, another thousand days, however long until they're perverse lust was satiated.

I opened my eyes again and glanced around. The room was big, long and open, white all over, of course, with about fifty beds that each had their own bio scanning machine. Other than the drum from the vents, the room was silent even with the few orderlies and the handful of other patients tied to their own beds. No one wanted to bring unnecessary attention to themselves.

Focusing on nothing in particular, my gaze shifted to a few drops of red on my pillow, at least it was supposed to be a pillow, the thing was little more than a hard plastic tablet with a flimsy sheet over it. So, the pricks hadn't managed to get every drop of blood out of me.

I stared hard at the tiny splashes of color. They were a painful contrast to the ever present whiteness of the asylum. I didn't take my eyes off the redness. Much like the fleeting pride I'd briefly felt, the dots of color were a glimpse of something above and beyond the hole I was stuck in. The color was truly beautiful. Funny, I'd never thought I'd see beauty in blood before that moment.

I sighed and a slight moan escaped my lips.

"Well don't you just look fantastic?"

I snapped back to the present and whirled my head over to my left. A man's familiar, smiling face stared sympathetically down on me.

"And by fantastic, I mean like a bag of crap dragged through the fires of hell and dropped off a skyscraper." He spoke softly and quickly, looking around before letting out a small laugh.

"Hey David." Even though it was only a tad above a whisper, when I spoke it felt like my throat was going to shatter. I made an ugly face still tried to show some sort of acknowledgment that I approved the man's presence. All I could think of was to give a short nod.

He grimaced. "Jesus, you sound even worse."

"Thanks, dick." I rolled my eyes.

Moving closer, with a smirk on his face, he grabbed a cup of water resting on the table near me and brought the straw to my lips. The moves on both our parts were quick and stealthy. I gulped the whole thing down in seconds while David made sure the orderlies were none the wiser.

"Thanks." I said again, this time much more genuinely.

Of all the twisted, troubled, malicious, insane, cunning, manipulating, selfish, diabolical beings in the whole forsaken place, David was the one, the only one I even remotely cared about. He was a good man, too good. His constant optimistic and upbeat demeanor didn't disturb the way Tom's attitude did. Somehow David remained a beacon of light, or, like the blotch of blood on my pillow, a speck of color in the world and I admired him for that.

He was always there to help me through my darkest times and his overall cheerfulness had pulled me back from the most horrible places in the back of my brain on several occasions. I knew I owed him my sanity. Again, I didn't believe in anything but I was thankful David was part of my pod. In short, he was my friend. Friend... a word that had almost lost all meaning since my brother died.

Despite the drabness and ugliness of the institution, David still appeared healthy. There was no denying he was a good looking guy, he knew it most of all and liked to flaunt the fact. He stood a couple inches shorter than me but was in as good of shape as one could hope to manage in this place. Had it not been for the fact that his pale skin hadn't seen the Sun in a year, he would fit right in with one of the old professional volleyball teams. His blonde hair was cut short like the other inmates but his deep blue eyes were as different from everyone else's as they could be. Not the color, or the shape but the true liveliness in them. It was his vitality that sometimes reminded me life could still go on in a place like this.

He did have his shortcomings though, nobody's perfect. David was overly hopeful in an almost gullible way. On top of that, he was the horniest person I ever knew. Sex, sex, sex. It was his passion. Nevertheless, he was a man of action and always seemed one step ahead of the keepers. He'd managed to keep in touch with several connections on the outside which proved to be extremely beneficial. His reach had helped to get in the good graces with several keepers by offering them various goodies and favors. The most common of which were tablets of clear, the hip new drug of the day.

Clear was sort of hallucinogen that was swallowed or allowed to dissolve on the tongue. It first came on the scene about ten years ago. David told me the potent stuff was made from the venom of some rare spider from South America. Typically a dose the size of a couple grains of salt was enough to keep a grown man flying for a few hours.

No doubt, it was through these favors that David just happened to be on custodial duty in the med ward while I was strapped to one of the beds. I let out a small chuckle.

David gestured my neck after setting the now empty cup back where he'd picked it up from. "What'd they do to you?"

I exhaled sharply. "Pfft, not this." Since I couldn't motion with my hands I glanced down in the direction of the gouge on my neck. "I can take credit for that one myself." I swallowed. "Nice, huh?"

My friend's smile vanished as he came to understand the situation. "God damn it, Jason. What the hell's wrong with you?" He moved closer, kicking his mop bucket aside. "Stop this lame ass self-loathing." He snorted in anger, a combination of disgust and disappointment. "Wake the eff up and open your eyes! Don't give into these pieces of crap. Don't let them win. Take some responsibility to yourself."

He paused, glancing around the room before going on. "Things are about to go down." The expression on his face changed back to his hopeful, almost giddy self. "Haven't you heard the rumors? Don't you feel it in your gut?"

I raised my eyebrows and slid my head back as far from David's face as I could. "What are you talking about? All I feel in my gut is the urge to throw up right about now." I shook my head. "Don't crack up on me."

David drew back a little himself. "I'm serious. You're really starting to piss me off."

"Hey!" I exclaimed as well and as quietly as I could. "Calm down. Is that what I get for that *gift* I got for you?" I paused. "By the way, how was she?"

David's demeanor changed instantly and the smile was back on his face. "Oh lord." He bit his lip and momentarily closed his eyes. "She was fantastic. How the hell did you manage to swing that one?"

"I paid off that young guard, Chris, Chris Berg with that crap you gave me. I've been saving it up." I smiled and knew what was coming, we'd had this talk several times.

"Clear is not crap!" David always defended the drug. "It's been around for a long time now and not once has there ever been any negative side effects. The stuff is awesome."

"Uh huh."

David huffed. "Whatever. All it does is make you feel like a billion credits, sharpen your mind, give a boost of energy and heighten your senses." He could see I still wasn't sold. "Ok, name one case where someone had a bad experience. Just one."

I shook my head. "I just don't trust the stuff."

"You don't trust anything." With a shake of his own head, he switched gears. "At any rate, I don't know how I'll ever be able to thank you enough. She really hit the spot, all the spots." David's eyes glazed over a little, lost in memory. "Damn."

Bribing Berg to smuggle in the prostitute was crude and I didn't understand my friend's insatiable lust but I couldn't think of any other ways to show my appreciation. It seemed everything worked out fine as planned. Yea, it was risky. If we'd have gotten caught, Berg would have lost his job, or his life and I would spend the rest of my life, outside therapy, in a tiny box.

I nodded. "No need to thank me. Hell, I'm surprised you haven't done the same thing for yourself."

David raised his eyebrows. "Way too risky. I'm not quite as crazy as you are, yet."

"Yea," I bit my lip, "I feel like I'm losing it for sure. Only a matter of time now…"

"Will you stop that? I mean it, stop it!" Serious David was back. "You don't deserve this. We'll get out."

"I do deserve this." My anger started to build, not at David but at myself. I could see Forate's fat face as I said the words. "I'm a god damned murderer, ok? I'm done. I did the crime and now I'm paying for it."

"Bullcrap!" My friend snapped through clenched teeth. "You told me what happened before they threw you in here. Maybe you did go too far but I would've done the same. They killed your brother, an innocent man." He paused. "Hell, I'm no better but I know damn well we don't deserve this."

"Come on," a skeptical expression popped up on my face. "All you did was beat up your corrupt commanding officer. That's hardly in the same league with what I did."

David set his jaw and nodded while mopping the floor around my bed, pretending to be busy. "I beat the son of a bitch to within an inch of his life." He snorted. "Doubt he'll ever walk again." He looked at me and winked. "Oh and I slept with his wife."

I rolled my head and stared up at the ceiling. "I'm not surprised."

Yea, and I don't regret it. Not one bit. The guy was a scumbag who abused her and his power."

I turned back to him. The man was beaming.

David nodded, confidently. "I did the world a service that day." He sighed.

"But now you're here." I stated.

His eyes narrowed a little. "For now."

He was so optimistic. I wished I could be the same but guilt and my latest therapy session did a number on my brain. They made me feel worthless, weak, evil. They were traits I despised and they described me, reminding me of the injustice I laid down on those people.

"Damn, I need to get moving." David said. "Anyways, he's on his way here. The whole place is in an uproar getting things perfect."

Curiosity replaced the despair running through my head. "Who's on his way?"

"Utterly clueless." David smiled and shook his head. "You need to listen more. I keep telling you."

"Who?" My voice raised a bit and I nervously looked around to make sure no one was paying attention.

"Shh." Davit put his finger to my lips. "Cross, August Cross. He's coming to visit Morbal and check things out around here."

I'd heard the name before but didn't get the connection. I only knew a little about Cross, mostly just that he invented the

Cell Truth and took over one of those new islands. I shrugged. "Big deal. Some rich little prince comes to town. So, who cares?"

Then I remembered how anxious Morbal sounded on the intercom phone before my last torture session. He was all worked up over Cross. It still didn't really matter to me but if he was coming over to have tea and crumpets with the monstrous doctor, I figured Mr. Truth should be run over by a truck as well.

Still, August Cross did have his own island, his own nation, free of Tehlasrin. Part of me suddenly realized how much I really wanted to live there and I wasn't sure why. I dismissed the thought. Christ, everyone with at least two brain cells in their skulls probably wanted out of the GU.

David brought me back to the present with a grunt. "There's no time to explain. They're eyeballing me, I have to go." He forcefully jabbed the mop into the wheeled bucket then turned to me again. "Just keep your ears and eyes open and be ready."

"Ready for what?" I was part annoyed and part curious.

"I'm not totally sure."

I rolled my eyes as the annoyed part took over.

David sucked on his teeth. "Just be ready!" He headed off, "See ya."

I watched him go and mildly enjoyed how he greeted each of the other strapped down men in the ward. Most of them told him to buzz off in not so kind words but it didn't faze my friend. I smiled.

A few moments later and I was back in my own head. It wasn't long before my foul mood returned. Thankfully, I eventually fell back asleep.

-

It was just my usual bad luck that the one time I was lucky enough to be having a good dream something awful had to wrench me awake. In my slumber, I was free, filled with the strength and will to fight out of this hellhole. I was on my way to Cross's island, Aswain.

It only took two words, spat out from the creature I hated so much, to rip me back awake. "Hello, brother."

I jolted with such force, I was surprised the straps holding my wrists down didn't burst. My teeth clenched and my lip curled. Forate's face filled my view, inches from mine. I wanted to dig my fingers into his dark eyes and rip them out.

The monster smiled and wagged his index finger in the air, like a father does with his child. "Come now, Thrine. Why are you so mad at me? You don't hate me, do you? Why would you?" His huge, meaty hand stroked my head as his thick eyebrows rose up until they were lost in his shaggy bangs. "Is it because you hate yourself and you know in your heart we're the same?"

I didn't give a response. Eff him. All I felt was defiance for the bastard, even more resistant than I'd felt before my last therapy session.

Forate sucked in his bottom lip and drooped his eyes, trying to look sympathetic. "You poor, pathetic man. We were so close last time. You nearly made it. Nearly tossed away all your cares and became free." He sighed.

Rage boiled in my gut. My chest heaved up and down as I forced air in and out of my lungs, trying to not let him get to me. My face flushed.

"Don't be mad at me, brother." He sounded defensive, wounded. "I love you. We're connected. You and me, we're the same. Look around. You, more than any of the pathetic fools in this place are set to follow my ways. You're not like them. You're special, like me."

Another patient a few beds down from mine, who'd remained silent until now, shouted at Forate. "Hey! Shut your mouth. I'm sick of your measly little voice." A laugh. "You love him? Well then have at him and be done with it. I won't watch."

Forate's expression changed immediately. His eyes rolled back into his head before he closed them. They opened up a second later and looked completely manic. He winked at me. "Excuse me a moment."

My heart started to race as the beast man strode over to the other bed. The poor fool laying there had no idea what sort of hornet nest he'd just pissed off.

"Yea," the patient went on, "you heard me. Bitch."

In a flash, Forate brought his fist down on the patient's nose, busting it to hell. Red sprayed everywhere, reminding me, in a sickening way of the blood drops on my pillow.

The man cried out in protest, calling for help. He must have been new here. Everyone knew the keepers weren't there to help. "Guards!" He yelled. "Get him away from me!"

Forate calmly motioned the two orderlies looking at him. "Turn around." His voice boomed. "If anyone interferes with me I'll rip your heads off. All of you."

The keepers scampered away like frightened mice.

The monster focused back on his victim. "Thrine!" He yelled. "Watch. This is power. This is for you. Accept who you are: An animal in a savage world ruled by strength. That's the only truth to everything. Deny it and you'll only continue to suffer and be ruled."

Forate side-stepped to his left and centered himself over the patient's left knee. The big man hummed as he drew his right fist high into the air. The humming grew louder and more feral until it turned into a growl.

The bloody faced man on the bed squirmed, powerless to do anything. "No, please, don't!" He pleaded. "I'm sorry. I'm sorry! PLEASE!"

I doubted Forate heard him at all. It didn't matter. The fist came down like a hammer, crashing and then crushing the knee beneath it. The horrible sound of shattering bone filled the air before being replaced by screams of pain.

Forate bellowed. "SHUT UP!" In a sudden rage, he ripped the bolted table holding the scanning device clean out of the floor and threw it against the nearest wall.

The patient continued to wail in pain. Forate covered the man's mouth with his hand. "You can't cry when you can't breathe. Right, Thrine?"

I knew all he wanted was a reaction out of me. He won, I couldn't ignore him and let the stupid patient suffocate. "STOP!" I yelled, remembering how messed up my throat was. "He's had enough."

The beast whirled around to face me, a wide smile on his face. "Has he now? How about you?" He turned to the orderlies and clapped his hands while the busted up patient continued to scream. "Shut him up! Drug him, or kill him, I don't care. The Doctor is with his guest and I don't want him to get interrupted."

The keepers hurried over to the injured man, each with syringes filled with what I knew were strong drugs. The wailing patient would probably never walk again. Maybe he would, with proper care but that was far too much to ask for in this place.

Forate glided back over to the side of my bed. "Do you see now? You're weak because you're sick, confused, little brain pretends to care." He poked the center of my forehead with a blood stained finger. "Stop lying to yourself. Stop thinking you can help anyone. You can't!"

I sighed then swallowed while my heart raced. If only I could get up and fight the bastard. Tell him how wrong he was. No, it wouldn't do any good and I wasn't really sure he was wrong. Instead, I just sunk deeper into my bed. Forate hurt and used that man to get to me. Angry tears of defeat welled up in my eyes. I hissed. "I do care, I do want to help." I latched onto my anger, my hate. It was all I had. "I'm NOT your brother."

Forate planted his bloody hands on the sides of my face. He spoke in a growling tone. "That's because you're blind to the truth. You refuse to accept that you're a killer." He huffed.

"Why fight it? Why fight me? WHY? I could kill you so easily right now."

"THEN DO IT!" I snapped.

He ignored me. "But the Doctor and I see great potential in you. You WILL be like me. Free, strong, ALIVE!"

The beast man calmed himself a bit. "It's just so damn frustrating seeing you like this." He bit down, hard, on his bottom lip and winced in pain.

I watched the anguish on his face and realized the many scars on his face were most likely all self-inflicted. The slash on my neck started to sting all over again, reminding me how similar we were.

Forate went on after finally releasing the clamp on his lip. "I see the old me in you and I just want to *squeeze* it out of you." He applied more pressure to the sides of my head. "The only constant in the world is power. Those who have it rule, those who don't are ruled. Those who are ruled are weak. Those who are weak, suffer."

I moved my face, trying to shake him off. "Get your hands off me. Or kill me, whatever. I hate you."

The man suddenly burst into laughter. "You're such a fool, such a child. It's time to grow up."

He finally took his hands off me and I wanted to shower myself off.

"Oh no, Jason Sworn." It was the first time he'd called me by my name in months. "We won't ever kill you. You'll be with us forever. The Doctor is a great man, he'll make you all better. He'll set you free."

An icy chill ran up and down my spine.

The big man sensed my uneasiness, of course. "Today's session was good, tomorrow's will be better. I can't wait. You'll see." He clasped his hands together. "Don't be afraid. Just one more session and it'll all be over." He drew in a loud breath through his nostrils and looked around the room. "Oh and brother," he went on, looking back at me, "you won't even have to thank me."

I closed my eyes and shook my head. "I beat you once and I'll beat you again. You can't break me."

A sudden, powerful slap stung the left side of my face, forcing my eyes open. I could taste blood from where my teeth had sliced the inside of my cheek.

"Look at me when we're talking, Boy." Forate was pissed as all hell now. "You think you're smarter than me? Than Doctor Maledro? You don't know... you don't know what we know." He laughed.

I froze. Something in the way he spoke terrified me more than usual. What was he getting at?

Forate nodded. "Everything will be all better soon. The Doctor will free you from your cares." He paused. "We know who you care about, who you think your friends are."

I gulped and thought of David. Oh Christ.

The big man's eyes squinted. "Did you really think you could fool us? We know you better than you know yourself. When he's gone, your friend, the weak Jason will have nothing left to cling to and will simply die."

Now I didn't say anything because I was genuinely speechless. I had to get out of here, out of the medical wing and back to my pod. I didn't know what good it would do but I had to warn David.

"That's right," Forate started. "You just tuck yourself in and have a good night's rest." The monstrous son of a bitch actually leaned over and kissed my forehead. "Things will be all better soon. You just wait."

With that, he stood up and headed out of the ward. I couldn't believe it but the insane bastard actually sang the words 'Just wait till morning' over and over. He skipped away like a child.

A full blown panic attack grabbed me by the heart and lungs. I felt like the world was about to end. I couldn't hardly breathe. Desperate, I called for the nearest keeper. "Hey! I'm feeling better. I want to get back to my pod. I'm hungry and I don't want to miss dinner."

Stupid. No one ever asks to get fed in this place.

Without saying a word, the keeper marched up to me and stuck a needle in my arm. I passed out in seconds.

# Chapter 3

Whatever drug the keeper gave me only knocked me out for about three hours. Part of me wished it'd been stronger. If I couldn't get back to my pod to warn David I'd rather be unconscious. Lying awake here for the past couple hours, absolutely helpless, was driving me into a silent frenzy.

The depressingly boring clock planted into the bare, white wall across from my bed constantly reminded me how long each minute was. The grey digits said it was two forty-eight a.m. Not that it mattered. The inside of this place was always the same, day or night.

I bit my lip and dug my nails into the bed. Forate's visit had me completely rattled. What the hell did he know? What would happen to me? More pressingly, what would happen to David? He was a good man and didn't deserve those effers torturing him any more than usual. What could I do? How could I do anything? Even if I could do something, what would I do?

I screamed in my head. Rage.

The cycle of questions repeated themselves over and over, echoing in my throbbing brain until a group of keepers finally marched into the medical ward and right up to my bed. Instinctively, I pretended to be asleep, not wanting to be noticed. This place had conditioned me that way. Being noticed, or worse, being exceptional in any way was a curse here.

The nearest guard shouted. "Three-nine-six-zero-four, wake up!" He shoved my head with his shock gloved hand. "Get up! WAKE UP!"

I barely opened my eyes while the other patients in the ward grumbled their disapproval of the noise. I looked at the noisy one while a couple other keepers fumbled with the straps on my wrists. Mr. Shout's face reminded of a devil mask I remember wearing one Halloween as a little kid; red faced, bloodshot eyes, curled lip and clenched teeth. All he needed were the little horns.

He screamed at the top of his lungs, right in my face, spraying me with spit, "WAKE UP!"

Another patient complained. I spared a quick glance and noticed the guy was new to the ward. He hadn't been here when Forate busted up that other one, who, by the way, was nowhere to be seen. Had this one seen what happened he might have known to keep his trap shut. But no. "I'm trying to sleep, mother effer!"

Without a moment's hesitation, Devil Face spun on his heels and rushed over to the man, sputtering obscenities the whole way. I could hear his shock gloves power up. In seamless fashion, he placed his right hand on the patient's face. The voltage blasted through the bound man's face, frying him. The poor bastard didn't even have time to scream. I guessed he was dead.

The bullying murderer straightened, drew in a deep breath and turned to the nearest orderly. "Get rid of the body." He looked back at me. "OUT OF BED, or so help me…" He charged his gloves again.

"Hey," another keeper started, "the Doctor wants this one alive, remember?"

On top of the grossly unjust murder I'd just witnessed, the mention of Morbal really pissed me off. I jumped out of my bed, quickly and angrily… a mistake. The shock blasts I

received, mixed with the lingering trauma from my latest
therapy bout, the sedatives pumping through my veins and the
fact I hadn't eaten in nearly twenty-four hours created a
dizzying cocktail. The instant my feet touched the floor my
head spun and my legs turned to jelly. I crumpled, face first
onto the cold, white floor.

A couple keepers laughed but their angry, pig faced
superior rushed over to kick me in the ribs. "Get the eff up!"

The blow hurt like hell but all it really managed to do was
fuel my rage which was already nearly at the boiling point. I
pushed myself off the floor and propped myself up on my
elbows while slowly lifting my head. When my eyes met the
keeper's, he shut his mouth and stepped back two paces.

Gathering himself, he snapped at the others, gesturing mc
with a nod. "Pick him up."

With a low growl, I shrugged their hands away and willed
myself to stand on my own, all while keeping my gaze fixed
on the leader's face. Pain and disorientation be damned, I'd
had enough. The dead man lying on the bed several arm spans
from me demanded justice.

"Don't look at me like that, you pathetic, little snot." The
leader hissed, slowing finding his courage. His eyes narrowed.
"Who do you think you are? I don't care if the Doctor wants
you alive. The world won't miss you when you're gone."

He moved toward me, hands reaching for my face, the
lethal buzz from his gloves filled my ears. In a blink, I rammed
the full blunt of my clenched fist hard against his nose,
breaking it and knocking the little would be tyrant to the floor.
His head smacked hard, knocking him unconscious.

"Jesus!" A startled voice cried out from behind me.

Coolly and seamlessly, I glided around, glanced at the
surprised face, grabbed the back of the man's neck, pulled it
down and brought my knee up. The met with a cataclysmic
result. Another keeper collapsed.

Now, the other two keepers and the three orderlies were
coming to their wits. Although fighting and combat came

naturally to me, and my training was alive and well remembered, ready to be put to use, I had a choice to make. A snap judgement... fight or flight. Outnumbered five to one, I ran.

Rushing through the doorway, it was ironically fortunate that I'd spent so much time in the medical ward. I knew the exact way back to my pod's chamber, not an easy thing in a place so big and bland where every hall, every turn looked the same. I hurried down the hallways, hoping to lose the guards and that they wouldn't know where I was headed.

Now I needed a strategy but all I could think of was to get to my pod, take out the guards there, get David, fill him in and get the hell out of the asylum. The plan was simple and very foolish but it was all I had.

"What the? Hey!" A patrolling keeper exclaimed when he saw me. He scrambled to charge his gloves.

It took a few seconds for the things to load so I turned up the speed, charging as fast as my bare feet could take me. My eyes locked onto the center of his body as a bellow escaped my lips. I hit him like a train. He flew back good seven feet before crashing to the floor. He aimed to get up but I didn't let him. The second I was close enough, I kicked him in his head, knocking him out cold.

I hurried on my way. Almost there.

Skidding around the last corner, my heart abruptly sunk. Forate's giant body stood, cockily in the middle of the hallway. He had David by the neck, his giant paw of a hand nearly circling the entire circumference. Four other keepers stood around the two. The abomination of a man giggled like a school girl.

"Right on time." His nasally voice said before he licked his lips.

All the momentum, all the energy I'd had drained away. The wear and exhaustion in my body caught up to me. I was like a deflated balloon. My shoulders slumped and my knees buckled. I fell to a sitting position.

Forate laughed and the team of guards who'd I escaped from finally caught up with me. Gasping for air, the five men looked just as startled as I was to see the big man.

The nearest one stuttered. "Ah, uh, Sir!" Nearly terrified beyond the ability to speak, he motioned me. "We were just, ah, retrieving -"

The big man exhaled sharply and raised his free hand in the air. "No." He shook his head. "You failed. The good Doctor Morbal has a world to run. He can't afford failures." He blinked, turning from me, to David and back to the keeper.

I took the brief moment to spare a glance at David, hardly able to believe it when he actually winked at me. The corner of the man's mouth curved into the slightest of smiles. *Not as crazy as me.* My ass.

"So, let's see here." Forate continued in a lecturing tone. "One, two, three, four, five of you, hmm?" I could almost see the wheels of demented, perverted craziness spinning in his big, fat head. A smile sprung on his scarred face as he pointed out two of the men. "You. Both of you. You two will pay for this." With a satisfied nod, he gestured an area to his left. "Step over there and remove your gloves."

The men obeyed like beaten, broken spirited slaves. As ordered, they removed their weapons and tossed them over toward Forate.

"Good." He said in a pleased tone before extending an open hand to the other three men. "You three, shock and stock these two. The Doctor will deal with them." He looked at David and me again. The smile on his face grew twice as large. "But not yet."

Gaining the wits to stand back up and as hard as it was to think clearly, I desperately looked for some way out of this as the five men filed away without another word. My eyes eventually locked onto the discarded pairs of shock gloves resting near Forate's feet.

David caught my attention when his eyebrows rose. I knew he had the same hopelessly foolish plan rattling in his brain.

"Think you could pull it off?" Forate's voice boomed the question, startling me. I flinched. He chuckled. "Don't I deserve more credit? Go on. Go for it. Come on, Thrine. Let's see how dumb… or smart you really are."

I spared a couple of heartbeats to consider my options. Absolutely none of them were favorable. Screw it. Better to go down fighting… There were few things I wanted more than killing the monster. This was our chance for justice and freedom. I went for it.

I dashed for gloved and prepared to dive but didn't get anywhere near that far. David's body slammed into mine before I could make the leap. Forate had whipped him around and speared his body into me. We both crashed to the floor, fumbling around.

Forate smacked his lips as he stepped atop the gloves on the floor. "That was fun but play time's over. Let's go."

-

David and I were marched to an unfamiliar part of the asylum and into a space that was set up like a classroom. A dozen desks faced a lifeless grey view screen that covered most of wall it was pressed into. We were forced down into the middle two chairs in the front row. My friend and I spared a quick glance. He looked as dumbfounded as I felt.

Why here? What was the point of all this?

I looked around a bit more and noted a large desk that sat in the corner of the room to my front left. Four keepers positioned themselves around it while Forate, the big bastard, stood facing us with madness in his eyes.

David exhaled a bit louder than normal and appeared ready to say something. Quick as lighting, Forate slapped him upside his head before a single word could escape his lips.

I was about to protest with a curse or two before suffering the same sting.

The beast man put his thick, right index finger against my lips, "Shh." He said. "One word and I'll start ripping pieces off you." He pulled his hand back. "That would be a shame."

My already hanging shoulders slumped lower. Defeat. We were done. Still, the anticipation, the waiting was torture. All I could hope for was that everything ended quickly, that I'd be killed before seeing David, my friend, mutilated and murdered. I knew that was too much to ask for. Chances were that I wouldn't be killed at all. I'd either be tortured worse than ever before, locked in a cage or finally lose what was left of my mind... turned into another Forate. Probably all three would happen. I swallowed hard.

Speaking of him, the man was now rocking back and forth on the balls of his feet, whistling some stupid tune, staring at us. The only time he removed his gaze was when he looked at his watch.

Finally, the door to Forate's left, my right, opened and Morbal slithered into the room. He headed over to the desk and set a bag he'd been carrying down on it. Then the Doctor turned to us and shook his head. "Disappointing. So damn disappointing."

Turning back toward the door, he called to someone outside the room, "Bring him in."

Two additional keepers entered, dragging a very sorry looking Chris Berg. The young man's terrified eyes looked like they were ready to pop out of his skull. When his captors reached Forate, Berg fell to his knees and started to sob.

Morbal clucked his tongue. "So, I imagine you can all guess why we've come together this fine morning, yes?" He took two steps over to Berg and started petting the man's head. The Doctor's evil filled eyes darted between David and me, his sharp, rat like face smiled. "Go on. You may speak."

David shifted in his seat. We looked at each other then back at Morbal without a word.

Forate grunted as the Doctor squinted his eyes while speaking. "Very well, have it your way." A slight pause. "You've betrayed me, all three of you. But even more so, even worse, you've betrayed yourselves. I'm here to help, to cure you." He glanced at Berg, shoved his head then looked back at us. "Well, you two at least. This one is hopeless, useless. But you two are sick; criminals with rotten minds. Insane, delusional and a danger to Tehlasrin, the wonderful society we've worked so hard to build."

I couldn't help but scoff at that, causing Morbal's eyebrows to rise. Tehlasrin? Wonderful? What an effing joke.

"Let's begin with Mr. Holt." The Doctor paced back and forth, obviously unable to contain the joy he was having. The prick was loving every second of this.

David's grip tightened. I could see his tendons stretching as he clasped the desktop. Then and there I realized how much he'd suffered here too. I knew he felt the same dread I'd been fighting with since the first day I'd arrived.

"You're a deviant. A fiend, obsessed with sex. We've worked so hard to rid you of your maddening lust. I thought we were making great progress." Morbal nodded as his face showed a disheartened expression. "Then you had to throw it all away, giving in to a moment of weakness with that *whore*. Disgusting." He moved closer to David, looking deep into his eyes. "Was she worth it? Worth your soul, your freedom?" He sneered while rubbing his chin, seemingly deep in thought. "We now have no alternative. I'm not a man who gives up, ever, especially not so easily. I REFUSE to surrender. You WILL be cured today."

My heart pounded against my ribs. What were they going to do to him?

Morbal sighed. "And you, Mr. Sworn." Saying my name was like an icicle being jammed into my spine. "Our last session was nearly a miracle. You were almost there. So close." He turned his head ever so slightly toward the hulk standing next to him. "Right, Forate?"

"Yes, Doctor." The behemoth nodded with a smirk, his eyes glistened with insanity. "So damn close."

Morbal's gaze burrowed into me. "We'll do better today. We WILL reach the pinnacle. We'll lance out the weak parts of your mind that are holding you back. The thoughts and feelings which are already withering away. Can you... smell it, Mr. Sworn? The dying remnants of your diluted conscience?" His eyes nearly closed in ecstasy. "Mmm."

I could only listen, nearly petrified. Sweat trickled down the sides of my face.

Morbal pressed on. "First we'll remove that pathetic sense of justice then we'll eliminate your cares." He smiled, eyes fully open now, his hand patted Berg's head again. "Would you like to know how? Yes." A nod. "You'll witness the slow, deliberate, calculated destruction of this traitor and then the final liberation of your friend. Those experiences will grant you knowledge, clarity. They'll teach you, help you shatter your delusions until you can no longer deny reality." He smiled. "When there's nothing left to hold on to, there's always the truth. The true nature of reality. My truth, which I want to share with you and everyone else." The man beamed. "At long last, the weight on you will be gone and by God you'll be FREE!"

"Like me." Forate said with a grin that spread clear across his ugly face.

Pride oozed from Morbal. "Two little birds freed with one stroke. You see, when I say 'liberating,' Mr. Holt, I mean we'll physically take away the instrument of your lust." He licked his sick, dry, thin lips. "Oh, I know, it's rather elementary but effective and necessary after you so brazenly disregarded my other techniques." He nodded in the general direction of David's groin. "When that distraction is gone so will your addiction. You'll be open to seeing the world the way I see it. The way it really is. MY way."

His eyes were back on me. "Do you see now? Your friend will be transformed. In essence, the man you know will be dead and you'll become free of the burden that comes from caring about him." He straightened, placed his bony hands on his almost non existing hips and nodded, satisfactorily. "Today is the first day of your new lives."

He let his sense of accomplishment hang in silent air for a moment. "Forate. Take this traitor to the surgery room and get everything ready. We'll meet you soon."

The tank of a man collected the Berg as he whimpered. His smile was like some hungry, demonic wolf, leering over a cowering victim.

"Please!" The young man finally found his tongue. "I didn't mean to... it's just, I did it for the clear! It's too expensive, I only wanted a little." He reached out and clasped his hands around Morbal's left ankle.

"GET HIM OFF ME!" Morbal shrieked.

Forate yanked the man away who still pleaded.

"PLEASE! I won't do it again, oh God, please!"

The Doctor looked at Berg with absolute hatred. "I KNOW you won't do it again." His eyes narrowed. "Take to heart that you'll be doing Mr. Sworn a great service. One more sacrifice for my forgiveness."

Morbal waved his hand and Forate took him out of the room. I could hear him screaming for what seemed a long time. The Doctor let things quiet down before speaking again. "I'm amazed you've been able to smuggle in all that clear right under my nose, Mr. Holt. Naughty, naughty. You'll be much better behaved after you're... fixed." He laughed.

"I hate you." I said with a snarl, breaking my silence. My body trembled with rage. The vents began to hum louder.

"Jason." David said. "Don't. Don't let them get to you."

Sensing the threat we posed to the Doctor, the keepers in the room all charged their shock gloves.

I don't know how, but David's words helped, like they always did. I felt stronger, clear, less afraid, and ready to fight.

Morbal picked up on it and surprised me when he stamped his feel like a toddler throwing a tantrum. "Will you

STOP? STOP IT! These fantasies of yours refuse to relent and will only bring pain to your life." He was flustered, angry and frustrated as hell. "You're a conquered man. Accept it! Both of you! What you're feeling now is your disease's last ditch grasp at life. Let it die!"

I looked at David, knew he was on the same page as me, ready to strike. We both turned back to Morbal.

His beady, dark eyes sparkled with madness as he gritted his perfectly straight, white teeth. "THEY WILL DIE! I am more powerful. ME! You can't beat me."

The muscles in my legs were ready to spring… then all hell broke loose.

A deafening explosion went off and the entire building shook. Desks and bodies flew in every direction and my body was lurched to the floor. My head smacked the edge of one of the desks, briefly knocking out my vision.

Morbal's voice was frantic. "WHAT THE HELL?"

The blackness slowly left my eyes and I was able to see David *move*. Despite the earth shattering eruption he was up on his feet, fighting for his life, for our lives. He grabbed and picked up a desk before slamming it into the nearest keeper's head. Another guard came at him. With amazing speed, he grabbed the man's left wrist with his left hand and brought his right palm up to blast against the man's elbow. The force was strong enough to bend the keeper's arm the wrong way, breaking and splintering bones. Screams filled the room again.

The other guards were attacking and I saw Morbal cowardly slink out through the doorway. David hurled a second desk at the Doctor's head but missed his head and body by inches. The weasel fled, hollering orders as he ran.

I watched it all like it was a movie, none of it seemed real and my head was still spinning and no doubt bleeding from the blow I'd taken. David's voice snapped me a little out of my daze. "Get off your ass and help for Christ's sake!"

Bringing myself to my feet, I hurried up behind the nearest keeper and punched him, hard in his right kidney. The man crumpled over a little and my next strike landed against the side of his face. A couple of his teeth and some blood hit the floor before the rest of him.

Pairs of shock gloves came for us. I followed David's example and used the toppled desks as weapons, picking up two of them and once and sandwiching the nearest keeper's head between them. Another guard reached for me and came within an inch of my arm. Quickly, I grabbed the outside of the glove, at the man's wrist where there weren't any shock points, and squeezed. In a couple seconds, I was able to overpower and turn his own weapon against him. In essence, the prick shocked himself and dropped, convulsing. Good.

Sparing a glance around the room, I saw only David and I were left standing. We took a moment to listen to the chaos going on all around. People were screaming, laughing and yelling amidst bangs, crashes and more explosions.

David nodded and spoke in a slightly arrogant tone. "I told you. Time to check out."

I smiled and the small laugh that escaped my lungs was the best feeling I'd had in years. "Don't be a dick."

"Come on."

I took a step and then my legs gave out, bringing me back to the ground, exhausted. The fight took what little was left out of me. All I could do was curse, desperate for any semblance of strength, enough to get me out and free.

A couple heartbeats later, David was alongside me. He pressed something against my lips. "Open and swallow, NOW!"

I grunted in slight protest, knowing what he was doing but I didn't resist even as he spoke. "Damn it. If you don't take this, it's over. No choice. Do it!"

The thin pill felt like a grain of dry rice going down my throat. Clear. Most of it dissolved on my tongue but I it all went down with a couple swallows. In seconds, my muscles came back to me. I blinked and stood up. David was already on his feet.

"Where the hell did you have that stashed?" I asked.

David made an ugly face. He didn't need to answer.

Whatever. I nodded, feeling amazed. Life coursed back through my body. I felt good. "Ok, let's go."

My friend put his hand out. "Wait." He looked around at the men sprawled out on the floor. "Grab some shoes. It's just barely spring and we're on a mountain in Colorado." He glanced at me. "Wouldn't be good to have our feet freeze."

An odd sensation hit me. I knew where the asylum was but before now, it didn't matter. It felt like I was waking up from a year and a half long nightmare.

I picked a pair of shoes off one of the larger keepers and they fit me for the most part. Oh well, no time to try them all on. David was laced up and ready. He and I were soldiers and knew speed was key in times like this. Time to move.

"Hey David!" An unknown voice called out from the hallway outside the room.

My heart skipped a beat and I armed myself with another desk. Turns out, it was another patient. A young black man with a smooth face and a deep voice. The newcomer scanned the room with raised eyebrows. He nodded at us. "Good job. We're on clean-up duty but everyone needs to bolt soon. The guards here are clowns but they have a big number advantage."

"Right." David said. "What's the plan?"

I was confused but kept my mouth shut.

"Head toward the western exit and run your asses a kilometer south as quickly as you can." The man said, handing David a crudely drawn map, pointing at a small red dot. "Get here. All the security doors have been shut down but that probably won't last. The escort won't wait forever either so hurry up."

"Got it." David nodded, folding the map up and tucking it under his pants' waistband.

"Ok, good luck." With that, the man nodded and darted away.

I stepped alongside David. "Who was that?"

"No time." He shook his head. "Let's do what he said."

We swiftly started on our way, down the many blank, white halls. Everything was amok. The once immaculate, organized, silent asylum was now a scene of outright rebellion. Any keepers David and I came across were quickly taken out, knocked out or left crying and bleeding.

It was a little troubling seeing some of the patients that were about to be freed into the world. Some of them were obviously raving lunatics. Still, I figured even they didn't deserve to be here as Morbal's twisted playthings. That and the rest of the world was far from a perfect place so to hell with it.

David and I rushed down another long, messy, bloody hallway when a sudden pain hit me in my gut. I stopped and shouted over the roars of combat and chaos. "WAIT!"

My friend turned and looked at me as though I'd sprouted horns. "WHAT?" He yelled.

"I have to go back." I said, to my own disbelief. "I can't leave yet."

"Are you crazy? Come on, quick! There's no time!"

I shook my head. "No, I can't let them torture him."

"WHO?"

My hands clenched into tight fists. "Berg. He's not a bad man. He helped us. I can't leave him with them."

I thought David was going to call me every name in the book and leave me right then and there. He should. I was an idiot and freedom was so close. Instead, the look on my friend's face changed to one of realization and he nodded.

"You're right." He took off running the way we'd come and I followed. "Jesus, HURRY!"

-

We reached the surgery room in good time, passing scores of keepers and patients sprawled out on the floor. The commotion had died down a little, reminding me time was short. No doubt many of the prisoners were either recaptured or making a mad dash for freedom.

I swore under my breath. David and I should be outside too. Instead, some stupid, overbearing sense of justice had a hold on us and we were here trying to save a man who didn't give a damn about us.

Morbal's voice boomed over the loud speakers. "All keepers, all keepers! Secure all patients in you assigned wings. Use of extreme force has been approved. Once everything is secured, report in to the operations assembly room."

David pointed at a couple downed keepers. "Grab their gloves. No telling who's in there." He pointed at a pair of large, swinging doors which led into the surgery room.

I obeyed and let out a deep breath I hadn't realized I'd been holding, even while running. Once we were both armed, I looked at him.

"Let's do it." He said with a nod.

We barged through the doors together, as ready as we could be for however many enemies there were waiting for us. The large, long room was empty, or so it seemed at first.

At the far end there appeared to be a body lying on a bed. It, he or she, was completely covered by a large white sheet. There was a table next to the bed with a wicked selection of sharp, shiny surgical blades and tools on it.

My heart thumped and my eyes took in every inch of the room. David crept around, silent as a cat, searching...

I whispered. "Maybe everyone took off after the explosions went off."

"Wait by the door and zap anyone who comes in." David ordered. "I'll check the table."

"Ok." I posted myself on the right side of the entrance, out of view to anyone might peek through either of the two small windows, one on each door.

The adrenaline rush I felt from the drug I'd swallowed made it hard to keep still. I worked on keeping my attention evenly focused and split between the door and David. I saw him hesitantly glide closer to the table. He reached to pull the sheet off the body…

A balled fist, followed by an arm shot out and struck David directly in his chest. He grunted and fell back a good distance before landing in a sitting position. A large, familiar figure rose from under the bed where the covered body laid. Forate. He lunged for my wheezing friend, giggling.

David moved just in time, causing the big man to belly flop on the cold, sterile floor.

I charged in to help. By the time Forate was back on his feet, I was close enough to plant a strong right hook flush against his large, square jaw. He barely flinched. Christ. Instead, the son of a bitch looked at me and made a 'kissy' gesture, sound and all, with his lips.

I swung again, this time for the mass of his gut, planting three good, incredibly quick blows before he roundhouse kicked me square in my chest. Now I was on the floor, gasping for air like David had been. Forate's strength and agility was impressive, I had to give him that. It didn't seem natural.

No David was on the offensive and I heard him charge up his shock gloves. The large bastard heard them too and stepped back toward the bed he'd been hiding and waiting under. He pulled the sheet off and I could see Berg's face but no sign he was still alive.

Forate squealed in delight. "Come on. COME ON! You little bitches!" His hands moved without taking his eyes off David, like they worked separate from his brain with eyes of their own. They found a couple especially lethal looking surgical knives that were laying on the table. He waved them in the air.

David slowed his attack, searching for an opening and uneager to let the blades tear into his skin.

I got up and charged my own gloves, moving next to my friend. The three of us shared a brief stare down until Forate broke the silence.

"You little cowards! Look at yourselves... you outnumber me! Surely I'm no match for two strapping men like you!" He waited. "No? Cold feet? FINE!" With that, the maniac whipped the blade in his right hand straight at my face. I moved, an inch away from the thing as it whizzed by my face, close enough to where I could feel the cold wind on my ear.

The attack distracted me, giving Forate the opening he wanted. He charged, like a bull in a ring, impossibly fast! When he was close enough, he dropped and swung his leg around to meet David's knee with his foot. My friend fell back down, crashing to the floor with a loud thud.

I attacked, jabbing my charged right palm at Forate's body but he was too quick and spun away. Counterstriking, he swung the blade in his left hand up at me and sliced through the cheap fabric on my pants, just missing my skin again.

The big man rolled to his right and snatched David's ankle. When he was back on his feet, the beast tugged and whipped David's body around. Amazingly, he was able to lift my friend up a good four feet into the air before slamming him back down, practically head first.

The move left a small opening on Forate's left and I took it, charging and pressing both hands flush against his chest. The blasts of electricity discharged and coursed through his huge body. The man let out a great roar and fell backward, crashing into an empty bed and taking it to the floor with him. The blade fell from his massive hand and clanged on the floor.

I recharged my gloves without wasting a second. No way was the bastard dead, besides I could see his chest heaving up and down. Not for long. I moved in for the kill.

Unfamiliar with the devices, I spared a split second to look down at the gloves on my hand, reloading them. In that part of an instant, Forate actually managed to get up and rush me. Weaponless, he swung his giant fist at my face. I tried to duck, too slow. The blow landed against the left side of my skull, momentarily knocking me silly, staggering from the blow just barely able to see the second assault. This time I was able to avoid the hit and even countered with a swing of my own. An uppercut that landed flat against the man's chin. I heard some of Forate's teeth crack.

He bellowed a fierce growl and plowed his left fist into my gut. I keeled over, unable to breathe. Forate's leg came up and kicked my chest. My body shot backward and I crashed to the floor. He stayed on me without any hesitation, ripping the gloves off my hands, tossing them away.

Forate nearly slapped me senseless before he began mashing my stinging face into the ground. To my surprise, he stood up and backed off.

I groaned and fought to get to my knees, sparing a glance at David. He hadn't moved and his eyes were closed.

Forate stood over me. "That's IT!" He spit a couple pieces of broken teeth at me. "I can't waste any more time playing with you." He bent down and picked up one of the blades that was laying by his foot. "A shame. We could've had so much fun together. Still, I'm not going to lie. I'm going to really enjoy this."

He held the blade in his right hand and brought it up toward my face, drawing closer and closer. I tried to move away, unable to stand, but before I could get far, Forate had his left hand around the back of my neck. "No more running. No more chances."

I lashed out, bunching, straining, and trying to scramble away. Failed. Finally, I grabbed the man's right wrist with both my hands, trying to keep the knife from cutting me. I couldn't over power him. It was only a matter of moments now.

Someone hollered from behind Forate. The large man twirled, releasing me. I saw Berg spring off the bed, armed with a strange, sharp, large, hook shaped utensil of his own. Forate swung his knife but was too slow. The keeper dodged the swing and then stuck his own weapon into Forate's large barrel chest.

Berg dropped to the floor and rolled away from Forate's wild, angry, retaliatory strikes. The beast didn't go down but his face showed fear.

A fresh wave of adrenaline, fueled by Forate's disorientation, helped me get back to my feet. I attacked again, punching and pounding on the wide, scarred face until it was little more than a bloody pulp. Finally, the maniac fell.

Berg's blade handle still protruded from Forate's chest. I planned to bring my foot down on it, aiming to shove it straight through him. I drew close but the animal let out another bellow and wrapped his huge arms around my legs, pulling me down to the ground with him.

Despite the blows and the knife buried in his chest, he still manhandled me. He soon had his immense hands around my neck again and I couldn't breathe. Frantic, I punched, scratched and clawed as much as I could. It did nothing.

Forate laughed with delight as blood ran down and off his face onto mine. My vision started to cloud when Berg attacked again. The keeper kicked the monster right in its mouth. Annoyed to say the least, he released me again and snatched the small, young man.

Roaring, Forate tossed Berg's body. It smacked hard into the surgical table and then crumpled on the floor.

Air raced back into my lungs and I pressed a small attack, pushing, punching and struggling. The bastard was still on top of me, keeping me pinned to the ground. He snarled and backhanded me across my face. The hit jerked my head back and it hit the floor, hard. Forate reached for his chest and pulled the blade out. Blood gushed from the open wound.

"Now," Forate hissed through bloody, broken, clenched teeth, "let's finish what you started, eh?" The sharp edge moved toward my throat, right where I'd cut myself a day earlier.

Before the weapon could dig in, David rushed up next to Forate and placed both of his gloved hands on the sides of

Forate's face. The electric waves of death surged through the beast's head, cooking everything in it.

The blade slipped out of his hands before Forate's huge body splattered on top of me. David helped me get out from under the lifeless mass.

We allowed ourselves a few seconds to gather our breath. We needed to get moving.

"Think there's still time?" I asked. "Is that contact still out there?

David frowned. "Only one way to find out. Either way, I'm not hanging around here. Move."

"I can help."

We both looked at Berg after he spoke. His face winced with pain. "I know the quickest ways around here."

"We want the west exit." David said between heavy breaths.

Berg nodded. "Ok."

"Let's go." I said, not caring to wonder how I even had the strength to stand, let alone run.

David smiled at me. "That's the spirit."

Berg led the way and we sped after him. The hallways were mostly silent except for a few keepers who wailed in pain here and there.

Morbal's voice blasted through the speakers again. "Forate! Forate, report to the operations assembly room at once!"

I looked at David and he grinned.

We ran hard. We ran to freedom.

# Chapter 4

I escaped hell and finally breathed free air again. I'd almost forgotten what it was like. My senses came back to me and I could actually *feel* again. The smell of the ocean, the touch of a spring breeze on my face and the heat from the Sun was nearly overwhelming. The days of white walls, stale air and daily torture were finally over.

I made it to Pacificus to start a new life… I hoped.

David and I were standing outside, waiting to be judged. Judged on whether or not we'd be allowed into the island nation. Pessimism, an unfortunate, constant colleague of mine nagged my brain the whole time. My gut was a havoc of nausea and uneasiness.

As nervous, hopeless and tormented as I was, my friend seemed the exact opposite. Of course. David Holt, Mr. Optimist. I swore under my breath. How did he do it? I looked at him. His smile was impossibly huge, eyes darting around taking everything, especially everything female, in.

We stood in the middle of a long line leading to a group of people who worked for August Cross. They were busy interviewing, probably interrogating more likely, new arrivals that had come over on the boat with David and me. At a glance, I guessed there were about five or six hundred men and women hoping to enter the new country.

I shuffled another few paces forward and looked down at my dirty shirt, ripped, stained pants and oversized shoes. Pathetic. I looked like a bum. It was embarrassing but my only consolation was that I didn't look any worse than the others in line with me. We were all refugees.

The workers weren't wearing uniforms, not like the servants of the state in Tehlasrin. There, individuality of any sort was discouraged with absolute disdain. Here, the men and women wore their own clothes, business casual, comfortable, some with ties some not. They looked happy, cheerful expressions on their faces, greeting each new person with joyful pleasantness. Beyond that though, I noticed their eyes most of all. They were piercing, studied us closely, watching, seemingly knowing.

I stopped my thoughts right there since they were starting to give me the creeps.

Aside from their interrogators was a small army of soldiers or mercenaries or something. They, men and women, patrolled around the entire dock, also observing. Even their uniform was lax compared to what I was used to. Dark blue caps on their heads and long sleeve, navy blue shirts with silver badges over the left breast. They were armed, heavily but still nodded, greeted politely and smiled. Happy guards... this place was weird.

My palms started sweating. My 'glass is half empty' brain took hold. The pleasantness set me on edge. It seemed fake. It all must be a hoax, a trap to lure in unsuspecting fools who'd be forced into slavery. I should run. Turn around, skip the boat, leap into the ocean and swim as fast and far as possible.

I was about to step out of line when David spoke. "Hey, you alright?"

When I looked at him, my nerves started to settle. I remembered why I was here. I didn't leave the line. Odd, somewhat powerful feelings in my gut told me I belonged here. I didn't want to trust them but between the yearning to be here and David's easy confidence, I couldn't fight them.

"Yea." I finally replied. I couldn't deny this was exactly where I wanted to be, where I felt we should be. I *belonged* here.

Recent history played over in my head. After getting out of Morbal's asylum, we reached our contact. I wasn't sure where we were going but one word kept resonating over and over through my head; Aswain.

As it turned out, we didn't really have much choice in the matter. Our contact leader, a spunky, short-tempered woman, told us this was exactly where we were going. She led us through a series of rendezvous, taking us through a zigzagging westward bound journey toward the Pacific Ocean. The woman was named Fier... yes Fier Wren. Sounding like 'fire' only spelled differently, she pointed out several times. I guessed the name was made up. What parent would name their kid Fier?

At one point, one of her subordinates confessed that he and the other contacts worked for August Cross. He also noted that it was indeed Cross's operatives who had planned and carried out the asylum attack. It was all supposed to be extremely 'hush hush' and confidential so Fier chewed the guy out. After an especially colorful and threatening verbal lashing, she turned to David and me and told us keep our mouths shut, especially while we were still in Tehlasrin.

I asked her why we were even broken out in the first place and she didn't give an answer, just a shrug and a slight nudge from her head. Ok. Then I asked what the GU would do if they found out. Wren smiled and pulled out a thick wad of cash, telling me the local guards wouldn't be a problem. That wasn't really what I was asking, I wondered what the Union would do to Cross but whatever.

David asked what we were supposed to do once we reached the island and Fier told us we'd find out soon enough. Again, had it not been for the odd desire nudging me toward wanting to go to Aswain, I would've protested. After a couple seconds of thought, I figured it didn't matter, there wasn't anywhere else to go. Tehlasrin had me black listed as a murderer and now a fugitive. It'd only be a matter of time before I was caught and probably put back in Morbal's asylum or someplace even worse, if that were possible.

Berg wasn't with us. After a quick scan of his blood, Fier flat out told him he wasn't invited to Aswain. Strange. The guy didn't really seem to care either way and was off on his own after our first stop. I bet he was happy to be free from the cramped, smelly, dirty transport we were all jammed in. There was Fier, three of her colleagues and seven other escapees with David and me. Crappy as it was, it still fared infinitely better than my pod's quarters.

Naturally, David spent most of his time shadowing Fier's every move. The woman had the fortune of being the first female to cross his path outside the asylum. It didn't help matters that she was quite attractive. The other men were all over her too but my horny friend had a knack at cutting them off at every corner. Fier didn't show the slightest interest in return, all but outright ignoring him.

I couldn't really care less. My head and body were absolutely exhausted. All I wanted was sleep and that's what I did. The only time I woke up what when I needed to eat, relieve myself or make a dash for the next transport in our journey. They said our trip from Colorado to Aswain, which sat in the Pacific Ocean about a hundred and thirty miles west of Oregon, took four days.

One thing I noticed was how easily we passed from checkpoint to checkpoint. Fier's seemingly endless supply of money bought all the corrupt guards we came across. The Tehlasrin soldiers were delighted to see us. They were supposed to stop and arrest us but instead greeted us like old friends. It was another case of how pathetic, rotten and dirty the Union was but, for my part, I was glad the men and women, our enemies, cared more about lining their pockets than doing their jobs.

Seeing the money made me think about Cross. *August Cross*. I couldn't understand the man. Why would anyone spend so much on a bunch of escaped mental patients? Either he had so much wealth it didn't matter, we were being lured in to become slaves on his island or he was just plain insane.

"Oh wow." David purred lustfully, pulling me back to the present. "Look at her!"

My eyes traced his line of vision. He was looking at a thin, disheveled young woman with a bruised face and filthy, ratty hair. She wasn't hideous but no beauty for sure. I looked back at David and saw him lick his lips.

"Hot." He gasped. "Not like Fier but I'd still love to lick-"

He was cut off when a group of people suddenly started shouting in protest. The group demanded our attention.

"This isn't fair!" A man yelled.

Another in his group, a woman, pleaded. "We can't go back there. They'll torture us!"

"Please!" A kid, sixteen at the most, cried, "Let me stay! Don't send us away!"

There were a dozen of them being herded by several guards back toward the boat. The soldiers tried to calm the group down, telling the distraught bunch that they were sorry but had no choice and there wasn't anything they could do. The genuine politeness didn't help any. The exiles grew more desperate the closer they got to the boat.

One of the refugees, a short, burly, middle aged man let out a small roar. "NO! This is BULL! This is our last chance! This is supposed to be sanctuary!" Something about the guy was grossly familiar...

"Jesus," David started, "that guy looks like Forate."

I nodded and watched the big man lunge at the nearest guard, tugging her down to the ground. David tensed up and my hands balled into fists. Conflict lit a fire in both of us, nearly forcing us to act. My friend took a couple steps toward the action when the whole group folded in on itself. The guards swarmed the small rioters then succinctly and efficiently bound their hands.

The soldiers' speed and accuracy was impressive, so was their overall gentleness. My brows rose halfway up my forehead. Had something like this happened at Morbal's asylum, or anywhere on Tehlasrin, the small group would've been flat out killed. This was much different. The guards didn't inflict any harm, didn't show any maliciousness nor did they use an ounce of force beyond what was necessary.

Beaten, the bound group marched back the way they came. There were some grumbles but no more physical outbursts. Amazing. Even then, the guards still apologized for the unfortunate situation.

I stepped forward in my line still watching the group. I wondered why they were rejected while two thoughts fired off simultaneously in my head: First was an incredible respect for the guards; second was the fear that I'd be the next one cast off, back to the asylum.

Why wouldn't I be kicked off? What new, free, successful country would want someone like me around? I was a murderous mental patient and a fugitive. I sighed, turned, looked ahead and swallowed all with a sick, deflated expression on my face. Christ. Half of me feared being taken in and the other half feared being bounced out. Typical.

David slapped me on my chest. "Hey! Cheer up." He was smiling, of course. "We're almost up!"

The guy always seemed happiest at times when I was filled with dread. How the eff did he do it?

A moment later, two of the interviewers, or screeners, or whatever, became available at the same time. David gave me a wink before skipping off to the female employee leaving me some guy who'd interrogate me.

I sat down in the chair across from the man with a small desk between us. The person's face showed a dangerously friendly smile. He had short, bushy brown hair, a small matching goatee and brown eyes. He studied my eyes while the ambient sound of the crowd behind me faded away to nothingness. I sat there, locked in silence.

He finally spoke. "Hi!"

The word came with such enthusiasm it made me jump. I managed the slightest of nods.

He laughed. "Sorry. My name's Joshua Sands, call me Josh. I'll be your adjustment counselor for the first few weeks of your new life here."

My eyes narrowed. "So I'm in?"

"Well, almost." He nodded. "We just have a few things to check out."

*Great.* I tried to muster some strength in my voice but came off too strongly. "What do you want to know?" It was almost a growl.

The interviewer, Josh, sat back in his chair and sighed. He seemed disappointed but the smile didn't leave his face. He spoke calmly. "Try to relax. We're not going to hurt you and there's nothing to be afraid of. Most of us were where you're at when we first arrived here." He nodded. The guy had a young face but his seasoned tone was confident, experienced and almost soothing. "I know how you feel."

I gave the slightest of nods and let out a breath I didn't know I was holding.

"That's better." He moved up again in his seat and danced his fingertips over the keyboard in front of him. The back of the monitor faced me so I couldn't see what Josh was looking at or typing. "Ok."

A quiet moment lingered into an uneasy spell. He looked at me, into my eyes, studying me more closely.

I swallowed and squirmed a little in my seat.

Josh blinked, easing up. "Go ahead and please place your right hand on the desk, palm up."

It was hard to tell what raced faster, my heart or my brain. Why did he want my hand on the desk? What did I do? What did he know? What was he going to do? Should I refuse? What would happen if I said no?

The man snorted and bit his lip. He looked around at everyone before zeroing back on my face. "It's a crazy world. Things are messed up. I know you've been through hard times" As he spoke, his hands were busy pulling out a small needle that tipped the end of cable which ran directly into his computer.

Seeing where my attention rested, he glanced at the cable. "Ever seen one of these? They're pretty new."

I didn't budge, frozen by a blend of suspicion and dread.

He leaned closer and showed off the instrument. "It's a new type of hardware that works with the PDRI-"

"The Plasma Database Registry and Information." I blurted, numbly.

The man nodded. "Yea."

My eyes shifted back and forth from his face to the needle. The PDRI was an enormous electronic file on everyone in Tehlasrin. Everything, and I mean everything from day one of everyone's lives was recorded in there. All anyone in power had to do to learn a person's deepest, darkest secrets was scan a sample of DNA.

"That's a Union tool." I barked behind gritted teeth. "Only the GU uses it. I thought you, this whole place isn't part of them."

The man's eyebrows perked up. "We aren't, not by any means. However, the tool has been helpful to Governor Cross. We've made good use of it, keeping potentially dangerous agents out of Aswain."

A very large lump formed in my throat. *Dangerous agents*. Sort of like murderous escaped mental patients. I shook my head, feeling my eyes threating to tear up out of sheer frustration. "How the hell did you, or he, Cross, even get access to the database then? Tehlasrin is corrupt as hell but come on…"

"The Governor has a lot of influence in the world." He nodded. "None of this would be here otherwise." The man smiled again, gesturing the newcomers. "Look around, we need to know at least a little about people before they move in.

"Right." The word reluctantly escaped my lips.

"Think about it," Josh went on, "I'm sure you've met some nasty people who could and would cause a lot of harm."

Forate, Morbal, my old military unit, the keeps, hell, just about everyone. I was no better. That was it, my chances of living here were gone. I was done. The whole prospect seemed ridiculous now, a bad joke. There was no way the Union would allow Cross access to their prized data and even less of chance I'd be allowed in. I slapped the back of my hand down on the desk. "Fine. Let's get this over with."

The other man exhaled deeply. "I'll know a lot more about you in a few moments but first I think you should be less suspicious." He nodded. "I can tell that's hard for you and I understand but wouldn't be great if you were able to surrender a little trust once in a while?" He swabbed the end of my thumb and chuckled as he poked it with the needle." Have a little faith. It's liberating."

I barely felt the small prick and was surprised when the needle was pulled away. "That's it?" I asked.

His eyes were glued to his monitor when he spoke. "That's it. Less than a drop. Pretty cool, huh?" He rubbed his chin and glanced at me. "Just give me a few moments to read up here, Jason."

A wave of heat flushed through my body when he said my name. The registry was working just fine.

The expression on Joshua Sands' face grew stern. "Morbal's?" He grimaced and sighed. "I'm so sorry. Of all the hells on the planet, that's one of the worst." His eyes, seemingly knowingly, shifted to my neck before he continued reading.

I reached up and rubbed the wound, feeling both angry and ashamed.

"Information on your time at the asylum is rather sparse which only further shows Morbal was doing things in there he didn't want the world to know about." The man's tone was growing more and more serious. "You already know Governor Cross was behind the break out so I can tell you I'm proud of the good we've been able to do. Maledro Morbal is a monster."

"Yea, I know."

He cleared his throat. "Your past has some serious history to it." He looked at me. "That's not news to you, though."

I paused and barely spoke above a mumble. "Enough history to kick me out?"

Josh raised his eyebrows. "Almost."

Almost? A rush of fresh air filled my lungs.

The man's smile returned. "The Governor trusts my team of councilors." He nodded back and forth at the others sitting behind desks around us. "We have a lot of say and responsibility. We decide who gets in and we take our jobs extremely seriously. We take everything into consideration."

I nodded, unsure what to say.

"Jason," he sat up straight and bore his gaze deep into my eyes. "I'm leaning toward allowing you to stay but I see traits of clear in your blood."

Oh crap...

"The reading is faint but it's there." The man poignantly placed his index finger down on the desktop, emphasizing what he was about to say. "It ends here, right now, NO exceptions. No more clear. There's not to be a speck of that drug in our country. If we catch it on you, you're immediately banned." He squinted. "Sound fair? Understood?"

I nodded again. "Yes." I thought of explaining the very good reason the drug was in my blood but knew it didn't matter. I only hoped David wouldn't get rejected.

"I don't know what you've heard of Aswain but it's unlike any place on Earth and we need to protect it. My colleagues and I are the first line of defense." He smirked. "I know you can appreciate that."

"I do."

His demeanor lightened. "As for your history. I can see why you did what you did, the reason you were arrested and sent to the asylum." The man's eyes narrowed. "The database sheds a little light but I can read the rest right off you."

A confused look painted my face.

"We all have great talents here." Josh said. "I'm usually able to understand people better than they understand themselves. You have talents too. In time here, you'll figure them out."

"So," I paused, "I can stay?"

"Direct." He laughed. "Yes, I'm allowing you in. Everything in your record checks out and I believe you'll become a valuable part of our country. Still, I'll need to keep in contact with you to make sure you're adjusting well, given your past."

Relief was slowly filling me up as the reality of the moment sank in. "That sounds reasonable."

Joshua Sands opened a drawer in his desk and pulled out an unmarked, white box. He quickly placed several items in it before punching some keys into his keyboard. Papers began springing out of a nearby printer. He folded the sheets up and slid them into the box. Finally, he pulled out a business card and handed it to me. "This is my work number. Call me, every day at 11am."

"Ok." I said, thinking, remembering I had nothing but the baggy clothes I was wearing. "How do I contact you?"

Josh laughed, heartily. "You'll see one of the keys to thriving here is efficiency." He patted the box. "There's a transport train waiting to take you to your new living quarters. The box has information on your address, your ID, a mobile phone, credits to local clothing and grocery stores and a bank account."

Dumbfounded, I felt like someone suddenly whapped me across my face with a fluffy, feathery pillow. I only blinked like a big dope.

The man snapped his fingers. "Wake up! Listen, lots of others to get through today."

I focused.

"Governor Cross has put everything into this country and we're a free enterprise nation." His eyes narrowed a bit. "We help you get started but you need to make a living for yourself. We're not a charity. We all need to contribute. Get a job and do some good."

I found my voice. "Of course. I'm not a free loader."

"There's also and information disk on everything going on here with multiple leads on employment openings." He tapped the box again. "Given your past and what's most available, I'd recommend looking in the security or construction fields."

"Right." My head was starting to swim. Everything was moving so fast.

My bewilderment seemed to amuse the other man. He chuckled. "You'll need to get a photo taken to go along with your identification in the next week. Your apartment is temporary if you choose to move elsewhere. It's small but not bad… everything's new here."

I actually giggled. "I bet it'll be a whole hell of a lot better than what I've been used to."

Joshua nodded. "True."

He slid the box over to me and I gently placed both my hands on it before pulling it closer. A whole new life was inside that little, cardboard cube, my life. Incredible. I looked at the other's face. "Is that it?"

He smirked, "That's it," Then craned his neck to look behind me. "Yep, busy, busy day. You move along, I have a lot of others to, how did you put it, interrogate?"

On the last word, Joshua gave a little, knowing wink that sent a chill down my spine. I never actually said anything about interrogation. Christ, it was like he could read my brain.

I nodded and stood up.

"Oh," he started, "one other thing. There's information in the box on our various recuperation centers. You've been through a storm of nightmares. I want you to pick one out and give it a visit tomorrow." He paused. "This isn't a request. Do it. They're good, great people that can help your mind and body cope with all the changes and the shock you've endured. They'll also help you recover your strength."

Sounded a lot like more 'therapy' to me. My stomach turned but I only agreed. "Ok."

Josh waved a dismissive hand in the air. "Go on, follow the signs. The next train heads out in fifteen minutes. David is waiting for you."

My brow furrowed. "How..?"

"Don't forget to call me, I have you in my database." With that, he tapped the side of his left temple then turned to greet the next newcomer.

I shook my head, shooing away the blend of confusion and curiosity about Joshua Sands, only to be replaced with the excitement and exhilaration that hit me the second I stepped through a final scanning portal and into the new country. My head whirled while a huge smile spread across my face despite feeling like I was about to pass out.

"Gonna stand there all day?"

I cut my eyes around to see David leaning against a clean, freshly painted pillar. He looked as pleased as I felt, face beaming. "I told you there was nothing to worry about."

I raised my eyebrows and let out a deep breath. "Yea."

"Come on," he said, "the train is this way."

There were signs everywhere telling us where to go. I rolled my eyes. "How'd you guess that?"

He laughed. "Don't be a dick." When we were within arm's reach, he planted his right hand on my shoulder, squeezed and gave me a little shake. "We made it!"

I smiled, nearly laughing and tearing up at the same time.

"Wonder if we'll live close to each other?" He pondered.

"Hmm," I looked down at my box. "No idea."

David nodded. "Let's check on the train." A couple quick steps later he said, "I hope there're a bunch of young women around us, ripe for the taking." His eye twinkled. "I've got a lot of catching up to do." He looked at me. "We BOTH do."

"Right." The word was barely above a whisper. Everything was just too bizarre. Nothing felt real.

David laughed. "Geez, you're really out of it. Let's go look for some places where we can get a few drinks after we're settled. My treat. I still owe you one." He sighed. "They took my clear away."

That woke me up. "Stay *away* from that crap." I spoke in as serious a tone as I could muster.

He nodded with reluctance. "I will. That gal, Lucy, my counselor, made her point back there." He huffed. "I just don't get it. The stuff is incredible. It's harmless."

I looked at him with raised eyebrows. "Harmless enough to get your ass punted off the island."

"Since when did you become such a goodie-goodie?"

"David…" I started.

He smiled. "Ok, ok. Don't worry. The stuff isn't addictive. No clear, no way, no how." He studied me, seeing approval. "Better?"

"Just don't eff with these guys."

We made it to the train, talked, exchanged phone numbers and poured over a map of the area we'd be living in. The two hour ride breezed by. Still, I mostly felt out of sorts the whole way. I was exhausted right up until I found my new apartment, washed myself in my new shower and passed out in my new bed. Those drinks would have to wait.

# Chapter 5

Even after a day and a half here, I still had trouble
believing my good fortune. I survived mental and physical
torture on a daily basis, escaped the asylum, fled the GU and
was allowed to live on the last free nation in the world. On top
of all that, I had my own place, furnished, a refrigerator packed
with food and a closet full of my own clothes. Jesus.

I ran my hands through my recently washed hair. It was
short, Morbal had seen to that, and I decided I was going to let
it grow out a little. Still, it didn't require any work but a quick
toweling off after showering. *Showers*. Nice, hot, long showers
were another delight I'd been sorely missing. They were
almost as spectacular as the food on the island. Every meal I'd
eaten had been amazing.

I considered heading back to a place called *Wally's* for
breakfast. They served the best pancakes and bacon I'd ever
had. It was hard to say if they were better than the
cheeseburger and fries at *Sweet Eats* I'd had for lunch the day
before though. Finally, the pizza and beer at *Fox Pizza Pub*
was astounding too.

It was wonderful actually being able to enjoy food again.
My taste buds, like every other part of me, felt like they were
returning to life. I literally tasted freedom and it was delicious.

It was just incredible, all of it. A large part of me felt like it was so much more than I deserved. In the back of my brain, a voice kept asking if I was really worthy of all this. Why should I get so much after everything I'd done? Still, Cross and his people were offering and I was taking. Only an idiot would toss away a winning lottery ticket.

Most of my first day here was spent taking care of various odds and ends. I shopped a bit and exercised several times. Nothing too strenuous. It would take a little time to get back into the shape I was in before being locked up. I ran a couple miles and worked out a couple sets of push-ups, pull-ups and a good set of core stretches. It was hard but felt great.

Other than that, I ate, had a photo taken for my ID, called Joshua Sands twice and watched some of that informational disk. The damn video, as informative as it was, reminded me of some lame, phony tourist advertisement. Everyone looked so happy and everything seemed so clean and fake. It all looked, well, perfect. The zinger was, as far as I could tell, the thing was completely accurate. The way things looked in the video was really how things were. Crazy.

According to the disk, Aswain's economy was growing rapidly. Private businesses were springing up as quickly as the buildings used to house them. Shops and trades of all kinds were thriving. The current population on the island had just topped two million and most were starting families.

I smirked after reading that, thinking of seeing David or me as family men. Neither seemed likely. My friend was likely far too wild and free, a real tomcat, to ever settle down and me… I was just too angry, brooding and difficult for relationships. I pitied whatever woman who was foolish enough to think of wanting to start a family with me. The smirk faded. Whatever.

Aswain used a unique currency called the Gem which was separate from the GU's Dollar. Money here was backed by various precious metals and goods. The country obviously traded a lot with Tehlasrin, greatly furthering growth and development. The island's main export was a new form of advanced, clean energy called etherspring. Curious, the video didn't give a lot of information on the stuff.

No one was homeless and employment was one hundred percent for everyone between twenty and sixty years old who'd been on the island more than two weeks. I blinked, considering that, wondering how long statistics like that would last. I also wondered if such a fact was even ethical. One hundred percent? Work or leave. That pessimistic voice was at it again, telling me the place, as remarkable as it was, was just another totalitarian system waiting to show its fangs.

I shook the thought away. The employment fact mostly worked to light a fire under my ass. David's too. We knew we needed to find work or we'd get booted. I'd already looked into some construction crews whereas my friend was leaning toward the security force. In actuality, for me, being a guard or a cop, or whatever, felt more comfortable but the thought of wearing a uniform left a sour taste in my mouth. The worst things I'd seen in the already horrible, dark, evil world were done by people in uniforms.

I paid particular attention to part of the video that showed maps of the country. The main island, which had about as much landmass as the old state of Michigan, was sort of shaped like kidney bean with the indented side on the west coast. Off that coast was a smaller, separate island called Shard Island. The disk explained that the smaller island was mostly undeveloped at this time with several resorts and just two cities. The largest, Ravenfall, was smaller than even the smallest city on the main island.

Oddly, the northern end of the big island had a steep mountain range with peaks over a mile high and the southern end was just barely above sea level. The entire southern coast was reinforced with an amazingly intricate and, I bet, very expensive system of levees to protect against large storms and rising tides.

There were lakes, rivers, streams, forests and parks dotted all around the island with several cities, towns and farmlands scattered about.

David and I lived in the capital, Prospous and what I'd seen so far was awesome. Everything was brand new with a blend of odd shaped skyscrapers and small cottage like buildings. It was a perfect mix of a futuristic metropolis and a small town from the old fairy tales.

As per Joshua's request, I visited the nearest recuperation center. The place smelled of candles and incense. It was weird and the lighting was dim with odd acoustics but surprisingly soothing. There was a woman working there who almost put me in a hypnotic state of relaxation. I'm not sure what she did to me but I felt her place objects on different areas of my body. She massaged my head and played different harmonic sounds that I'm sure would've been annoying had they not made me feel so calm and good. When I got out of there I felt much more alive and energized.

David visited the center too. I'm not sure what he got out of it because he didn't share much on his experience. Instead, he asked me to go to a bar with him but I turned him down. I was so overwhelmed by everything, all I wanted was to be alone and let things sink in. I took the time to take in a few more sights and got a closer look at some of the locals.

Most of the people I came across were from America but there was quite a diverse mix of skin tones and accents. People from all parts of the world made the pilgrimage to live here.

They seemed normal at a glance but when I looked deeper a lot of them were, I don't know, a little 'off.' Hell, it was probably just me, I'm the *off* one, but aside from their odd, abundant happiness they smiled and stared a lot, always studying, seemingly deep in thought. Some were a little skittish, happy but on constant guard; alert. Maybe they were just the new ones, like me.

I listened in on groups of people that stood around in random places engrossed in deep political and philosophical conversation. One group formed out of nothing when a couple pairs of people passed each other on the street.

At one point a young man who was part of a small circle of five suddenly screamed in fear and ran off down the road. I watched the others holler at him, asking him to come back and telling him "it was ok." Strange.

All in all though, I didn't notice as much as I could've. My time alone, the first real time I had to reflect on my situation as a free man, was partially busy remembering my brother.

The pain of his loss was renewed now that I was free. I'd been locked up ever since two days after his death. During my imprisonment I focused my thoughts on my hatred for Morbal, Forate and the entire ugly situation. The torturing bastards brought back some memories to me but they were vague and distracted. I wasn't able to fully reflect on my remorse.

Now, when there was nothing else to occupy my brain, there it was: Mark's slaughtered body and the murderers who hurt him. It was inevitable that I'd next remembered my savage acts of revenge. It was almost unbearable, like razor blades slicing away at my stomach from the inside. The thoughts were part of the reason I'd been exercising so much. The physical strain and mental discipline kept my head busy.

On that note, I focused back on the clothes in my closet. After breakfast, David and I made plans to meet for dinner around 8pm, fifteen minutes from now. I grabbed a new pair of blue jeans, a tight fitting dark blue long sleeve button up shirt and a pair of black shoes.

I threw everything on and inspected myself in the Mirror. Not bad. Despite all the rigors I'd been through, I was still a head turner, even with that giant slash on my neck. With an approving nod I grabbed my wallet and a slick, black leather jacket and was out the door, working to keep Mark out of my head.

The worst thing about the whole situation with my brother was that I really *wanted* to remember him but I had to run from the pain. I felt like a coward and that really pissed me off: Despair, sadness, regret and anger; a nice cocktail of crappy emotions for sure. Freedom didn't erase grief, I guess.

-

David's apartment building was a ten minute walk away, part of the same complex as mine. There were five buildings in total, all similar, all twelve stories high, all filled with living units identical to each other.

The early spring night was cool but the air felt good and thanks to my new clothes I strode with a bit of pride. An adorable young woman passed by and smiled at me. I gave a faint smirk I'm sure she missed. I liked women and had natural urges toward them but I knew they were more trouble than they were worth. Right now, I had too much on my plate. I reached the intercom outside David's building and pushed his call button.

"Hey man." David said, cheerfully. "Be right down."

I turned around and looked out into the complex's courtyard. The area was lit up well enough so I could see several large trees, bushes, benches, tables and a big fountain in the center of everything, gushing water several feet into the air.

I shook my head; Joshua said this was one of the least attractive areas in the country. It seemed damn fine to me.

A sudden wispy voice startled me. "Hello." I nearly jumped out of my skin, startled by a gangly, sick looking man who showed up out of nowhere. I studied his face. His large, dark eyes seemed hollow as they focused, unblinkingly on me.

He moved closer and licked his lips. "You're new here. I can tell." He swallowed hard. "You need to know what's going on. Here take this."

I looked down at his bony hand and saw it held a brochure of some sort. I didn't reach out to take it. Instead, I just looked back at him, sure my face showed an appropriate scowl that was in line with how I felt.

The stranger made out a quick, nervous tick while withdrawing his offer. "Ok fine. But you listen." He hissed. "We can't remain independent! We need the security and graces of Tehlasrin. How long can we last -"

The very mention of the GU made my lip curl. "Get the eff out of my face!" I hissed, furious, ready to toss the little bastard into the nearest wall. "That place can go to hell for all I care."

I heard the building's door open behind me and turned my head enough to see David come out. When I turned back to face the scrawny man he was gone.

David stepped out ahead of me then looked back at my face. "What's wrong?"

I huffed, cooling my temper. "Nothing, I guess. Just some guy telling me we need the Union's protection." I snorted. "Idiot."

"Come on, let's get moving, I'm hungry." David started for the street before continuing. "I've heard a little of that from people here and there." He sounded disappointed. "They're part of a new movement who call themselves the 'Unifiers' I think."

I nearly spat. "If they think the GU is so effing great, why'd they leave?"

David shrugged. "I don't know. I guess they're trying to be free like us but they want to be able to see their families more easily."

I chewed on that for a moment. "Oh. Yea."

"Yea." David imitated. "But, others I've spoken with think they may be Union operatives trying to create a crack in the foundation here." He shrugged. "Who knows?"

I shook my head. "There you go again. How the hell do you always know more about what's going on than I do?"

David stopped and looked at me. "I may have told you this before, but, ah." He paused, looking around. "Come closer."

I moved in, curious, expecting him to whisper some new secret to me. When David's mouth was about an inch from ear he spoke, loudly. "Because I listen to people!"

I gritted my teeth and jerked my head away. "Jesus Christ, prick!"

"I'm tired of telling you the same thing over and over." He pretended to be annoyed but David was smiling, glad I fell for his little trap. "Pay attention! You're not stupid, so wake up."

"Bah." I said, starting to walk again. "You were a lot more relaxed when you were on clear." Now I was smiling.

"Don't be a dick." He shot back.

Victory. Any time David said that, I knew I'd zinged him. "So," I started after we reached the sidewalk running along the main road. "Where are we going?"

A steady stream of vehicles ran up and down the street, ending the relatively silent atmosphere and David had to raise his voice a bit when he spoke. "Mmm," he began, "an Italian restaurant called Bella's." He stopped turned to look at me with excitement pointing his index finger at my chest, a huge smile on his face. "Oh! After we eat you have to go out for a drink with me. There were some people I had a few drinks with last night you've got to meet."

I shrugged my shoulders and gave a lazy "Yea alright."

David nodded. "Cool, they'll be at a bar called *Clovers*. Dinner first though." He started walking again. "I hear this place has the best lasagna on the island."

I nodded, instantly intrigued. "Sounds good to me."

"Should be." He let out a deviant chuckle. "Won't be as good as what I got last night though."

"Huh?" I furrowed my brow, thinking for a moment he was talking about a dessert or a new drink. When I saw David's wolfish smile, I knew he meant something different.

"Oh man, let me tell ya."

I laughed. "Did you at least get her name? A number maybe?"

He just smiled, looking straight ahead. "Names weren't really import -"

He was cut off when a pair of young men rushed past us, ramming their shoulders into ours. I snarled, "Hey! Watch it!" and looked at David, he didn't seem too bothered by the interruption. Instead, I could tell the wheels in his brain were spinning, playing over the activities from the night before.

We pressed forward and I broke the short silence. "Where is this place?"

"Oh, um," David snapped back to the present, "just up the road a couple block -"

Another inconsiderate plow into my shoulder. This time by a heavyset woman huffing as she frantically hurried by.

Now I was genuinely furious. "Goddamn it! Watch where you're going!" I growled, almost ready to run after the woman. Instead, David put his hand on my arm and stopped walking, studying the air to see if anything was out of ordinary. He looked at me, confused.

"Out of the way!" I turned to see another man rushing directly toward me. It would have been easy enough to move out of the way but I was pissed and fed up with being pushed around. I held my ground and faced the man.

To his credit, he changed his direction to go around me but my temper had the better of me and I wasn't going to let him by. I was sick of the constant, rude interruptions. When he was close enough I reached out, grabbed his shoulders, stopping him in his tracks, and threw him down to the ground.

"Jesus, Jason!" David began. "Calm down."

I shook my head. "No, someone needs to teach Mr. Speedy here a lesson."

The man scrambled to his feet. "You son of a bitch!"

Despite the darkness I saw him reach into his jacket and pull out what I instantly recognized as a pistol. Without thinking and quick as lightning I kicked the gun out of his hand. Before I could follow up, David planted his well-trained fist flat against the man's jaw. The guy's head fell back, unconscious.

"What the hell?" David started as I hurriedly picked up the weapon.

I didn't take my eyes off the man. My heart pounded as I spoke. "Where the hell are those security guys when you need one?"

Then all hell broke loose. From behind me, in what seemed a few blocks away, an explosion went off and the night air erupted into gunfire. Without thinking, I scrambled for cover and darted against the nearest wall. David was right beside me.

"WHAT THE EFF?" David exclaimed, eyes wide as saucers.

I held still, scanning the air like an alert guard dog, immediately in reaction mode. My mind raced. "Something big is going down." I looked my friend in the eye. "Come on."

Common sense be damned, I hurried in the direction of the chaotic outbursts with Speedy's pistol still in my hand.

David chased after me. "Hey! What the hell? Where are you going? Stop!"

I didn't stop. "Come on!" I repeated, unwilling, almost unable to stop. Despite his protests, David followed, seemingly just as pulled to the action as I was.

We rounded one last corner and quickly planted ourselves against a nearby wall. There was a motorcade of slick black cars surrounded by men and women raining fire on them. The lead car was burning, no doubt the source of the explosion we heard a few moments before. A couple shooters looked at David and me but ignored us, instead keeping their focus on the cars.

Several armored soldiers emerged from the remaining cars and returned fire. My instincts burst to life. This was a planned hit. An assassination. No doubt, the attackers were after someone of importance.

More of them rushed past David and me to join their fellows. My ears perked up when they spoke. "Get the Governor! Kill him!" They aimed their weapons at the nearest group of guards and fired.

*Governor.* My mind whirled. They meant Cross; he was in one of the cars! I looked at David and, in a beat, saw he and I were on the same page; he'd made the connection too.

It was hard to know for sure whose side I should help but I tagged the attackers as the 'bad guys.' They were the ones lashing out from the shadows, firing wildly in a public place, aiming to kill the man who'd mainly made everything here possible.

I quickly and rather gracefully cat-footed away from the wall and slammed the butt end of my pistol into the back of the nearest attacker's skull. By the time his partner knew what was happening I planted the weapon against his nose, shattering the soft tissue.

Moving in perfect unison, David was with me, helping secure the men's weapons and making sure the first one I hit was out of commission. I pounced on the second, landing a couple more blows against his face for good measure.

Now it was on, we were officially involved and bullets started tearing our way, just barely missing. I returned fire, the familiar feeling of firing a gun surged through me. David shot back as well. Our targets tried to get out of the way but, caught in a crossfire, were cut down by an assault from the nearest vehicle.

"Christ, get down!" David hollered, frantically gesturing the guards. "They don't know whose side we're on!"

I dropped and flattened myself against the newly laid pavement, turning my head to lock eyes with my friend, wondering if we should find a place to hide the rest of the battle out. I wanted to help but also wasn't eager to get gunned down by same people we were helping.

Luckily, or maybe it wasn't luck, maybe the guards were much more aware than David and I gave them credit for, the nearest soldier shouted in our direction. "You two! Get the eff over here! Stay low!" We obeyed without pause and raced, nearly on all fours, toward the car. When we reached it, I slammed my back against it and scanned the area David and I were just in. It was now swarming with several attackers.

I fired off a few rounds toward the crowd, not knowing if I hit anything, and slid along the perimeter of the car to its side. I bolted behind the nearest open door for cover. Of course, David was right with me.

The firefight was fast and chaotic. The tempo changed when a small rocket launched out of the darkness and plowed into a car three vehicles behind the one I was fighting from. The deafening explosion pelted me with debris.

"Get the Councilor!" an authoritative guard shouted. "Get the Councilor! We've got an APC coming up at the rear! Get him there, now! Go!"

I spared a glance back and saw a small group of soldiers surrounding a very disheveled and shocked man. Amidst the madness, I wondered if it was August Cross. When I noticed the attackers' attention mostly direct itself toward the small group I knew they'd found their target.

One of the guards glided around the side of the car David and I were planted against and fired into a crowd of attackers. Suddenly and out of nowhere, one of the assassins showed up right in front of the guard, aimed his weapon at the soldier's face and fired. A quick blinding light washed over the guard's head as he fell to the ground.

David grabbed the attacker by the neck and slammed his face into the rear window, shattering both the glass and the killer's face.

"Where the hell did he come from?!" I screamed. David's eyes nearly boggled out of his head. "Jesus, look!"

I followed his gaze and saw the guard was still alive. His face was intact and there wasn't any blood. It was impossible.

How could he have survived that blast? "Are you alright?" I yelled.

The man was dazed, his eyes rolled back in his head but he managed to nod. Then he passed out.

Still shocked, I turned my head. The team with the Governor moved as one toward the armored vehicle, bodies, both guard and assassin, were dropping everywhere.

David punched me in the arm. "They're going down too quick! Move!"

I didn't have time to think any further what we'd witnessed with the guard and rushed toward the Governor. His group was diminishing quickly. We fired our weapons and tagged several targets. I found an abandoned rifle on the street just as my weapon ran out of bullets.

We were a car length from Cross when the last of his guards fell to gunfire, howling in pain. He ran at full speed toward the APC until one of the attackers cross checked him into the nearby car. The assassin lined up his weapon, a second away from burying a bullet in the Governor's head.

"Ahh!" David yelled. Out of bullets, he threw his weapon at the would-be killer's head. It just missed. Still running, I aimed my weapon and pulled the trigger. A lucky shot: The attacker's lifeless body launched backward and crashed to the ground.

For less than a heartbeat, my brain absorbed the kill. I hated killing but I'd done it a lot during my military years. Then there was Forate… In a flash, quick as lightning, I rationalized my actions. They were justified, either saving the lives of innocents or eliminating crazed, murderous monsters. But that wasn't completely true with Mark's killers. I forced the thoughts away. Now wasn't the time.

"Get him! I'll cover us!" I yelled and opened up my weapon, spraying a volley of death into the shadows. Bullets blasted back at me. A nerve-wracking second later a large number of soldiers unloaded their weapons at the attackers. Either they were all killed or they were smart enough to give up because that was the end of the near death encounters for the night.

We reached the APC and scrambled inside. "He's in!" the guard nearest me yelled. "Go go go!"

With that, the small tank like vehicle was off and I was able to breathe normally. I looked at David. "You alright?"

He didn't answer and instead glared at the man we'd saved. His brow furrowed. "You're not Cross. Who are you?"

To his credit, the man had the fortitude after what he'd been through to smile. He had a narrow face, thin lips and large oval eyes that were almost elfish looking. His black hair was slicked back, undisturbed by the chaos, no doubt filled with styling product. "I'm sorry to disappoint you. Being that I'm not who you assumed, do you regret saving my life?" He had a British accent which caught me off guard.

David blinked, momentarily stumped by the comment. "No, not at all." He tripped on his words a bit. "I just thought you were, I thought they were after Cross. Is he here?"

The man wiped his sweat soaked face. "No." He took turns looking at David and me, still breathing heavily. "He was supposed to be but had other plans come up and sent me in his stead." The man paused, reflecting.

David spoke again. "Who are you?"

He raised his eyebrows. "I was about to ask you the same thing."

"Drop your weapon and identify yourselves! Now!"

I darted my gaze from the man whose life we saved to the barrel of a riffle eight inches from my face. My weapon dropped to the floor and I raised my hands.

"Calm, Captain." The man said in a soothing voice. "Easy. These men just saved my life. You can stand down. We're quite safe now, yes?"

The barrel moved away and I breathed again. I looked at the Englishman and nodded. "Thanks." It was only a hair above a whisper.

My brain settled a bit as David introduced us. I didn't catch much other than our names and the fact that we were new here.

"Well," the man began, "how timely and fortunate for me that you chose to live here. Welcome to Aswain and again, thank you." He smiled. "My name is Simon Krane, Mayor of Prospous and chairman of Aswain's council."

He stuck his hand out and I shook it before David did the same. "You're very welcome, Mayor Krane." David said in a suddenly formal tone. "It's nice to meet you."

"Please, just 'Krane' will suffice." He laughed. "I'm not big into titles. I share that attribute with Mr. Cross or August as he'd have you call him." He winked.

Now that it was confirmed the man was an authority figure, and a politician at that, I instantly became less keen on continuing the conversation. Krane's type always made me uncomfortable.

"So, where are you taking us?" I asked, bluntly.

Krane didn't seem to notice. "You know, those were some fantastic moves out there. I'm highly impressed." He shook his head. "It looked like you were actively dodging those bullets." He looked at me and raised his eyebrows. "And that shot! The one while you were running at me, splendid."

I shrugged. "It was more luck than anything."

"I doubt that!" Krane spouted with a hearty laugh. David chuckled too. The Mayor's mobile phone started ringing and he addressed us. "One moment please."

I wondered who'd happen to be calling this Mayor right after an attack. I looked at David, he was focused on Krane's conversation.

"Sir," Krane began. "Yes, sir, I'm fine, thank you." He paused. "I'm not sure, they moved me out of the area rather quickly and I haven't heard anything. We're nearing headquarters now." He nodded. "Yes, sir. I'll report in as soon as I'm settled." Another pause. "Thank you, August, that really means a lot."

He looked like he was about to end the call. "Oh, sir! One moment please."

I knew what was coming, I just knew it. Part of me was excited and the other part embarrassed, almost ashamed. If my guess was right; Krane was about to speak highly of David and me. Receiving praise made me achingly uncomfortable.

"My life was quite literally snatched from death's clutches by two bystanders, civilians, new to the island." He smiled. "Oh yes, I know for a fact. They were incredible. We wouldn't be talking right now if not for them."

My palms started to sweat.

Krane's eyebrows perked up again and he shot glances at David and me. "That sounds excellent! I'll give them the good news. Ok, talk to you soon, sir. Cheers."

He ended the call and smiled at us. "Well, gentlemen, it appears you both have a very fortunate and opportunistic lunch with Governor Cross tomorrow."

I let the news hit me and barely flinched. David showed another one of his huge smiles. "That's great!" He paused. "Where? When?"

Krane laughed and pulled out a small scanning device. "Here, press your thumb to this." He put it in front of me first. Almost reluctantly I planted my thumb and felt a slight prick. I knew it was taking a drop of my blood. David took his turn after me.

"There, now your addresses are in my system and a car will be over to pick you both up at 11:45am." He put the device away. "All taken care of."

"Great. So, *where* are you taking us?" I asked again, annoyed.

Krane furrowed his brow a bit when he looked at me. "They're taking me to security headquarters." He sighed. "I'll most likely be stuck there for a while. They won't let me simply head back home after an assassination attempt."

I began to panic, fearing I'd be stuck there for hours too.

"Well, I think that's for the best." David chimed in.

I grunted and gestured toward David and myself. "What about us? I just want to be on my way, damn it."

The Mayor let out a small chuckle. "Well, if any of the assailants survived, I doubt any of them got a good look at you two. So you should be clear to go." He pulled his mobile phone out again and looked at me while punching some buttons. "I don't see any risk for either of you."

"Good." I snapped.

"Robert." Krane began. "Get one of the unmarked cars ready. I'm sending a couple gentlemen to you and I want you to take them wherever they ask." He paused. "That's right. Yes I'm fine. Thank you." He set his phone down again.

David stirred. "Sorry for Jason's behavior, he gets pissy when he's hungry."

The two men laughed while I fumed.

My behavior? I scoffed and looked at Krane, sick of the whole situation. "Excuse me, but we were just nearly blown to bits and I don't feel like wasting time with you or any of your guards."

The Mayor raised his eyebrows. "Don't worry. You're free to go. Sorry."

I saw my friend shake his head. "Christ, Jason, relax."

"Oh, stop kissing his ass." I spat. "Relax? We just get here, to this island and not two days in we're in the middle of a war." I glared at Krane. "What kind of place is this?"

"Hey, hey!" Krane said with his hands in the air. "It's alright, I understand. You saved my life; I don't want to hold you up."

"Again, I'm sorry." David said.

The Mayor chuckled. "There's absolutely nothing to apologize for. You saved *my* life and given the caliber of the politicians in the place you just came from, I don't blame you for not wanting to have anything to do with me right now."

I shut up the rest of the trip, refraining from punching my brown nosing friend in the mouth. What was David thinking, lapping at this guy's heels? We didn't know anything about him or his true motives.

The two carried on until the tank reached the security station. It was clean, professional, busy and impressive even with my foul mood. Everyone and everything moved in perfect unison, like a healthy bloodstream. *Efficient* was an understatement.

To the Mayor's credit, he did a good job of hiding David and me from the press that was buzzing all over the place. We ducked into the car he arranged and sped back the way we came.

David told the driver to drop us off at the restaurant we planned on going to but I interrupted. I just wanted to go home. My nerves were shot and I was too worked up to eat. I was tired, bewildered, confused and upset with him. He needed to grow up, apologize and remember who his trusted friends were.

I was pissed right up until I fell asleep.

# Chapter 6

I was still in a foul mood when I woke up early the next morning. An especially aggressive work out didn't help get any of the frustration out either. I was annoyed and angry the rest of the morning right up through the drive to August Cross's home where we were to have lunch.

David and I were led into the backyard and seated at a large table under a shaded deck off the back of the house. The house was one of several Cross owned. It was nice but not nearly as over the top as I expected. It was a single layer brick home, about two thousand square feet that sat on a good piece of land with a very sturdy and very guarded gate surrounding the property. Large oak and maple trees filled some of the space but the yard was still open with perfectly trimmed grass that looked like a golf course. Brightly colored, flowering bushes lit the yard up and the sounds of birds filled the air.

Beautiful. It was heaven. I couldn't keep from admiring the place. Not too big or fancy. It was perfect. Had I been given a little time to just sit in silence and appreciate the peacefulness of the area, my mood might have improved. But no.

"Jason, what the hell is wrong with you?" David spoke, condescendingly, once we were alone at the large table.

He sat across from me two chairs down from the head of the table. "You've been a real ass ever since we saved Krane."

I rolled my eyes, not interested in talking.

He huffed. "Well you'd better show Cross some respect. This is our chance to make an impression with the man who made all this." He waved his arms, gesturing everything in a large circle.

I looked at David and folded my arms. "No sweat. I'll try to kiss ass like you. It'll be tough but I think I can do it."

"Whatever." He sat back in his chair, acting like he'd given up. The façade only lasted a second before he was leaning forward again, aiming a finger at me. "Try to remember this is the man who broke us out of the asylum, show some gratitude. If you want to blow it for yourself, go ahead. Christ."

I smiled a little on the inside. Even though his sucking up was annoying as hell, it was still obvious he cared about me. I remembered everything he'd done for me in the past and lightened up a tad. "Alright. Alright, I'll try." I said, letting the tension in my shoulders relax a bit.

"Try what?" A foreign voice boomed at us from inside the house.

I turned to see a man in full military dress step out onto the patio. He was tall, nearly six and a half feet with a solid build, bright red hair and a thick, equally red mustache. Underneath the hair, was a worn and withered face that looked like it had been through hell. His grainy skin was dotted with scars and pockmarks. As aged as his face looked though, his eyes were beaming: Green, electric and sharp.

David and I remained silent.

"Try to kill the Governor? Hmm?" There was a Scottish ring to his voice.

I furrowed my brow, trying to absorb the accusation.

"Excuse me?" David asked, obviously taken aback.

The man took his time getting to the seat at the far end of the table. "I've studied up on you two." His eyes cut back and forth between us. "I don't trust either of you."

I shot my gaze back and forth between David and the big man. The feeling of ease I'd finally managed was gone. "Ok. So who the eff are you and why should we give a damn what you think?" I stared into his eyes.

David kicked me under the table. I didn't take my eyes off the uniformed stranger.

He laughed. "Watch yourself, boy-o."

"Well, I see you met Chief." A new voice said from the same doorway the red-haired man had come through. The tension in the air immediately loosened up when I looked at the newcomer. He was a stark contrast to the soldier. Smiling, he had big, brown eyes and wavy, brown hair that fluttered in the breeze. I sized him up at about five-eleven and a hundred and sixty-five pounds. His face looked young, happy and alive. If I had to guess, I'd say he was in his early twenties but I had a hunch he was older than that.

"You'll have to forgive him." He gestured Mr. Redhair. "He's blunt and overly protective of me but I owe him my life several times over."

The man walked up to me and stuck out his hand. "I'm August Cross. It's nice to meet both of you."

I shook his hand and David did the same before Cross sat down. I heard the big man grumble when I locked hands with the Governor.

Silence hung in the air for a moment while we sized each other up, trying to get a feel for each other. My palms started to sweat.

"I hope you like fish." Cross broke the silence with a lazy wave of his hand. Several men and women burst through the doorway carrying plates of food, drinking glasses and bottles of wine. They placed the food before us, poured our drinks and vanished as quickly and silently as they'd arrived.

I glanced at my food and took in the smell. It looked and smelled terrific.

David smiled. "Sir, this is too much. Thank you!"

Our host smirked. "Please it's the least I could do for the valiant men who saved such a valuable and close friend." He worked his fork and knife and took a bite. "Oh, and you can call me Cross, or August. I hope you don't mind if I call you both Jason and David. Formality isn't really my thing."

David laughed. "The Mayor said the same thing."

"It's a common theme around here," The Governor said through a smile.

I shot a quick glance at the large man, Chief. He seemed pretty damn formal. A sigh escaped my lungs before digging into my meal and I could feel Cross's gaze on me.

"Is the food not good?" He asked. "I could order you something else if you'd like."

I took a bite and it was absolutely delicious, nearly melting in my mouth. "No, the food is fine." I didn't want to sound too gracious.

"Ok then." Cross put his utensils down and took a sip of his wine. "What's bothering you?"

I looked at him and raised my eyebrows wondering why he even cared. "Nothing. Don't worry about it."

I wasn't sure, since I was distracted by another grumble from the big oaf in uniform, but it looked like Cross winced a little. Then he smiled. "I'll ask one favor from you two." He paused, taking to turns to eye both of us. "Please be honest with me. I want to enjoy this meal."

I chewed on the request and figured it would be best to keep from lying. Something about his tone told me he meant business. After all, this guy, Cross was the man who invented the Cell Truth. He obviously didn't like deception in the slightest.

Cross pressed again, a bit harder this time, his gaze was more intense. "So what's the matter?"

I looked and David who shook his head, ever so slightly at me. The gesture annoyed me. Screw it. He wanted honest? He could have it.

"Alright." I stared at the Governor. "I'm angry."

Cross's eyes widened. "Oh? Why is that?"

I snorted, defiantly. "This place, everything. It's just a hoax, isn't it? You and your video pretend it's a perfect little heaven world. You let on that everything's safe, secure and that this is a free nation."

Cross took another bite of his meal. "Mmhmm. Are you saying it isn't?"

"No it isn't." My voice raised and I sensed the big man stir in his seat. "That little mishap yesterday proved it." I shook my head. "I don't remember the video saying anything about assassins running through the streets killing mayors."

"I see." Cross said almost nonchalantly.

"And you." I pointed at him with my fork. "What are you? Just another dictator, master of his own little nation? What are we? Pawns for you to rule over? Servants?"

"Jason!" David exclaimed.

Cross flashed a glance at my friend. "Let him go on. I admire his honesty."

I continued. "It's so stupidly obvious. This isn't a democracy at all. You rule and your say is law." I shrugged, let out a sigh and looked down at my plate. "I was dumb to think otherwise. This whole place is a joke."

"I'm sorry you think so, Jason." A beat. "I'm not going to bother defending myself or my decisions. Instead, let me tell you what I fear."

Curious, I looked back up at the Governor.

"Two things." He nodded. "Harm to my children and a losing my freedom."

My brow furrowed.

"What happened last night was horrible." Cross said somberly. "But it's a risk we have to take. Now I could bottle this island up, tight as a drum. I could force everyone to walk straight lines when and where I want. I could impose martial law. I could put squads of troops on every street corner."

I bit my lip, seeing where he was going. I began to feel foolish.

Cross blinked then looked off into open space. "But that's not the type of world I want to live in. It's not a world I want anyone to live in." He looked back at me. "Freedom doesn't equal security. Freedom is risky but well worth it. It's dangerous and it's wonderful. So, I decided to do the best I could with the resources around me."

I nodded, my anger cooling off. "Yea."

Cross smiled. "Come to think of it, even with all the security in the world, I could still drown in a bathtub, fall and break my neck or even get hit by a meteor." He went back to his plate. "We're all mortal, no one is ever completely safe and it's foolish to pretend otherwise."

I sighed again.

He went on. "Still, I'm sorry you had to go through that ordeal last night." Cross smiled. "Ironic that two newcomers would not only be caught up in but also become heroes in the worst outbreak of violence in Aswain's short history." He shook his head and resumed eating.

I watched him chew and almost smiled. Somehow the man had actually turned my attitude around. Rather easily too. How did that happen? Damn it. I was glad but I felt completely schooled, scolded. I felt like an idiot. The guy didn't do anything wrong. The attack wasn't his fault. He was right. If you live in a world with less rules that's less bottled up, crap is going to happen. That's the price. I was stupid to have not realized that on my own.

Cross seemed to pick up on my change of thought. He swallowed. "Oh and in regards to my being a dictator -"

"Sir." The military man interrupted. "You don't need to explain yourself to these two. Everyone with half a brain knows you're a good, noble leader."

"Chief, please." Cross spoke calmly. "I invited you on your request. Be civil. I do need to explain."

The soldier looked down at his plate continued eating. I did the same.

"Jason." The Governor drew my gaze again. "My say does go for the moment. We're in a delicate stage right now and I'm trying to build a foundation here. It's not easy, trust me." There was his smile again.

I popped a bite in my mouth. "Yea, I bet."

"I always keep my eyes and ears open to keep in touch with peoples' concerns." Cross shrugged. "You can think of me as a dictator if you want but that's not my aim. I'm just trying to keep freedom alive in the world. I hope I'm doing a good job."

With that, we silently ate our meals for a good piece of time. Uncomfortable in prolonged silence, David eventually spoke. "Um, thanks for freeing us from the asylum." He swallowed. "I don't think we'll ever be able to repay you."

I shot glances at both men's faces. The Governor smiled. "Well, official policy is that I have no idea what you're talking about." He winked. "Unofficially, you're welcome. And, you've already repaid me by saving Krane's life."

David stirred. "The Union must suspect you. Aren't you afraid they'll take action? I mean, you can't fend off the whole world."

Cross gathered his thoughts and then he chuckled. "No, I'm not afraid. Not yet, anyways. For the time being I know Tehlasrin won't do anything about Morbal and his center. Morbal himself, on the other hand, has already moved against me. I have no doubt he was connected the botched attempt on Krane's life." He paused, a hint of a smirk on his face. "But he failed, and Aswain's not as much of a pushover as you may think."

"Why did you do it?" I asked bluntly. "Why risk the security of your country? Why bring down the wrath of psycho like Morbal for a bunch of criminals?"

Cross set his jaw and seriousness washed over his face. "Because I could. Because it was the right thing to do. Those who we freed, who now live with us here were only criminals in name, named by a criminal organization. And, I know what kind of man Morbal is."

That was all he needed to say.

After our plates were empty, Cross leaned back in his chair and sipped his wine. "Anyways, I mentioned a bit ago that I do the best I can with what and who I have to work with."

I licked my lips and shared a quick glance with David.

"A successful person uses all available resources in the most efficient and beneficial way." Cross continued. "I've studied the PDRI reports on both of you."

A heatwave rippled through my body and my palms started to sweat. Even though I didn't have a mirror close by to confirm it, I knew my face had turned bright red. People knowing about, thinking about and talking about my past was never a good thing.

"Yes," the Governor went on, almost in a whisper. "I know."

"Damn straight we know." Chief blurted. "I can't believe we're even talking to these two, Sir!"

"Chief." Cross said in a calm, pleading tone.

"This one," Chief motioned to me, "a god damned killer. And that one," a shot a finger at David, "a drug addict!"

"Chief!" Cross finally raised his voice. "I want you to leave."

The big man's expression looked as if Cross had slapped him across his face, both surprised and hurt. "Sorry, Sir."

I saw the Governor grimace. It was sort of the same look he had when I lied earlier. "No, you're not sorry. I can tell." Cross shook his head. "You're excused."

Without another word, the large man stood and left the way he'd come.

After the distraction, I realized I was shaking. My history played through my head in a series of stinging, painful, ashamed flashes. I felt dirty, evil and unworthy of being in these pleasant surroundings with someone like Cross. Even though I still didn't really like him much, I couldn't help but respect him. He seemed to be a good man which was more than I could say for myself.

"Jason." August's voice was calm again, clear and soft like the gentle breeze that ran through the beautiful yard. "I know your history. It looks bad at a glance, however, I have a knack for reading people. I'm good at seeing things for how and why they really are." He looked my face up and down. "I don't blame you. It wasn't the real you who did what you did. You were nearly driven insane by pain, anger and grief. The injustice of what they did to your brother…"

"You don't blame me?" I spoke in a distant, hollow tone. As hard I tried to fight it, my mind visited the events again. Only this time, I envisioned Cross watching them, thanks to PDRI, on a computer monitor.

-

Mark Sworn was always in the middle of something. Always fighting for one cause or another which he believed to be just and worthy of action. A generally happy and optimistic man, only blatant corruption and injustice brought out his angry side, usually working him up into a frenzy.

Be it a bully in school, unkindness amongst his peers or the totalitarian policies of the GU; he was the first to point out and attack what he saw as evil or unfair. I respected and admired his valor, coolness and bravery.

He had a great sense of humor that helped him deal with all the wrongs in the world and he was the only person that could consistently make me laugh. As mad as he'd get, it was only a matter of time before he was able to constructively, albeit sarcastically, mock the situation. Bright and accountable, he often reminded me that life was only as fair as we made it. Injustice and evil was only the result of good people doing nothing to fight it. That fight could be with fists, words, ideas or even just simple smiles or helping hands.

My big brother. I don't think he was afraid of anything. From my mid-teens on, I was physically bigger and stronger than him but was never nearly as bold. He took action on issues I wanted to but was too timid. He would stand out from the crowd to champion the underdog while I hid in the back with others too afraid or unsure on what to do or say.

Modest at his core, he was also a great leader. He'd confess that he didn't have all the answers' but as far as I could tell, he was always, always on the 'right' side.

Mark Sworn was my hero for as long as I could remember and I tried to be like him though I could never measure up. He sure as hell didn't think so. He told me he was proud of me a bunch of times. I'd blow him off or ask why he'd say such things, not really believing him. He'd say it was because I was a noble man. Noble. Me. Well, maybe he wasn't always right…

He never lectured me but I knew he disapproved when I joined the Tehlasrin military. I didn't really care what our parents thought; they never showed any interest in our lives but Mark's opinion did matter and his lackluster approval hurt. I explained, almost selling, that my choice gave me a chance to help my future while protecting people from the various outbreaks of crime and violence.

I knew he didn't buy it. He didn't like seeing me on such a tight GU leash. Still, I saw it as an opportunity to help others. It was a way for me to be more like him, to defend those that needed help.

Unfortunately, Mark's wisdom was accurate. My 'authority' was only as justified as those above me.

Each of the four years I served got progressively worse. I went from defending people's homes and capturing madmen to being part of a suspicious and corrupt goon squad of thugs.

Even though I tried my best to be fair and honorable, receiving a few commendations along the way, I couldn't keep from growing to hate those I was associated with.

When the Union passed a new law banning charities, any funding outside the GU's corrupt rule and tax heavy grip, my brother took action speaking out against the policy. Tehlasrin didn't want any group gaining favor with the masses other than itself. With the new law, even the few privileged people who wanted to help others couldn't.

Mark went through the usual channels, asking the regional magistrate for permission to speak. He would never have gotten permission had he not bribed the authorities. In the end, he got his chance. His opportunity to try to make difference for what would be his last time.

During the speech, a group of soldiers, from my very squad no less, plowed through the small crowd of people in a large armored vehicle. They claimed to have only wanted to disrupt Mark's speech but along the way they 'accidentally' ran over a small child and his mother, killing them instantly.

Mark lost it. He raised hell, screaming at the corrupt, abusive soldiers and punched one in the face. My squad mates weren't amused. At first they only taunted, pushed and shoved my brother around. But like a vicious pack of hungry wolves, their rage grew. One soldier took Mark's leg out at the knee. When he fell to the ground the slaughter officially began. They kicked, stomped, and beat every inch of his body.

Finally, as my brother, busted up and bleeding, tried to crawl away they slammed the butt end of their rifles down onto his skull. His beautiful skull which housed his magnificent, honorable, genius brain, everything he was and would ever be... It shattered under the assault. He died right there, lying in a pool of his own blood in the middle of the street. Murdered.

I found out three hours later. My commanding officer called me into his office and told me what happened in the most uncaring way possible. The scum sucker almost laughed at one point.

I sat there in a state of shock when he told me the three soldiers would be 'disciplined.' I knew better, I knew there wouldn't be any repercussions for Mark's killers. The Union didn't care.

Later on, while I sat in the dark in my small dorm another soldier in my squad called and told me that was exactly the case. The murderers had gotten off without even a slap to their wrists.

The next day I didn't leave my room, I didn't sleep or eat. There was no tiredness, no hunger, no joy, nothing. All I had was sadness and hate. I'd lost the only person I'd ever loved, the only person who ever loved me, the best man I ever knew.

I lost my mind.

The caller did tell me the soldiers who killed Mark would be debriefed in my CO's office the next day at ten in the morning. When that time came, I gathered the ability and will to get to the station and marched directly into the office. It's hard to remember what I was thinking. All I have now was a vague memory of a sense of duty or a force that drove me to act. The force didn't feel like it was under my control. Again, it's hard to remember what going through my head. Unfortunately, I would remember what I did next.

When I entered the office, the three, two men and a woman were sitting around laughing and enjoying each other's company.

They haphazardly acknowledged me and half assed attempted to joke with me. Without saying a word I walked up to the nearest man, pulled a large, six inch, serrated knife out of my pocket and buried it into the top of his skull. The twist I gave at the end ensured he wouldn't have any chance of seeing another day.

The woman's screams filled the room while the others tried to take defensive action but I had surprise, strength and rage on my side. I was unstoppable, a monster far worse than Forate would ever be.

I do sort of remember being surprised to find I was armed with several knives. The second found my female squad mate's throat and made short work of it, slashing the tissue to shreds. The force of my attack nearly took her head off.

My third victim lunged at me, trying to knock me off balance. He failed and received a blade in his heart for his efforts. He also lost part of his face after my teeth clamped down on his cheek, sunk into his flesh, ripped and tore.

My commander was the last to die. I wasn't as hateful toward him so I simply buried a few rounds in his head from one of the dead soldier's pistols.

There, amidst the pile of dead bodies, I collapsed and cried out in anguish. Butchering them didn't bring my brother back and the killings didn't make me feel any better. Instead, I just hated. I hated myself. I hated everything.

-

The horrible memories slowly faded away so I was able to pull myself back to the present. August Cross and David were engaged in conversation. I don't know how long they were talking but I was gracious they'd left me alone to my thoughts.

"So you personally funded this whole place?" David's voice was heavy with awe. "That must have cost billions of dollars."

"Trillions." Cross smiled then shrugged. "It's taken most of my family's fortune but I also called in on some favors that helped pay for some things. Whatever the cost, look around, it's worth it. Freedom is worth it."

David nodded and smiled. "I'll drink to that." He downed his glass of wine.

I finally found my tongue and looked up at Cross. "You don't blame me?" I repeated from before.

The Governor seemed quite excellent at multi-tasking because when he looked at me he was back in my world, far away from the conversation he and David had been having.

"That's right." He said, quietly.

"Jason." David spoke softly. "It's alright, man. This is a new start for all of us. Your brother would want you to have this. It's ok."

I swallowed and locked eyes with Cross. "He should be here, you know. Mark belonged here."

The man nodded. "We all belong here, for now. Someday, maybe we can help other places be like Aswain."

I furrowed my brow, skeptical.

Cross let out a deep breath and slapped his hands on his lap. "So, speaking of Aswain, what do you two really think of the place?"

David laughed. "It's unbelievable. I love it." He shook his head. "It's the first place I've ever truly wanted to call *home*."

Cross looked at me, expectantly, waiting for my answer. I buried my pride and gave the man what he wanted. "It's like a dream." A few troubling issues still tickled the back of my brain. "Although..."

The Governor raised his eyebrows. "Yes?"

"Oh, never mind." I bit my lip. I wanted to ask about the 'odd' things I'd seen: People running and screaming, men showing up out of nowhere and soldiers surviving bullets to the face. But I didn't push it, not now. I was too out of sorts to deal with that right now.

Cross shrugged. "Ok then. To get back to what I wanted to propose a while ago, I've studied both of you and I, um, noticed you're still not employed."

David and I exchanged looks.

"Given your skills and abilities I'd like you to work for me, directly." He smiled. "I'd like to assign you to my top level security force, my intelligence team."

David's impossibly huge smile was back on his face.

Alarms went off in my head. This was too much too fast. "What?" I asked. My face contorted with disbelief. "Top level security? Us? David and me? You don't even know us."

Cross lazily looked at me, he seemed bored, like he'd heard this type of thing a lot. "Yes, you. Trust me."

He paused a moment seeming like he expected more questions. When none came, he continued. "You've both demonstrated your heroic nature and I'd like you to offer personal security to various leaders on the island, officials and even myself at times. You'll also be asked to investigate crimes and other unfriendly parties." He smiled before carrying on.

"There's a lot more to it than that and if you accept there will be quite a bit of studying up you'll need to do. Our security system isn't too complicated but there are levels of protocol."

I blinked. David looked dumbfounded.

Cross raised his eyebrows, waiting. "I'm a man with lots going on and not a lot of time to wait for answers."

"Sorry, I, I just can't believe it." David shook his head while he spoke. "I don't always think the same as Mr. Optimism over there," he gestured at me, "but, ah, yea. I don't know how you can trust us that much."

August Cross blinked. "Why don't you just trust me? Let me do the worrying." A pause. "So..?"

"Of course we'll take the offer!" David looked at me, giddily. "Right?"

After the roller coaster of emotions I'd been through, the overall favorableness of Cross and the fact that the offer was one only a fool would refuse, I agreed. "Of course." I looked at Cross. "Thank you."

He leaned back in his chair and exhaled. "No. Thank you."

A man came out through the door, walked up to Cross and whispered something in his ear. The Governor nodded and the man left.

"Well," he began. "I have some other engagements to attend." He stood up and nodded at both of us. "Thank you for having lunch with me. There's a driver waiting to take you where you'd like to go." He paused. "Jason, I believe Joshua Sands is your admittance counselor?"

I nodded.

"Right, he's a good man, one of the best that we work with. I'll assign him to you two. He'll prep you on your new positions and tell you where you need to go and when." He spoke while pulling his jacket on. "I'll tell him you two will be ready to start in three days. I want you to have a little more time to familiarize yourselves with everything."

I may have imagined it but it looked like Cross winked when he finished speaking. David seemed to catch it too.

"Sir," he started, "sorry, I mean Cross."

August looked at him, expectantly.

"Is it true?" David asked before licking his lips. "What I've heard about the *specials* around here?"

I was lost. "Specials?"

David flinched, obviously flustered. "The people that live here... are some actually specials?"

Cross grinned. "You're going to be part of my intelligence team; you may want to find that out before you begin." He addressed both of us. "You have three days, gentlemen. I'll be seeing you both soon."

With that, he was gone. The last, almost cryptic, conversation left me confused but I put it out of my head. David and I headed for the waiting driver.

# Chapter 7

David and I took advantage of our chauffeur and ran him all over Prospous. I tried to familiarize myself with as much of the city as I could. My jurisdiction would cover the entire island but the capital city would be the main hub of activity.

An energetic excitement filled the air. People of all sorts filled the streets, heading to and from work, taking care of personal needs and filing in and out of various stores. Every corner was packed in with movie theaters, shops, restaurants, grocery stores, different spiritual centers and so on. The place was so *alive*.

I took special note of any security men and women we passed and observed how helpful and pleasant they were. I hoped I could be as polite.

Naturally, David was absolutely thrilled. He could barely contain his excitement and reminded me of Mark on Christmas morning when he was a kid. My friend had a real knack with people, speaking with almost everyone we passed, shaking hands, joking and engaging in small talk. It was a good thing he was around. I didn't really feel like talking to anyone but it was good to see others and hear how they talked and thought.

After a few hours of exploration, David's phone started playing some obnoxious, upbeat song I'd never heard before. The conversation was brief before he snapped the phone shut and beamed at me, excitedly telling me there were some people I had to meet.

Reluctantly, I agreed to go with him since I'd flaked out the last couple nights. Not that I was angry or even tired, I just would've preferred to have some time on my own to let everything sink in. But no, we explored a few more areas of Prospous then we were off to meet David's friends.

The Sun was setting when we entered the small but seemingly popular bar called Ruby Moon. David's name was called out as soon as he was through the door by a group of elderly people seated at a large round booth in the back corner. We headed over and found two empty seats waiting for us.

"David!" A smiling, kind looking, grey-haired old man said excitedly. "So good to see you again!" He stood up and stuck his hand out at me. "You must be Jason, we've heard a lot about you."

*These* were the people I had to meet? They were ancient! I expected a bunch of young, vibrant, joyous types, mostly women, celebrating and talking loudly. But no. There were five of them, all dressed in what looked like upscale clothes from a century before I was born.

After a short, confused pause, I shook the old man's hand. His grip was stronger than I expected. Despite his age, his eyes were alert and his voice was strong, vibrant and bold. I had a feeling he was the type who'd run a victory marathon on his hundredth birthday. "Hello."

"Please sit down." He sat back down in his own chair and gestured the others at the table. "This is Beth, Harry, Jack and Sally. My name's Bill."

I looked at them in turn with a nervous smile. Being the center of attention around a bunch of strangers wasn't my cup of tea. With a quick nod, I said, "Hi."

The woman furthest from Bill, Sally was her name, spoke after a quick swig from her drink. Her bright red lipstick and even brighter eyes stood out, even in the dimly lit bar. "Well, well, well." She winked and lowered her voice. "You are a special one, I can see that plain as day. No wonder Cross picked you. The hero who saved Mayor Krane!"

Startled, I quickly turned to David, not happy they knew about our heroics from the night before. As usual, he just smiled. "It's ok, Jason. These guys know just about everything that goes on here."

"Yes." The old man, Jack slurred. He was heavyset with a thick beard and small glasses. "That's our job which includes making sure the drinks are satisfactory." He laughed, raised his glass and then downed its contents.

"Slow down, Jack, none of us feel like carrying you home again." That was Beth who spoke in a squeaky high pitched voice. She was petite with a large poof of white hair, big eyes and extremely thin lips.

I smiled, not knowing what else to do.

"So," Bill began. "How did the meeting go with August?"

Jack slammed his empty glass down. "Slow down, you nosey old bastard. They haven't even ordered yet." He raised his hand and motioned for a waitress.

"Don't let him fool you, gentlemen." Sally started. "He just wants another drink for himself." She looked at Jack. "Any excuse, right?" There was a round of laughter.

The waitress came, took our orders, left, then returned with our drinks. I kept it simple, ordering a pint of the house beer called *Rubybrew*. It tasted fantastic.

The five continued to roast each other and I could tell they were a tight group. David mostly sat and listened, smiling, chiming in here and there. Each time he spoke the group paid close attention, genuinely interested. I had the impression the old folks liked having fresh company around.

Eventually, Bill repeated his earlier question. "Well, how was it? What do you think of our Governor?"

My eyes drifted down to stare at the tabletop and I took another drink; thinking how to answer the question.

"I was impressed." David said. "He seemed calm and polite but also self-assured and to the point."

"Indeed," Bill said. "He's a great leader. We're all proud of what he's done."

The fifth member, Harry, had been mostly quiet aside from laughing. He turned his gaze my way, studying me intently and spoke in a low, rumbling voice. "Jason, what did *you* think?"

I nodded. "I like him." The words surprised me when they came out. "And that's saying something, I usually don't like anyone."

They were silent for a beat before Sally spoke. "Well I hope you like us." She winked again.

"It's ok, very practical." Bill nodded at me. "Trust is earned not immediately granted." He partially rolled his eyes. "Titles... what good are they? Pointless. It's the fruits, the merit that count."

I raised my eyebrows, liking the man's point. Still, he might've misunderstood me so I clarified. "I didn't say I trusted him, I don't even know him. But I did like him. He seems honest and direct." Qualities that reminded me of Mark, I thought to myself.

The group murmured sounds of agreement and I heard the word 'honest' whispered a few times mixed in with chuckles. Bill spoke again, eyes darting between David and me. "You accepted his offer, right? Did you take the job?"

Too fast, they knew too damn much. I sat back in my chair and folded my arms. "How do you know about that? How did you know we were the ones who saved Krane?" My eyes dashed over all five smiling faces. "Who the hell are you people?"

David laughed.

Harry boomed. "I like him."

The room was starting to make me feel uncomfortable.

Bill held his hands up, palms out. "I'm sorry, Jason. You're right. It's not fair that we know so much about you and you know nothing about us." He looked at David. "You haven't told him anything?"

"I thought about it but figured I'd let him meet you first."
David smiled. "Jason isn't good at listening anyways."

"Right." I said, finishing my drink.

Jack's head perked up the instant my empty glass hit the
table. "Another round for the young man!" he shouted.

"You two aren't the only ones at this table who work with
August." Bill made a circle with his finger, gesturing everyone
seated around him. "We're his official historical research team.
We're also personal counselors of sorts."

The man could tell I was confused so he went on. "Cross
has hired and brought on many of the brightest minds on the
planet. Everything from human relations to security, to
technological advancement to philosophers… The Governor
has quite an outstanding group of people to work with." He
chuckled. "I hope the five of us can measure up. It's our job
and our passion to know as much about the past as possible."

"And the present," Beth added, "and thereby the future."

Bill nodded. "Yea." Suddenly looking serious. "There's
much more to history than you'll read in any textbook, Jason.
We try to piece things together."

"Ok." It was the best reply I could think of. It all seemed
rather odd. What was he talking about? Some secret history? I
didn't buy it. As far as I could tell, they were just a bunch of
old people who made a living of studying history and getting
drunk.

Bill gathered his thoughts. "This is an interesting world,
knowledge is a powerful asset. There're mysteries the general
public hasn't the faintest idea about. So, we look for answers.
We call ourselves the Golden Cup."

I felt a contorted look spring on my face when I spoke.
"The Golden Cup?"

"It's the best gig in town, believe you me." Jack said,
happily, with a little salute.

I looked at him just as my new drink showed up. David
tapped my shoulder. "These guys know stuff about everything.

I keep trying to pry information out of them but they're good at changing the subject."

I sighed and lowered my voice, sounding disappointed. A dark cloud started to form over me. "Mysteries, huh? So is that why we're here? Are you checking us out, making sure we're trustworthy?"

David snorted. "Lighten up."

Bill smirked. "No, we don't need to, Cross already did that."

I shrugged and lifted my fresh beer, shooing my muggy suspicions away. "Fair enough." I looked around the group. "So, is there anything you can tell us about this true past?"

Sally giggled. "In time, maybe. But if I were you, I'd be more interested in learning about the true present."

I set my drink down a little too hard. "Why make a puzzle out of this?" I smirked. "Is it some sort of game? Everyone seems to know, or pretends to know things. What is it?"

The Cup exchanged secretive glances.

I rolled my eyes. "Fine. Whatever. Forget it." My gaze shifted to David. The beer was encouraging me to be a little more talkative. "What was that thing you asked Cross? Something about specials? What was that about?"

When David spoke he took turns looking at each of the old people. "I was hoping they could tell me, but they won't say."

I shook my head. "Ok then, what do *you* know?"

The others smiled and listened while David spoke. "Not much, really. Just things my mom used to tell me when I was a kid. I heard a bit about it at Morbal's too. And I've heard stuff around here."

He looked at me. "Hell, we've seen things, strange things. Either we're both crazy or something's going on."

I thought about the time spent stuck in the asylum. That should've been enough to make anyone crazy. I shook my head, frustrated. "But what the hell are 'specials?'"

"Shh, shh, shh." Bill calmed me down. "Listen. Some things in the world can't be told, they have to be seen." He smiled. "Try not to worry about it."

I rolled my eyes and finally gave up, deciding instead to just relax and enjoy the night. The day had turned out to be a good one and I didn't want to spoil it. For all I knew, these old people were just nuts. Still, they were entertaining and continued to buy me drinks so I went with it.

At one point David left the group to get acquainted with a pair of young women who entered the bar. Jack passed out. I didn't really remember how I got home but when I finally collapsed in my bed, I slept soundly.

-

A light, cold spring rain fell on me as I walked down the busy sidewalk along Eagle Street. The road was home to several shops, stores, coffee houses and bars. I don't usually use the word 'cute' to describe things but that's exactly what the strip of buildings were. The chain ran a few miles from the crowded downtown area and was a town in itself.

People hustled around, trying to escape the rain but I moved at a normal, steady pace. The cool wet drops were more refreshing than anything after the busy day I'd had. It started with a vigorous workout and then a lengthy session with Joshua Sands.

David and I met the man at his office on the eastern edge of Prospous County, about thirty-five minutes from our apartments. Joshua congratulated us on our new positions and ran over the basics of Aswain's security body. There were three levels; the county guard, the state marshals and the intelligence agents. The last was the most selective group. It was small and would soon include David and me, as strange as that was.

The man was busy as hell. His phone was constantly buzzing and messages popped up on his computer after almost every sentence. He told us most of the interruptions were new citizens making their daily check-ins and I was glad I wasn't the only one on 'probation.' Well, I wasn't anymore. The counselor told me I didn't have to check in anymore unless I had questions.

After a good four or five hours of learning about Aswain's government, economy and security, Sands finally wrapped things up. He finished by setting our meeting time and place for the next day. Afterwards, David practically begged me to hit a few bars with him but I was too tired and said I'd meet him later that night. Drinking and socializing at three in the afternoon wasn't my thing.

I headed home and worked out again. After a long, relaxing shower I decided to head into town to do a little shopping. The thought of buying a few movies or some music or something sounded good. Something mindless, I wasn't really sure. I wanted to be alone. Peace and quiet; I hadn't had much since I'd arrived at the new country. Actually, I hadn't had much since... well ever.

There was a store up ahead that sold all that stuff and I was almost there. A light drum of thunder rumbled through the grey clouds overhead as a smile sprung up on my face. Even in rain, the island was cheerful and happy.

I watched the people around me, the people I'd soon be serving. They looked 'normal' and by normal I mean they looked like people I'd seen in films from days before all the turmoil that fouled the world. They looked like they lived enjoyable lives. Couples ran together, giggling in search of dryness and parents marched their children around. Kids splashed in puddles and adults laughed. Yea, despite the weather, this was the 'sunniest' setting I'd ever seen. No wonder I couldn't help but smile.

I neared a little coffee shop which I normally wouldn't have noticed had there not been two burly men standing outside the door. The one nearest me looked Native American with light brown skin and long black hair. The other stood shorter but also had dark skin. He looked Middle Eastern; neither smiled.

I looked them both in the eye when I passed. The big Indian nodded and the other sized me up. I kept walking and was nearly back to thinking about movies when one of them called out.

"Sworn!"

I drew in a deep breath and turned around, instinctively curling my hands into fists. It was a reflex. I was used to fighting anyone who knew my name. The shorter man waved me over. I puffed up my chest and casually headed back.

"A man inside would like to speak with you."

I shot glances between them. "Who?" I was going to follow up with 'And why?' but before I could get the words out, the door was open and I could see August Cross sitting alone at a table. He had a large coffee cup and a book resting in front of him.

I took a step inside and the Governor waved me over, a smile on his youthful face. The moisture in the air had his wavy brown hair especially out of control. There was an attempt at a part a little right of center but the length and curliness made the effort essentially pointless.

Cross shot his hand out before I sat down. "Jason! Good to see you again so soon."

I shook his hand. "Hello, Sir."

"Call me August."

I thought about my upcoming job and went into protector mode, glancing around the coffee house. It was shocking and stupid that the leader of the country would be in a public place, sparsely guarded only a couple days after an assassination attempt.

Cross laughed, reading my eyes and body language. "Relax, Jason. Have a seat." I obeyed, still on edge. "I'm not afraid to be out in the open. I wouldn't live any other way. Aswain is a good place." His tone was serious but quickly lightened. "Besides, most people don't even know what I look like."

And most people weren't named 'August' which he'd just blurted out in the open. I didn't press the issue and merely nodded. "Ok then."

"So," Cross began before lifting his cup to his mouth. His eyes widened. "Oh! Would you like a cup? The brew here is excellent. My treat."

I shrugged. "Sure, I'll have what you're having."

Cross smiled and raised his voice. "Raj, get my friend a house blend, lots of cream and sugar."

"Right." Came a voice from behind the bar.

The beverage arrived and I tried it. Outstanding. I nodded in approval.

"Good, huh?" He took another sip.

I shook my head and smirked. "Does everything in this place taste so great? I swear I've never had food or drinks like this."

Cross let out a satisfactory sigh. "That's what you get when people are happy. You get the best from them, the best in life."

"I guess so." I took another sip and my taste buds danced. "Damn."

"How was your first day of class?" He laughed.

He meant Sands. "It went well."

"*Well*." A pause. "Not very convincing."

I forgot how good Cross was at reading me. "It was long. Informative but I was glad when he let us out of there."

"I understand but I'd encourage you to remember what Joshua tells you. You're going to have a lot of responsibilities on your plate." He set his cup down. "But you'll be fine. I know you're up to the task."

"I don't know how you know that but you're right." I took another delicious gulp of my coffee. "I'm a quick learner."

"Good. What else have you learned?"

He caught me off guard again. His questions weren't ever what I expected. I thought for a moment. "I met the Golden Cup yesterday."

The Governor laughed. "Quite a bunch, aren't they? I'm always blown away by how much knowledge they have." He paused for a moment, thinking. "I trust you got along. They're good people."

"We got along and we got drunk." I grimaced. I wasn't used to drinking that much beer.

Another hearty laugh from Cross. "Yep, that's them. The group loves to celebrate life as much as they like to talk. We're fortunate to have them here."

I changed the subject. "So what are you doing out here today?"

"Birthday shopping for my son. Though I'm usually out on the town." He shrugged. "I was taking a little coffee break since I'd passed my favorite shop and then saw you walk by. Small world." He winked.

I stirred. "Yea. Still, I think it's a bit risky for you being out here alone."

"I'm never alone." There was a slight, very slight tinge of longing in his tone.

"How has the investigation into the Mayor's attack gone?" I asked.

Cross sucked on his teeth for a second. "Not too well. You'll learn more about it once you're on the job." He paused. "We weren't able to take any survivors. We're working on it."

"Hmm." I squinted a bit, thinking.

"Question?" Cross asked with raised eyebrows.

I nodded. "Do you think they were part of that Unifier group?"

The man shook his head. "No. The theory has been tossed around but I know the leaders of the movement. They aren't a violent bunch."

"You *know* the leaders of a group wanting to join the GU?"

Cross furrowed his brow. "Of course I know them. Some of their leaders personally gave me information on their meetings and rallies. They don't want to join the Union; more like a partnership." Now his brow rose. "I happen to disagree with them."

"Anyone with a brain would disagree with them." I said, sharply as another question swirled around in my head. I struggled for the right way to ask it.

"What is it? Don't hold back, say what you're feeling."

I looked at Cross. "So, you allowed the group to organize and speak. The same group that wants to bring the country down?"

"Says who? They don't want to bring anything down. I've fought to create a free country here. That means everyone gets to speak and act so long as it's civil." He slowly drew in a breath and his eyes widened. "Now... if they were involved in the murder attempt, I'll have to deal with them accordingly."

I chewed on that for a bit. On one hand I respected Cross more than ever. On the other I was a bit curious and maybe slightly alarmed that the group felt they had to bring their information to the Governor before speaking. Something didn't add up if the country was indeed a 'free' place. That and the way he said he'd 'deal with them' sounded a little like a tyrant to me.

The man didn't look at all like any tyrant though. The messed up hair, the youthful face, quick, innocent smiles, big, curious eyes and his clothes... This was the second time I'd seen him and both times he'd been dressed in casual, comfortable clothes. He wore a pair of khaki pants, a loose fitting, cotton, blue sweater and a pair of cushy sneakers. Most tyrants had over inflated, bloated egos. They'd dress in expensive, flashy clothing to show off. Not this guy.

"Well," I started, getting back on track, "I'd keep a close watch on them, the Unifiers I mean."

"Yes, you will." Cross nodded.

I smirked and silence hung in the air for a piece of time. Cross broke it. "Where are you headed today, if you don't mind my asking?"

"I was heading out to buy a movie or two to watch." I answered. "I'm not really sure what I'm looking for but I'll find something."

"*Crystal's* has a good selection." Cross said. "It's just down the street a bit."

"Yea," I nodded. "That's where I was headed."

"Oh. There's also a good computer software store next door with all sorts of games, puzzles and information discs."

I shrugged. "Thanks, but I'm still leaning towards a film. I don't feel like thinking anymore today."

Yet another laugh. "Tell me about it. It's nice to just shut down sometimes."

I agreed.

"Well then," Cross started, "I've taken up too much of your time so I'll let you get on your way. I need to get moving too."

He stood up and started to leave when a question popped in my head. "Sir, I mean August, quick question."

He stopped moving and looked at my face. "Yes?"

"You're out here on your own with just the two guys," I shot a thumb in the direction of the two hulks outside the door, "so why did Krane have such a huge group guarding him the other night?"

"Yea, that was different. He was headed to a leadership conference. The event was publicly known and called for additional security. I was supposed to go but something urgent came up and I couldn't attend." He trailed off a bit, thinking again. "Krane took my place. Thank God he didn't get hurt. I wouldn't have forgiven myself."

I thought about the guards and the attackers that night. A lot of them were hurt and killed. I guess that wasn't really Cross's fault.

A weird smile sprung on Cross's face. "That surprises you? I don't act much like your average *tyrant* now after all, do I?"

I wasn't sure why, but I blushed. People around here had a terrific knack for picking up on my thoughts. I wondered about David's 'special' people thing again.

Not sure what to say, I kept it simple. "Thanks for the coffee."

"You're welcome. I'll see you again soon."

# Chapter 8

David and I spent more time with Joshua Sands over the next couple days where we covered our new jobs. He reminded us several times that we were going to be both investigators and secret service officers, bodyguards for high up officials. He said we'd also be the overseers of other security personnel.

I still couldn't wrap my head around the fact that two newcomers like David and me would be granted so much authority so soon. However, Joshua, who uncannily picked up on my thoughts again, explained it wasn't power or privilege we were being granted, it was responsibility we were entrusted with. He reminded us that Cross moved fast when making decisions, self-doubt wasn't his thing. He trusted us.

Sands took us through a tour of the security headquarters where Krane had been dropped off the night he was attacked. We were given a rundown of building then passes into the deepest section of the base, the intelligence wing.

I nearly backed out of the job when I found out that big stiff, Chief, was the commanding officer. I guessed working under the man would be hell since he seemed to despise us. Of course, when I voiced my consideration to David, he blew my concerns off and talked me out of quitting. Sands had nothing but nice things to say about the big Scotsman and even shared stories of the soldier's past heroics. As impressive as they were, I still wasn't fully sold or the least bit thrilled.

We were told that unlike the other, lower level, security officers, we wouldn't be wearing uniforms. Instead, we were given additional money to purchase business casual type clothing. Our jobs were to blend in and not draw attention to ourselves or whomever we were escorting.

Joshua talked fast and I could only absorb half the information he shot at us. I wasn't worried though, I'd always done best at learning on the job, hands on. I did catch the fact that our group was small, though. With David and me there were only thirty-five intelligence agents. Again I couldn't believe I was part of such a small, elite team.

Other bits of information played over in my head during the light-rail ride to *Clovers*, another bar David had discovered and wanted to hang out at.

The train stopped and I stepped out into the cool evening air, scanning for the bar. As with *Ruby Moon*, this place was small and would have been hard to notice without the parade of people filing in. I headed for the door.

"Mr. Sworn?"

I stopped and turned around. To my horror I saw a woman with a microphone, a man with a camera and another man with a beaming light that assaulted my eyes, burning them.

The woman smiled. "Hello, I'm Melissa Cole with Channel Nine News."

"No." I said instantly, squinting my eyes and jutting my hands out to barricade myself from the reporter and the damn light.

"Just a few questions. We have witness accounts that say you were involved in Mayor Krane's defense. Is this true?" She spoke even faster than Joshua while shoving her microphone in my face.

I backed up, annoyed and angry. "I don't know what the hell you're talking about. Goodbye." I turned to leave.

The woman raised her voice. "Mr. Sworn! You're a hero! Just a few comments, please!"

My brain raced. Part of me wanted to continue lying and denying, part wanted to run away and another part wanted to grab the camera and smash it to pieces.

Suddenly, seemingly out of nowhere, a man showed up and stormed between the news team and me. He wore thick sunglasses even though the sun had set hours ago.

He spoke in a low commanding voice. "Excuse me, Ms. Cole, but you have your facts mixed up and this is a matter of utmost security still under investigation. Please leave this man alone and have a good evening."

The reporter looked angry. "We have a free press here, you know? This is not the damned GU, August Cross -"

"Governor Cross has stated that the protection of Mayor Krane's life is of utmost importance and that facts will be released as they come to us when it's safe to do so." The man interrupted. He stuck his chest out and moved toward the team, forcing them away from me.

She didn't appear to like that either. "No, this is wrong. What's your name? Who gives you the right?"

"Please Ms. Cole." He spoke slowly and calmly while fluidly reaching into his jacket pocket to pull out a card. "Please contact this representative in the morning. He'll personally keep you updated on the events you're investigating."

Ms. Cole closed her mouth and studied the card. She raised her brow.

"And please leave uninvolved citizens alone for their safety." The man added with a nod. "Have a good evening."

The team left and the man in sunglasses turned to look at me. I smirked, curious who the guy was but not wanting to push things. "Thanks."

He stared at me. "Have a good evening, Mr. Sworn." With that, he was gone.

I let out a deep breath and entered the bar. It was small and crowded. The blend of all the different conversations and music sounded like a muffled flock of birds chattering away. I scanned the place and pinpointed David standing with a drink in his hand alongside the Golden Cup.

I sighed, tired of the old bunch. Instead of heading over to David, I planted myself in a lone available stool at the bar and ordered a beer.

Time passed and it was nice sitting there, sipping a few drinks without having to talk. Despite its size and how unique the crowd was, I ignored everything but the bartender, my drink and the telescreen which gave the day's weather and news. I zoned out, daydreaming for an unknown piece of time.

I was eventually interrupted by a tap on my shoulder. I pulled myself back to the present and expected to see David's smiling face when I turned around. Instead, there was a tall, wide eyed, elderly man blinking back at me. The top of his head was bald as an egg and his perfectly trimmed goatee was white as snow.

"Mr. Sworn? Can we talk for a moment? Please." He gestured to a dark corner in the back of the bar. "I have my own table. Please."

I don't know why I followed him; I was quite content where I was, but the next thing I knew I was sitting across from the man sipping my beer. I suppose curiosity had gotten the better of me.

The man smiled and stroked his small beard. "My, my name is Pat Crow. It's nice to meet you." He nervously licked his lips and looked at my glass. "Would, um, would you like another beer?"

My eyes narrowed. "What do you want?"

The man flinched, almost jerking himself out of his seat. I could see the color drain from his face even in the dim light. "Did you see that? Right there!"

I looked behind me and saw a few couples drinking and enjoying each other's company. I looked back at the man, figuring he was either drunk or out of his mind.

He frowned. "Of course not." He rubbed his hands together. "I can't stay long, so I'll be brief."

"Good." I was blunt and ready to leave.

The man swallowed. "I know you saved Krane. I know you're part of Cross's intelligence team. I know you have great strength."

*Screw this.* I started to stand up, done with the old man. "I have no idea wh-"

Crow put his hands out, begging me to stay. "I know! I won't tell anyone! Listen, I'll ask this once." His eyes suddenly doubled in size, staring at something behind me. "Oh lord! What is that?"

I didn't turn this time. Instead I sat back down. "What do you want?" I growled.

"Ok, ok." He reached into his pockets and pulled out some pieces of paper along with a wad of cash. "I'm rich, very, very rich and I want to hire you for a job." He looked at the money. "Here are a couple thousand Gems. And here," he slid the papers over to me, "are pictures of the men who stole an item from me. I need it back."

I scowled. "And just how am I supposed to help you?"

Crow's eyes widened. "You're on the Governor's intelligence team!"

"Shh." I put my finger to my lips and looked around to see if anyone was paying attention to the old fool.

"It'll be easy to find these men." He paused with his mouth hanging open, anxious to hear my answer.

I wished I wasn't so buzzed from the alcohol. My brain was unable to think clearly enough to turn down the cash, I took the money and glanced at the two pictures, each showed a different man. I put everything in my pocket.

"And this," he slid another card over, "is my contact information and a picture of the item I n, n, need." His mouth fell wide open. "Oh dear, not again, not YOU!" He buried his face in his hands.

I took the card and picture and almost laughed at the old fool.

"Is it gone?" Finally, he pulled his hands away and blinked a few times. "The item is called the Soulphire, a blue gem -"

"Soulphire?" I asked.

The man gulped. "Yes, a blue gem the size of your thumb. The men in those pictures were the last ones seen with it." He leaned forward and looked at me with pleading eyes. "Please get it back to me. I'll pay you fifty thousand Gems for it."

I looked at my thumb then into the man's eyes. Crazy, completely crazy. But, he seemed harmless enough so I humored him with a nod. "Ok, I'll look into it."

The old man laughed gleefully. "Oh thank you, my friend. Thank you!"

I started to feel uncomfortable and was glad to see the man get to his feet. He slid his jacket on. I stood up too and felt the effect of the beer I'd been drinking, strong stuff. I swaggered and tried to think.

"Wait." I put my hand on Crow's shoulder and he nearly jumped out of his skin. "Why do you want this thing so bad?"

"The Soulphire?" He looked down at me; the bastard must've been six and a half feet tall.

"Yea."

He bit his lip, tears welled up in his eyes. "It's the only thing that'll make the ghosts go away."

I didn't know whether to laugh or feel sorry for the guy. *Ghosts?*

"Goodbye, Mr. Sworn." I watched the crazy man shuffle out of the bar. Doubtful, I wondered if he was as rich as he said. Then I remembered the wad of bills in my pocket.

Quickly brushing off the odd encounter, I headed back to the bar. My stool from before was filled but others had opened up. There were three empty ones in a row and I chose the middle one, glad to have a little elbow room.

I ordered another beer and glanced over to where I saw David earlier. He was still there, smiling and laughing it up with his new, old friends.

A raised voice from behind caught my attention.

"Damn it! Just leave! Go!"

I turned my head and cut my eyes around to see what was going on. It took me a moment to recognize the loud, angry woman. Fier Wren. I followed her gaze and saw a very sorry looking man sulking away with droopy shoulders and an even droopier, sobbing face.

With a snort, the woman marched up and plopped herself in the stool to my left, not recognizing me. Hell, she didn't even look at me. A couple seconds later, an old and all but forgotten feeling stirred in my gut... and below. I wished she would notice me. I studied her face, her hair, her arms, her hands and her mouth, feeling a powerful longing. She had short reddish-brown hair, not quite shoulder length in the back that dangled a little in the front over her eyes. It perfectly conformed to her cute round, youthful face. It was hard to tell in the bar but I remembered she had lovely hazel eyes, a cute little nose and lips that were just right, not too thick or thin.

She had a nice, athletic build and stood about five foot seven. Dressed for the bar, she wore a snug pair of jeans and a green sweatshirt that hugged her body well.

Oh eff. I couldn't believe it, I was actually aroused. I hadn't had feelings like this for such a long time...

She turned to look at me and I felt myself blush.

"Well?" She spat, loudly. Her eyes darted over my face. "Wait... I know you."

I raised my eyebrows.

Fier looked me up and down. "Huh. Nice to see you're not still in those rags you were wearing the last time I saw you."

In an intoxicated, trancelike state I muttered the word "Morbal's."

She grimaced and looked around, alarmed. "Shut the hell up! Jesus."

I stared at her lips, done being surprised with my lusty feelings. They were there and that was that. God, she was so... "Beautiful." Oops, I said that out loud.

Fier let out a small growl, the anger on her face made her even sexier. She snapped her fingers. "Hey! Wake up!" She shook her head. "I thought you were immune to this. You didn't show any interest during our, ah, trip."

I had no idea what she was talking about. Instead, my half drunken, rusty brain desperately clawed for something gentlemanly to say. I looked at her hands. "Can I buy you a drink, Fier?"

"You're not listening." She sighed. "Ok, pay attention."

She paused and looked into my eyes. I smiled, wolfishly.

"You're under a spell, do you know that?" She spoke at me like I was a child.

It was the last thing I expected her to say and the oddness of it shocked me a bit. That, on top of the old man talking about ghosts, was enough to snap me from my love struck daze. I shook my head. "What are you talk -"

"Shush." She interrupted. "Quick. Take your hand and rub the back of your neck at the base of your skull. Do it!"

I obeyed.

"Good. Keep going." Fier nodded.

Things cleared up as I rubbed. I noticed the woman's appearance wasn't quite as enticing as it had been a moment before. A couple of her teeth were a little crooked and her skin was far from perfect.

I turned to face forward, a bit dazed and confused but mostly embarrassed. I'd been behaving like a fool. My eyes wandered around the bar to avoid Fier's stare. They settled on a strange, heavyset man planted two stools down to my right. I could hardly believe my eyes. He was actually wearing a top hat. Loud, his voice and hearty laugh boomed through the bar as he told jokes to the people around him. Most annoying of all was how he spoke with his mouth full. Each time he smacked his big lips I felt a shiver run down my spine.

I looked away and tried to block the guy out. I eventually focused back on Fier.

"That's better." She said. "The whole 'you're so beautiful' thing was nice for a while but it's gotten old. You're cute but I'm glad you aren't totally obsessed with me anymore. Though I'm sure you're confused as all hell, huh?"

I bit my lip. "Look, I'm sorry. I don't know what I was thinking."

Fier smirked. "You weren't thinking; your body was reacting. I told you, you were under a spell, of sorts. Don't worry about it, it happens to almost everyone."

My head started to hurt. "What happens to everyone?"

"You're just completely clueless, aren't you?" She laughed and shook her head.

I grimaced, not amused by her cockiness. "Clueless about what? What spell?" I rubbed my temples. "Jesus, what the hell is wrong with everyone here?"

"Nothing's wrong, we're just... special." Her eyes scanned the bar while she took a drink from her glass. She quickly ducked down. "Damn it. That horny friend of yours almost saw me!" She curled her lip. "I'm in no mood to fight him off. He has a knack for finding the more lively spots."

I studied her, ignoring her last sentence. I had a feeling the woman could give me some real answers and I was going to pry. I spoke slowly and as clearly as my half-drunk speech would allow. "Ok. So what *exaaactly* makes them special?"

Fier set her glass down. "You know, I'm not really a professional in this area. Bottom line; I don't really care. I focus on the tasks Cross gives me and deal with everything else when I have to."

"Fair enough." I liked the way she thought. "But what makes them special?"

"Them? You? Me? We're all special, Jason. None of us would be here if we weren't." She paused to let me absorb what she said.

I realized that other than including me in the mix, she didn't tell me anything. "Me? Ok then, what makes me special?"

"Hmm, let's try this." She gestured to the fat, lip smacker to my right. "See him?"

I nodded.

"His name is Ronald J. Ruthelstone. You know why I know that? It's not due to his charming personality or ravishing looks. If you call him anything other than Ronald J. Ruthelstone he'll get offended. If you do it again, he'll get angry." She snorted. "Do it a third time and you'll find you suddenly have the worst headache of your life."

"What?"

Fier laughed. "Oh lord, I hate trying to explain this stuff." Her face was serious again. "Look at me. You don't lust for me anymore do you?"

I considered the question, quickly trying to think of way to answer. No one had ever asked me if I 'lusted' for them before.

"But you did." She went on. "It's one of the things that make me special, I guess. I just wish I could turn that damn thing off."

I could tell I looked as lost as I felt.

"Over there," Fier continued, "see that little guy that sort of looks like a puppy in the face? His name is Charlie. He's got some of the quickest reflexes I've ever seen. I've heard he can even dodge bullets."

I looked at the man, amazed at how much his face resembled a pug. I blinked the image away and looked back at Fier. She continued.

"The red headed girl." She pointed. "My friend, Blix. Don't yell around her, she can hear insanely well."

I looked at the woman, she was a bit heavyset with long hair and big, thick glasses. A closer look showed she had earplugs in her ears. I raised my eyebrows.

"The bartender, Rex. He'll sometimes know what you're thinking before you do." Fier continued.

I looked at the man behind the bar who was listening in on the conversation. He winked at me. I made an odd face.

"That young guy over there in the blue sweatshirt, I think his name is Kyle." Fier said, "He's got a real knack with animals. I swear he can *talk* to the things."

I straightened myself in my stool. "Ok, I'll bite. So what's special about me? What about David?"

She shrugged. "I don't know. What can you do? Have you noticed anything odd or spectacular about yourself or Mr. Whambam over there?"

"No, nothing." I paused. "Only thing I've learned about myself is that I hate to see people suffer. Nothing special about that."

"You're wrong." She smiled and I again found her face more than pleasant to look at. "I told you, you wouldn't be here if you weren't special. Remember that quick little blood test you took when you got here?"

"Yea."

Fier gestured me with open arms. "Well, you're here! That means you have special traces in your blood." She took another drink. "Oh and your friend? Yea, he's got the same thing I have only in male form. I felt it immediately. I was so sick of rubbing my neck by the end of that little trip with you guys."

I couldn't believe it but I was actually buying this crap. I looked at David. "I'll be damned, no wonder it's so easy for him." I scratched my head. "But seriously, I can't do anything like that, like any of you."

Fier rolled her eyes. "No, you just hurl yourself into danger to save a man's life. You put yourself in impossible situations and come out alive, right? I'm guessing the incident with the Mayor wasn't the first of its kind."

I thought back through my military past. Blurred visions of infiltrating heavily armed bases and dangerous camps rolled through my head. I also thought about Keeper Berg back at the asylum. I risked my life and my freedom going back for him. No matter the risk though, it was the only option. I *couldn't* leave him. Maybe she was right, but I didn't see how that meant anything. "So?"

"So? A lot of us here, especially those in the security force have a strong drive to protect others, to do what is right." She raised her eyebrows. "Sound familiar?"

I took a moment to think about that one. "I guess." Then I thought about the old man. "What about whatshisname? Ah, that tall old guy, Crow?"

Fier scoffed. "Pat Crow? Did he talk to you?" She laughed. "The guy asked me to work on some side project for him, to get him some jewel." She shook her head. "I knew better than that. I feel sorry for the fool dumb enough to take his request."

She looked at me. "What did he say to you?"

I had trouble finding my tongue. "He um, hmm. He said something about being able to see ghosts."

"Yea." Fier said with a shiver. "Some can do that here too. I doubt they're really ghosts, most likely traces of images from the past or something. I don't know." She rubbed her head, shivering a little. "I'll take my so called gift over that one any day."

I tried to soak everything up but it was just too wild. "I don't believe it."

Fier shrugged. "Oh well, doesn't matter, I guess. But you're going to see some strange stuff here, if you haven't already."

I certainly had… After taking another gulp from my glass I asked, "What about Cross? What's his deal?"

"Let's just say I wouldn't lie around him if I were you. He really doesn't like that." I waited for more but that was all she said.

Fier gestured toward David. "He seems quite buddy buddy with those old timers. They know a bunch; you should ask them about this stuff."

I nodded. "Yea, the Golden Cup. They never want to say much." I rubbed my chin. "So they only let these special people in here, huh? Strange. I wonder what Cross is planning."

"I don't know and like I said, I don't really care." Fier looked at me with an intense seriousness. "He's a good man and made this place possible. You remember that."

I looked at my glass and studied it for a short period, gathering my thoughts. "Seems a lot of people know about the whole Mayor thing David and I were involved in." I set my eyes back on Fier. "How do you know about it?"

"I'm on the same level you and Loverboy are about to join." She gestured with her head toward David. "It's my job to know. Though I'm a bit different. Cross sends me on more covert, out of town assignments. I'm a bit 'out of the loop.'"

"Like breaking people out of -"

"Shh!" She interrupted. "You'd better learn to keep your big mouth shut."

I flushed, "Right, sorry," then changed the subject. "How long have you been here?"

"Two years."

Even though I believed she could be as nuts as old man Crow, I still couldn't help but like her. In fact I admired her. I enjoyed her company, her presence. I wanted her...I rubbed the back of my neck again.

Fier laughed. "Now you're getting it. Good boy."

As clear headed as a man could be after more than half a dozen pints of beer, I didn't appreciate her condescending comment. I was not a 'boy.'

Silence hung in the air for a piece of time. Unfortunately, during that time the big man to my right kept yapping away. The smacks continued.

Fier hollered over me. "Hey Ronald J. Ruthelstone!"

He turned with a huge smile on his round face. "Yes, dear?"

"Don't talk with your mouth full!" She yelled. "You're making me sick!"

I smiled. Spell or no spell, I liked the woman.

"Hey, there you are! What the hell, man?"

I looked at David and saw his gaze shift to lock onto Fier, right in her eyes. He smiled wider. "And look who we have here! Wow! How have you been, Fier?"

She closed her eyes. "Very well, thank you." She rubbed the back of her neck and pretended to look at her watch. "Although, it's late, time for bed."

David raised an eyebrow. "Sounds like a great idea."

I stepped in, for her sake. "Oh hey, sorry. I didn't see you. You've been here the whole time?" I saw Fier smile out of the corner of my eye.

David glanced at me. "Yep, over there." He gestured to where he'd been standing then his eyes were back on Fier.

"Goodnight, gentlemen." She headed for the door.

David snapped to attention. "Please. May I walk you home? It's dangerous out there, assassination attempts and all."

I stood up and grabbed my friend by his shoulders. "She's a big girl."

Fier shifted her gaze between the two of us and finally rested her eyes on me. She nodded and was almost out the door when I yelled. "Oh, hey!" She looked back. "Thanks for, um, the talk and, ah, everything. Especially that, ah trip."

With another brief nod she was gone.

David turned to me with a hurt, betrayed look. "What the hell was that all about? I don't know if you could tell, but I was making a move there."

I smiled. "Sorry. She's had a rough day. She wants to be left alone."

"Damn." David huffed. "I hope I see her again."

I laughed. "You will."

# Chapter 9

It was the first day on the new job and I felt totally lost and out of place. I was unsure what to do, where to go, who to see or where anything was. Worst of all was having to ask for help and explanation on things that weren't clear. I didn't like it at all. I preferred to know my tasks so I could knock them out with minimal interactions. Done and out.

My stomach was a tight, gnarled, twisted mess the entire first hour. The strangeness of Aswain, particularly its people, didn't help matters. Apparently, according to Fier, everyone on the island had strange gifts or powers. How the hell was I supposed to protect others, much less myself from any would-be nasty 'specials' as David called them?

Even though I drank a lot the night before, I remembered everything the woman told me. I hoped she was joking but doubted it. Maybe she was crazy. That would be fine too. I tried to convince myself that what she told me was a load of bull but it didn't work. I'd already seen and felt too much. This place and the people here were *different*.

Eff.

David and I walked into headquarters right at 8am. To my annoyance, we were wearing almost the exact same thing; black dress pants, black socks, black shoes and blue button up shirts. If I wasn't so nervous, I might've been embarrassed.

Not that it mattered but I didn't want the two of us to be noted as 'those guys,' one and the same, two peas in a pod and so on.

We were told we'd be on call twenty-four hours a day, seven days a week but our typical work period was broken up into eight hour work days Monday thru Friday. I'd heard this was the standard work week back before the whole planet went to hell. The schedule sounded nice to me and I kept reminding myself I'd have the weekend off when the butterflies, more like dinosaurs, in my stomach started acting up.

Surprisingly, David didn't look much better than I felt. I'd have thought he be all about this, new beginning, new people, new tasks and so on but I could tell he felt more than a bit bewildered and off balance He still maintained a smile on his face though but it wasn't as bright and wide as normal.

I didn't have time to tell him everything I'd learned from Fier the night before. That was most likely a good thing for his sake, less to worry about. He could just focus on the new job.

We entered the base after our light-rail commute and were immediately greeted by one of our new superiors. The man eyed us up and down before reminding us that we weren't supposed to follow any particular dress code. That was followed by a giggle. Ass.

The man, John Durn, Captain John Durn, was the most round person I'd ever seen. He was short, maybe five-eight with an oversized belly, a near perfectly circular head and round glasses over large eyes. His short brown hair was thinning to where it just barely covered his scalp. I almost laughed at the sight of him but managed to hold it in.

He led us to the information room and introduced us to several computers that had the goods on everyone in Aswain. He ran us through various programs and instructed how the machines worked.

Each terminal came with a DNA scanner along with an advanced photo identification device. The thing was amazing. You could just stick in a picture of anyone from any time in their lives and it would recognize the image then give you the person's history.

The tool was invasive and reminded me of the Union but what the hell did I care. We were on the intelligence team after all.

John eventually left David and me alone to work the program for a piece of time, running checks on newcomers to the island. He'd said he'd be back in a few hours and it was now eleven o'clock.

Working the machines, I felt like a spy prying into people's lives. The newcomers I went through were from all over the place. Asia, the Middle East, the Americas, everywhere. The pages of information each file showed that David and I weren't the only ones who'd had difficult, disturbing pasts. Some people arrived here from other prisons or asylums like us and others were free and able to come over on their own. The records didn't go into a whole lot of detail on the initial page but with a bit more digging I could find out everything about anyone.

Bored at one point, I was curious and punched in Chief's name. Nothing but a blank screen with the word 'Restricted' came up; same with Cross. I wasn't surprised.

All in all, everything was easy to follow and rather self-explanatory except for something called an 'H count' which was listed for every person. David and I had no idea what it meant. Most people ranged between three and seven. When I looked at my own file, I saw I was a ten. David was an eleven. We could only wonder what the number meant.

I thought of scanning the pictures that old man, Crow, gave me of those two supposed thieves but each time I went to make a move, David would start chatting and looking at me. I didn't want to get him involved in my business, especially after what Fier said. I knew I should drop the case all together but the money would be nice. I wasn't a materialistic man but I did imagine myself having my own car. Driving again after all this time made me nervous but the crowded light-rail was getting old.

I was about to punch up Fier's information when the sole door to the room slid open. An icy-hot shrill raced down my spine when the big Scot, Chief barreled in. John was in line behind him followed by, of all people, Fier Wren. I quickly cleared the search I'd just started.

I saw David straighten up when he noticed the woman. "Holy …" He nudged me. "Look who it is!"

I acknowledged her with a quick nod. Her relatively short auburn hair dangled along the sides of her face. She had on a cute black business skirt, black pumps and an attractive red sweater that fit her well. Very sharp. She was impossible not to notice, so sexy, so… I quickly rubbed the back of my neck and focused my attention on Chief.

Fier stepped up alongside the big man and dropped off another stack of bios that needed to be checked. She looked at David and me, a silly smile on her face. "Don't you two just look adorable?"

Chief scowled. He was wearing the same military uniform he had on during our lunch with Cross. His clothes stood in contrast to everyone else's relaxed look and made him look like he had a real stick up his ass.

"If I had it my way," he started, "I'd keep you two tucked away in here. Keep you both from screwing up my team. But, God knows why, the Governor likes you, so we're stuck together." A disgusted look painted his red face.

Nice way to start things off, I thought, biting my tongue. My natural instinct was to tell him to shove it. David cleared his throat, knowing all too well I could snap at any second. He smiled and nodded. "Sir, give us a chance and we'll prove our worth."

David was a good man, much better than I'd ever be, but I felt ill when he sucked-up like that.

Chief curled his lip, pushing his thick red mustache into an odd slant. He grunted. "We'll see. I'll be watching." He stomped up close to me. "Come. Time to meet my team."

I walked up to the door and stopped, not sure where to go. David was beside me.

"Move it!" Chief bellowed. "We're heading to the assembly area."

I turned to look at the man. John and Fier were behind him again. "Ohhhh kaaaaay." I couldn't keep the attitude out of my tone. "Where exactly is that?"

Chief's jaw tightened. "Christ's sake. Didn't study the base floor plans? I'm not surprised. Well," he stepped directly behind David and me, "if you want to be treated like children, so be it."

I felt a large hand grip the back of my neck before receiving an unfriendly shove. I looked out of the corner of my eye and saw David was in the same vice. "Move!" Chief roared.

A surge of anger boiled inside me. Now I really hated this man. We were led, more like forced, a good distance and I felt my face flush each time someone passed us. This was not the first impression I wanted to send. Chief quickly moved us past several labs, offices and cubicles connected by long hallways. With each step, the man's grip on my neck made me hotter and angrier. I tried to shake his hand off a few times but that just made him squeeze tighter.

He stopped abruptly. "Here." He manhandled my neck, forcing my head to turn. "This is the men's room. We don't have a little boy's room for you two, unfortunately. Do you have to have a wee?"

I fumed as my muscles started to shake with rage. Everything inside me, my brain, my gut, my instinct demanded I turn around and rip the guy's head off. I barely fought the demands off.

Behind us, John chuckled. David and I didn't say a word. Chief yanked our heads straight again. "No? Ok then, keep moving."

I wondered how David was holding up through all this. Knowing him, he was most likely thrilled. Probably enjoying the tour.

At the end of yet another hallway was a large, no doubt several feet thick, metal door with guards posted on each side. The door was familiar. Joshua had shown it to us a few days earlier but didn't take us through. I glanced over the intricate security lock device. Lights of every color danced over several buttons.

"Stop!" Chief yelled before finally releasing his hold on our necks.

He bolted up to the lock and danced his fingers over the pad. The move was followed by a series of vibrations, clanks and bangs. There must have been a dozen or more heavy locks releasing their hold.

I glanced back at Fier. She seemed nervous, maybe she was worried for David and me, but gave an encouraging nod. I wondered if she'd studied up on my history, my temper.

I caught a glimpse of John as well. He gave a quick 'thumbs up' and smiled. Hmm, I guess he was on my side too. Maybe Chief was a prick to everyone.

The C.O. was back behind David and me a beat later as the door fully opened. I felt the initial brush of his fingers on my neck and snapped, whirling around to face him.

"Alright, *Sir*, that's enough!" I bellowed. "I think we can make it from here."

Chief squinted. "You thought wrong, Sworn. Eyes forward!"

When I saw the genuine concern on Fier's face and the look of horror on David's; I sucked up my pride and obeyed. The large hand was back on my neck, just below my skull. I gnashed my teeth.

"Maybe next time you'll prepare yourself, boy-o." Chief spoke in a low, smug tone. "Move!"

We proceeded through the thick door into a narrow hallway with red strips of light running up and down the walls. The hall led to another heavy security door. Chief stopped about a yard from it and bellowed. "Chief!"

A misty green beam of light shot out between David and me, a little above our heads. I looked back and up at Chief to see the light run up and down every contour on his scowling face. A few seconds later the red lights turned green and a digitized, female voice said "Clear." The door opened.

A very large and very open room was sprawled out before us. I was so dazzled by the security device and then the new room I hardly even noticed Chief's shoves, moving us into the new, large chamber.

We stood on an elevated platform with a three sets of stairs that led down to the main floor. Rows of intricate communications stations, computers and other devices filled the space.

Men and women hustled around, punching information into various computers or speaking into different microphones and headsets. Some of them acknowledged us, a few smiled and others laughed.

My eyes dashed over everything. It looked like a NASA control station I'd seen in old movies. Glowing electronic maps filled the side walls and the far wall was made up of three huge theater sized screens that hung side by side by side. It displayed a large map of Aswain and Shard Isle.

I noticed an odd, somewhat hidden, inconspicuous black door in the far lower left corner of the room. There was a sign above the door that read 'TRANSPORT.' I was so amazed by the technological buzz of the place I couldn't help but wonder if they'd actually created a teleportation device of some sort. I doubted it, but still wondered like a dazzled, astonished child.

"To the conference room!" Chief's annoying, deep voice pulled me back to the present and I realized my mouth had been hanging open. "Move it!"

Still on the platform, we were pushed to our right along the wall toward a doorway that led to a good sized room with a large table in the middle. I counted about fifty chairs around it.

David and I were forced down into the two nearest seats. "Sit down." Chief ordered. He headed back out of the room while John and Fier each took a seat across from us.

I grimaced and rubbed the back of my neck, not to suppress any lusty feelings but to soothe the burn left there from Chief's forceful grip. "Is he always like this?" I asked.

John shook his round head. "No, not really."

David sighed and I rolled my eyes. "Great." We said in unison.

I heard Chief's booming growl from outside the conference room. "Anyone who can spare the time, come into the conference room!"

"He's usually grumpy, but, he really seems to have unique feelings for you two." Fier said with a little, smartass grin on her face.

David perked his head up after the smile. His demeanor visibly lightened. "Hey. How come you never told me you were on the intelligence team?"

Fier looked at him. "You never asked. You didn't seem to care what I did. Every time we met, you just had one thing on your mind."

I looked at my friend and saw the devious, almost guilty smile that popped up on his face.

Before he could reply a group of men and women who'd been busily running around and working in the intelligence room a few moments before entered. They each took a seat.

Finally, Chief came back in. He remained standing. A man was with him who looked quite out of place. He wore an expensive looking suit and had a thick head of wavy gray hair, a smooth, hard face and deep, dark eyes. He stayed standing as well with his hands clasped behind his back.

"Well, here they are." Chief said to everyone without an ounce of excitement. "Our new recruits. And by 'new' I mean straight off the boat. I've asked you all to read up on them so you know their history."

A warm flush immediately overflowed my face and my eyes retreated, dropping down to stare at the blank tabletop. Embarrassed, I felt like I'd been thrown into a room of strangers completely naked.

Chief cleared his throat. "Sworn, Holt! These are your Captains. John Durn, Sarah Keen, Fier Wren and Clark Ashe."

I forced my gaze to meet Fier's surprised to hear her name specially noted. I had no idea she was a captain. Hell I didn't even know there were 'intelligence captains.'

"Each report to me but they're authorized to make orders and decisions of their own." He snorted. "If you're lost and I'm not around, they can walk you to where you need to go."

I looked up at Chief with blazing, hate filled eyes. "Thanks." I snarled through locked teeth.

The others who were there introduced themselves and seemed pleasant enough. We were then given a little recap of our jobs over the next half hour or so. It turned out the large room with all the monitors is the intelligence command center which helps organize all other security personal, Aswain's defense and helps track citizens when needed.

"That's enough of all that." Chief blurted after Ashe gave David and me a few pointers on various duties. "We have a nation to secure and these two can learn as they go... I hope. Anyways, we have some executives and officials that'll need a security escort. I've sent out your assignments so you'll all need to check your logs."

I was curious if I'd receive an assignment. Headquarters was interesting but I preferred to be out and about. I wanted to see the world while on the job, actually do something I felt had meaning.

Chief noticed my attention had perked up. "Nothing for you two." He smiled. "You greens need more schooling."

The well-dressed gray haired man finally spoke. "Chief, are not these the two who saved Krane?" He regarded us as he took a deep breath in through his nose. His voice had a thick accent too it that sounded Russian. "I bet they are more than ready, yes?"

"I'll say who is ready and when, Yuri." Chief retorted.

The man shrugged. "Very well." He continued to regard us as the rest of the people in the room filed out and stuck his hand out to me since I was closer. "I am Yuri Volkov, Mayor of Tauros."

I stood up and took his hand, glad I had a firm handshake to match his. I remembered reading or hearing that Tauros, about sixty or seventy miles south of Prospous, was the main manufacturing city for Aswain. All the raw metals, concrete, plastics and woods used for construction were processed in that city. I imagined the place must've been and still is just a flurry of activity judging by how much and how quickly Aswain had grown and developed.

"Jason Sworn." I said with a nod.

Durn coughed from behind me. "*Agent* Jason Sworn."

I looked at him and he winked while Volkov shook hands with David.

"Durn." Chief started. "I want these two familiarized with escorting procedure along with the locations and layouts of all security stations in the country." He eyeballed us and raised an eyebrow. "Issue them their weapons too."

"Yes Sir." The Captain acknowledged. He looked at David and me. "Let's head back outside the command center. Less clutter out there."

Durn walked by and I positioned myself to follow him when that damn hand grabbed hold of my neck again. I didn't think, I couldn't think. I simply reacted, whirling around and shoving both hands, palms out, right into Chief's barrel of a chest with as much force as I could muster. The big man flew back and crashed into one of the conference room chairs. He and the chair tumbled to the ground.

"Oh sh -" I heard David begin.

I stood my ground and puffed out my chest, looking down on Chief. Part of me wanted to pounce on him and attack but the smile on the big man's face stopped me.

Chief casually stood up and dusted himself off. He looked at me. "Well, well. You've got balls, that's for sure." His eyes sparkled. "But not many brains." He pulled out a nightstick which had been dangling off his belt and held it while looking at me.

I stood my ground, anticipating an attack. Instead Chief put both hands on the stick, one at each end and, with literal ease, snapped the thing clean in half. I gulped. The stick was like a small baseball bat and he broke it as if it were a toothpick.

Volkov clapped while chuckling. "Very impressive. Now why don't you let these young men on their way and stop pestering them?" The Mayor didn't seem at all upset that I'd just knocked the head of Aswain's intelligence on his ass.

"I'll let that little tantrum go this time, sonny," Chief said quietly and slowly, ignoring Volkov, "but I won't be so lenient next time."

Yea, the nightstick display was impressive and I'd have to be a fool to not be intimidated but I refused to show it. Instead I just scoffed. "Yes, *Sir.*"

Chief squinted. "Get the eff out of my sight."

I turned, followed Durn and smiled. Chief's hand wasn't anywhere near the back of my neck this time.

-

I honestly tried to forget about Pat Crow. I wanted to keep the money, throw the pictures and cards away and then lie to the old man if and when he ever asked about my progress. But

I couldn't. I was a pessimistic downer and a jerk but I wasn't a thief. That, and I was bored out of my mind.

Finally, on my third day on the job, I got the chance to investigate the guys who supposedly stole the blue gem Crow wanted. After a quick glance around the large room, I nervously placed the first photograph on the scanner. I was alone and the hum from the different computers filled the large empty room.

David was out on his first actual assignment. Lucky Bastard. The other intelligence agents were all still busy investigating Krane's assassination attempt. I was stuck here, checking up on new arrivals again. It was obvious I was being punished, stuck with mindless remedial work. In hindsight, maybe I shouldn't have knocked Chief down. Christ.

The monitor lit up and information splayed across the screen. The first picture was of Scott Wright, a construction worker, white male, age 23. He was a good sized, six-four, two-hundred thirty pounds. The report noted he resided in Marchfield, seventy miles east of Prospous. Some bolded, red text stated he'd been missing from work for eight days.

The next picture was of Shawn Ryan, another white guy who was thirty-six years old. He was smaller than the first, only five-ten, and worked in the agriculture department. His house was all the way south in Breadstone, over one hundred fifty miles south of the capital. He was also listed as missing from work. Interesting.

I looked deeper into the men's data, searching for similarities. It didn't take long. Both were prison escapees from Tehlasrin and drug addicts with violent tendencies. Ryan had been in Aswain four months and Wright had been here for two. They were both nearly kicked out of the country but did well in rehabilitation and were allowed to stay.

I snorted and shook my head, disgusted. *Cross just about let's anyone in here.* Then I thought of myself. I was no better and I was on the effing intelligence team!

I re-focused.

The bank accounts for both men had a sudden boost in them six days ago and they'd been spending a lot of Gems at a bar called Club Aces on the southern outskirts of Prospous County. Their accounts showed they'd spent money at the bar every night for the past seven nights.

I grinned. This was almost too easy. I guessed they were a couple punks who found out about this Soulphire, met up, stole it, sold it and then got back on their drug kicks. That or they were just unreliable workers and old man Crow was crazy with a grudge against them.

I printed up a quick rundown of the information I'd processed and stuck it in my pocket. A couple moments later John Durn ended my loneliness, startling me.

"Agent Sworn?" He regarded me with a slight pause, reading my face. I wondered if my guilt was noticeable, knowing full well I wasn't supposed to be working on any independent investigations. Durn seemed to put it out of his head. "Chief wants everyone to meet in the conference room. Come on."

I nodded and stood. "Whatever you say, Captain. I'm really starting to hate this room."

Durn smiled. "Three days of background checks will do that to you. Don't worry; I think Chief's beginning to only really not like you instead of hating you."

"That's a relief." I rolled my eyes.

We moved quickly and reached the intricate touch pad security panel. I looked at Durn and he raised his eyes. He wanted me to give it a whirl. I was about to protest but when his eyes narrowed I decided against it.

It took a couple tries but I eventually got it. Each of us had our own code to enter and mine was a series of numbers followed by some letters then colors then more numbers. The next part was easier.

"Jason Sworn." The scanning beam ran over my face. I fought the instinct to close my eyes but the retina scan was an important part of the reading. The inner door opened.

"Good, very good, Jason."

I smirked. "No sweat."

We headed toward the conference room and I watched the other agents file in. I spoke in a lowered tone. "Sir, where's Fier?"

"*Captain* Wren is on another special, ah, recruiting assignment." Durn pursed his lips a moment, thinking. "That's all you need to know for now."

"Fair enough."

We walked in the room and I locked eyes with Chief. He looked the same as always, military dress, tough as nails and pissed off. I sat down as far from him as I could.

"Sworn." Chief called from the head of the table.

My stomach turned. "Yes, Sir?"

"Why aren't you armed? Where's your weapon?" He was up now, heading toward me and I started to sweat. On his way he turned his head and called out. "Jamal! Alert every agent out on assignment right now. I'll be starting soon."

I glanced to see who he was talking to. Jamal was as lanky and as dark as Durn was round. The man's black skin seemed to shine blue in the light and I marveled at how quickly he worked his mobile phone. A second later, Chief was towering over me.

"Stand." He spoke in an almost soft tone. I obeyed. "When Governor Cross told me he was going to put you on my team I thought it was a bad idea, a horrible idea. I thought you and your friend were dangerous and untrustworthy."

I blinked. This was nothing new.

"Now I believe I may have been wrong." Chief continued. "Now I see you're just plain incompetent!" His volume tripled on the last word. "We are on duty every second of every day. We're the protectors, the watchers, the brains of Aswain's defense network. You are to be armed and ready to fight and die at any moment! Do you understand me, Agent Sworn?"

I nodded. He had me and there was no excuse. I could see the others around me were all armed. I had taken my weapon off at the beginning of my daily set of background checks, figuring I didn't need it. A mistake.

"Sorry, Sir."

Chief scowled. "All you are is sorry." He headed back to the front. "Agent Brown! Do you have them yet?"

"Yes, Chief." Jamal's low voice reverberated through the mostly empty room.

I looked around and saw there were only fifteen of us here. Must be a busy day. Not that I'd have known, tucked away to my remedial duties.

Chief quickly snatched up and eyed a sheet of paper that was lying on the table. "Wren, Ashe, Yoki, Holt, Ahlar, are you all present? You haven't acknowledged yet!"

A series of 'Yes Sirs' came through and I focused on the name 'Holt.' I wondered how David was doing on his first real task, beyond envious.

"Good." Chief barked. "Let's start then. As most of you know there have been multiple reports of citizens missing work. Some have been found miles away from their homes and others… others were the ones killed during Mayor Krane's attack."

I felt my brow furrow. Missing work… just like the guys who stole Crow's gem.

Chief snorted. "Even more alarming, some of these reported missing people are security personnel. Level two marshals and level one guards all over the place haven't been seen for a week or more." He paused and I saw his shoulders slump. "Also, Agent Kara Childers can't be located."

There was a collective gasp in the room.

"Kara?" Another agent, a young man with slick black hair, asked. "I thought she was on assignment in America."

Chief nodded. "She was but she disappeared shortly after returning. I've personally investigated the case but so far I've come up empty."

This was a huge deal, any idiot could tell. I looked at Durn who nervously rubbed his chin. A missing agent, with the information available to them, was a major snafu.

"Pay attention!" Chief could see his team was anxious. "Now. Focus. Some of these people have been found committing crimes and attacking officials so we're going to assume that they're all either part of an insurgent group or dead."

Captain Sarah Keen, a motherly, rather harmless looking black woman who appeared to be in her mid-forties, raised her hand. She was dressed in comfortable clothes, blue jeans and a sweater and was a tad overweight. If I'd have passed her on the street I never would have guessed she was on any security team, much less an agent and then a captain at that. But then again, that was the point, right?

"Yes, Captain?" Chief gave the woman a respectful nod.

"Do we have any leads on this 'insurgent' group? Do we know anything about them?" She spoke in a soft, melodic voice. "What do they want? What does Governor Cross have to say on this?"

"No leads yet. This is all very new and even though the group seems to have just sprung up over the past week, we know better." Chief started pacing back and forth. "This movement is organized and it's had time to talk with, corrupt and organize its followers. My guess is that it's been developing for some time. Governor Cross is doing all he can to find answers and so are we."

"I see." Sarah nodded. "What are our orders?"

Chief stopped pacing and raised his eyebrows. "We're going on full alert. We're going to be in constant contact with county, city and township security heads. We're going to step up protection for business owners, officials and council members."

The large man slammed his fist down on the table, creating a loud boom that echoed through the conference room. "I want to do more but Cross demands we merely stay on high alert."

"More?" I couldn't help but blurt the word.

Chief curled his mustached lip. "Yes, Sworn. More. This has potential to snap the very foundations of this nation, the last bastion of freedom on the whole blasted planet. I want to find it and knock it out quickly. I want to lock the place up and run thorough checks on every living soul." He squinted. "The Governor said that's too much, too soon."

I nodded and considered the situation. Cross was right. Chief was talking about martial law and I've seen firsthand how fun that was.

"At any rate," Chief went on, "you'll be getting a stream of updated reports listing who're missing and where they're from. So be ready to work above and beyond normal hours, got it."

The team and several voices from the room's intercom system agreed. I just nodded again.

"Ok then, let's get busy."

The other agents and I stood up to leave when Chief bellowed over the murmurs that had started. "Oh I almost forgot." He groaned, and I mean it was an actual groan. "Sworn, come here."

I laughed at my own misfortune. What now? I thought I was free and clear. What did I do wrong this time? I took my time walking up to Chief now wishing to retreat to my boring duty.

The large man didn't look at me when he spoke. "We're shorthanded and it's been requested by Mayor Krane that you escort him tonight on a small business trip."

My mood instantly brightened. An actual assignment!

"Where to, when am I supposed to meet him?" I spoke quickly and Chief finally looked at me. I could see the disappointment on his face.

"Here's the mission file. You'll pick him up at 8pm and then escort him to a secure location in south Prospous County." He thrust the file out at me and shoved it into my gut.

I grabbed it and looked the man in his face, unable to keep from smiling.

"Sworn." Chief said in an almost pleading tone. "Don't screw this up."

I bit my tongue.

# Chapter 10

"So," Simon Krane began while flipping his mobile phone shut. The guy had been through a marathon of phone calls ever since being picked up. He didn't seem to mind, in fact, he loved it. A cheerful smile was on his face. "How's the job treating you?"

I shrugged, not caring to get into how bored I'd been the last few days. "It's interesting," a pause, "though I'd hoped to see a little more action."

He raised his eyebrows. We sat next to each other in the back of a spacious security car. The windows were heavily tinted and I was told the thing was bullet proof.

"Really?" He asked in a raised tone. "I'm surprised, what with everything that's going on. I'd figured they'd have you running all over the place."

"This is the first running I've done." I blurted the words out quickly and with attitude.

The Mayor shrugged. "Ah, well. It must just be because you're new. Good for me though. I'm glad you were available tonight."

Hell yes I'm available. I was so eager for the assignment I arrived at headquarters a half hour early for my rendezvous with the driver. From there we headed to Krane's office and picked him up at 8pm sharp. Now we were heading south toward the Prospous / Tauros County border. It was about a forty-five minute trip and we were nearly there.

I took a moment to study the man I was protecting. Judging by the number of calls he'd gotten in such a short time, I knew a lifestyle like his would be a living hell for someone like me. Endless talking and planning while staying so upbeat and enthusiastic wasn't my thing in the least.

The Mayor, in contrast to Cross, dressed very formally. Suit, tie, the whole thing. Tonight he wore a matching, flashy gold colored jacket and pants set. His black hair was perfectly groomed, slicked back like the first time I saw him and his eyes seemed even bigger and more elf like than the night I helped save his life.

His style was very professional and but also very rich, almost snobbish. Still, his attitude didn't come off that way so he was alright in my book.

I glanced at that back of the driver's head. He looked to be in his early forties and the only words he'd said all night were "You Sworn?" That was fine with me; Small talk wasn't my cup of tea either.

Everything was moving along just fine but the night had me on edge. It wasn't the task that bothered me. Escorting Krane was simple enough and there hadn't been any attacks on him since the other night. I was on guard but not especially alarmed, everything seemed well in hand. Still, I didn't know exactly where we were going and Chief's parting words kept ringing through my head. *Don't screw it up. Don't screw it up.* Ugh. I was worried the bastard would put a jinx on the whole thing.

Then there was old man Crow. Even though our exact location wasn't clear, I couldn't help notice we were in the vicinity of *Club Aces*, the seemingly favorite hangout of the two alleged thieves. Out of curiosity, I'd printed up a few quick maps of the area earlier in the day. I knew damn well I should just put the case out of my head but I also knew there was a good chance I'd be stepping into the club for a drink later in the evening. Such was the life of a bull-headed fool like me. Too informed to be ignorant and too stupid to stay clear of trouble.

Going to the bar would no doubt lead to a confrontation and my stomach was a blend of excitement and anxiety. After the mundane past few days, a little excitement sounded wonderful. I wondered how I ever managed all those months in the asylum without really going insane.

"You're a quiet man, aren't you, Agent Sworn?" Krane snapped me back to the present.

I looked at him and nodded. "Usually."

"The concept is quite foreign to me. I like to talk." He laughed. "I often wonder what quiet people are thinking. What do their minds do with all that time?" He gave me an intent look and a smile. "Well? Do you mind indulging my curiosity? What occupies the quiet mind of Agent Jason Sworn?"

I didn't expect the sudden interest in my thoughts and wasn't about to mention Crow or the Soulphire. I let out a small grunt, gathering my thoughts. "Um, I guess I'm just mostly wondering where we're going."

"No one told you?" Krane asked. "Not even Chief? It was in a report or something?"

I nearly rolled my eyes. "If it were then I'd know."

He chuckled. "Of course." A pause. "We're headed to meet Mr. Wang Otaki, a prominent business man and a giant in the construction field. Most of his work has been in Tauros, Lionsgate and Sunrise but now he wants to start a project in Prospous County." He gave me a second, making sure I was following him.

"Ok." I was going to leave it at that until another question popped up in my head. "As mayor, do you just oversee the city of Prospous or the whole county? I've heard you're Cross's number one man."

The Mayor laughed, seemingly tickled by my wording. "As one of our top intelligence agents, shouldn't you know all this?" A beat. "I'm the leading chair of Aswain's council, just under Governor Cross. That means I have a say in affairs all across the country. But... My primary watch is Prospous, both the city and county." His eyes widened. "Anything more would be far too much to handle." He laughed and lowered his voice. "Don't tell Mr. Cross that, though. Sometimes it seems like the man's a machine."

I nodded. "Ok, I've got it."

"Alright then, back to Mr. Otaki." Krane moved his hands a lot while he spoke, very animated, almost annoyingly so. "He wants to build in my County. The council and everyone else in Aswain encourages growth, but thanks to our friendly competitive atmosphere, this is causing a slight stir in Prospous."

I was putting the pieces together. "I see. So Otaki wants to butter you up for the rights to build in your county and you have other developers that also want the job."

"Other developers that are actual residents in Prospous County. They feel they should have first dibs." He laughed. "Ah, the merry world of money and politics."

I thought about the whole situation. Back in Tehlasrin, the person or party with the most credits and clout would always get the goods. That left ninety to ninety-five percent of the GU's people with essentially nothing but slave wages and long work weeks. I wondered how things worked here. I hoped they were different. Eff, they *had* to be different.

"I'm meeting Otaki for drinks in the hotel lounge where he's spending the night in Goldthorn. It's on the county border. The place is well protected and you'll be free to go a short while after we arrive." Krane's phone, which had been quiet for too long, buzzed again and he looked at it while finishing his point. "I'll let you know when you're free to head home. Excuse me a moment."

Krane read the text message on his mobile and I thought on the name of the city we were approaching, *Goldthorn*. Club Aces was right smack in the middle of that town. My palms started to sweat. Coincidental opportunities like this don't come up very often...

The mayor looked up from his phone with a quizzical expression after seeing my face. "Is everything alright?"

"Yea," I let out a sigh. "I'm fine, Sir." I didn't like feeling so transparent and worked to change the subject. "So, um, why did you request me for this trip?"

There was a slight pause while Krane continued to study me. "Has anyone ever saved your life?" He asked finally.

It didn't take long to recall the list of people that had saved my ass over the years. Most notably, David. "Yea."

"Right then." A short nod. "Wouldn't you feel more comfortable with that person, a person you know is accountable, able and trustworthy, rather than someone else or a complete stranger? These are delicate times." A serious expression sprung up that made him look like an entirely different person. The look was, for lack of a better word, intense. "This world hangs in the balance, Jason. Big things are happening all the time and it won't take much to shift the entire alignment."

I pulled myself away from the Mayor, literally taken aback by the sudden shift in character. Strangely, as quickly as the man's demeanor changed, it shifted back to what I knew as normal.

"Actually there were two of you that saved me, correct?"

Rhetorical. I barely moved. "Yea."

"I wanted Mr. Holt to come along as well but ironically he was busy watching and protecting a couple of the business men and women who are opposed to Otaki's desires." Krane sighed. "You're friend has had a busy day, I'm sure he's in bed by now."

"Pft." I made the sound while turning my head to look out the window. If David was in bed he certainly wasn't alone. I was curious who he'd been guarding. We hadn't spoken all day. Now I knew.

A few quiet minutes later, the lights outside the tinted windows grew brighter and our vehicle slowed. I looked out to see an impressive, shiny, black glass building with valets and bellboys busily hustling around doing their jobs.

I looked over at Krane whose nose was already buried in his phone again. "Stay here until I ask you come out." I spoke in a deep, serious tone, all business now.

An almost startled look of surprise splashed up on the Mayor's face.

When our car stopped, I opened my door and stepped out. The cool night air swirled around me and I scanned every face, doorway, car and crevice. Looking up the façade of the building, I saw it was roughly shaped like a pyramid, about twenty stories high and covered with windows. Damn. Snipers could be behind any one of them. My brain focused on my weapon which was pressed against the left side of my chest under my shirt.

The gun was a brand new model, hot off the assembly line which used some new advanced technology. The thing was almost a laser gun but not quite. I couldn't keep images of old science fiction movies from popping into head when Captain Durn was explaining the thing.

It was shaped like a pistol only much thinner with a noticeable gap, a hole in the middle of the barrel. It used long lasting, multiple shot energy capsules which could launch waves of heat and electricity powerful enough to kill or, with a shift in settings, weak enough to merely knock the target unconscious. As far as Durn knew, it was the first line of weaponry made using the new etherspring energy. Only the Aswain intelligence team had clearance to use them at this time. Here and now, alert and protecting Krane, I was ready to use it at a moment's notice.

Luckily, everything appeared safe. "Ok, Sir, things look clear. You can come out."

The man looked a little annoyed when he stepped out of the car. "Relax, Jason. This is a secure place."

"I'll be the judge of that. I'm not paid to relax." Memories of Krane running past burning cars with bullets whirling by him played through my head.

"Wow." Krane gave me a little salute. "You *are* good. Cross and I were right about you." He gestured toward the door. "Let's head inside. Tyler will wait for you out here. He'll take you home." He gestured back to the car and I guessed 'Tyler' was the driver's name. "This won't take long. I promise you'll be out of here soon."

I straightened and stepped in front of Krane when I saw a man and woman, each wearing extremely expensive looking business suits, power walking toward us. Their eyes were glued on the Mayor who side stepped around me. I grunted.

The oncoming woman wore a professional smile. She was a tall, thin and graceful, looking like she came from India. She had perfect posture, long straight black hair, a face that was pleasing to look at and some of the largest brown eyes I'd ever seen. "Mayor Krane, it's a pleasure to meet you." She reached out and shook his hand. "My name is Nitya Rai and this is Jeremy Staal. Mr. Otaki is expecting you. Please follow us."

The man, Staal was short and thin with an odd 'bunched up' looking face. Everything, his eyes, nose and mouth seemed smaller than they should be. His eyes were what really stood out since they were so tiny. His brown hair was long and wavy in contrast to his small face and seemed to sit on his head like an oversized tablecloth.

Rai and her partner each shot glances at me and I only glared back. They led the way through a busy maze of luggage, people, walls and staircases until we reached what turned out to be a very luxurious lounge.

Men and women sat around on couches and at tables, talking and sipping drinks, some smoked sweet smelling cigars or cigarettes. I didn't mind even though I hardly ever smoked myself. The blend of smells gave the dim lit room a mystical aura that felt very comfortable.

We zigzagged around couches and tables until we reached Mr. Otaki. The man was already standing in anticipation of Krane's arrival. He was Asian and small, both short and thin. It was hard to guess his age, anywhere from forty to sixty. His eyes showed wisdom, his face was stern and his hair, which was graying, long and wild, showed energy and creativity.

We stopped when Otaki and Krane were within arm's reach of each other. They locked hands and the businessman gave a quick bow. "Thank you for coming, Mayor Krane. I know you are as busy a man as I am. I truly appreciate this." He spoke with a very heavy accent.

"Mr. Otaki." Krane began. "You've done so much for our country; it's my honor to finally meet with you." The flattery was thick enough to cut with a knife. I realized the Mayor could even kick David's butt any day in brown nosing.

Otaki gave another short bow then cut his eyes around at me. "I don't want to waste your time, Mr. Mayor." He finally looked away from me. "So let's talk business… in private. I have a secluded booth in the back corner."

"Of course." Krane nodded.

An alarm bell went off in my head. The corner the man gestured was too dark and hidden away. Too dangerous. I leaned forward to speak quietly in Krane's ear. "Sir, I don't like this. I have a bad feeling."

Otaki stopped walking and turned to look at us. "Is there a problem?"

I furrowed my brow. "That's for me to decide."

Rai and Staal both stirred. Otaki puffed his chest out before speaking in a much deeper tone this time. "Do not disrespect and dishonor me. Who are you, anyway?" His stare was intense even from someone so small.

I raised my eyebrows, not at all intimidated. The man may have been rich and powerful but that didn't sway me in the slightest.

I was about to speak but Krane beat me too it with a loud, fake cough. "He's with me... A good man but overprotective it seems."

"He should learn to keep quiet when important men discussing business." Otaki stared into my eyes and I blazed back at him, angry as hell.

"Important men?" I said mockingly. I shot glances between Jeremy and Nitya before settling back on Otaki. "Listen here, you little -"

"Excuse me!" Krane raised his voice, followed by a quick laugh. He grabbed me by my arm and pulled me away from the businessman. When he spoke again he was calm and quiet. "I appreciate your enthusiasm but I'll handle this. We're safe here and you're free to go home. Tyler is waiting. Thank you, Jason. Chief will receive a glowing report. Well done."

I let out a deep breath, trying to calm myself. "Alright, fine, if you say so. I'm not comfortable with this, though."

Krane furrowed his brow. "What do you mean?"

I wasn't sure how to explain it but I felt uneasiness in the air. It was a strange feeling I'd had from time to time over the years. It felt threatening, scheming, menacing. Unable to pinpoint or properly articulate it, I gave up. "Forget it." I shook my head and shifted gears. "Sir, about *Tyler*," It felt odd using the name in such a familiar way when I didn't even know the guy, "will he take me wherever I want to go?"

Krane slumped his shoulders and cocked his head to the side. "Jason. You don't have to stay in the area for my safety, I'm fine. Trust me."

I almost laughed, almost. Instead I just waited.

"I suppose he'll take you where you ask but he'll be heading back soon. The man is my chauffer, not yours." Krane shot a quick glance at Otaki. "I have to get back. Take care and have a good night." He winked and headed back toward Otaki.

It was then I noticed the two associates had been listening in on the Mayor and me. Their stares alarmed me all over again. I scoffed. "Anyone ever tell you it's not polite to stare?"

They walked over to me, unresponsive to my question. "This way Mr., umm I'm sorry, I missed your name." The Indian woman said with a raised eyebrow.

I snorted, "No you didn't," and stomped a few paces. "I can find my way out."

"We're headed out too." The man, Jeremy said. "Mr. Otaki likes his privacy."

"So what do you do for the Mayor?"

I looked the woman in her big, dark eyes. I wasn't sure how I should answer. I decided to keep it short. "Security." I asked a question of my own before she could pry further. "What about you?"

She smiled. "Security, for Mr. Otaki."

I glanced between the two of them. "Good job?"

Now she looked annoyed. "It's both honorable and lucrative."

"Good." I looked forward, signaling I was done talking.

"Heading to see some sights in the area?" Jeremy asked. "Business or pleasure?"

I looked at him, threateningly, not about to answer. We reached the exit and the man swooped ahead of me, opened and held the door. When I walked by he smiled, almost wickedly. "Have a great night."

I ignored him as best I could and marched toward the waiting car.

-

*Club Aces* was loud, large, dimly lit crowded and smoky. Electronic music filled the air causing people to have to yell to be heard over the thumping beat. The group was made up of mostly young men and women in their early twenties. A lot of them writhed around, provocatively, on the dance floor adding to and creating a lusty aura of sex and intoxication. I'd heard of the term 'hooking-up' and this place seemed made for it.

The place was filled with energy, life and jealousy. People flirted and fought with each other to attract potential partners. The men were puffed up and cocky and the women were teasing and sultry.

I hated it.

Despite all the obnoxious distractions, I'd been watching and stayed focused on one man who was leaning against the opposite end of the square bar gulping down drink after drink. Scott Wright.

He wasn't hard to spot. The man was even bigger in person than his bio let on. He had a mean look on his face that kept others clear of him as he made moves on various women who'd sauntered too close. It seemed Mr. Wright was Mr. Wrong every time.

I sipped my own drink, and waited. Anxiety fluttered in my gut but now that I was here, on the job, my predatory instinct took over. I was on the hunt and had my prey in sight. I waited for the right time to confront him about the Soulphire.

"Hey honey. You look like you've had a long night."

I hardly glanced at the obviously drunk woman who tried and failed to speak seductively into my ear. She had to yell to be heard at all and I wanted to slap her for the abuse to my eardrum. "Eff off," was all I needed to say. She swaggered away, onto the next available male body.

The bartender nearest me overheard the exchange. She made an odd face and gestured my empty glass. "Want another one?" She stepped into my line of vision with Wright.

"No." I barked, shifting my head to keep the man in sight.

The bartender turned to look where I was focused. "Oh I see." She sounded disappointed and totally had the wrong idea.

I rolled my eyes.

She looked at me, quizzically. "You looking for something?"

The question caught me off guard. "What?"

"I can tell, little gift I have." She nodded. "You're after the orb aren't you? Funny, you don't look that stupid."

I made an ugly face. "I don't know what you're talking about. Why don't you just piss off and serve some drinks."

The woman muttered something under her breath and moved over to a customer asking for another shot of liquor. I spared a second to study her when I felt a tap on my shoulder. I quickly turned my head and saw a young man with wild eyes and ratty hair.

"Hey." He said. "I can help you find the orb for some money. You have any money?" He licked his lips and moved in closer to me.

I shoved my shoulder into his chest. It wasn't meant to hurt him, just get the point across that I didn't want him near me.

He complained and backed off. "Fine. Forget it. Jerk!"

I didn't have the time or care to wonder much about the man. Instead I went back to watching Wright. The current song, heavy bass mixed with loud squeaky highs ended and was replaced by another which sounded just like it. I squinted when Wright slammed his empty glass down and headed away from the bar. I guessed he needed to piss and cut through the crowd after him.

I was right. The bathroom was a disaster and smelled of stale beer, urine and vomit. As gross as it was I was surprised and pleased to see it was empty, except for Wright and me. He was parked in front of a urinal taking care of business and I stared at his back.

"Wright." I boomed, my voice echoed through the room.

He turned his head slightly and slumped his shoulders, zipping up. "Man, I've seen you watching me. I don't swing that way."

I ignored him. "I hear you have an interest in rare gems."

A serious and angry look sprung up on his face. "Who the eff are you?"

"The rightful owner of the Soulphire wants his property back." I stepped forward, adrenaline blasting through my veins. "Where is it?"

"I don't know what you're talking about. Now turn around and leave before I hurt you." He stepped toward me as best he could, swaying from the alcohol in his blood.

I didn't budge, glaring into his blurry eyes. "*Where* is it?"

He lunged at me and roared. I sidestepped just in time and almost laughed when the fool face planted on the dirty, pissy floor. He scrambled up, angrier than ever, and threw a punch at me. I made a slight move, dodged the blow and then grabbed his extended arm. In a heartbeat, I had the arm locked behind his back. I could have broken it, but I wasn't to that level yet.

Wright growled and tried to back me up against the wall. Big as he was, he was drunk and uncoordinated. I pushed back and slammed the man, face first, into the opposite wall. His body planted hard against it and I kept him pinned there. He struggled to free himself but couldn't overpower me.

"I'll ask you again." I hissed into his ear. "Where is the Soulphire?"

Wright spit and I saw his mouth was bleeding. "I sold the effing thing."

"To who?" I shoved him into wall again, harder this time.

The door opened and a familiar face stepped in, Shawn Ryan. He wasn't alone and his eyes boggled. "What the hell?"

I focused on Ryan and his two companions. Now things were getting serious. Quickly, I brought Wright's head down and slammed it against the nearest sink. While his body fell to the floor, seemingly knocked out, I bolted over to Ryan and grabbed him by the front of his shirt. I picked him up and slammed him to the floor with as much force as I could muster. He groaned in pain.

"Kay, get help!" The nearest standing man said to the other, who ran out the door. The remaining man looked ready to fight but I didn't attack. Christ, things were getting out of hand.

I put my hands up, palms out. "Look, my issue is with these two. They stole something from a friend of mine."

The man's lip curled. He wasn't buying it.

"I don't want to hurt them, I just need information." I continued, knowing it was pointless. Now I just wanted to get the hell out of here. I was in over my head.

A flash later, the man, Kay, and four others entered the bathroom. A couple were armed with clubs and they all had manic looks in their eyes. I knew the look well, having seen and made it many times myself. Too late. I was going to have to fight my way out of this.

I darted back against the far wall, deep into the bathroom and pulled out my weapon, making sure the setting wasn't one that would kill anyone. Before the group could react, I squeezed off two shots, bringing down a couple of the men.

I expected the others to flee but instead they charged. They were quick and on me before I could line up another shot. I saw a swing come at me and ducked my head only to land smack into another blow from a club. Stars blurred my vision and I hit the floor. When I could see again several pairs of feet were rushing toward me.

Amazingly, the one concern that played through my mind at that time regarded my weapon. I knew I couldn't take the whole group and I knew I couldn't let the bastards get their hands on the state of the art gun.

Luckily, Durn had foreseen this type of scenario and showed me a nifty little self-destruct button on the device. I pressed the small knob and held it tight for a few seconds while the men grabbed, punched and kicked me. I could feel the thing heat up and had to drop it once it started to burn my flesh. It clanked on the ground and literally melted into a small grey, metallic puddle.

"What the?" One of the startled men said.

The distraction allowed me to sit up and lean against the back wall. Blood ran down the side of my face. "Listen." I mumbled. "I just wanted to ask some questions. I don't have any problems with any of you."

"Oh." A short but well-built man said with an evil smile. "You do now."

My head screamed with pain but I wasn't about to give up so easily. I somehow managed to get to my feet as the group of men started to move in closer again. After the little show with the melting gun, I'm sure they wondered what other surprises I had up my sleeve. Unfortunately, I didn't have any.

Mentally and physically preparing myself as best I could, I balled my hands into tight fists, snarled and charged the group. They were shocked by the move and I managed to land my fists against a couple faces, breaking a couple noses but they soon fought back and beat me down again.

Before I passed out I heard someone say "Call the Mistress."

# Chapter 11

Pain throbbed through my head, persistently banging over and over, pushing, shoving and aching into wakefulness. The pressure mounted with time as I slowly opened my eyes, trying to figure out what the hell was going on. Then alarms started ringing in my brain. I remembered things. I remembered escorting Krane. I remembered *Club Aces*. I remembered I was in deep crap.

I jolted and sat up too quickly, causing a black tunnel to cave in on me and swallow my vision. The dark world spun in circles and I groaned in pain, burying my face in my hands. Disoriented, confused and concerned, I stopped everything and took in a few deep, slow breaths.

When I could finally see, I noticed I was lying in a puddle of water on a dirty cement floor in the middle of a large, mostly empty, brightly lit room that looked like a cellar. All that occupied the space was a single chair and a table with a computer and monitor on it. That was it, except for myself and the five men staring down at me with hateful eyes.

I saw a set of stairs behind the men that led up to a flimsy looking wooden door. It appeared to be the only way in or out of the place. There weren't any other doors and no windows. I wondered what I was doing here. I wondered what the men wanted with me. I wondered how much time had passed. I wondered how I could have been so stupid to get myself into this situation in the first place.

I took turns looking each man in the face. "So?" My voice echoed in the room and then reverberated through my aching, beat up head. I grimaced. "What do you want?"

No one spoke.

"Ok, fine." I'd been through hell at Morbal's, interrogated and tortured by the worst. I wasn't going to let these clowns intimidate me. Sick of sitting on the floor, I struggled to my feet. I could sense the stir of alarm in my captors but I didn't pay it much mind. Boldly. I shuffled over to the lone chair and pulled it back to where I'd been laying. Like a sack of potatoes, I plopped down into the chair and crossed my arms. Finally, I huffed. "What time is it?"

"Shut up!" the man in the middle of the five said.

I almost recognized some of the faces. I'd seen them on the 'missing persons' report Chief had sent out after our short meeting. So, maybe Ryan, Wright and some or all of these guys were part of that insurrection group. Maybe the same group that tried to kill Krane.

"Who are you? All of you? What are you doing here?" The same man from before sprayed an angry mist of spit when he yelled, "I said shut up!"

"Or *what*?" My eyes narrowed, burying my gaze into the man. The group could obviously take me out but I was too angry and proud to be bullied. "What do you want from -"

One of the men had a mobile phone and it started ringing. I stopped talking and shifted my attention to the man. He pressed a button and spoke. "Yes?" I watched his eyes slowly close as a strange smile formed on his face. "Mmm. Yes… Ok. It's clear and everything is ready, come down when you wish."

He suddenly pulled the phone away with a hurt look on his face. "Goodbye." He whispered.

"Well?" Mr. Shut Up asked.

The phone owner's eyes boggled. He spoke fast while smiling. "She's coming. She's close. She'll be here soon."

Now all the men were stirring and a couple actually moaned. "I can't believe I actually get to see her!" The smallest of the bunch squealed in delight. It seemed they'd all forgotten I was even here.

A light went off in my head and my depleted adrenaline somehow started to percolate again. This was as good a chance as any to get out of here. I planned my attack in a heartbeat, lining up which prick I'd attack first. Then... then the door at the top of the stairs opened and I could literally smell her... It was the sweetest, most intoxicating and arousing smell in the world.

My mouth involuntarily dropped wide open as I watched her glide down the steps. I marveled at her feet and the sexy black pumps she wore. Her legs were so perfect I wanted to take a bite out of them. The black skirt she wore stopped a few inches above her knees and showed the luscious curve of her hips. A tight fitting, white button up shirt covered parts of her upper body and half of her arms. It exposed a little bit of her sweet, flat, mesmerizingly sexy stomach and was open a bit at the top to grant me a slight peek at her breasts. Her hair was golden blonde and her face was angelic with large, emerald green eyes.

I sank into my chair, unable to even think of escape. I'd never felt so enamored before and honestly thought I was in love. The woman oozed sex and I was lost in the sea of her being. All I could do was sit there and gaze upon her like an unworthy, pathetic admirer as she waltzed up and stopped to stand by the lone table, about three feet in front of me.

She smiled at me and seductively raised an eyebrow. "They didn't tell me you were so cute. Aw." She moved closer and brushed her hand against the wound on the side of my head. Her touch was electric. "That doesn't look too good."

She moved my head to the side with the slightest nudge and looked at my neck. The old wound had healed but the scar would be there forever. I was delighted to see her interest in the mark. She stared into it and sensuously slid a finger up and down the line the blade had left. Now I was the one moaning.

"Lovely." She purred. The woman kept her eyes on me and raised her voice. "Carrie. Come clean our guest's wound."

I hardly even noticed the new arrival. A young woman bolted down the stairs with a small kit in her hand. Even as the newcomer knelt by my side and cleaned my head, I kept my gaze locked on the absolute beauty, the love of my life, standing in front of me.

The angel moved back to the table and hopped up on it to sit down. She crossed her legs and dangled them in front of me. I felt like I was going to melt into a gushy puddle right there but at the same time I was ashamed I hadn't offered her my seat.

She sympathetically cocked her head to the side. "What's your name, Sweetie?"

One of the other men sprung to life and rushed up to the woman, fumbling with something in his hands. I had to tear my eyes away from her to focus on the object. It was my wallet. The information in there was all phony. It was a precautionary measure for all agents. My fake name was Aaron Waters and I hated it. The man told his Mistress, no, *my Mistress* the name.

She glared at him and her eyes were filled with fire. "DON'T interrupt. Go back and stand where you were." She shifted her gaze. "And Brye... stop that."

I followed her line of sight and saw the man she'd addressed. He'd been busy giving his pelvic area a deep massage while he stared at the Mistress. I couldn't really blame him, part of me wanted to do the same but I'd be too embarrassed.

For an instant, I suddenly became alarmed again. My present situation poured back in around me and I felt a hot wave run down my spine. The woman and the others were holding me prisoner and I needed to find a way out. But then, she reached her foot out and rubbed it on my leg. I quivered as my eyes rolled back in my head and another lust filled moan escaped my lips.

She smiled. "Mmm, that's nice. What's your name?"

"Jason." I couldn't lie. It was hard enough just to find the ability to speak at all.

My Mistress let out a small laugh. "Very nice name, very strong. Do you have a last name, Jason?"

I felt so stupid for leaving that part out. "Sorry!" My voice cracked a bit and I wanted to shoot myself. "Jason Sworn! My name's Jason Sworn."

She looked at my fake ID and smirked. "I see. And what do you do, Sexy?"

My heart felt like it was about to burst when she said the word 'sexy.' I opened my mouth to speak but somehow, something, somewhere stopped me. I swallowed, confused. "I, um…" I bit my lip.

My Mistress, no, the woman across from me stirred and furrowed her brow.

I felt lost, not sure why I couldn't tell her my job. Or was it… I didn't know why I wanted to tell her my job. Who was this woman? Something remembered she was my Mistress and I should do whatever makes her happy. Then I thought how ridiculous that sounded. I started breathing quickly.

"Jason." The woman's voice was calm and in command. "Look at me."

I disobeyed and instead looked at the woman on her knees beside me, cleaning the dried blood off me. She was working hard to get the dried blood off the back of my neck, right at the base of my skull.

My mouth dropped open even further until it hooked up into a smile. I reached back and started rubbing my neck as forcefully as I could stomach. Things cleared up. The incredible lust I felt was replaced by the pain I'd all but forgotten from my now cleaned wounds.

I looked the sexy woman in her eyes. "Who the hell are you?"

I didn't take my gaze off the woman when one of the men hollered at me. "Hey! How dare you speak to her like that? I'm gonna kill you!"

She turned her head. "You!" She pointed at the man. "Be silent, turn around and face the wall! You've lost the privilege to look at me!"

I couldn't help but laugh. "Wow. You're a pretty girl but come on. Going a little far don't you think?" I under exaggerated for effect. The little sexpot was light years beyond pretty and I still wanted to jump her bones right there. But now I knew I was being manipulated and managed to rip the thoughts out of my head. Well, some of them.

Her eyes narrowed. "And you're and interesting man, *Agent Sworn*." She paused to watch the startled look spring up on my face.

"So you know?"

She winked. "Oh yes, I had your blood run a while ago."

I gritted my teeth. The damned Plasma Database Registry and Information file. She wasn't supposed to be able to do that. Only high end personnel and the intelligence team had access. Well, so did Tehlasrin. Unless she was with them or had spies in the county's network. My brain scrambled and she enjoyed every second of it.

"How did you get access to the PDRI?" I decided to be direct, no time for games.

She ignored the question and nodded. "Yes, I knew but I wanted to test you. The little neck rub thing doesn't work with me for most men, or women." She gestured toward the young woman who was putting her cleaning tools away. "Carrie."

"Yes Mistress?" She looked up with large, sappy eyes like a begging puppy.

I snarled when I saw the manipulative woman's smile. "Who do you love, dear?"

"You and only you, Mistress. I love you so much. I want you, I need you!" The girl had an opening and she was running with it.

The Mistress raised her hand. "Enough. Leave us."

The young woman stood and left without another word.

I didn't know what to make of it all. Either these people were all insane with lust or there really was some weird magical spell cast on them. Maybe both. Whatever it was, I needed to focus.

"Ok, then. Who are you?" I asked again.

And again, she ignored my question. "So you work for Mr. Cross. I'm surprised you'd plunge into something so wholeheartedly when you have no idea who or what sort of man he is." She raised her eyebrows. "I don't take you for a fool but that's what you're acting like."

I squinted. "What are you talking about?"

It was another useless question. She pretended to not hear a word I said. "How do you know about the Olorus Orb? Why do you want it?"

There was that effing orb thing again. "I don't know what the hell you're talking about. What is it?"

"Does Cross know about it then?" She sprung off the table and stood up straight. "Did he send you?"

I bellowed. "Send me to do what?"

The woman moved in extremely close to me and our noses almost touched. I could smell her even better now and, whatever god there was help me, she smelled delicious.

She spoke quietly, barely above a whisper. "Come now. I know you were looking for the Soulphire. That means you want the orb or control of it. Does Cross have his own device?"

I leaned forward and almost head butted the woman, hell, I considered busting that pretty face open. I was starting to really get pissed off. "What the eff is the orb?"

She moved her head back and away from me, turning to look at one of her minions. That's all they were. Somehow they'd been completely bewitched by this woman. "Call Kara, ask her what she's found out."

A jolt ran through me. Kara Childers? The missing agent. "Is she still alive? What have you done with her?" The woman finally acknowledged my question and I had a bad feeling I wasn't going to like the answer.

"I showed her the truth, Agent Sworn." She resumed her seat on the table and clasped her hands over her right knee.

I tried to fight it, but the confidence she let out and her attractiveness kept washing over me in waves. God damn, I wanted her bad. I pulled myself back together. "What do you mean? I'm really sick of all this cryptic talk. Just spit it out."

The woman blinked a couple times. She was studying me and I had the faintest feeling she was reading my thoughts. "You're hiding information from me because you want to protect a man you think is noble and fair." She nodded. "Kara was the same but you seem a bit more stubborn. You're being difficult."

I scoffed. "Get used to it."

"I like when guys play hard to get. All the more *fun* to break." The smirk she gave me made her the sexiest little devil in the world. I couldn't help but let out a little laugh. I knew this woman was dangerous but damn, I had to respect how cool she was. What a piece of work.

I snorted and tried to get my tough façade back. "Ok, let's play some more. What's this truth you're talking about?"

Without taking her eyes off me she called out to the others in the cellar. "Leave us." A series of protests filled the air and my eyes widened. The other men were afraid I'd attack her and I should've had the same idea. Instead, I wasn't proud to admit, all I thought was that we'd have the opportunity to really get to know each other, every inch of each other. I even went so far as to hope I'd be able to perform satisfactorily; it'd been a long time.

"I said GO!" Her voice was a commanding shout now and the men reluctantly obeyed. When they were gone she looked at me with an innocent, pleading look. "I trust you won't try to hurt me, Jason. All I want to do is show you the truth about August Cross."

Now, with the more intimate atmosphere, I let my guard down a little and nodded. "Ok. Then will you let me go?"

"Well," the woman slid off the table, moved behind me and began rubbing my shoulders. My muscles melted under her fingers. "I hope you won't want to leave after you see this."

She removed a hand from my right shoulder and I heard something click before the computer monitor came to life. "These files weren't easy to get. I'll offer some narration to fill in the gaps. Pay attention."

I watched the screen. What I saw enraged me. The sounds and images went on for more than an hour showing Cross conspiring with the founders and leaders of Tehlasrin. Cross helped dictate some of the totalitarian mandates, he cut deals to further his own power and he even worked to help put dictators in positions of power. The man had a hand in every crooked deal and helped make the GU the hell it was today.

I was stunned. Every time I asked the woman a question she told me to keep watching. The last part almost made me puke. It showed the Governor spending time with Morbal going over new potential inmates. They laughed while reading over various personnel bios. Morbal's sick, rat face smiled demonically as he marveled over the new torture subjects.

I thought of all the pain the inmates suffered there, are still suffering today. Cross helped put them there. He knew what Morbal was doing, he had to know, and he still went ahead and contributed to it.

Rage poured over me like a tidal wave. A small part of me tried to defend Cross, tried to rationalize what I was seeing. I had known Cross visited Morbal. The man was responsible for blowing David, me and countless others out of there. But the way he worked with other leaders, the GU system and Morbal showed August Cross was far beyond untrustworthy.

He used everyone for his own gain. My jaw was clenched so tightly I thought my teeth were going to shatter.

The video finally ended. "Why?" I hissed.

The woman slithered around me, running her hand over my neck, shoulder and arm. "August Cross only cares about one thing; Power. He worked with Morbal and then used him for his own gains, freeing several victims so they'd serve him here. It's all win-win for him." She squatted down in front of me with her hands on my thighs and I gasped. She smiled. "So devious but so clever. He's a genius and a monster."

I stirred. It was so hard to think clearly. My head ached, my insides were twisted from what I'd seen and my heart raced from having the most perfect woman in the world kneeling in front of me with her hands on my lap.

I exhaled sharply. "I, I don't know what to think." It was the truth. I felt clueless and vulnerable. I tried to put the pieces together. I remembered the Golden Cup telling me what a great man Cross was. I remembered Krane telling me how hard the Governor worked. I remembered Fier telling me how much Cross sacrificed for us all and how Aswain was the best place on Earth.

Fier. I tried to remember all the weird stuff she'd told me, all the things I'd seen. This whole place was different and the people here were too. She said only people that were 'special' were allowed in. What did it all mean?

Then I remembered the feelings I had before I met Cross. How blatantly obvious it was that Aswain was nothing more than a fancy dictatorship. I remembered how much power Cross really had. His desire for power matched the videos the woman showed me.

"Oh, Jason." Her pleading voice captured my attention. "You're so conflicted. I know. I know what you want. I know your dreams and I want to share them with you."

She crept up a little closer, pulling herself up my lap. Her chest rubbed against my knees, which were now trembling.

"Oh yes," she breathed. "You want to help others, you want justice but you also want peace."

Her eyes stared into mine and my head gave a little shake. I couldn't believe what I was hearing. She really knew me, she understood me.

"Shh," She brushed her lips against mine. "Let me help you. I know how hard it is to have conflicting dreams. You want both peace and action." The woman slipped her tongue out and ran it, ever so slightly, across my top lip. "I can show you the way."

When I spoke it was a whisper. "How? How do you know all this?"

She didn't answer, instead she said, "You're a unique man, Jason. So strong and noble. You resisted me. You intrigue me." When she spoke next her lips were brushing against mine. "Thank god, I can't believe I may have found my equal. Please. Let me show you the way. Trust me."

"I," I tried to speak but her lips were fully on mine now and we kissed, long and deep. My cares slipped away and with it went my pain, sorrow and obligation. This woman was incredible. She was the key to happiness, I knew it. If she said Cross was a bad man, it must be true. I knew any revolution against him would change everything about Aswain but it had to be for the best. The Governor was blatantly corrupt.

I moved into the woman and kissed her even deeper. My hands ran up and down her back from her neck to her ass. I squeezed and she moaned.

Oddly enough, amidst all this passion, I remembered David, my best and only true friend. I thought of how happy he'd been since we arrived on Aswain. Give or take everything else, my friend's happiness outweighed it all. How could I take that away from him?

My brain detached itself from my body which was a dense forest of tingles and exploding endorphins. I knew I had to decide, right then and there on Aswain's fate. Was it really that bad? I hadn't seen any real injustice and it seemed to be a good place, a great place. Hell, it was a heavenly place. I couldn't turn my back on it. I couldn't turn my back on David. Not yet, not until I had more information.

I inhaled sharply, pulled myself back and opened my eyes. I didn't know if what I saw was real or if I imagined it but for an instant, I saw a shadowy figure of a man hovering behind the woman. The image sent a shiver down my spine.

"Jason?" Surprise filled her voice.

I pushed her away and she fell flat on the floor in a sitting position. I shook my head and swallowed. "I'm sorry. I just don't know. This doesn't feel right."

The woman had a scorned look on her face. "Doesn't feel right?" Her eyes ran up and down my body, twice over my waistline area. "You're body begs to differ. Why reject me?"

I was still buzzing from the encounter I'd abruptly ended and put my hands up, palms out. "I'm not rejecting you. I just need time to think."

I sounded like an idiot and realized I'd just thrown away a shot at true happiness. My stupid, suspicious, pessimistic brain had ruined it for me again. It seemed impossible for me to ever be happy. I cursed.

"Time to think?" The woman was standing and stamped her feet. "I'll give you time to think. COME!" She yelled and all the men from before, plus a few more, filed down the steps. They circled themselves around me.

A wicked smile sprung up on the woman's face. "I gave you your chance to join me freely but you threw it away. Now you're going to learn the hard way."

I squinted. "So it was all a lie then. You're no different. You're just as power hungry as Cross." I shook my head. "I bet you're just as bad as Morbal. Bitch."

She spat on me. It smacked against my cheek but didn't faze me in the slightest, it only validated my suspicion. She was like Morbal, just as cold, just as calculating. Granted, her methods were much more pleasurable than the rat-faced bastard but her aims were the same. They both wanted to twist, corrupt and control others. She was just like the others who craved power and cared only about themselves. I nodded satisfactorily, knowing I'd beaten her.

"You only think you've beaten me!" She shot back.

Ok, now I knew she was reading my thoughts. There was no way around it. I swore under my breath. How do you fight something like that? How can I stop thinking?

She slapped me across my face. It was much harder than I expected and I realized the woman was stronger than she looked. I shouldn't have been surprised.

Now the sweet smile was back. "Oh Jason. I'm sorry it has to be this way but I'm not giving up on you yet."

I shook my head. The woman's sudden shift in moods made her come off as a schizophrenic. I rubbed my stinging cheek. "Thanks for caring."

"You say you have no idea what the Olorus Orb is?" She giggled. "Well you'll know soon enough." Her eyes left me and planted onto one of the men behind me. "Lock him up. I'll be back with the inventor."

"Yes, Mistress." A male voice responded, obediently.

The woman looked back at me again. She leaned forward and brought her face down right in front of mine. "Don't go anywhere, Jason." She planted her lips on mine again and moaned.

Damn myself, I enjoyed it.

# Chapter 12

I knew I was dreaming but didn't really care. My lucidity didn't keep me from enjoying the peaceful, comfortable ride my brain was on. I was happily floating down a smooth river of warm mud. Everything was perfect and I felt completely relaxed without a concern in the world. Nothing bothered me, not even the fact that I couldn't move my arms or legs. My head was quiet and unstrained and that was all that mattered. It felt great. Every moment was delightful. The bliss lasted a while until a shower of freezing ice crystals splashed down on my face.

The cold sting jolted me awake. I opened my heavy eyes to see a dirty faced, angry woman standing over me with a bucket in her hand. I stared at her sensing something familiar about her. It took a moment for the name *Kara Childers* to come to mind.

I'd only seen one picture of her but the person in front of me hardly resembled the image. She looked awful. Her eyes had big dark circles around them and seemed to sink into her skull. Her short brown hair was a ratty mess and her clothes, blue jeans and grey t-shirt, were filthy.

"WAKE UP!" She screeched in a shrill, tormented voice that was filled with pain, anger and desperation.

The shriek rattled my brain. I winced after a short delay. There was something seriously wrong with me. My head swayed and I had to fight to keep my eyes open. The air around Kara swirled in and out of focus and I felt like I was going to fall over. I probably would have if my hands and legs weren't tied down to the chair I sat in.

I felt pain in my right arm and slowly rolled my head to look at it. There were fresh needle marks and I finally figured out I'd been drugged. There were also dozens of small ice chips on my arms and lap melting into small, cold puddles. I looked back up at the sorry face in front of me.

Recent events came back to me again. "Kara?" My own voice sounded strange in my head. "Is that you?"

She made a hideous face, showing several of her dirty teeth and snarled. "YOU!" She screamed. "Did you have sex with her? With *my* Mistress?"

I could have. I don't know if I said it or thought it but I guessed the former since a flash later the agent had the barrel of her gun pointed at my face. Drugged or not, now I was alarmed. I shook my head and the world shook with it.

"You don't deserve her! You're not good enough! I'm hers, not you!" Her finger squeezing a little harder on the trigger.

I swallowed. "Wait! No! No, we didn't have sex. Put the gun down."

Surprisingly, she obeyed and I could breathe again. My nerves relaxed and the drug nearly put me back to sleep. Kara slapped me back to full wakefulness.

After the sting passed, I felt warmth on my face and turned my head. Sunlight was hitting me from a small window. I wasn't in the cellar anymore.

"Where am I?" It was mostly a mumble.

Kara paced and chewed on her fingernails. "You're safe."

I perked up. "Safe? You got me out? Why am I still tied down?" My brain fought to think clearly. It seemed the harder I tried, the less things made sense.

"Because my Mistress wishes it so."

I groaned. "I thought I was safe."

"YOU ARE!" She screamed again. "We tied you down to keep you from causing any more trouble. We can't have you hurting anymore of the Mistress's pets."

Damn it. Now I remembered. I'd gotten into another fight after the green eyed woman left me alone with her guards. This was my punishment; drugged and bound. I wasn't safe at all. I'd seen enough crazy people in my time to know Kara had gone way over the edge.

"What happened to you? Chief and the others are looking for you."

She spat. "Ha! Those fools. I don't want to be found. I have my Mistress. I, I…"

She suddenly panicked and shoved her hands in her pockets, searching for something. She pulled out what looked like a stocking. An ease washed over her while she rubbed it against her cheek. "My Mistress."

Oh Christ. The 'Mistress' had weaved her spell, or whatever it was on the poor agent. She wanted to do the same to me. Hell, she almost did. I started to sweat.

The drug's fog started to lift. I spoke softly. "How did she get you?"

Kara jerked her head around and looked at me with manic eyes. "She didn't get me. She freed me. She picked me. She loves me. We're going to spend our lives together. We're going to save the world. We're going to kill Cross and his servants. She loves me so much and I love her!" She spoke to fast for my cloudy brain to keep up before abruptly bursting into tears.

Whatever world Kara's brain was trapped in was a hell I wanted no part of. I struggled with the bounds on my wrists. No use, they were tied up nice and tight.

Kara caught the move. "Enough! You can't get away. Just shut up and wait. My Mistress will be here soon and she'll take care of you. She's going to use you. We're going to use you."

I shook my head and let out a sarcastic chuckle. The woman wanted to use me? That sounded familiar. Morbal wanted to use me too. So does Cross for that matter. It didn't make sense. I wasn't anything special. Why was everyone so interested in me?

"God damn it! HURRY!" Kara threw a tantrum, flinging her arms, kicking her legs around and swearing up a storm.

I grimaced. "What?"

She stopped in a crouched position and turned to me, looking furious, like she wanted to rip my throat out. "Not you, idiot! The team. We're moving you to a better place."

"Better? Where?"

She roared. "Ask me one more god damned question and I'll put a bullet in your head, I swear to God!"

Something told me she meant it so I shut up. Besides, I guessed I'd learn more from her by just watching and listening. David would be so proud.

The tormented agent paced back and forth again speaking nonsense so I let my thoughts wander. It was David, or at least my memory of him that kept me from falling under the green eyed woman's spell. It was also my friendship with him that kept me sane in the asylum. Damn. If I got out of here, I owed the man a drink, a lot of drinks.

Kara continued to rant. "Come on! Move this bastard now! I want you! My Mistress!"

The door opened and a few men came inside.

"WHAT?" The crazed agent yelled.

The nearest man surveyed the room. "Everything ok?"

"You son of a bitch! Of course it is!" Kara whipped her gun out again and pointed it at the man. The color drained from his face. "Where is the moving team?"

"The, they're on their way." He put his hands up, backed up and bumped into the men frozen with fear behind him.

She lowered the weapon and collapsed in on herself. I took the moment to damn myself. This was my fault. I marched right into this mess and totally blew my first assignment. Way to go, dumbass.

"He's too alert." One of the other men said, gesturing me. "It's time for another dose." He moved over to a set of cabinets in the corner of the room and pulled out a small bottle of clear liquid and a syringe.

I tensed up while watching him, helplessly. The man headed over to me with the loaded needle when gunfire erupted from somewhere outside the door. Screams followed and my heart skipped a beat.

Kara sprung back to life. "Watch him!" She flew through the door, almost ramming into the wall.

The man nearest me dropped the syringe and pulled out his pistol. The others did the same. They swore at each other.

"What do we do?" One man asked.

The third man moved behind me. "We watch this guy and kill him if things get out of hand." He planted the barrel of the gun against the back of my head. "Shut the door!"

The gunfire grew louder and more frequent. I could hear the distinct sound of ether weapons discharging. They'd found me, somehow. Still dazed, my head swam with a blend of fear and excitement.

The door opened and another guard burst in. He was nearly shot down by his three companions. "Sweet Mistress, they're close!" His face was filled with terror. I snickered. "What are we going to do?"

The voice from behind me was cool and collected. "You know what we have to do, you stupid prick. We're going to fight and die in the Mistress's name."

The four men took up position around me, each pointing their weapons at the door. Moments passed that were filled with encroaching sounds of chaos. "Let's kill him now!" An especially frightened man whimpered. "He's the one they want. Let's kill him and go!"

"Shut up!" Ordered the calm voice. "She wants him alive."

Silence. I could almost hear my heart thumping. I licked my lips and waited for what felt like an eternity. I heard a light tap on the outside of the door and everyone in the room flinched. "What the eff was that?" The man who had gotten the needle asked.

His answer came soon enough when an explosion blew the door off its hinges. The thundering boom killed my ears. Parts of the door flew at me and just barely missed my head. Luckily, a big chunk hit the man to my right and knocked him to the floor.

In the next instant the room was filled with gunfire and ether blasts. Men around me dropped one after another. To my surprise, it was David who rushed into the room, alone with the most serious look I'd ever seen on his face.

He smiled when he saw me. It didn't last though. Mr. Calm was still alive and had ducked down behind me. His gun was pressed against my head. "You stupid -"

David leapt to his left and fired. The energy whizzed by my right ear and I could feel the heat singe my hair. Then I heard a thud and smelled burnt flesh. I didn't have to see, I knew Mr. Calm wasn't with us anymore.

"David!" I hollered. "Holy -"

"Shut up." He bolted over to me and took a knife to my restraints. "We're getting out of here." He cut through the ties on my ankles and left wrist when he looked at my face. "Jesus, what did they do to you?"

"What?" I wondered if I'd been beaten up some more.

David shook his head and took care of the last tie on my right hand. "You look stoned. Did they drug you?"

I nodded and was about to answer but something else caught my attention. I yelled. "LOOK OUT!"

More bad guys charged into the room. David didn't hesitate. He was on his feet and spinning in a flurry of rage at the attackers. I don't know when he pulled it out but his nightstick was his left hand and he was working it like a pro. The stick landed against an enemy skull, then thudded another.

The guards were helplessly caught by surprise. David moved so fast they couldn't even get a shot off. Another one dropped. Two left.

My friend dropped to the ground, aimed his weapon upward and fired. The discharge made a hole in his target's chest. Before the last one could react, David swung his legs around and took the man down at the knees. Without the slightest pause, he rolled up the man's body, aimed his weapon at the guy's face and blasted him.

I watched it all, high as a kite, marveling at David's skills. He was the best man I'd ever known and now he was the greatest warrior too.

I was free a couple seconds later. "Can you walk?" David asked, between gasps.

I exhaled sharply. "Of course I can." I leapt out of the chair and the room flipped over. I crashed to the floor then groaned. "Maybe not."

David swore something fierce before he scooped me up. Gunfire continued outside. "Work with me damn it, come on!"

I ordered my legs to function and it took every bit of focus I had to just lean on David enough to hobble along. His left arm was around me as we darted through the doorway.

I took in my surroundings. The place was a mess. Debris littered the floors, furniture was overturned and there were several small fires burning which created a smelly, smoky atmosphere.

It was hard to think, but the place looked like a police station. There were hallways, rooms, desks and cells. The only light came from sunlight that seeped through several windows.

Despite my handicap, we moved at a good clip and David seemed to know where he was going. An angry female face popped around a corner. She moved to aim her gun at us but didn't make it. David shot her and she dropped. I felt his grip slipping. "Damn it, Jason! Help me out."

I wrapped my right arm around him and slung myself up, trying to plant my feet back on the ground. "Give me a gun." I barked.

"You can't even walk, what makes you think you can aim?"

He was right, but I still wanted a weapon. At least I could pretend to feel useful. We moved on and I could see more light up ahead. "We're almost out."

When we were finally outside the bright sunlight burned my eyes. The scene was filled with bullets, energy blasts and bodies scattered about. I saw a couple of the Mistress's men take aim at David and me. I pulled my friend down to the ground a split second before bullets ripped through the empty air we'd just occupied.

I was pulled over to a small brick wall that looped around the building. A couple enemies came into view and David fired. One dropped and the other ran off.

"Stay down." He ordered before glancing over the wall.

"Over here!" He hollered. Not at me but out away from our covered spot. "I've got him. Come on!"

Several Aswain guards rushed toward us.

A vicious, almost inhuman roar tore through the air. I turned my head to see it was Kara and she was rushing the team of Cross's soldiers. She fired her weapon as she ran and hit a few soldiers.

The others scattered and David fired at her, missed then shot again. She was too quick.

The drugs in my body kept me planted against the wall and all I could do was watch her move. It was both amazing and horrifying at the same time.

I didn't trust my eyes but she seemed to move in and out of existence, popping up in front of the nearest guard and killing him or her. I slid up further against the wall, wishing I could bury myself into the bricks. I normally wasn't afraid in the heat of battle but I was so drugged and defenseless. I could barely see straight and my muscles felt like jelly. It was like being stuck in a nightmare where a monster was chasing you and your feet were stuck to the ground.

Kara kept zipping from guard to guard, shooting or stabbing them with an especially lethal looking knife.

David lunged at the woman. He wrapped his arms around her and pulled her to the ground.

My brain spaced out and numbly took in the soft, green grass, the calm, blue sky and bright, shining sun while the two tried to murder each other. I eventually snapped out of it and decided I was done being helpless. I pushed myself off the wall and crawled toward the wrestling pair. I wasn't sure what I was going to do but as luck would have it, I came across David's weapon. I picked it up and aimed.

"David, move!" I shouted.

Kara saw me and barred her teeth. David shoved her and rolled away, giving me the opening I needed. She charged me. Aiming was hell but I fired anyways. The energy brushed against the side of her head, knocking her to the ground. She stopped moving.

"David, you ok?" I asked between heavy breaths.

He sat up, his own chest heaving, and gave me a 'thumbs-up'. "I'm fine." He reached out. "Give me the gun."

I tossed it to him without thinking. My friend caught it, stood up and stumbled over to Kara's body. He aimed the weapon at her face.

"Stop!" A familiar Scottish accented voice called out. "We need her for questioning."

I looked at Chief. Amidst all the carnage he looked exactly the same as always; angry. He marched up and put a hand on David's shoulder. "At ease, lad. All the others have been killed or killed themselves rather than be captured." He nodded at Kara. "She's one of our own. We need her to talk."

He looked at me and scowled in disgust before calling to some nearby guards. "Lock her up."

I was alive and safe. Now, looking at Chief I knew I was in trouble.

-

"I've heard enough! Keep your mouth SHUT!"

I looked up at Chief's angry, red face and grimaced. "I'm right here. Do you have to yell? My head's killing me."

He grunted. "You little bastard! You have no respect for authority. Well don't worry. You won't have to anymore. Not from me at least." There was a malicious spark in his eye.

I swallowed, picking up on Chief's meaning.

"That's right. You're through. Done. I don't want you on my team anymore." He took a seat across from me and folded his arms, both beaming and furious at the same time.

I rubbed the sides of my head. The constant throbbing almost made me throw up. At least the room wasn't brightly lit. The dimness helped keep my eyes from hurting a little.

We were in a good size office with expensive looking, comfortable furniture. Chief and I sat next to each other in chairs that were planted in front of a large wooden desk. There was a large window behind the desk and I could see it was sunset. The soft golden light filtered in through the mostly closed blinds.

The room also smelled nice, a sweet combination of the Leather from the chairs, the wood of the table and a light hint of incense. If I weren't in such deep trouble, I would've been enjoying the atmosphere.

Instead, my face was flushed, my heart raced, my knees shook and my head felt like it was going to either explode or implode. I wasn't sure where exactly we were or what we were doing here. There were lots of other areas where Chief could scream and yell at me. So, I was done. Ok. I just wanted him to spit everything out and be done with it. I'd had a hellish day and just wanted to sleep.

David had helped load me into an ambulance back at the battle scene after things settled down. The medics ran an IV through me with chemicals that were meant to nullify the drugs in my system.

They said I'd be all better soon but they couldn't help the disaster my head was in.

I slept a few hours at the hospital and woke up still plagued by this monster headache. Shortly after eating, David picked me up in a patrol car and brought me to headquarters. He walked me to this office and as far as I knew, was still waiting outside.

My friend wasn't at all happy with my recent decisions. He laid into me pretty good during our short drive, calling me names worse and more colorful than stupid, irresponsible and foolish. I didn't even try to argue. He was right, I was dumb.

Now I had to pay for it.

I sunk further into the plush leather chair. David never even bothered to ask why I'd gone to Club Aces. I guess he didn't have to, it didn't really matter. Maybe he knew already. Damn, I screwed up, big time.

I cut my eyes around to meet Chief's. "What are we waiting for?"

His response was only a prolonged exhale through his flared nostrils.

Since there was nothing better to do, I continued rubbing my head. This was the worst ache I'd ever had and that's saying something. Christ. I wanted to rip my eyes out.

Finally, the door behind me opened up and August Cross entered the office. Great, now I had to endure him yelling down at me.

He moved around the desk and sat down in the large chair there. I guessed this was his office. He probably had lots of offices. Hell, the whole island was his.

A rush of memories flooded through my aching head. The videos of Cross I'd seen came to the forefront of my thoughts. As nervous and ashamed as I was, I still felt enough anger and disappointment to wonder what kind of a person the Governor was. How could he work with those awful people? He actually played a part in creating the Union.

I looked at the man. He seemed perfectly calm, almost happy. August Cross: The beneficiary from the torment of billions of people around the world. I wanted to slap his arrogant face.

"How are you feeling?" He asked.

"Like hell."

Cross nodded. "I see that. The doctors didn't help?"

"Not much." I said sharply.

"Watch your tone, boy." Chief bellowed.

I whipped my head over to face the big man. "Or WHAT? You're going to threaten me again?" I snorted. "Seems you're all talk. Do something or shut the EFF up!"

"Calm! Everyone keep your eyes on me." Cross called out, raising his hands in the air, palms out. He glanced back and forth between Chief and me. "What's bothering you? Where's the pain?"

I thought about that. Pain was everywhere, every part of me hurt but I kept my answer short. "My head aches."

"What were you doing at that club?" Cross asked coolly.

Here we go. I sighed. "Being an idiot."

"I won't argue with that, but I'd like specifics, Jason."

I decided to be direct and honest. The sooner I could get this over with the better. "I was looking for a crystal called the Soulphire for an old man named Pat Crow. He said he'd pay me a good sum of money if I got it for him."

"I see." Cross frowned. "How much money?"

"Fifty thousand Gems."

The Governor slumped his shoulders, disappointed. "You risked your life, freedom and career for that?"

"Hey!" I started. "It may be chump change to you but it's a lot to me."

"Do you have any idea what this Soulphire is or what it does?" The man was unfazed by my aggressive tone.

I shook my head. "I don't know. The people at the club kept talking about some orb thing. They must be connected somehow."

Chief grunted. He and Cross exchanged glances. "The orb." Cross said quietly. "And what led you to the club? What made you think the jewel was there?"

I grimaced. "Crow gave me some leads, information on two guys, Wright and Ryan. I found out they'd been hanging out there a lot."

"I see." Cross's face was unreadable and his cool stare made me even more uncomfortable than the situation already called for.

I swallowed. "Were they at the battle scene?"

"Yes." He said with a slow nod. "They're dead now."

I sighed. Damn. I was responsible for that. Well, partly. They were the ones in league with the sexy green eyed psycho.

"I can't believe how completely inept you turned out be." Chief spat out. "No private investigations. You knew that! Because of you, seven soldiers, good men and women, are dead!"

"Chief, calm yourself." Cross spoke with warning.

The big man didn't take it. "We should've left you there! You should've been the one who died for your stupidity! Who the hell do you think you are?"

I looked at the man and could see the genuineness on his face. He was right and the guilt was starting to crush me. "I'm sorry. I thought it would be a simple task. But you're right. I was stupid. Christ, I'm sorry."

"What's done is done." Cross spoke in what came off as a callous tone. He didn't care. Chief was an ass but at least he felt compassion. Now I wanted to throttle the Governor.

I curled my lip. "I'm not surprised you don't care, Cross. How are you going to spin this to your advantage?"

Cross raised his eyebrows.

Chief bolted out of his seat and balled his hands into fists. "You ungrateful little twit! GET UP! I'm going to -"

"SIT DOWN!" Cross demanded, slamming his fists on the desk with force that shocked me. The whole damn thing bounced. It was the first time I'd seen the man angry. The Scot obeyed, grumbling.

The smaller man looked back at me. He looked a whole hell of a lot older right then. "You have something to say to me? What did you learn in your captivity? Tell me."

I blew out a heavy breath. "There was a woman there, they all called her their Mistress. She showed me some interesting things about you." I looked at Chief. "You may want to know too, know who you're working for."

Cross slowly shook his head. "So, a woman holds you captive and you believe everything she tells you? Jason, I thought you were smarter than that. I'm disappointed."

"I saw it. I saw what you've done. I saw the work you did to help create Tehlasrin, its crap laws and practices." I was livid now. "I never fully trusted you, but I wanted to believe in you, god damn it."

Cross rubbed his chin. "I don't know what she showed you but I can guess. I'm sorry you had to see all that. There are aspects of my past I can't expect you to understand."

"I understand perfectly." I hissed.

"No, you don't." The anger was gone but the seriousness was as thick as ever. "Jason, I did what I had to do. I *hate* Tehlasrin. I want it abolished and I'm working toward that aim every day." Suddenly, he looked sad. "Things were set in motion that couldn't be stopped, only altered. I did that. I won't bore you with all the details but trust me when I say the world would have been much worse had I, and others with me, not taken action."

He could tell I wasn't buying it.

"Without doing what we did, without the negotiations, the deals and the bribes, there would be no Aswain and the GU would be so much more hellish."

I let out a little laugh. "No Aswain? Oh, I'd hate for you to not have your own private little kingdom. That'd be awful."

Chief gritted his teeth. He spoke to Cross but kept his eyes locked on me. "Sir, he's hopeless. Let's be done with it. Let me have at him. I'll bash some manners through that thick skull of his."

Cross ignored Chief. The action alone seemed to deflate the big man. "Jason, I want the whole world to be like Aswain. I know it's hard but you have to trust me."

I looked down at the ground and shook my head. I couldn't trust him.

"You're just beginning to wake up." That drew my gaze back. Cross had a pleading look on his face. "The world isn't what you think it is. You know that, deep down. Hasn't anyone told you about the people here yet? Haven't you seen and felt more since the last time we met?"

Damn it, I felt myself softening up. I felt weak. "I don't know about all that. Everyone could just be crazy."

Cross surprised me with a laugh. "You know better."

"Ok, what is it then? Tell me?" Curiosity had a good hold on me, even momentarily blocking the headache out.

Cross was silent for a moment, seeming to gather his thoughts. "You have to experience it yourself. I could tell you things but it would be like teaching algebra to a toddler. You wouldn't grasp it. You'd think I was insane. I'm sorry. Again, you have to trust me."

"Why does he have to trust you, Governor? He's done. Out. Hell, lets lock him up now, or throw him off the island." He was almost growling now. "We don't need his taint here, messing up all the good you've done."

Again, Cross seemed to not hear his security head. "But you're right about one thing, Jason. I am going to use your experience and the events that followed to my advantage. To not do so would be an injustice to those who died."

I was lost and felt like an ignorant kid. "What are you talking about now? How?"

"Tell me about this… Mistress."

I described her and relayed everything I'd felt and gathered from her. The Governor nodded.

"Hmm, her name is Samantha Forrest." He paused, it seemed like his mind wandered a bit. The look on his face was filled with sorrow. "At one time, I thought she would be a great partner, a good friend and an important ally. I was wrong."

I interrupted his thoughts and locked my eyes onto his. "What's your relation to Morbal? I know you busted us out of the asylum but you two seemed like such buddies in those videos, laughing, planning..."

Cross shook his head. "Again, you don't have all the information. I despise the man, everything he is and stands for. I had to do something." His tone grew livelier. "Do you think it was easy or enjoyable? I had to learn everything I could about him and his damned prison. Maledro Morbal is one of the more prominent GU leaders in North America. I needed to earn his trust. It was the only way to successfully free you and the others."

I chewed on that for a moment. It sounded reasonable.

"It was one of the most difficult covert operations I've ran but it had to be done." He snorted. "Morbal is one of the worst men I know. I don't have to tell you that."

"So what's with this woman?" I asked.

Cross closed his eyes. "She may be one of the worst *women* I've ever known. And now, thanks to your blind actions I know she's on our island. In our sanctuary." He opened his eyes again.

The word sanctuary rang in my head. I'll be damned, it was the perfect way to describe Aswain. I started to feel foolish again.

"Try not to beat yourself up, Jason. No one's perfect, we all make mistakes." He spoke next in a near whisper. "So many have died, it's nearly too much to bear."

"Sir!" Chief was annoyed as hell. He desperately wanted Cross's attention.

The Governor looked at him. "Yes?"

"You're going to let him off, aren't you?" He shook his head. "I can't believe this."

"Chief, I respect you and trust you with my life, you know this." Cross began. "But I asked you join us to help you understand. I wanted you to learn something. I want you to trust Jason as I do."

I couldn't believe what I was hearing. "You're not going to fire me, jail me or banish me?" My eyes darted between the two men.

"No, Jason." Cross said softly. Now Chief was the one slamming his fist on the table. "But I need you to trust me. I know it's hard, especially for you. I'm not giving up on you. I need your help, now, more than ever."

I wasn't completely sold but I nodded. "Ok." I sucked up my pride. "What do you really want from me?"

Cross laughed again. "First I want you to respect Chief. He's your commanding officer and I hold him in high esteem."

I looked at the man and he looked like he wanted to bite my head off. I gulped then nodded.

"Second, I want you to end this side job investigation of yours." Cross raised an eyebrow. "This Soulphire is much more important than fifty thousand Gems. I have a feeling we're going to need it to stop Forrest's plans."

"Right, you got it." He didn't have to tell me to drop the investigation for Crow. I'd learned my lesson. The next time I saw the guy I might just bust his old face open.

"And third, I need you to keep me informed on anything you see or hear about Forrest and her team. She's extremely dangerous and seems to have an interest in you... like Kara." He paused and a shiver ran up my spine. "She may try to contact you again. Be careful."

"Ok."

"Now, you say your head is hurting you even though your medical evaluation says your body should be clean." Cross nodded and reached over to press a button on his desk.

"Yes, August?" A voice said.

Cross cleared his throat. "Please ask Chloe to come in."

"Will do."

A couple seconds later a very tiny and happy looking woman entered the office. She had short brown hair, wide blue eyes and a huge smile on her face. I guessed she was in her late twenties. She wore lavender medical scrubs and stopped after a few steps into the room. "Hi, August. Who do you need me to look -" She paused when she saw me. "I see. Hello!"

I failed at an attempt to smile. "Hi."

She giggled. "Don't mind me, keep talking and try to relax." She came off as a zealous cheerleader.

The merry woman bounced over behind me and started rubbing my head. I turned around to look at her and she forcefully manhandled my head forward. "Look ahead, please." She spoke in a very high, almost squeaky voice.

I reluctantly obeyed and then I felt such a soothing wave flow through my head my eyes almost rolled backward.

Cross laughed and clapped his hands. "She's good, huh?"

"Uh-huh." I purred.

I heard Chief shift in his seat. "No point in talking anymore, look at him!"

"Oh I'm sorry!" Squeaky voice, Chloe said. "I'm almost through the first phase, he'll be back with you in three, two, one... there!"

I snapped back to attention. She was still rubbing my head but the initial rush of pleasure passed. Now it was just sort of embarrassing sitting in front of my superiors, talking policy with a strange woman rubbing my head.

"I think we're almost done here, anyways." Cross said.

"What happened to Kara?" I asked. "Is she dead?"

Cross shook his head. "No. We're working with her. Thankfully, we're making progress but taking things slow. Her mind is a mess."

"It's good your friend didn't kill her." Chief grumbled.

I shot my gaze at him. "It's a good thing she didn't kill David."

"Of course it is." Cross said.

Chief made a 'pft' sound with his lips. "That man, David is almost as foolhardy as you, Sworn. He charged inside that compound as though he were invincible as soon as he found out you were there."

A light went off in my head. Another question that needed answering. "How exactly did you find me?"

"You can answer that, Chief." Cross had his serious face back on again.

The large man shifted in his seat. "I had you followed."

"WHAT?" I was shocked and insulted at the same time.

Chloe coughed. "Calm please. Working here."

Chief nodded, a proud look on his face. "Yes. The whole night. I admit it, boy-o, I didn't trust you. I didn't want you to screw up your first assignment, so I had you followed, watched and monitored."

I heard the woman behind me scoff. "That's not nice at all, Chief!"

He looked at her. "It saved his life."

"Who followed me?" I didn't know if I should be more curious or angry. There was plenty of room for both.

Chief brought a small radio up to his mouth. "Come in."

A moment later I saw a large, familiar man glide in through the door. It took a second but I remembered him, mostly by the sunglasses he wore. It was the mysterious guy who got that reporter off my back several nights before.

"You?" I felt my eyes bug out.

The man nodded. His face showed no expression.

"This is Poet Kyle. One of my personal team members." Chief's voice was filled with pride.

I squinted. "Poet?"

"That's what he calls everyone on his small, special team." Cross said with a smile. "They're good."

If stares could kill, Chief would've dropped dead right there. "You knew the whole time where I was? It took you that long to get me?"

"Yes." Chief said flatly. "You effed up and I used you like a guinea pig. Don't like it? Too bad, it's done."

Cross groaned. "No. Actually, we were extra cautious getting into position. We wanted to minimize the damages."

"See." Chief said, smugly. "We *think* before we act."

I was livid and my head started hurting again.

"Lots of pain in here." Chloe said in a warning tone. "It comes from your anger. You'd better lighten your mood or this will never get better."

I looked back to give the happy woman a nasty stare.

Her pretty little face lit up with smile as she smacked me on the top of my head.

# Chapter 13

I didn't believe in luck, especially good luck. So I couldn't say the events that followed my capture were lucky but they were certainly welcome. I wasn't kicked off the island, I wasn't locked up, hell, I wasn't even fired. To top everything off, the next day was Sunday.

My head was still a bit of a painful war zone from the blows I'd received and I was fighting with my guilt over the people who'd died saving my ass. It was a good thing I didn't have to be productive. I could hardly think much less complete any tasks.

The Aswain intelligence team was on overdrive looking for the green eyed woman but Cross, having seen the condition I was in, gave me the entire weekend off.

I spent all day Saturday and most of Sunday lounging around and sleeping when my head allowed it. It wasn't easy. A damn voice in my head wouldn't stop reminding me how stupid and irresponsible I was. It was hard shutting the voice up. The more I tried, the louder it got. Every now and then I was able to surrender and drift off to sleep.

David had been called away both days, working his butt off with the other agents. He was finally given Sunday night off so I met up with him at *Clovers*. I showed up an hour early and nursed a pint of beer, locked in thought. I was eventually able to stop dwelling on the men and women who died.

It was painful but death was part of the risk of being a soldier. It sucked but I wasn't the one who killed them. Forrest's fanatics bore the blame. Besides, Cross moved on so I would too.

I thought about Aswain's Governor for what seemed the millionth time. I felt better about him after our little meeting but I still wondered how good he really was. Maybe he shrugged off the deaths because he didn't care. Hmm, he acted so sincere in regretting their loss. Maybe he was able to put aside things he couldn't change. Maybe he'd been around so much death, it didn't faze him anymore. I didn't know and it was maddening dwelling on it so I tried to stop.

I also dedicated a good deal of thought on Thursday night, the abduction night. The whole thing didn't sit right and I had a strange feeling I'd been set up. Even if I didn't make a move on the two thieves I guessed they would've still been after me.

Maybe I was just being paranoid but I couldn't help it. Everything was a little too convenient. There were too many of them… too fast, like they were gathered together to get me.

Maybe Crow was in league with them. Maybe Ms. Green Eyes wanted to torture and corrupt another one of Cross's agents. Maybe Kara was still able to pull the agents' daily task reports so she knew where I'd be. Maybe I was being followed by more than Chief's sunglass wearing 'Poet.'

Lots of maybes… I turned to my friend, sick of thinking. "You look tired."

He sighed. "Yea, we've been running around looking everywhere for leads. Chief's making us follow every single tip we get."

"Find anything?" It had only been two days but I was already out of the loop.

David shook his head. "Not really. A couple agents visited Club Aces last night."

I perked up. "Really? And?"

"Not much. Most of the people there knew each other. Maybe they're all with Forrest or maybe none of them are." He furrowed his brow. "There was some rich old contractor at the bar who didn't really fit in."

A wave of heat surged through me. "Who?"

"Some rich guy named Otaki." David studied me. "What is it?"

"That's the guy Krane was meeting the night I escorted him. What was he doing there? Who was he with?" My voice trailed off a bit.

Otaki and his associates didn't like me one bit and seemed interested in where I was headed. I could've been way off but my intuition told me the little man tipped off Forrest. I'd be back on the job tomorrow and planned on doing some investigating of my own.

David gave a quizzical look. "I don't know. A couple others were with him. Bodyguards maybe."

"Did they do anything that stood out?"

"No." He seemed tired of the subject and yawned. "They left shortly after the agents showed up. Otaki eyeballed them for about ten minutes. They guessed he knew they were security."

I shook my head in disbelief. "They let them go?"

"They weren't there to watch Otaki. They were there to check out the place. The man didn't do anything wrong." He looked confused. "What's the big deal?"

"A hunch." I paused to gather my thoughts. "Something's off about Otaki. He and his guards acted odd that night and they were interested in me."

"Huh? Interested?" A light went off in David's head. "You think Otaki may be with Forrest?"

"I do."

"Any proof?" I could tell he wasn't buying it.

I huffed. "Not really. But he was there and that's a place I doubt he'd visit normally. Why would a rich sixty year old be hanging out in club like that?"

I actually had no idea how old he was but sixty sounded good for my case.

"I don't know. Maybe he just wanted a drink."

I didn't press the matter further. I'd already planned to get my own answers. "What else did they find?"

"The agents were keeping a low profile and didn't want to blow their cover. But they overhead a few whispers about that orb thing." He shrugged his shoulders.

"I wonder what the hell that is. The orb." I tried to think and it made my head hurt all over again. I polished off my drink. "Wonder why it's so important."

"Dunno." He looked around for a waiter; I could tell he wanted a beer. I smiled. "Don't worry I have you covered."

"Is this for saving your life?" He laughed.

I nodded. "Damn straight."

David smirked. "You know, Chief gave me quite a lashing for rescuing you."

"Wait. Weren't they coming anyways?" Part of me expected David to tell me they were going to leave me there.

He gave me a look that said 'don't be an idiot.' "Sure they were. But I, ah moved things along a bit quicker. Ok, a lot quicker." He slapped his palm on the table, suddenly angry. "But I'm not going to apologize! I couldn't leave you there. Who knows what would've happened?"

My stubborn stupidity had also gotten my friend in trouble. "Sorry."

"I was pretty pissed at you the other night but I'm over it." He shrugged. "Just try to show a little consideration for yourself in the future. It'll make my life a lot easier. I think I pulled a muscle carrying you around that effing place."

I shook my head and laughed. "You were a machine in there. I wish we had a recording of the ass kicking you handed out. Those were some moves."

The light was dim but I think my friend blushed. "Hey, it's what I do. They were messing with my buddy. Nobody messes with my friends."

"Well, again, I think I owe you my life."

"Don't worry about it." He waved his hand and blew the whole thing off. "Oh!" He said, suddenly excited. "They finally set up our desks at HQ."

I raised an eyebrow, not really caring. "Cool."

"Yea, nothing fancy, just a couple office cubes side by side to make a sort of pod." He smiled. "It's nice having a work station of our own."

He was right, I supposed. It would be nice not feeling like such an orphan at work anymore.

My mood lightened and David fidgeted. "Alright, where the hell is that waitress?" He asked.

I stood up and scanned the bar which was surprisingly slow tonight. It was Sunday night and I guessed most people were relaxing the night away in preparation for the upcoming work week. "There she is." I waved.

The young woman popped over and smiled. Cute, nice build, early twenties, long brown hair and large, happy round eyes. "Yes?"

"A couple more of these please." I handed her my glass.

She took it and batted her eyelashes at David. "Right." She backed up a few steps then headed toward the bar. Seeing her reminded me of Forrest. I shivered and tried to think of something else.

"So," I started. "How's Kara doing?"

David looked back at me, he'd been checking out the waitress too, especially her pretty figure from behind. "Huh?"

"Hello, David." I waved my hands in front of his face.

He smiled. "Oh sorry." Then he shrugged and motioned toward the girl. "Hell, I'm beat. No energy for anything tonight anyways."

By 'anything' he meant a romp in the sack. I repeated my question.

"Kara? Oh she's locked at headquarters." David raised his eyebrows. "She's completely nuts. Totally lost it."

"Yea." I grimaced. The woman was wasted, like Forate. "Have we learned anything from her?"

"Dunno." David saw the waitress head back with our drinks and halted the conversation. She set them down and gave my friend a bright smile which might've included a wink, it was hard to tell from my angle.

"There you go. Let me know if you need anything else." Her attention was locked on David. I might as well not even have been at the table. She bounced away.

David licked his lips. "Mmm, mmm, mmm." He took a drink and focused back on me. "Anyways. Chief and Cross have been working on her. I'm not sure what they've learned."

I kept my thoughts to myself, hoping some good came from her. If she spat out some good leads it would partially justify my stupid move.

David knew me well. "Hey. I hope she talks too." He sighed and leaned back in his chair. "These people are insane."

I blinked. "Who?"

"Forrest's bunch. The rest of them killed themselves rather than be caught. They must've done it to protect her." He shivered. "Spooky. They made it on the island so they must've been normal at one point. I wonder what happened to them."

"We're the ones who should know, I guess. That woman is something else." I paused. "If some of the people here are really *special*, Forrest is one of them."

He studied me, curiously. "Really."

I was going to go on but I heard someone call David's name, then mine. I turned and saw the Golden Cup had arrived to claim their usual spacious corner booth.

"Oh man." I gave David a look and he could see how annoyed I was.

He smiled, grabbed his beer and stood up. "Come on, Jason, they're not bad. I'm tired as all hell but I haven't seen them in a few days. Let's go chat."

I sighed and then groaned. "Fine." I didn't dislike the old people but I was enjoying the relaxing, friendly conversation.

Now I'd have a bunch of old, nosey people studying me and asking questions. Ugh.

We headed over and found a couple empty seats. They were all there. Sally's make-up was as lively and flamboyant as ever. Jack had a near empty glass in his hand. Harry studied me intently. He sat next to Beth whose large, round, white hair looked like either a puffy dandelion or an enormous halo around her head. Bill sat up straight with his hands folded, resting on the table. Smiles all around.

I made a face, feeling odd. They looked like a pack of owls observing me like I was a juicy mouse, ready to be snatched up.

"Well. Jason." Bill started. "We're all pleased to see you alive and well."

I scoffed. "So you've heard, I take it. Heard about what happened to me. The whole ordeal, right?"

"The whole thing." Sally said.

"It's our business to know." Jack said with a wink.

Harry grunted, a low rumble that was almost a growl. "Stupid, Jason. Very stupid."

I cut my eyes around to glare at him.

"Ease off, you old badger!" Sally made a dismissive wave toward her colleague then looked at me, her eyes beaming. "Don't mind him, sweetie. We're just glad to have you safe and all in one piece."

Beth cleared her throat. The sound was high and almost comical. "Ms. Forrest is a dangerous, dangerous woman. We don't know how she got here or what her plans are but you watch yourself." She pointed an old finger in the air.

They spoke in such perfect sequence it was almost like their responses were scripted or they were each part of one collective mind. I nodded. "I will."

Bill shifted in his seat, drawing my attention. His brow was furrowed. "Jason. You don't have to answer if you don't want to but I, or *we* are curious. What did she want?"

Great. I knew it, here we go. I didn't want to be questioned, lectured or have to retell the events again. I just wanted to relax.

"Aw, it's ok." Sally purred. "Bill, you're making him uncomfortable."

She gave me a warm smile and I returned it. The old woman was like a grandmother I never had. Her kindness helped me feel better and at ease. I looked at her, feeling bolstered. "No, it's ok." I glanced at everyone sitting around the large table, including David. "I don't know what she wants. But whatever it is, it isn't good. She has it out for Cross. That's for sure."

"Hmm." That was from Jack. I wasn't sure what it meant.

I scratched my head, thinking out loud. "She wanted me."

There was a slight gasp from the group after the inadvertent sexual innuendo. They must have known more about Forrest than they let on. David chuckled.

I continued. "I know the type. She wants power and enjoys controlling and dominating others. Hell, her minions call her *Mistress* of all things." I bit my lip, formulating my thoughts. "She wants to shake things up here, in Aswain."

Bill nodded, a serious expression on his face. "As we feared. We've had the same conclusions."

I drew in a deep breath and let it out slowly. "Yea. But still, I think most of all she wants Cross dead." I tensed as the images she showed me played over in my head.

"Naturally." Harry bellowed.

Bill cut his eyes around to glimpse his partner before they rolled back over to me. "It would be easier for her to rattle the country's foundations if Cross weren't with us anymore."

"Indeed." Beth squeaked. "Such a dreadful thought."

I pressed a bit. "Why does she hate him?"

Jack chuckled. "Because he's in charge and stands for everything she despises. Cross wants people to be free and happy." He raised his eyebrows. "Forrest has given herself over to the dark. Now she feeds off other's misery. Bitch."

"Watch your mouth!" Sally scolded.

"But it's true!" Jack full out laughed before drowning it by downing the rest of his glass. A few drops fell onto his thick beard.

I pretended to laugh but my head was trapped thinking about Cross and those videos... I looked up after a few moments and saw Bill gazing at me. The old man raised a hand in the air and the group hushed. "The nation aside, I think she's rattled *you*, hasn't she? You're losing faith in Cross."

I never had a lot of faith to begin with and wasn't in the mood to lie. So I said, "I'm trying not to."

Uneasiness came from David. "Jason, c'mon." He started. "Don't you remember Morbal? The asylum? The GU?"

I nodded.

"Look around." His face lit up. "This is heaven compared to all that. People are actually happy here. Do you really think it'd be this way if Cross were evil?"

"No." I said, quickly and flatly, taking turns to search all six faces around me for some glimpse of understanding. "You don't know. You didn't see what she showed me."

"We understand." Harry said.

Bill rubbed his chin. "At least I'd wager we do. Cross has an eventful past. I've never met a man who worked so hard for so long. Some of the things he's done would look ugly to those that don't have all the facts. He's had to pretend to be like them so he could better fight them. Undercover, so to speak."

"Be like who?" David asked. He was lost, understandably so. He couldn't know what we were talking about. He hadn't seen the videos and I never went over the specifics with him.

"The greedy bastards that run Tehlasrin." Jack bounced his head up and down and curled his lip. "Bunch of no good snakes, all of them. Oh, if I could get my hands around their necks I'd -"

"Jack Green, contain yourself!" Grandma Sally was at it again.

Bill continued, ignoring his friends' antics. "August is the noblest man I've ever known. And I've known a lot of people. What he did took him to the brink of exhaustion. It nearly killed him, holding up the façade for so long."

I bit my lip and tried to decide how much merit I put in Bill's testimony. He seemed biased, a loyal fan of the Governor.

"August needs our help, more than ever." He paused, blinking a couple times. "I know it's not easy but you should put some faith in him. He's put his in us. We can only be at our best, our most helpful when we're committed. I think we should all commit to protecting Aswain." His voice was a whisper. "Or it'll all be gone."

The normally boisterous group fell silent and I sat back in my seat. The weight of the old man's words pressed down hard. I thought of David, how happy he was, how nice Aswain is. I didn't want that to die.

The waitress from before approached our table. No doubt she was well accustomed to the Cup's knack for running up hefty bar tabs. The eerie silence seemed to throw her off. She carried a tray with several empty glasses on it. "Can I get anyone anything?"

"Hell yes!" Of course it was Jack who spoke. He sat up straight. "Your timing is perfect, my dear. Too serious around here. A round for the table!" He made a big circling motion with his right hand.

The waitress smiled and headed off. A second later I heard a loud crash behind me and quickly jerked myself around to see what caused the commotion. The young woman was on the ground surrounded by an overturned table and broken glass. She let out a shrill yelp and reached down toward her right thigh.

I looked at her leg. A large shard of glass was lodged deep in her flesh. She instinctively tugged at it.

"Don't!" David yelled but it was too late. She pulled the glass out and a gush of blood rushed from the wound.

I was instantly on my feet, rushed over to her and knelt by her side, inspecting the gash. I was no doctor but I knew enough to apply pressure to the wound. "Call an ambulance!"

"Stand aside."

I looked up at a short, slightly balding, middle aged man.

He knelt down beside me and motioned for me to move. "Are there any other healers here?" He called out.

"What?" My tone was both shocked and angry. I'd already tugged my belt off, preparing to create the best tourniquet I could muster. I spat out desperately. "WHAT ARE YOU DOING?"

Another person came into view, a young, heavyset woman. She shoved me. "Excuse me!"

I was close to shoving her back when I heard Bill's voice from behind. It was calm and collected. "Jason, move. They'll take care of this."

I spared a sharp, menacing glance at the man while the poor young girl whimpered in pain. He didn't understand the seriousness of the situation and I wanted to slap him silly.

He nodded, eyes wide. "Please, Jason."

"No!" I shook my head in desperate defiance, looking over the gaping cut again. By now there was a pool of blood on the floor. "For Christ's sake! Call an ambulance!"

The waitress started to panic.

I heard Bill talk some more while I worked to block the man and woman by me from poking and prodding the woman's leg.

"David. Please move your friend. It's ok. They're very skilled hailiorea healers."

A second later I felt David's powerful hands on me, dragging me back from the woman. I turned around and looked at my friend, feeling totally betrayed. His face was as white as a sheet and he looked at me with wide eyes.

"What are you doing?" I exclaimed. "She needs help!"

Harry roared. "Calm, Jason! Look!" He pointed at the injured leg.

I looked at the girl and the two people hovering over her. They moved their hands over the cut, almost making contact.

"She's going to bleed to death!" I fought and eventually freed myself from David's grip, aiming to move back to my former position. I was about to pull the two strangers away when my eye caught the wound. I gasped and my heart skipped a beat. It changed. The cut was closing up. Very slowly but undeniably, the two people mumbled words I couldn't make out while moving their hands in quick, circular motions.

"What? How?" I was shocked beyond the ability to articulate more. I held still and watched, jaw hanging open.

After a few moments, the man and woman pressed their hands on the waitress's leg and squeezed. They held the grips for a solid minute, eyes closed, faces contorted and focused.

The bleeding stopped. I couldn't believe it.

Finally the healers stood up and moved away from the woman. The wound was now nothing more than a scar.

It was a miracle! They actually, magically healed her.

By now the bartender, a cook and another waitress were checking over the girl and worked together to pick her up. She was out cold but breathing fine.

An awestruck dizzy numbness washed over me. I looked at the blood then took turns examining the two who'd healed the cut with nothing but their hands. They were both hunched over in their seats looking exhausted, panting heavily.

"I can't... how did? What did they do?" I babbled.

"Jason, David. Have a seat." I turned and saw Bill standing up, looking down on me. His eyes had that familiar cool, almost lazy look they often showed. I realized the healing we just saw was nothing new to him.

I can't remember getting off the floor but before I knew it, I was back in my seat, unsure what to say or think. I wanted to scream and laugh at the same time.

David spoke a word. "*Hailiorum*."

"Yes." Beth said in a tone that was a bit lower than her usual pitch.

I turned to look around the bar. Aside from the employees, David and the Cup, there were a dozen others sharing the space with me. A couple looked as surprised and dumbfounded as I felt but most were going about their business like nothing had happened. I looked forward and shook my head. It was true. All of it. All the things Fier told me, all the strange things I'd seen. It was real. To their credit, the Golden Cup gave David and me time to collect our wits.

I felt a sturdy hand on my shoulder and turned to see Jack's jovial face smiling at me. He licked his lips. "You know. I remember the first time I saw such a thing. I never knew how stupid my face looked. Now I know."

"Jack!" Sally said sharply.

The man chuckled and patted my back. "It's ok, kid. Take your time. Soak it up."

"They're really hailiorea?" David found his tongue before me. I wasn't nearly ready.

"Yes." Harry said in his deep voice.

"And so are you." Bill added coolly. "So are all of us."

I wasn't looking directly at him but I could see David shake himself out of the corner of my eye. "It's all true. My mother told me about them, err" he cleared his throat, "about us. But I never believed her."

"It's ok, son." Sally said. "This stuff isn't taught to us in school or on TV, unfortunately. It's impossible to grasp until you've seen it with your own eyes. Until you've experienced it yourself."

Jack removed his hand. "I imagine you've both seen things already but not this blatantly. I know how it is. Deny, bury, ignore. Do whatever's needed to keep the world in order so things make sense."

"Now you know." Bill said. "And now the real questions are going to start."

I looked at Bill and squinted.

He gave me an endearing little wink. "Here's my advice. Take it slow. Don't overload yourself. You've seen a thing that has opened your eyes. Let it settle and allow more information to sink in."

"But." David began.

Bill put a hand up. "Slowly."

I turned to look at my friends face. He was desperate for answers. "Ok." He nodded and let out a deep breath. When he spoke his voice was calm. "Who else knows about this?"

"It's hard to say for sure." Beth answered, her ultra-high voice had returned. "Everyone's different. Some know more than others. Some don't know anything."

I swallowed, finally able to speak. "What?"

Beth looked at me. "Cross knows what we know. Chief and most of the intelligence captains know quite a bit too I imagine."

"Fier tried to tell me." I sounded ashamed, like I was a fool for not believing her. I tried to think. That word... what was it. "What's a halrum?"

"Hailiorum." Harry corrected.

I looked at him without speaking and said the word in my head. Hay Lee Or Um.

Bill grunted. "Hailiorum is the singular, hailiorea is the plural. In short, we're people with exceptional talents." He motioned toward the mess on the floor behind me. "Like the two who healed young Miss Holly."

I thought the words again: Hay Lee Or Um singular, Hay Lee Or Eye plural.

I looked at David and he giggled like a schoolboy. "I need another beer."

"Ha!" Jack blurted. "Now you're talking!"

# Chapter 14

I woke up the next day, exercised, cleaned up, downed a couple aspirins and commuted to work in an understandably odd mood. It was hard getting to sleep after leaving *Clovers* and I had to convince myself all over again that what I'd seen was really real.

I eyeballed everyone that passed me on my way to work, wondering what 'magical' things they could do. What about me? What could I do? It was all so amazing. I had to keep pulling myself back down to Earth but my head wanted to stay in the clouds. It was a constant battle that went on the night before and all morning.

Yea, it took time but I eventually grew tired of the struggle and tried to just roll with it all. The world had changed and become even stranger than ever but I'd take things as they came. There was nothing I could do about it anyways. The world was what it was.

Screw it. So people here had special powers. Big deal. They were still people. In the end I suppose I felt relief. The things I'd seen made more sense now: People moving in and out of space, dodging bullets, the odd stares and others knowing my thoughts. I wasn't crazy after all.

My job would be more difficult dealing with a host of hidden wildcards but life had never been easy so what's the difference? I'd deal with each surprise as they came.

I remembered Fier telling me nearly the exact same thing. Her outlook made a ton more sense now. If bad guys could fly, I'd knock them out of the air. If they were invisible I'd wait for them to come to me. If they got the better of me, then the hell with it, I guess I just wasn't good enough.

David met me at the base's front entrance and led me to our new work stations. He looked like he hadn't slept a wink. There were large circles under his eyes and he hadn't shaved. He chuckled a couple times as we walked, grasping the new reality of the world in his own way.

We reached our office cubes in the deepest sections of the base and I inspected the space. David and I each had our own computer, phone, information terminal and scanner. His station was adjacent mine with a small wall separating us.

I adjusted my seat and then checked the phone. It worked. Then I studied a couple files that were organized on my desk. There were documents with information on potential connections to Forrest and a thick stack of bios that needed to be checked. It wasn't my favorite task but at least it was simple. I wouldn't mind taking it easy. My body was still a wreck from the beating I'd taken a few days ago.

No such luck. John Durn marched his circular self into my cube a few minutes after I sat down. "Jason, David. Come with me. Mr. Cross wants to see you."

David hopped out of his chair and I cursed under my breath. Cross, great. We followed Durn through the security doors and several busy halls. The base was a flurry of activity.

I looked at my friend.

He looked back, knowing what I was thinking. "It's been like this all weekend."

"Busy, busy." Durn said. He hustled into an elevator and pressed the number twelve, the top floor where Cross's office was. He smiled with his gaze fixed straight ahead as he spoke. "I understand you boys had quite an eye opening last night."

"You could say that, Captain." David replied.

I looked at the round man. He'd obviously known about all the magic stuff the whole time. I couldn't believe they'd keep such information secret. I surprised myself when I spoke words I meant to think. "What can you do?"

Durn looked over at me and laughed. His large eyes beamed. "You'll learn those things are usually private." He pursed his lips. "Sorta like religious beliefs or political ideals or recent sexual activity. Lots of people don't like blurting out or bragging about their gifts."

He looked back ahead and started humming.

I snorted, annoyed by the non-answer. We headed out for Cross's office, reaching it quickly. Chief was standing outside the door with his eyes locked on David and me. He folded his big arms, defiantly.

If the man didn't like me three days ago, he full out hated me now, full of anger and blaming me for the guards that died. What could I do about it? Nothing. I guessed the huge bastard wished I'd died in the fight. Oh well, too bad for him.

We stopped at the door. "Here they are, Sir." Durn said with a quick salute.

Chief nodded. "Go in. The Governor's waiting."

David opened the door and I followed him in. I could hear Durn going over some information with Chief as the door shut behind us.

Cross looked up from his computer and smiled. I couldn't believe it; he'd actually gotten a haircut. It was still disheveled without any particular hint of order but not nearly as crazy as it was the last time I'd seen it. He was also wearing a bright blue shirt which varied from his normal earth tone scheme.

"Gentlemen! Please have a seat."

I sat down trying to remember what Fier had told me about Cross's gifts. I recalled something about not lying to him. He hated that.

The man took turns studying our faces. "So, what do you think? The Cup told me about last night. I just want to make sure you're adjusting ok. I don't normally pry like this but I take a little extra interest in the mindsets of our agents."

"I'm still shocked." David said.

I shifted in my seat, still uncomfortable around the Governor.

My friend laughed. "I always thought my mother was just telling stories to entertain my sisters and me."

"Not quite." Cross smirked. He glanced at me and gave a little nod. "Oh, Jason. I wanted to tell you that Krane was impressed with your work Thursday night before the events at *Club Aces*."

I pulled back. Krane's praise didn't mean much to me right now and the comment caught me off guard, it felt irrelevant given everything else that had transpired. I figured Cross was trying to stroke my ego. I simply said, "Good."

Cross raised an eyebrow. "He practically begged me to not fire you. Ah well, I just wanted to let you know. We don't always hear about how appreciated we are. Anyways, back to the point." He licked his lips. "I want you to feel free to talk with Mr. Sands, any captain, the Cup or myself if things start getting too heavy or weird. We're here to help."

"Ok." I said. "I have some questions. Not sure where to start, though."

"That's understandable." Cross said, folding his arms.

I quickly got my thoughts in order. "That guard, the night we saved Krane... he really did get shot in his face, didn't he? He actually survived it."

The Governor nodded. "Officer Blake. Yes. He was able to channel his energy and it shielded him. It's an incredible gift very few of us have. He's still resting to this day, recovering his life force."

"Jesus." David said.

"Here." Cross handed David and me matching video disks. "These are not to leave this base, understood?"

We nodded.

I stirred. "You only let these *special* people live here."

The Governor nodded.

"And there're two million of us?" I shook my head. The number felt too big.

The man smiled. "Well, the blood lines have thinned out a bit, they've spread out. Part of the DNA chain gives most of us a strong drive to breed, to pass on our gifts."

*I don't want kids.* I thought.

"Not all of us, I suppose." Cross added, reading my thoughts. He motioned the disks. "They have information on the hailiorea. Watch them at your stations when you have time." He chuckled. "I don't know when you'll find the time but there you are."

I looked down at the disk and flipped it around in my hand. Cross liked informational videos it seemed.

"Listen." He went on. "We need to stay focused. Your mission remains the same no matter how much things have changed. Protect Aswain. There's a powerful hailiorum out there intent on causing havoc. We need to stop her."

David agreed. "Right."

I shrugged in a 'no duh' kind of way. Did he think I'd become a bumbling idiot just because I found out about these magic people? Or that I'm supposedly one too? He seemed to expect something from me so I decided to ask another question. "Cross."

"Yes?" He studied me, waiting.

"What? No, how did we become hal, whatever they're called?" I struggled with the word, "hailiorea?"

Cross looked at his watch. "Damn, sorry I have to be somewhere soon." He grimaced. "The Cup is working on what we are. We have ideas but nothing definite. Fifteen hundred years ago a group of people were born with incredible, seeming inhuman abilities and traits. They called themselves the Hailiorea. We're their descendants."

I squinted. "What did they do with these powers? How come we've never heard of them?"

"It's believed they used their gifts to combat malevolent forces." Cross spoke quickly, eyes shifting between the two of us. "It's supposedly all kept quiet to prevent panic. I don't know. I think everyone should know. Someday this will all be common knowledge."

"Why not spread the word now?" David asked.

The Governor shrugged. "In time. There're too many other big fish to fry right now."

"So what about the people on Aswain? Why not tell them right off the bat at least?" I asked. "Why didn't you tell us about all this?"

Cross blinked. "I told you before that you wouldn't have believed me or understood reality until you saw it for yourself. You were indoctrinated with your old mindset. It can't be changed from the outside with a few words."

"What can we do?" David interrupted. He referred to himself and me.

Cross sighed before starting. "There are four basic branches or types of hailiorea. You two are obviously mostly descended from the defender or justice line."

I furrowed my brow. "What the hell does that mean?"

He slumped his shoulders and shook his head. "I'm sorry, I know this is overwhelming. You'll learn more in time. For now, just spend your mental and physical energy on the present. We can talk more later or, like I said, get with the Cup or set an appointment with Josh."

No real answers, big surprise. I shook my head, tired of being clueless, of feeling so ignorant.

Cross picked up on it. "Watch the video, ask around. You'll learn more."

"Alright." I said finally. "Was this all you wanted to see us about?"

"Mostly." The Governor stood up. "John will be meeting with you in a bit, David." He turned to me. "Sarah has an assignment for you, Jason."

I made a face. I had no idea who Sarah was.

"They have leads for you to investigate today." Cross continued. "Stay focused."

David nodded. "Yes, Sir."

Cross locked eyes with us for a silent piece of time. "This is important."

"We understand, August." David was more comfortable calling the man by his first name than I was.

"Good. Again, sorry for cutting this so short. I wanted to see you and make sure you were both ok." He smiled. "I've been through this with a lot of people. You two are taking it exceptionally well."

I laughed. 'Exceptionally well' was one way to put it. I was a bit surprised myself but for the moment, I really didn't give a damn. I was tired of the emotional roller coaster I'd been on for, what? Two years? I was done.

"Ok, I have to get going." Cross opened the door and stepped out. David and I followed. "Go on back to your offices. Your captains will be there soon."

Ah, I remembered. Sarah was the motherly looking captain.

I was surprised and jumped a little when Cross planted his hand on my shoulder. His other hand was on David. "I'm proud out you two. I believe in you. Now let's crack this case and get Forrest. Good luck."

We headed back down into the deep corridors of the base. I looked at the disk in my hand thinking about the healing I saw at the bar. My brain kept trying to over think things, it wanted to be amazed and alarmed. I wouldn't let it.

-

After meeting with Captain Sarah Keen I spent an hour going over various reports, searching missing citizens and cross checking new arrivals. After that, I headed home for a quick change of clothes. The business casual look was too dressy for the location of the assignment the captain gave me. I was to meet a contact with information on Forrest at some sort of game hall. I went with a pair of blue jeans and a form fitting, comfortable green tee shirt and sneakers.

Keen was quick, direct and came off as cold. She gave me my assignment and didn't stick around for follow up questions. Either she was busy or she didn't care for me. I figured both were true. Everyone scrambled for information and I was still black listed for my stupid stunt at *Club Aces*. At least she didn't bring the fiasco up.

Now I was sitting at a flimsy booth in a mostly dark room waiting for my contact. It turned out, the man, Eric Rose, decided to meet me in an arcade. My ears were bombarded by an assault of horrible noises. The assortment of games each wailing out their own messes of music, beeps, explosions and screams. I'd never had much experience at arcades but it was like a casino for kids.

I took a drink from my soda and looked around. I didn't fit in, even with my relaxed clothes on. For starters, I was more than ten years older than everyone else in the place. I wasn't interested in playing any games and I knew my annoyed expression was hard to ignore.

"Where the hell are you, kid?" I grumbled to myself. A young woman standing behind the cash register glanced at me We were alone in the arcade's eatery section. I looked at my watch. This Eric was now fifteen minutes late and my patience was wearing thin. I started to wonder if I was in the wrong place.

A couple moments later, thought, I saw a tall, lanky young man walk by one of the windows separating the small section from the outside. He had *white* hair and some of the fairest skin I'd seen. A few seconds later and he was standing near my booth.

"You have to be Waters." It was hard to hear over the noise but I turned and nodded, feeling the distaste of my undercover name.

The young man sat himself in the booth across from me. By the snobby, stuck-up look on his face, the perfect form of his hair and the expensive looking clothes, which were covered with meaningless brand names that told the world he spent more than they were worth, I could see the kid came from money. Strike one.

"You're late." I spoke louder than I wanted to, but it was the only way he could hear me.

He shrugged. "Sorry."

I sighed. "And why here? Couldn't pick a quieter spot?"

"Hey, enough with the attitude. I'm here to help you guys out, remember?"

Cocky and arrogant, strike two.

I fought the urge to slap him upside his head. Instead I surprised myself with a diplomatic smile. "Well, we're paying you if the information is good."

Eric rolled his eyes. "I don't care about the damn chump change. You can keep it. I'm here to get back at the bastards who messed with my dad's organization and a bunch of my friends."

I furrowed my brow. "What?"

"You're on the intelligence team, right?" His voice was loud and clear over the noise. "Didn't you check up on me?"

"No." I said sharply. The idiot had broadcasted the words 'intelligence team' to the whole world.

Eric moved his lips but I couldn't hear what he said. I guessed it wasn't very flattering. I curled my lip.

"My father is one of the Unifier's leaders." The smugness in his voice was thick as wool.

I looked into the kid's rich, spoiled, ignorant eyes and wanted to rip into him, let him know what I really thought of his father's organization. I didn't, though, I kept calm and professional. My tone was even and cool. "Ok then. What happened and how can you help me?"

Eric looked around, making sure no one was listening, suddenly Mr. Secretive. I peeked at the sole employee; she was busy studying her fingernails.

He moved closer. "Remember that whole thing with the mayor? When he was attacked?"

I nodded. You bet your ass I remember.

The man scoffed. "And that incident in Goldthorn where some dumbass agent was captured, ending in a bloodbath?"

I literally bit my lip.

"Ok, well a few of my buddies died in both fights." He paused. "Well they used to be my friends, they were part of the movement before that bitch turned them into raving lunatics."

He must've meant Forrest. I nodded.

Eric seemed to expect me to speak. He continued after I kept silent. "I want her and her slaves to pay. We can't take her by ourselves so I decided to help you."

"Good." I said finally.

"My dad would kill me if he knew what I was doing but they were *my* friends! There're two guys who work for her who I saw talking to my friends. They vanished shortly after until their corpses turned up." A fire blazed in his eyes and I felt a little respect for the kid. Take one strike away.

I eyed his face up and down, it showed a familiar mix of sadness and rage. "Who are they? What are the men's names?"

"I don't know their names. One is a sort of young, short guy and the other... he's older, always wearing fancy dark clothes. Black hair and intense dark eyes." He looked down at the table then back up at me. "I'm going to find the sons of bitches."

I wanted to tell him to leave that to my team but part of me didn't want to discourage his resolve. He was a bit of a rebel and I related to that.

Back in the arcade, one of the machines let out a god awful wail followed by a series of explosions. I winced. The static was bringing my headache back with a vengeance.

Eric's face lightened. "Sorry about the noise. But there're people out there who don't want me talking. I figured this was a safe, inconspicuous place."

I nodded and rubbed my temples. "Don't worry about it."

"You never know who you can trust these days." He spoke quietly but I heard him clear as day. The remark made him seem a lot older than he was.

I moved in closer myself and encouraged the man. "Ok. What do you have for us? Tell me and we'll get out of here."

"Right." Eric licked his lips. "I know how that monster got on the island."

I raised my eyebrows. "Forrest?"

"Yea."

I gave Eric my undivided attention while he shared his relative information. Afterwards, we went our separate ways. Neither of us said goodbye.

I stepped out of the hellishly noisy arcade into the cool, fresh outside air. It was a cloudy, overcast day and the wind moved fast. A brisk chill glided through my body and I felt immediately refreshed. Funny how that happens. I was about to smile when my eyes passed over a face across the street staring back at me. The face was wearing a pair of thick sunglasses.

"Son of a bitch!" I stormed across the road, ignoring several honks from annoyed drivers.

The sunglass wearer chuckled. It wasn't Kyle, this guy looked Hispanic. "You'd better be careful, Agent Sworn."

I snarled. "What are you doing? Watching me again? Did Chief send you?"

"Chief sent us out three days ago and never called us back. We've been watching you ever since." He gave me a sick little smile then he motioned toward the arcade. "Find out anything good?"

I shook my head in disgust then stormed away. I wasn't going to tell him anything.

-

Durn popped his round head out through the door and called me in. I'd been waiting outside a room I'd never seen before for about ten minutes. When I entered I saw Chief, Durn and the other three captains, including Fier. So she was back. The woman gave me a quick little wink.

A tingling buzz started to grow in my gut and I marveled at how lovely her face was. So beautiful. Her auburn hair shined in the light. I smiled.

Sarah stopped me before I could think any further about her eyes and lips, her cute little nose and luscious figure... "Agent Sworn. Rub your neck, please."

"Sit down." Chief barked.

I took a seat at a table across from the others while giving the back of my neck a good massage. The room wasn't that big but it had enough space for a desk and the table with eight chairs around it. There weren't any windows and the lighting was a little dim. Amusing how bright the place, especially the glow around Fier, was just a few moments ago.

I locked eyes with Chief and my mood turned sour, immediately. A strong desire to punch him in his face grew. The bastard was still having me followed.

Instead, I remained still and he spoke. "Report."

I cleared my throat. "I met with Eric Rose. Did you know he's the son of one of the heads of the Unifiers?"

"Yes, yes." Ashe said. I hadn't dealt with the man much but he seemed to be a slightly less intense version of Chief. He was older than the rest with broad shoulders, bright red hair and a seemingly permanent scowl on his face. Grumpiness must've been a prerequisite for the leadership job. At least Fier and John weren't uptight all the time.

"Did he share any good information?" Sarah asked, eyes wide and serious.

I nodded and decided to let out the information quickly so I could get the hell away from their stares. "Yes. He claims to know how Forrest got on the island."

Durn perked up. "Interesting."

I shot a glance at Fier, feeling like she was my only ally in the room.

"Calm down, Jason." Sarah said slowly. "You're not in trouble. Relax."

That was an odd thing to say. I knew I wasn't in trouble, this time. I continued. "He said she came in through the shipping docs in Lowshore."

Lowshore was a port in the deep southern parts of Aswain. As with the other ports, it was a focal point for trade between the island and Tehlasrin.

Chief nodded. A grim look on his face. "Continue."

"Eric told me she tucked herself into one of the empty etherspring crates that returned from the Americas." I stopped, expecting a response.

"And?" Ashe said after a short silence.

I swallowed. "She was supposedly found by a couple guards and quickly bewitched them, or whatever you call it."

"Damn it." Chief grunted. "So careless. We should've known better. It's our own damn fault! *My* fault."

Ashe slammed his fist on the table and Chief went on. "I knew we should've had more reliable guards at every entry point." He growled. "We failed miserably."

No one argued with the big man.

"What happened from there?" Durn asked when he looked back at me.

"How long ago was this?" Sarah said before I could answer Durn.

I looked at her. "Eric said this was about four weeks ago."

The group of commanders squirmed. "He also said she immediately headed to Shard Isle."

"What for?" Ashe uttered, thinking out loud.

Chief grunted. "Is that it, then?"

"That's all he told me." I took turns looking at each of them. I decided to keep the bit about the two guys turning Eric's friends to Forrest's side to myself. There were no real answers there anyways.

Durn spoke when my eyes met his. "Did you believe him? Was he trustworthy?"

I thought for a moment, reflecting. "I believe him."

Chief stood up, grumbling, shaking his head. He walked out of the room without an audible word. I took it that the meeting was over. The rest of the small group stood up and filed out as well so I followed. I saw David leaning against a wall outside.

"Hey man." He said when he saw me. The familiar, movie star smile was on his face. Then he saw Fier and the smile grew. "Well, look whose back!"

I glanced between the two. For the first time in memory, Fier seemed just as happy to see David as he was to see her. Their eyes locked and I could almost feel the room's temperature rise.

I shook my head. "Ok. Both of you. Rub your necks, come on."

Fier shook herself back to the present and brought her hand up behind her head

David gave me a confused look. "Huh?"

"That's right, you don't know about that one. Here." I walked up to my friend and quickly squeezed the base of his skull a bit. "It's one of those hailiorum things. Apparently you're both sexual magnets."

David's eyes lit up when I finished my work on his neck. "Tell me something I don't know. But damn. That really works?" He looked at Fier and gave a wolfish smile. "Not much. How about you, dear?"

"That's *Captain* Dear to you, smartass." Fier said with spunk, tossing me a sideways smile along with a quick wink.

David gave a little bow. "Of course, Captain. Welcome home. I missed ya."

I shook my head and looked at my watch, it was a little after five o'clock. I looked at Fier. "So what's next?"

She sighed, slumped her shoulders and rubbed her temples with her right hand. "Plenty but I'm tired." She paused a moment. "Ah hell. Let's go grab some dinner. You guys like pizza? I haven't had any good food in days."

"Sounds good to me!" David nearly jumped out of his skin, more excited than a man should be for pizza. He was still just as sex crazed after the neck rub. Shocker.

I nodded, feeling strangely excited about having dinner with Fier myself. Uh-oh. "Yea let's go. It's been a long day, I'm fried."

Fier gave us a ride in her car which was powered by etherspring like all the other vehicles in Aswain. She was surprised I didn't know that already and I decided then and there to study up on things more. I was tired of everyone knowing more than me.

We reached a small, busy Italian restaurant called *Venetian Pride* fifteen minutes later and walked in. Fier looked at us. "Damn, I wanted to talk to you guys. Some about work stuff… Too many ears around here."

I shrugged. "Let's go somewhere else then."

"No." Fier shot out quickly. "I want to eat, I want pizza and I want it from here." She looked around the restaurant. "Hold up here, I'll take care of this."

I watched Fier lazily raise her hand in the air and call out, "Gigi!"

A well-groomed man perked his head up and bolted over. "Ah, Ms. Wren. Ciao. How fantastic to see you again, my sweet. Here for a little dinner?"

I almost laughed when Fier batted her eyelashes. Flirt. It seemed she didn't completely dislike her special allure. Part of me suddenly wished she'd bat her lashes at me. I rubbed my neck again, didn't help much.

"Yes, but I was hoping for a spot a little more private for my friends and me." She said.

The guy, Gigi, didn't take his lusty eyes off Fier. She was laying it pretty thick on the poor guy. I smiled.

He pointed a finger in the air. "I have just the place. There is an available private balcony off the second floor which should be very nice for you." He puffed out his chest, filled with pride. "Follow me, please."

We sat down and agreed on a couple large pizzas, one with all vegetables and the other with an array of meats. After the waiter left, Fier leaned back in her seat and let out another deep sigh. I couldn't help but catch her chest heave with the move under the cute form fitting green sweater. Lovely.

"Tired?" David asked in a soft voice. He made sure he sat on her side of the booth across from me.

She looked at him. "Exhausted." Then she raised a finger and lazily pointed it at me. "Your buddy here wasn't the only one who nearly ate it over the weekend."

A mix of shame and curiosity washed over me. I ignored the shame part. "What happened?"

Fier looked at me and I noticed she was subtlety rubbing her neck. It seemed David's effect was working on her again. "I got into a snag with some Tehlasrin goons. They took the bribe then wanted more." She shook her head. "They nearly brought the whole operation down."

"Damn." David's face showed concern. He inched closer to her.

I furrowed my brow. "What operation? You mean your mission?"

"No, I mean the operation of rebels in the Americas who help us stick it to the GU every now and then." She sounded annoyed. I guessed this was more information I should have known already. "My friend, Michael Vistear, nearly got killed too. It was crazy."

Thankfully, I wasn't alone in my ignorance. David seemed to know as little about it as me. "Wow, so there's actually a rebellion within the Union?"

She cut her eyes around at him. "Several rebellions led by a bunch of different people. Some are larger and better equipped than others. They're scattered and everywhere but they're coming together. Once they're more organized, they'll really be able to stick it to Union" She nodded and showed the faintest smirk. "I think Tehlasrin won't last long. Especially in the Americas; there're uprisings everywhere."

"And you know all these groups?" I asked, intrigued. "Who else goes with you on these missions?"

Fier let out a quick, sharp laugh. "Why, do you want to go? Be my guest."

"That's not what I meant." I snapped, annoyed.

She waved her hand in the air. "Just kidding. No, I don't know them all. And, no one else goes with me." She smiled brightly. "I'm such a lucky girl!"

"Christ," David said. "Sounds risky. I hope Cross pays you a lot more than he pays me."

"He does."

Now I was the one sighing. "So what? You must have quite a contact list of people over there, huh?"

"Yes, yes, yes." Fier said with a sharp exhale. "Look, I'm really tired. I'm not here to be questioned all night."

"Oh, sorry, dear." David said in a soothing tone.

"Stop calling me that!" Fier growled. "First off, I'm not *your* Dear, second, it pisses me off, third, I'm your commander and forth, if Chief heard you he'd rip your head off."

I cleared my throat and ignored Fier's little spat. "So why are you here? With us?"

Fier looked at me and her mouth dropped open a little. She held quiet for a moment. "Why do you ask?"

I raised my eyebrows. "You don't seem to be enjoying yourself. Why torture yourself?"

"I'm sorry." Her shoulders slumped a bit. "Both of you. I don't mean to be a bitch all the time."

I saw David's his shocked expression. "Never!"

"Come off it and give your neck a good solid rub down. And give me some damn room." Fier barked, spreading her left elbow out, pushing David away a bit. She looked between the two of us. "I know how I am. I'm sorry if I come off rough sometimes."

"Who doesn't?" I said with a smile. Hell, Fier was a cool breeze compared to hurricane that was my attitude.

She smiled back. "Truth is, Cross asked me to spend some time with you two. He wants to make sure your adjusting to all the *special* stuff ok."

"Oh, I see. You're here because you were ordered too." I folded my arms. Outwardly I showed a hint of disgust, inwardly I felt deflated. "Just like Chief's puppets."

David finished rubbing his neck and gave Fier a hurt look. "Is that true?"

She squinted at me, not impressed with my comparing her to a puppet. "Yes it's true. But." She paused for effect. "Cross wouldn't have asked me if he hadn't known I liked you guys. You're new and naive but you're both good, honest, direct people. I like that. Hell, with a little time we could become friends."

David smiled wide. He looked like he was going to say something but didn't.

I cursed. "I'm sorry about the puppet thing. I'm just sick of Chief having me followed."

"He's supposed to call those guys off. I heard Cross tell him that, personally." Fier's eyes lit up when she saw our food headed out way. "Thank God!"

We tore into the pizzas and spent a piece of time chewing rather than talking. I had to give my neck some work around my third slice when I caught myself longingly staring at Fier's mouth as she ate. It made me think of the hailiorum again.

"Hey Fier." I said after swallowing.

She glanced up at me from her plate. "Damn this is so *good*! What's up?"

"I'm not really bothered by the *specials* thing." I raised an eyebrow. "But I wonder... why does Cross only let them here? To live? Why not *normal* people?"

Fier nodded. "Did Cross give you that video? Did you watch it?"

"Not yet." David said.

"He gave it to us today but I haven't gotten around to watching it." I added. "Been busy."

Fier nodded then scoffed. "A lot of it doesn't make much sense and it puts me to sleep. As to your question, Cross has plans he hasn't completely shared with us yet. At least, not with me."

I rubbed my chin, thinking.

"Also," Fier started between bites. "The hailiorea have something to do with the production of etherspring."

"What?" David asked with a full mouth.

I perked up.

"Yea. Strange, huh?" Fier nodded with a look of awe on her face. "I don't know all the details but the Cup went rambling on one night about the relation in energy output to the number of hailiorea living on the island."

"Jesus." I shook my head. "If that's true then we're... I don't know. Like nothing more than living batteries."

David grunted. "Come on, Jason. You know better than that."

"Hey!" Fier said, interrupting my thoughts. "Ask the Cup about it sometime before you decide Cross is some evil Dr. Frankenstein. Don't take my word for it."

I let out a small laugh. Her comment put an abrupt end to the next round of August Cross mistrust before it even started.

"But you're a Captain in the country's intelligence branch. Shouldn't you know about all this stuff?" I gestured David. "Shouldn't we too?"

Fier raised an eyebrow. "I'm here to protect the country, rescue potential newcomers and lead and train clowns like you. That's my job. I'm busy enough as it is. So lay off, ok?"

"You're such a bitch." I tried to say with a straight face but failed.

We all burst into laughter and enjoyed the rest of our meal.

# Chapter 15

Work started off interesting the next day. I settled into my cubicle not ten minutes before Captain Ashe showed up to give David and me our first stakeout assignment. We were told to keep watch on a small Chinese restaurant named *Chins* which had been visited by a couple people on Forrest's watch list.

The task sounded fun and exciting. Ashe also surprised us with the keys to our own car. We were speechless. He told us that since we lived so close to each other we could keep the vehicle and share it between the two of us, for official use only of course.

I was thrilled, finally somewhat free from Aswain's public transit. Ashe didn't share our enthusiasm and acted as if he were giving us a used tissue.

We received files with bios and pictures of the two suspects then sent on our way. David parked the car in a lot across from the restaurant where we watched for Barry Solso and Nina Vans. They were both school teachers from Marchfield who had been missing from work for several days.

What started off as fun and exciting quickly became dull and boring. The stakeout wasn't what I hoped it would be and I was glad David was with me to pass the time. We talked a lot, played tic-tac-toe and took turns napping.

At one point, after a prolonged silent period, David blurted, "Damn I'd love to sleep with Fier."

I whipped my head around to face him, a surge of alarm coursed through me. I wasn't exactly sure how to verbalize how much of a bad idea the prospect was so I kept quiet. The news was nothing new, of course. It was obvious David wanted Fier from the get go. But now, the thought of the two together stung me right, dead center in my chest.

"She's so sexy and spunky, you know?" David looked at me and smiled.

I'll be damned… What I felt could only be jealousy. Had to be. To my horror, I realized then and there, without a doubt, I had feelings for Fier. Eff.

"Hello, Jason." David said, no doubt noticing my dumbfounded, spaced out expression. "You there?"

I blinked. "Yea, I'm here." Thoughts coursed through my head, not only about David and Fier but also about Fier and me. I played it cool. "Dangerous ground, buddy. She's your boss, nothing but trouble messing around there."

That was aimed at both of us, I thought, as was my next comment. "Besides, what makes you think she'd even go along with it?" I laughed, somewhat nervously.

David didn't see any possible complication with such a relationship. He was blinded by optimism again and as happy as could be. Thankfully, he brushed it off and all but ended the conversation.

There was a short silence then the subject changed to my kidnapping. I thanked him again for saving my life. The conversation moved on to fighting styles and various battles we'd been in. We also talked about my brother and David's sisters. He missed them more than he'd previously let on.

I guess the time in our new car could be labeled as typical male bonding. We were already as close as brothers but the hours together, with nothing to do but wait and talk, brought us closer. The world had become a busy place since we made it to

Aswain, it was nice to slow down and remember how close we were.

Our two targets never showed up and finally, around 2pm, my phone rang, startling David awake. It was Fier, she ordered us back to base immediately. Cross was conducting a meeting with of all intelligence personnel and other heads of security.

David drove us back to headquarters. I hadn't driven in years and didn't feel bold enough to give it a try. Luckily, he didn't have any problems behind the wheel.

We got back to base and headed in. Durn was there with his hand on his hips watching people pass by, directing a select few to where the meeting was taking place.

He gave us a quick rundown of 'take a right here and left there.' We reached a large, brightly lit conference room with multiple rows of chairs set up and sat down.

I recognized some faces but there were lots I'd never seen before. The intelligence agents were easy to distinguish from the uniformed security officers. My team had a mixed look to them, some wore jeans and tee shirts, and others wore suits and dresses. They'd been on undercover jobs like David and me and wore whatever clothing best suited each operation.

Cross stood at the front, near a podium with a microphone on it, chatting with Chief and Sarah. Fier and Ashe were seated up front facing the rows of seats. By the time Durn joined the other captains, most of the seats in the room were occupied. The large group chattered away until Cross raised his hands in the air and spoke.

"Good afternoon, everyone." He called out, smiling and giving the group a quick once over. He was back to wearing his relaxed, casual clothes and his hair was pulled back a bit, looking flat and wet. I guessed he'd simply taken a handful of water and ran it through his hair. "Thanks for getting here on such short notice. I know you're all very busy."

I studied the faces around me. They looked eager and expectant. I gathered this sort of meeting wasn't a frequent occurrence. I couldn't help but wonder how many were still clueless about the whole hailiorum thing.

Cross paused for a second and swallowed. He looked nervous. Odd. I didn't take him as someone with stage fright.

"I want to get everyone up to speed on recent events in one shot and then go over what we've learned. We've got an extremely serious threat in our midst and we need to act fast to catch Forrest before she causes more harm."

The very mention of her name made me flush. I couldn't help but reflect on the frightening and arousing time I'd spent with her. Lusty tingles ran through my body followed by a sharp pain in my head. I tried to block it out and focus.

The Governor paused and shuffled a stack of papers that were in front of him. "Sorry." He tossed the pages aside. "Public speaking isn't my thing."

A few people in the group chuckled and Cross scratched his head, laughing. "Anyways. We know Forrest has made several moves against us. She attacked Krane, abducted and tortured one agent then kidnapped another. She's also twisted and ensnared a number of people from all over the island."

I almost rolled my eyes. This was old news. I saw a sprinkling of hands raise in the air. Cross put his own hands out, palms first.

"Please hold your questions until later." He glanced around at the faces then continued. "It's been difficult getting anything out of Kara, she's such a wreck." Cross sighed and his eyes dropped down. He spoke quietly into the microphone. "Some of you may be new to this term, but it appears she's been shattered."

There were several gasps from the large group. I looked at David. His brow was furrowed and he looked as lost as I felt. Good.

"Hmm. I see." Cross said amidst various mumbles from the group. "Shattered is a condition we refer too when a hailiorum falls into insanity. Some of us have tried to save friends and family who were shattered and failed every time. Sadly the same can be said for Kara."

"What?" I said quietly, rubbing my head.

Cross licked his lips. "I'm not going to get into a big lesson here but we're all people of strong resolve and determination. When that *passion* and energy is twisted and broken, we become shattered. I've never heard of anyone pulling out of it."

Now I gasped. David looked at me, quizzically. "What is it?"

"Like Forate." I said loud enough for the room to hear.

August Cross looked at me with a sad look on his face. "Yes, Jason. Like Forate. He was shattered by Morbal."

David and I glanced at each other. He raised his eyebrows.

"Like I was saying," Cross went on, "We haven't gotten much out of Kara but we've learned a bit about this mysterious Olorus Orb."

I looked back at the Governor.

He grimaced. "We need to find it and destroy it. I'm not exaggerating when I say the object is otherworldly. I don't know how it works exactly but I know it's nearly completed and Samantha Forrest wants to use it to shatter more of us... maybe all of us."

One of the agents a couple rows in front of me blurted out. "Impossible!"

"Quiet!" Chief roared.

Cross put his hand out, gesturing the big man to calm down. He looked at the agent who'd spoken, a short, stocky, Asian man. "We've only uncovered the tip of the iceberg in regards to the complexities of our world, Agent Yen. At this stage, nothing is impossible."

There was a period of silence in the large room. Now I figured everyone must have known about the hailiorum. David and I seemed to have been the last to find out. Figures.

"So, Forrest wants to use the orb to gain power and influence. For now, that seems to be her aim. She wants Aswain and we need to stop her." Cross's face changed from a stern look to a smile. "On the plus side, our search for information has gone extremely well. We have leads on dozens of people and we need to keep it up."

I let out a breath I didn't even realize I was holding. The good news was literally a breath of fresh air. I was a bit troubled by the whole 'shattered' thing. Christ, to think any one of us could be turned into another Forate, or worse. Awful. It happened to Kara, it could happen to me too. I remembered how hard Morbal tried to break me. Forrest did too. I forced the thoughts away and listened to Cross.

"I'm confident we're moving in on Forrest and we'll find her soon." He said in an upbeat tone. "Her operation was shaken up after her failed abduction attempt. And we rescued Kara. Forrest is scrambling now and she's going to make mistakes."

I rubbed my chin, thinking. The woman didn't seem like one who would scramble. I hoped the Cross was right.

He went on. "Before I open things up for questions I want to remind you of our objectives. We need to find Forrest and the Olorus Orb. We also need to continue our search for her followers. We have to stay vigilant. We're all targets now. She could try to get at any of us and she'll kill you if she thinks you're of no use to her." He closed his eyes. "I've known Samantha for a long time." He opened them again. "She's a monster who may have been shattered herself. Don't allow her to sway your mind. Being shattered is a pain and torture far worse than we can imagine."

"Poor Kara." I heard Sarah say. She hung her head low.

Cross sighed. "It's clear that Kara was set up. Forrest had specific aims for her." He locked his gaze on me. "I believe it was the same with the other agent she targeted. Luckily things turned out to our advantage."

A strange feeling ran through me. So I was right, I was a target. But why?

Cross gestured a uniformed man who had his hand in the air. "Yes, Lieutenant?"

The guy cleared his throat before speaking. I couldn't see much of him other than his brown hair. "Who exactly is Samantha Forrest? The PDRI has nothing on her and I think we'd all like to know who we're going up against."

"That's a hard question to answer quickly." The Governor began. "Some of you know more about the hailiorea than others. I would recommend studying over your information discs on the subject."

My eyes washed over Fier and her expression remained neutral. She said she didn't like the documentary, now I wanted to watch it more than ever.

"Anyways," Cross continued, "I'll just say that she was part of the Tehlasrin resistance with me and many others. She's charismatic, bold and intelligent. She was a good friend and a great partner."

His voice was heavy with sadness and slowly fell to a whisper. I wondered just how much history he had with the woman. Cross's gaze fell to the floor. "At some point they got to her and she changed. She grew obsessed with power." He shook his head. "She became a controller."

I looked around at the faces surrounding me. Half seemed to know what Cross was talking about and half looked as dumbfounded as I felt.

"Who're *they*?" A gruff voice asked.

A woman piped up from across the room. "The Osilea?"

"What's a controller?" A third voice asked.

Cross bit his lip and shook his head. "I'm sorry. There's no time for an entire history lesson. Just know that she's dangerous, deadly, ruthless and powerful."

"Sir, sorry, August." Another man started, correcting himself after his raised hand was acknowledged. "You mentioned our investigations were going well. Can you expand on that?"

"Yes. We're tracking several people who're listed as missing." Cross said. "They seem to be congregating. It's our guess that they're banding together for their next move. We plan to be ready. Chances are Forrest will be with them."

"Isn't she smarter than that?" A female voice asked from behind me.

Cross raised an eyebrow. "We'll see. Like I said, she's always been bold."

I was surprised when David raised his hand. I shouldn't have been, he wasn't the quiet type and liked to stand out. I preferred to remain unnoticed.

"Yes, Agent Holt?"

"Do we know what else the Orb can do besides expand Forrest's influence?"

"Hmm." Cross looked behind me toward the far corner of the room. I turned to follow his gaze. Bill was there with a surprised look on his face.

The old man stood up. "The Cup has gathered that the Orb may be a connection to the ethereal world." He paused. "Inner space or outer space. It's hard to explain but we believe such devices are connected to other dimensions, maybe other worlds."

I could tell the whole room was confused now; no one had a clue what he was talking about. Bill bit his lip. "In short, the Orb could have multiple uses. It's powerful and dangerous. From our studies and research, we've learned that objects like it are incredibly difficult to create and even more difficult to destroy." He looked around the room. "It may be a bridge, window or doorway into other realms."

I shook my head, totally lost.

"It's also possible it might not even work at all." Bill added quickly. "We don't know. The Orb could merely be an artifact of sheer superstition."

"At any rate," Cross boomed, "we don't want it in Forrest's possession."

"Mr. Cross." A small voice said from the front row on the other end of the room. "What are these rumors we're hearing about the man in black?"

A bell went off. That kid, Eric mentioned a dark dressed man. I darted my gaze from the direction of the person, I think it was a man, who asked the question, to Cross.

The Governor blinked. "I've heard about him too. We're looking into it but having a hard time pinpointing him. I don't know who he is or why he's here. It's clear he's with Forrest and he's not a citizen of Aswain."

"I heard he can disappear for long periods of time." I shifted my gaze to the latest speaker. He sat directly in front of me. "Not like some of us that can hide ourselves for a few seconds. This guy seems to be able to literally go invisible."

"I've asked Kara about it." Cross said. "All she tells me is that he's a master of stealth. Kara has always been good at keeping herself unseen. This stranger seems to be far beyond her abilities." He raised his eyebrows. "That's saying something."

"We'll deal with the bastard when he shows himself." Chief boomed.

I nodded. "Hell yes." I spoke loudly without thinking.

Chief looked at me with an odd, amused expression.

Cross nodded. "Remember, ladies and gentlemen. We're the protectors of this place. If the world is ever going to break free from the shadow it's trapped in, Aswain's going to be the first beacon of light."

I agreed and felt a tinge of pride build inside me. Fighting and working with such a large group of likeminded people gave me sense of belonging. I'd never felt that before. It was nice.

"We're freedom's last line of defense." Cross continued. "Remember that, believe in Aswain and believe in yourselves. We'll overcome this obstacle."

The group expressed agreement. Some clapped.

The Governor let out a deep breath. "Ok then, let's get to it. You'll be hearing from your superiors soon. Thanks everyone."

With that, the meeting was over. The information wasn't groundbreaking and could have been relayed through an e-mail or a memo. I figured the real point of the meeting was to get everyone together to bolster our resolve. A pep rally of sorts. I didn't know about anyone else but it worked for me.

David looked at me. "Damn."

I looked him in his eye. "Yea."

-

David was called away shortly after Cross's meeting to resume the search for Solso and Vans. He wasn't happy with having to head out on his own but I was glad I didn't have to go. I could only handle so much bonding in one day.

I didn't envy the boredom my friend would have to endure but at least he got to take the car. That meant I'd be taking the familiar, crowded light rail home after work. At least I thought so.

It was coming up on four o'clock and I'd spent a good portion of the last hour and a half checking bios. It was hard staying focused on work. I kept mulling over the information Cross shared in the meeting.

My office phone brought me back to reality with a series of chimes and beeps. When I answered I hardly had time say anything before Ashe's demanding voice ordered me to his office.

I sighed after hanging up the phone and looked at the clock. A sinking feeling formed in my gut telling me I'd be putting in some late hours. I was vaguely familiar with where Ashe's office was and headed in its general direction.

My cube sat next to a bunch of other agents' work stations. They were usually empty since my team spent so much time out on assignment. Right now they were all empty leaving no one there to ask directions from. I exited the cluster of cubes through a security door and entered a spacious lobby still deep within the building.

I was surprised to see several people there that weren't on the intelligence team. I was more surprised to hear raised voices between them and then even more so when I recognized Mayor Krane and Mr. Otaki. Seeing the business man reminded me I'd forgotten to run a check on him. Damn

"No, I will not keep my voice low, Mayor Krane!" Otaki exclaimed. "I can't do this anymore!"

I moved in closer and noticed the others in attendance were watching the two. Mayor Volkov from Tauros was there, looking as sharp and rich as ever in his flashy silver suit.

Krane was saying something to Otaki which was just quiet enough to escape my ears. Otaki snarled and shoved his left hand against the Mayor's chest. A mistake.

I was on the little man in a heartbeat, removing his hand and spinning his body around so I had the arm locked behind his back. The man struggled to free himself and I looked into the eyes of his two bodyguards. I couldn't remember their names but they were the same two from the other night: The intense looking Indian woman and the young beady-eyed guy with extra wavy brown hair.

Rage filled their eyes and I could tell they were just barely smart enough to keep from attacking me.

Volkov marched up quickly, followed by several others. "Problem?"

"No problem at all." Krane said with a genuine laugh. I felt his hand on my shoulder. "Let him go, Agent. It's ok."

I eased up and stepped back alongside Krane.

Otaki whirled his little body around to face me and rubbed his sore arm. "I swear… I," he cut himself off. Rather than speaking, he just looked at me and shook his head. There was something odd about the look. I couldn't pinpoint it but I could only guess it was disgust.

"I'm sorry, Mr. Otaki." Krane said happily. He gave me a pat on my back. "He has a zealous knack for protecting me."

Otaki growled.

I mostly ignored Krane and stared down at Otaki with as much intimidation as I could muster. I spared a couple glances at his two guards standing behind him, letting them know I hadn't forgotten they were there. This builder was up to no good, I just knew it. Maybe it was my special magic talent. I was certain he'd set me up the week before and I wanted to throttle him for it.

"Excuse us." Mayor Krane spoke loudly and gave my arm a light tug, ending the stare down between Otaki and me. I blinked and looked at him. The happy, youthful, Elvin-like face smiled. "I'd like you to meet Mayor Volkov."

"We've already met, Simon." Volkov said in his thick Russian accent.

Krane straightened his back. "Oh." He looked at me and moved me, ever so slightly away from Otaki. "Have you met Mayor Burr from Ravenfall?"

I cut my eyes around to look at the woman. I guessed she was in her mid-thirties. She wore thick glasses and a proud smile. She was attractive but her large smile was almost too bright and her cute little ponytail seemed odd, like she was trying too hard to look younger than she really was. She winked.

Ravenfall, it took a moment to recall, was the capital of Shard Isle, the vacation getaway spot for Aswain citizens. I nodded at the woman. "No, we haven't met. Hello, Mayor." I reached out and she took my hand.

"How about Mayor Fjorn from Lionsgate?" Krane pulled me over to meet the man. He was tall, thin and there wasn't a hair on his head. We said hello to each other and Krane was on to the next introduction.

I stopped him. "Sir, I'm sorry but I need to be on my way. Captain Ashe is expecting me."

Krane gave me a hurt look. "Oh, I'm sorry. I don't want to hold you up. I'll introduce you to the rest of Aswain's mayors some other time."

"Good." I nodded again and was about to head off when Krane continued.

"We're meeting, the other mayors and I along with some prominent business men to cover some of the information August shared in your meeting today." He raised his eyebrows. "Seems it's time for everyone to be up to speed on Forrest."

I looked around at the collection of executives and politicians and felt my face flush. I couldn't help it. I didn't like or trust any of them. "Good idea." I said finally.

"We're also settling that development dispute. Otaki had the rights but backed out so we're handing the proceedings over to Mayor Burr." Krane's wide smile was back and he spoke with a sudden incredible excitement. He was like a male cheerleader.

I looked again at Otaki and grew even more suspicious. Why on Earth would he suddenly back out? Was the whole meeting a pretend move just to set up another agent? Me specifically?

"Burr was in construction and city planning before she got into politics. She'll do a fantastic job. You should see the wonders she's done on Shard Isle. It's a heavenly retreat." Krane went on and on.

I put my hands out in a 'slow down' gesture. "Sir. I really *have* to go."

"On your way then!" Krane gave me a playful shove. "Have a good meeting."

"Thanks." I took a couple steps then stopped and turned around. "Do you know which office is Ashe's?"

Krane burst out into a laugh. "No idea. I hardly ever get to come down here. None of us 'non intelligence' people do." He made small quote marks with his fingers. "The only reason we're here is because Otaki doesn't feel safe anywhere else. Such a paranoid man."

Otaki said something sinister in a language I didn't understand. I understood the tone though. Dick.

I waved. "Ok, thanks anyways." Then darted away.

-

I found Ashe before I reached his office. He was pacing back and forth and looked at his watch when he saw me. He grumbled something under his breath. The only audible word was "Follow." He led me back past the large command center and through yet another heavily bolted security door I hadn't noticed before.

We marched down a ramp that went another thirty feet or so deeper underground. It felt like we were plunging into a cave except the lighting at the end of the ramp was bright and intense.

There were a few armed guards posted past the door and beyond them was a long row of containment cells. Each was nothing more than a nine foot by nine foot cube with a bed, a toilet, thick looking metal walls and dense plastic glass separating the inside from freedom. The room sent chills down my spine and brought back memories of my time in captivity.

"Down here." Ashe said in a cold voice. I followed him past several cells and my pulse quickened. I didn't like the place and it almost made me sick to my stomach. "As you probably guessed, this is our headquarters' detention center."

I nodded, unable to speak. We reached the end of the long row of cells. They were all empty except the last one. I looked in and my eyes boggled. Had I not known any better I would never have been able to recognize Agent Kara Childers.

Her cell was a wreck. The bed was completely destroyed, the sheets and pillow torn to shreds and there were stains all over the floor. I guessed those had come from whatever food and drink she'd been given.

Kara herself looked no better. I felt waves of repulsion and pity looking at the woman. She sat on the floor and rocked back and forth in torn clothes. Several chunks of hair were missing from her bloody scalp.

"Jesus." I uttered through clenched teeth.

"We've tried to feed her, sedate her, keep her clean and maintain some semblance of order in her cell but she won't sleep and goes into continuous fits of rage." Ashe sighed. "God, she's a mess."

I looked at Ashe and saw genuine sadness on his bitter, old face. Then I glanced back at Kara. She was quietly crying to herself.

"Chief and Cross have been trying to learn anything they can from her but she's getting worse with each day." Ashe slumped his shoulders. "We don't know what else to do."

I licked my lips and wiped the sweat off my palms. I spoke, unable to take my eyes off the poor crazed woman. "Why are you showing me this?"

"Come." Ashe moved toward the wall opposite the line of cells. I turned to follow and spotted a small desk with a computer, a phone and flimsy looking chair. "Everyone else is out on assignment tonight. I'm putting you on guard duty."

"*What*?" I nearly shouted.

Ashe gritted his teeth. "Enough of that! Someone has to keep an eye on her. Since you're not doing anything useful tonight, it's going to be you."

I wanted to protest but I knew it wouldn't do any good. Now I really wished I'd been sent away again with David. For some, this may be an easy assignment but for me… the cells, the walls, the closed feeling and the torment Kara was going though all hit too close to home. The space was clean and brightly lit and reminded me of the asylum I'd nearly lost my mind in.

Ashe could see the anxiety on my face. He lightened up a bit. "Look, Sworn. It's only for a few hours, ok? Just keep an eye on her, see to it she gets fed. Not that that will do any good, and use the computer to pass the time."

I turned to look at the monitor without blinking, my mouth hung open and I nearly forgot how to breathe. I felt like I was having a panic attack.

"There are some bios for you check up on and some leads you can go over." Ashe continued. "Just stay busy and you'll be relieved in no time."

"How long?" I asked in a defeated sounding whisper.

Ashe nodded, firmly. "A few hours, no more."

I nearly jumped out of my skin when the man placed a sturdy hand on my shoulder. "It's alright. Those guards will stay posted at the end of the hall. Just try to relax, watch her then go home." He paused. "And feel free to take part of the morning off. Sleep in a bit."

If I weren't so freaked out by the whole situation I would've been surprised at how kind the Captain was being. Instead I just swallowed and sat myself down in the little chair. It was cushioned but far from comfortable.

"Ok then. We're short staffed tonight and I'm in charge so I need to get back to the command center. Call me if you need anything." With that, Ashe walked back the way we'd come.

My eyes darted around, taking everything in. I looked at the bios and couldn't even remember what I was supposed to do with them. I glanced at the monitor without really seeing it. Finally, my gaze drifted over to Kara. The woman wasn't crouched on the floor anymore. Instead she was standing up against the glass staring at me. It was hard to tell but I thought I saw a hint of a smile.

I swallowed hard. This was going to be a long night.

# Chapter 16

I hated the detention block. It was awful. The lighting was pale, the smell was sterile and the feel was hard and cold. All I did was stare into empty space for the first hour while my brain whirled in circles, threatening to totally freak out. It look a great deal of effort to keep enough wits to stay calm.

Kara staring at me every second didn't help matters either. Her gaze amplified the creepy factor of the place. Still, I eventually started to grow curious about who the woman was before Forrest got to her. I keyed her name into the computer database.

Kara Childers, twenty-six years old, born in Florida. She had as normal a childhood as one could expect these days and became part of a GU resistance group in her early twenties. She fought with the band for a few years before they were all killed or captured.

From there she spent a year in prison, not an asylum like me but a regular jail. I didn't know which was worse. I'd heard horror stories of other Tehlasrin criminal institutions. Her escape then exodus to Aswain was similar to mine and she made it to the island ten months before me. Like David and me, Cross quickly assigned her to the intelligence team.

I looked at the curious H level notation and saw she was a nine. I wished I'd remembered to ask what that number meant.

I was willing to bet a week's wage it had something to do with the hailiorea.

There were notes of several good, heroic deeds she'd accomplished, helping others and serving as an upstanding security guard. She was labeled as a kind, gentle woman with a calm demeanor and quick smile.

I looked at a couple photos of the woman from her file and then glanced at the woman in the cell. Nothing alike. She'd been completely twisted and her mind nearly destroyed. I closed my eyes, terrified and sickened that someone could be perverted and brainwashed in such a way. What a nightmare.

"She likes you, you know."

I opened my eyes and looked at Kara, shocked to hear her speak in such a cool, calm way. She was barely standing, swaying a little while leaning heavily on the glass wall. A maniacal smile replaced the tormented frown she'd formerly had on her battered face.

I knew she was talking about Forrest and ignored her. I wasn't in the mood to hear about how much the 'Mistress' liked me nor was I prepared for whatever head games she had in mind. Now wasn't the time.

She continued nonetheless. "You like her too, don't you? How couldn't you? She's so beautiful, a real angel."

I didn't answer. My instinct and nature was to argue but I knew it'd be pointless. It would end up being like debating a drunken alcoholic on how drinking was bad for you.

I sighed, through with Kara and decided to check up on a different target. I clicked back to the home page of the search engine on my computer and typed in the name 'Wang Otaki.'

After skimming through the man's summary I was annoyed that nothing seemed out of the ordinary. He was from China, had just passed his sixtieth birthday and was born into wealth. He was also listed as brilliant with an IQ near two hundred and an H level of eight.

He started his own construction business and worked for the GU a few years building various government buildings. I raised my eyebrows after reading he'd been one of the first people brought to Aswain and was also one of its first citizens. He used a large sum of his wealth and knowledge to build a good chunk of Tauros.

I snorted then let out a small growl.

Clean bio or not, I still didn't trust him. The lack of any suspect evidence put a damper on things though. I remembered hearing other agents talk about how they'd tracked targets through their bank accounts and decided to do the same.

A few clicks on the computer and my phone would send me a message every time Otaki purchased something. I'd know what he was buying and where he was buying it from. The move was invasive and felt wrong, maybe even illegal but again, I was an intelligence agent going with my gut. To hell with it.

Good. I leaned back in my chair and crossed my arms in a satisfactorily triumphant way. I felt better after accomplishing something worthwhile. It was only when I looked away from the monitor that I remembered where I was. I'd been so tied up with Otaki, I forgot about the prison cells around me. Kara held her zombie like stare on me.

"Let's go see her together." Kara said in a monotone voice. "I promise I won't be jealous. I'm sorry I pointed a gun at your head."

I shook my head. She was obviously lying but I wondered if she even knew it. Her mind was so far gone I was surprised she could even talk at all. I checked the time. 6pm.

A weak laugh seeped out from Kara's cell, forcing me to shift my eyes back on her. "The tables have turned, Sworn. Now I'm the captive."

I stared and considered the woman. Her plan of meeting with Forrest... Could it be useful? Maybe she could lead us directly to her. I quickly figured Cross and Chief had already considered that though. Chances were Kara had no idea where her mistress was. And I bet they didn't want to risk giving her even the slightest opportunity to escape.

"Why won't you talk?" Kara made a labored move and planted both hands, palms first, on the glass. Her breathing became labored and I thought her knees were going to buckle under her own weight. "You met her. She really *likes* you. That makes you special. Come on, we can love her together. Think of her body. So soft, so perfect. Her skin, her eyes, her hair. So beautiful, so sexy."

I gave my temples a good massage while Kara went into a series of purrs and moans, her head swimming with images of the monster she loved so much. I knew because the same pictures were running through my brain. I swore under my breath and fought to block them out.

My eyes glanced over the monitor again and caught the name 'Otaki.' I looked at Kara, suddenly having an idea. "Do you know Wang Otaki?" I asked.

"Who?" She snapped. "Who the hell is that? Who cares? What is he, your lover? Is that why you won't go to her right now?" Her speech quickened with each word until I was nearly unable to understand her.

I made a painful, disappointed face. So much for that theory. All the question managed to do was work her up into a frenzy.

Kara belted out a horrible scream and her legs finally surrendered. She fell hard to the floor and writhed around for a stretch of time.

Damn it, I couldn't help but feel sorry for her. I stood up and walked over to within an arm's length of the cell's thick glass wall. I glanced toward the guards seated at the far end of the long room. They weren't paying the slightest attention to Kara or me.

"Hey." I spoke quietly. "What's wrong?"

She let out a loud whimper and clutched her arms around her midriff. "My stomach, it's burning from the inside. The fire… it won't stop burning. It hurts! I need her right now. I need her so bad! Only she can make the pain go away." Tears streamed down her scratched, bloody cheeks.

I moved a little closer. "Kara, you need to eat. You haven't had anything in days."

"It's not the effing food, idiot!" She spat at me and started rolling around on the floor. "God, it hurts!"

The woman continued to thrash around, rolling through the debris that littered her cell and didn't show any signs of stopping. I couldn't take any more. This was pathetic. The whole situation was inhumane.

I turned and headed toward the seemingly blissfully ignorant guards, calling out to them half along the way. "Ok, that's it!" They turned to me, confused faces all around. "Hey! How about we get her some dinner?"

The nearest guard rolled his eyes in a way that made me want to punch him in his face. "Ok, fine. Just more for the cleanup crew to take care of."

I snarled. "Now!"

Another of the three guards picked up a nearby phone and spoke into it. He looked at me after hanging it up. "It's on its way, Sir."

I gave each guard a meaningful stare then marched back to Kara's cell. When I reached it she was huddled in the far corner leaning over the toilet. She was spitting into the bowl still going on about how much she needed Forrest.

"Kara," I said loudly. "She doesn't care about you! She was only using you."

She looked at me like horns popped out of my head. "What the eff are you talking about? You're a fool! You don't know anything! She loves me!"

I clenched my hands into tight fists and slammed them on the glass. This whole thing was starting to feel disturbingly personal. "No! She's a manipulative bitch! Look at yourself! She made you like this. Trust me, I know. The same thing almost happened to me." It felt weird being this open but I didn't care, I wanted to help.

"You only wish she chose you!" Kara curled her lip and crawled over to me, just on the other side of the glass. "You're jealous! You're nothing! You're not even worthy of looking at her!"

I dropped down my knees so our faces were level. "God damn, Kara." I spoke softly. "I'm sorry. I wish you could see past her crap. She tried to get to me like she got to you but I was lucky enough to escape." Her silence encouraged me. Maybe I was getting through to her. "This isn't good. This isn't you. Can't you see that?"

"Why are you saying this?" Her tone matched mine. "Why can't you just let us live with each other?"

I let out a deep breath, unsure what to say.

Kara gently placed her right hand on the glass. "Please."

I lifted my hand to meet hers through the glass. We shared a connection and looked into each other's eyes. I could almost see the sane Kara tucked deep down and away...

A man showed up with a tray of food and called out, startling me. I looked at him. He was young and his wide eyes were fixed on Kara. "This is for Agent Childers."

I nodded. "Thanks. Set it down and go." The guy obeyed and almost sprinted toward the exit. I looked back at Kara. "Alright, now you're going to eat some of this."

She scoffed and defiantly turned her head away like a bratty four year old.

"Listen." I said, not completely sure what I was going to say. "You eat this and we can talk all about Forrest, ok? I'm here to listen."

When Kara turned to face me again she showed a wicked grin. "Will you sit with me while I eat? Here, inside my cell?"

I squinted, weary of the crafty woman but also eager to jump at any chance to help her. Damn that hailiorum blood. She desperately needed food. I spoke with more confidence then I felt. "Sure."

I stood up and turned to shout at the guards. "I want two of you down here!"

The three men debated who would go and who would stay. Finally, two of them headed toward me. The nearest one spoke. "Yes, Sir?"

"Open the door, let me in, then lock it back up."

The other guard raised his eyebrows. "Sir, that's a bad idea. We don't have authorization for that."

I gave the man one of my most intense 'Don't dick with me' looks I could muster. Pulling out and handing my ether pistol to the guard, I said, "*I'm* giving you authorization. Open the door. Now."

The first guard fumbled with the electronic lock and I scooped up the tray of food. Kara was on her knees watching the whole ordeal. The other guard pulled his sidearm and aimed it at the woman. I wanted to tell him to put the gun away but I figured it was better to be safe than sorry. I remembered seeing her in combat, how she could zip in and out of vision. Surely she was too weak for that now.

The door opened and I quickly entered. "Close it!" I heard the bolts lock into place and stood staring at Kara, breathing her air, suddenly feeling stupid. It was a fight to regain my resolve. She didn't move while I set the tray down and lifted the overturned mattress to set it on its frame.

I turned to Kara, gesturing the bed. "Have a seat. It'll make eating easier."

The woman raised an eyebrow and slowly obeyed while I went back for the food. I shot a glance at the two nervous guards who now both had their weapons drawn. When I turned back toward Kara she was wincing in pain again, rubbing her belly. I sat down next to her.

"Ok, here. Have a bite of this." I cut off a piece of what looked like Salisbury steak with the plastic fork and lifted it to her mouth. The dish also had a pile of sliced red skinned potatoes and green beans. Everything was liberally covered with gravy and smelled quite delicious. I became faintly aware that I hadn't eaten anything since morning.

Kara opened her mouth and took the bite. I smiled which was a mistake. The gesture pissed her off and she spit the meat out onto the floor. I sighed. "Why are you doing this? This isn't a game, damn it."

To my surprise, Kara laughed. "It doesn't matter. I'm going to die."

I curled my lip. "Yea, we're all going to die. Now shut up and eat. Remember, we had a deal." I speared a potato slice with the fork and brought it to her lips. "Eat."

She snatched the bite off the fork, chewed and swallowed.

"Good." I said. "Now, what do you want to talk about?"

"The only thing worth talking about." She said and I cringed. "My Mistress is the only thing worth even thinking about. I guess -" She cut out and groaned, clutching her chest. I thought she was choking but then she spoke again. "You don't understand. You -"

Kara suddenly whipped her left arm out and knocked the tray onto the floor, scattering her dinner all over the place. Her face contorted into a twisted expression of pain. Her mouth was wide open and looked like it was going to scream but no sounds came out. She fell to the floor and convulsed.

"Jesus!" I shouted, turning to the guards. "Get a doctor down here now!"

The men fumbled around, unsure what to do.

"Call for help, for Christ's sake!" I screamed at the top of my lungs then fell to the floor beside Kara. I grabbed hold of her body and fought to contain the violent spasms so she didn't hurt herself further. All I managed to do was keep her head from continually banging against the floor.

"Kara! Kara!" I yelled. "Easy, easy! What's wrong?"

She wailed in anguish. "My stomach's exploding! AH!" An animal sound of pain echoed from her throat. Her eyes locked onto mine. "Jason! I'm sorry!" Her eyes welled up with tears that raced down her contorted face. "Oh God, I'm sorry! You're -" Another deep rooted grown, "right. This isn't me."

"Shh," I tried to calm her and spoke softly, gently stroking her bloody, sweaty forehead. "It's ok. Just hold on. Help's coming."

Kara gave one last convulsion and tugged herself out of my arms, rolling and crawling away. She lifted herself to her knees then crumpled to the floor. She didn't move after that.

"Kara!" I yelled, racing over to her and checked for any signs of life. Nothing; no pulse, no breathing. "Oh no, come on! KARA!"

I didn't notice the cell door open or the medic that rushed in. By the time the doctor had me away from Kara and was able to examine her, the former agent was dead. The doctor looked at me with an unreadable expression.

I sat on the bed, held my head in my hands and trembled. "Jesus…" I felt like hell, sad Kara had died. But even more than that, I was scared, terrified again that what had happened to her could happen to me.

-

I woke up to the sound of arguing voices and when I opened my eyes, the bright lights burned my brain. I'd momentarily forgotten where I was until the recent past came back to me. I felt sick to my stomach all over again.

Kara had died in my arms after a fit of pain and torment. Ashe had rushed to the cell and immediately suspected that I'd murdered her. He accused me of either taking revenge or of being in league with Forrest, killing the woman before she could give Cross any useful information. So much for trust.

Naturally, I grew defensive, loud and aggressive, standing my ground and defending my innocence. The Captain got in my face and I shoved him. He wouldn't have fallen had he not tripped over Kara's lifeless body. He hit the back of his head on the cell's glass wall and started bleeding. I had no intention of going that far but what's done was done.

After that I was herded into my own cell. I shouted in protest and challenged Ashe with giving me a Cell Truth test so I could prove I didn't kill Kara but he didn't want any part of it. The man was pissed as hell and I knew he enjoyed locking me up.

I nearly lost my head after the locks bolted shut. I was back in prison like Morbal's asylum, like Kara before she died. Yep, I was close to panicking into a fit of rage. Instead, amazingly, I was able to suck in and blew out a series of breaths, venting a lot of the adrenaline out of my system.

I sat on the bed and thought about David, and Fier, and Cross. Surely they'd get me out of here. I hoped. Thankfully, I maintained control long enough to lie down and drift to sleep.

Now I was awake again and my eyes adjusted to the light. Once I was able to see, I read the time on my watch, 1:30am. I'd been out for around seven hours. My stomach rumbled in protest after sitting up.

Ignoring my hunger, I tried to make sense of the loud, angry voices having at each other. They came from further down the detention block where I couldn't see any faces. I recognized Ashe's voice but not the other's.

I started pacing around in my cube, angry, frustrated and sad for Kara. I hadn't been this bad off since breaking free of the asylum. Fed up with it all, I slammed the heel of my fist into the glass wall.

The arguing stopped and I heard footsteps headed my way. The first person I saw was August Cross. His face was flushed red and his eyes blazed with intensity. The recently shortened hair on his head was a disheveled, twisted jungle. He pointed at the nearest guard. "Open the door." Then he looked at me. "Jason, sit on the bed."

Part of me wanted to plead my case right then and there, but the seriousness on Cross's face told me I should just shut up and do as I was told. I sat down and the Governor was right next to me seconds after the cell door was opened.

The situation was oddly similar to the way I sat next to Kara only now I was the prisoner. I shuttered.

"Look in my eyes and give me your hands." He ordered. I hesitated and furrowed my brow. "Hurry, Jason. There's no time."

I reluctantly put my hands out and he grabbed them. The strength of his grip surprised me. I kept my eyes on his but still noticed Ashe and Chief file into the cell. They were watching us intently.

Cross was quiet for a few seconds, studying my face. He drew in a deep breath through his nostrils before he finally spoke. "Did you kill Kara Childers?"

I blinked and shook my head. "No, I didn't -"

"Do you know how she died?" Cross interrupted.

"No."

"Do you know who killed her?"

"No, I don't." I was beyond uncomfortable and my hands were starting to hurt under the pressure from Cross's grip.

He nodded. "One more. Are you glad Kara is dead?"

"No! I didn't want her to die. I tried to help her." I grimaced.

Cross abruptly let go of me and stood up, there were tears in his eyes which baffled me. He turned to look at Captain Ashe. "He's fine, just like I knew." Then he regarded Chief. "Prepare the team and ready the attack. I want you on the move in fifteen minutes."

Chief stood up even straighter than normal and clicked his heels. "Yes, Sir."

My mouth dropped open and I was now completely awake. "Attack?"

Cross looked at me. "I want you suited up in full assault gear and in the command center in ten minutes."

"Why, what's going on?" I stood up and headed out of the cell, excited and confused as all hell.

Cross ignored me. "Ashe!" he roared. "Take Jason to the armory."

"Let's move!" Ashe commanded, bolting off for the doors leading out of the detention block.

I stuttered a bit, moving forward but turning back to look at Cross a few times. I was completely lost and wanted to ask more questions.

The Governor pointed a finger at the doors. "Go!"

I turned and ran after Ashe, shouting. "Why are we going to the armory?"

"Shut up. Hurry up!"

Lost, I eventually quit trying to make sense of things. Something was obviously going on and there was a battle to attend. Ashe and I ran through the command center and into yet another heavily secured room filled with body armor, helmets and weapons.

My eyes dazzled over the display. Every wall was stacked with offensive and defensive items. There were a dozen other men and women in the large room, suiting and arming up.

Ashe ran to the nearest wall and starting throwing gear at me. "Put these on, quickly!" The heavy bullet-proof chest armor slammed into me and would've knocked into my head had I not gotten my arms up in time to block it.

I studied the piece for a second and looked around to watch the others putting similar items on. It wasn't rocket science and I had the chest gear on in no time. There were also pieces for my shoulders, forearms, thighs and shins. Finally, Ashe lobbed over a thick pair of combat boots.

After I slid my feet inside and laced them up I looked up and saw a helmet being held in front of my face. I snatched it, put it on then looked at the person who handed it to me. It took a second to recognize David's serious face behind the faceplate of his own helmet.

"Hey!" I said loudly to my friend. He was already geared up. All the armor, including the helmet was a dark beige color. "What the eff is going on?"

David studied me. "Are you armed?"

I realized my weapon was still with the guard. I shook my head. He rushed over to the weapon rack and handed me a nightstick, two ether pistols and a few extra recharge packs. "They go here, at the bottom of your chest piece." David said pointing at a row of small slots, pockets of sorts on the armor.

"Two minutes!" A voice roared. It was easy to make out Chief's base heavy tone.

I checked my pistols to make sure they were loaded then placed them each into their own holster on the sides of my thighs. I tucked the additional ammo into the pockets and slid the nightstick into its home against my right thigh. I looked up at David, expectantly.

He checked me out and did a quick rundown of my gear. David moved behind me and tugged on the fasteners around my arms, legs and chest. When he was done he gave me a hard knock on my head. "All set. Let's move."

I didn't know where we were 'moving' to so I followed my friend and a line of others back out through the armory doors and into the command center. Everyone filed toward the mysterious doorway with the word 'TRANSPORT' planted above it. Butterflies did more than dance in my stomach as I marched in line through the doorway.

After a brisk walk through another hallway I couldn't believe I found myself in what appeared to be an underground rail station. There were several train cars there with combat gear wearing soldiers marching in. I blindly entered the same car David went into.

There was a buzz of voices but I couldn't make out any of the conversations. My head was whirling. It was one thing to go into a battle when you had time to plan and mentally prepare yourself. This was totally different. I had no idea where we were going or what we were doing. That and I had only just now discovered this new subway system. In short, I was bewildered.

I could hear and feel the drum of the train's power coming to life. My heart raced and I could feel it slamming over and over against my ribs. It was like the feeling you get slowly heading up, up, up the first ramp of a rollercoaster, anxiously awaiting the big drop-off. Only this was a hundred times more intense.

David turned to me and spoke. He had to shout in order to be heard over all the commotion. "I heard this train can take us to any major point in Aswain, fast as a jackrabbit."

I nodded but doubted he could see the gesture.

"Calm down! Breathe. We're moving soon."

I moved closer to him and shouted. "Moving soon to where?"

Chief's voice echoed loudly through the rail's intercom system. "Everyone, turn on your ear sets and microphones. Only, repeat *only* speak if absolutely necessary. We want the channel clear for commanding officers."

My face flushed, having no idea how to activate anything on my helm. I turned again to David for guidance but he was lost too.

I felt a hand shove into my right shoulder and turned to face its source. I saw the top of a helmet, the person was several inches shorter than me. The face of the helmet looked up and moved into view. It was Fier.

"Here, switch them on like this." She hollered. "David! Effing pay attention!"

The woman reached up under the left ear covering of my helmet and flipped a couple switches. A second later I heard a calm, collected voice, which I pinpointed as Captain Durn speaking in my ear.

"Departing for Eaglebase in T-Minus one minute." His voice was cool and even. "Assume transport positioning."

"To talk, you press this button on your microphone." Fire tugged on a small arm that jutted out from the side of the helmet toward my mouth. "It's best you two just shut up and listen, stay off the airwaves but if you have something to report, this is how you do it."

"Got it!" David yelled.

Fier nodded. "Good, I'm off to check on the others."

I quickly reached out and grabbed her arm, bringing her back closer to me. "Where are we going?"

I could see her wicked, sexy little smile through her faceplate. "We've got her. We're going to take that whore out!" With that she pulled her arm away and headed off.

I turned to David and could see the surprise on his face. Durn's voice droned in my ear. "Set all weapons to the highest incapacitate setting. We want to keep the death count to a minimum. The highest setting could be fatal to anyone with heart conditions but we can't risk any lower setting. The renegades are assumed to be heavily armed and dangerous."

Holy…

# Chapter 17

I wasn't exactly sure how fast the train moved but the thing was hauling some serious ass. The distance from headquarters to Eaglebase was around forty miles and we covered it in about ten minutes. On the way, Durn gave a quick overview, telling us the base was actually a huge etherspring generating factory, the largest in Aswain.

I remembered Fier telling me a bit about how the clean, efficient energy was generated from the actual citizens living here. The prospect still gave me the creeps but I didn't know how much of it I actually believed. Right now, in all the armored excitement, none of that really mattered.

We exited the train and quickly cat-walked through a maze of otherworldly looking devices and gizmos. It was like we stepped onto an alien spacecraft. There were large, electronic beams running along the walls and across the ceiling which gave off a soft, eerie, purplish glow. Here and there were bright, bulbous orbs of light that surged with power. The damn things hurt my eyes if I looked at them too long. The whole place didn't seem real.

We were ordered to move as quietly as possible into position so as not to tip off any would-be bad guys to our presence. Chief was setting a trap and I sure as hell didn't want to spoil it.

Apparently, there were numerous tips from sources that confirmed Forrest planned to take down the facility. Eaglebase generated enough energy for all of Aswain and then some. The excess was exported, used for trade with Tehlasrin. Knocking out the plant would be a large blow to the island's operations.

The base rested at the foot of the towering, mountain range called the Light Peaks. They made up the entire northern part of Aswain's main island. To the south of the factory there were three main entrances. We were ordered to fan out in teams and cover the doorways.

There were scores of other guards in hiding, stationed outside the base, scattered throughout the heavily wooded area. The plan was to let Forrest's team move in and unwittingly get themselves surrounded. It sounded simple, but I knew better. Battles were never simple and I hoped my fellow soldiers were good at their jobs.

David, Fier and a dozen other agents were directed to the westernmost entrance with me. After passing by another series of buzzing purple energy beams and futuristic looking, high tech control panels, my team set up position. We tucked ourselves in, taking cover behind walls and terminals.

The train we'd exited minutes before was now being loaded up with the civilian workers for quick transport to safety. Everything seemed well planned and now all we had to do was wait. I took deep, calming breaths and heightened my senses, preparing myself for the upcoming battle.

David was in a machine-like mode, all serious. I wasn't used to seeing him this way but it was the same look he had when he freed me from Forrest. The cheerful, smiling David was tucked away.

Several quiet minutes passed and I couldn't help but wonder if the attack was actually coming. It was possible the tips were wrong or maybe Forrest had caught wind of our trap and pulled back. Still, I didn't lower my guard in the slightest.

"All teams are in position." Durn's electronic voice said in my ear. "Stand by."

I looked at Fier, she was the commanding officer in our group. Her eyes blazed with intensity and she held incredibly still, like a cat ready to pounce on an unsuspecting bird. She, like David, had shifted into a force of sheer, lethal will.

I checked my weapon for what seemed the hundredth time. It was fully loaded, set on the highest stun setting and ready as ever to unleash its energy. The blasts ranged in color from white, the lowest setting, to deep, dark blue, which was the kill mode. I knew from some shooting practice time I'd put in that the current setting would launch a soft blue colored beam that would knock a full grown man out for hours.

Durn's voice started again, it was still calm but quicker, with a hint of excitement. "Confirmation, repeat confirmation. Enemy forces have entered the premises. The front gates have been compromised."

My palms started to sweat. I wondered what happened to the poor saps stationed at the gate. Maybe there wasn't anyone there. That would look stupidly obvious. I fought the urge to ask Fier about it but the woman didn't even blink after Durn's last message. Christ.

"Enemy units approaching all three entrances!" Durn exclaimed. "All field commanders move in to position! Outer guard teams watch for reinforcements."

My heart thumped hard against my ribs as I gripped my weapon tighter. They were just outside the large sliding doors. I swore I could almost hear them.

"Base teams, prepare for intruders. Open fire only on your team commander's order!"

A moment later the large doors began to vibrate. I held my breath, listening to a faint buzz that came from the metal plates. The center of the doors began to glow a soft orange color, slowly turning to yellow then bright white. Finally a huge circular section of the door gave way and crashed to floor. The bang made a noise was especially loud compared to the utter silence from a moment before.

They'd attached some sort of thermal device to the doors and melted a large chunk away. The technology showed Forrest's team was well equipped. I grimaced.

A helmet wearing head peeked through the hole and I nearly blasted it. Fier's voice whispered in my earpiece, stopping my trigger finger. "Hold."

A second later, there was another head, then a third. The first intruder boldly stepped through the compromised doorway and scanned the area, keeping as low as possible. He moved in further, quietly searching.

The man must have been confused as all hell; things were too quiet. I was afraid he'd smell the trap and retreat back through the hole but luckily, or maybe unluckily, he took a few more steps inside before waving his arm at his companions, beckoning them inside. More people came through.

The group was made up of both men and women and were about thirty yards from our concealed positions. I could see they were armed with pistols and old model shotguns. Oddly enough, some didn't look like they were armed at all. Why..?

Next, the intruders with guns slinked back, out through the hole while the unarmed men and women stayed inside. I looked at their eyes. They looked hallow, dead, sad, almost love struck… like Kara.

*Oh no.* Sick, tickling tingles ran up and down my neck. I remembered how dreadfully crazy Forrest's people were. They were willing to do anything for her. Anything. Anything to others or themselves. The realization, or was it premonition, washed over me. They were going to blow themselves up.

I looked at Fier, she still hadn't moved. She didn't see what I saw. Eff it, there was no other way. I wasn't going to wait for any green light, I aimed my weapon at the nearest unarmed attacker and squeezed the trigger. The body fell to the ground and then all hell broke loose.

Blasts erupted from my entire team knocking down intruders left and right. The bodies were unconscious before they hit the floor. They fired back but they didn't hit anything. We were well covered.

Fier roared into her microphone. "Damn it! Who fired? We weren't ready!"

Durn's voice joined in. "Western team! What happened? We weren't set!" His voice paused. "Field commanders move in! In, in, in!"

Whatever else the Captain was saying got drowned out by a sudden huge, thunderous boom. The building shook to its foundations. The vibrations rattled my brain and my teeth. I was surprised none of them shattered.

Other explosions sounded from elsewhere in the factory and I knew I'd been right. The other teams waited too long. The attackers at the other entrance points had got in far enough to set off their explosives. Damn it.

I switched my microphone on. "This is Sworn. Unarmed enemies are strapped with bombs, take them out now!" The attackers in our area were all either asleep, dead or had retreated. I sprung out from my cover and dashed for the melted doorway.

"Sworn!" Fier yelled. "What the eff are you doing?"

I looked outside. Aswain guards were picking off the last of the intruders that had assaulted our wing. I could see the burning red glow from further down the base that lit up the dark night. Smoke filled the air.

Turning back to my team, I spoke into my microphone. "The central and eastern entrances have been broken!"

Durn's voice drown mine out. "All western team! Ensure your zone is protected and then move eastward! Field teams, remain outside. Base team move back toward the central control station!"

David swore, loudly. "C'mon. Back this way! They're in the base! Listen!"

I strained my ears through the thick helmet covering them and the buzzing voices in my head. Sure enough there was gunfire coming from inside the plant.

Fier waved her arm. "Let's move!" She bolted through the doorway that lead deeper into the base.

We rushed in a mad dash, with little organization, toward the center of the plant. By now the plant's sprinkler system was on in full force, drenching everything. The deeper in we moved, the smokier and hotter it got.

"This is Fier." She barked into her mouthpiece while running. "West team is nearly at the control station. Center and east may be out of commission."

No duh.

"We'll set up and dig in once we're at the station."

"Roger that." I shouldn't have been surprised to hear Chief's voice. "I have my team here now. We're monitoring you."

"Almost th -"

Fier was interrupted by a volley of bullets that suddenly screamed toward us. A couple of my unit mates howled in pain and dropped to the floor.

"Cover!" Fier roared.

Those who were able to do so kissed the ground and returned fire. The streaks of light from our ether weapons whizzed through the smoke filled corridor.

I was lying in a cold puddle firing my weapon when I saw an indentation cut into a nearby wall. I scrambled for cover, raising myself to one knee, continuing to shoot. I was almost there when I felt what seemed like a giant fist, ram itself into my chest. I flew backward and crashed to the ground.

"Jason!" I recognized David's frantic voice. He tugged on my ankle and slid me over to the wall. It was hard to see through the smoke and the dark but I felt his hands on me, running over my chest.

Breathing felt ok and nothing really hurt. "I think I'm alright." I sat up and discharged my weapon some more at the attackers, sparing a quick glance at my chest. The body armor was smoldering. A bullet had slammed into me, right over my heart. The vest saved my life.

David let out a string of obscenities then turned to the attackers. To my horror, he stood up, armed each hand with a weapon and rushed the onslaught. The blasts from his pistols were dark, dark blue, full kill mode.

I considered hollering at him to get his dumb ass down but instead, I got to my feet and followed his lead. Screw it. Better to die fighting than huddled in a corner. To my surprise the rest of my able bodied team joined the charge. Under David's berserk lead, we mowed over the attackers.

I mostly paid attention to my own targets but every time I caught a glimpse of David, I saw how fluid his movements were. It was like a choreographed dance. Each step ended in a killing blow. He *couldn't* miss and a good dozen attackers fell to his fury.

The hallway fell silent a couple beats later. Fier raced up beside David and me. She swore out of shock and then turned back to her team.

My eyes followed her gaze. There were four from our group lying on the ground, sopping wet, a couple writhed around and groaned in pain. The others were still and silent.

"David, Jason, Keely, Craig, Sumir," she listed, "come with me. The rest of you stay here and guard them." Everyone nodded and Fier headed further down the hallway. "Move!"

"Main station is under attack!" Chief's voice echoed in my ears, through the static and gunfire. "We're being hit hard!"

My heart raced even faster. I didn't know what exactly would happen if Forrest's army accomplished their mission and I really didn't want to find out. I ran harder, passing the rest of the small group.

Fier yelled at me. "Sworn hold up! The control station is just up ahead."

I stopped and saw the latest corridor we'd been rushing through led to an open room. The smoke hadn't reached this area yet but water was still coming down heavily. I had to wipe my faceplate off to see clearly.

"Chief! This is Fier." She spoke after she and the others caught up with me. "What's the situation?"

Chief bellowed in response. "We're tied -" His voice was drowned out in gunfire. I could hear the blasts in my earpiece and up ahead of me. The effect created a disorienting loop of feedback.

"Repeat!" Fier shouted. "We're just outside the west door. I can't get a visual of what's happening in there!"

"- just me and a couple others left." Chief went on. "Bastards have us pinned down -" Static. " – about ten of them holed up behind the main panel junction."

"Ok." I looked at the young Captain. She nodded and huddled us up. "Quickly. Through the door there'll be a large panel with control devices on it to our right. That's where our targets are. Chief's team will be to our left about fifteen yards away." She looked off into empty space and spoke into her microphone. "Sir, we'll be moving in ten seconds. Give us some cover then lay low."

"Roger."

Fier looked back at us. "Let's get them."

I reloaded my weapon and pulled my second out. "Let me go first."

"Me too." David said without hesitation.

Fier didn't argue. Hell, someone had to go first.

I heard the distinct sounds of ether pistols going off in rapid succession. That was our cue. Chief's team was distracting them as best they could. I hoped it would give us the opening we needed.

We followed Fier's lead and inched up to the doorway. She held out a hand. "Three, two, one. Go!"

I let out a mostly involuntary battle yell and rushed in with as much determination, focus and inconsiderate, brave stupidity as I'd ever remembered having. I blasted the first intruder before she even knew I was coming. The second started to turn to look at me. The third was zapped by David's weapon. The rest tried to reorganize themselves but we had them completely off guard.

There were nine of them that had Chief's group pinned down. Now they were just a bunch of unconscious or dead bodies sprawled out under the spraying water. I looked back for Fier.

She was huddled over one of our team, Craig I believe, who'd taken a bullet to his throat. I grimaced as the man let out an awful gurgle before falling silent. Eff.

Chief popped his head up followed by the two soldiers left with him. "Secure the room! Take cover and watch the doors!" He ordered. "Durn, do you copy?"

"Yes sir!"

I saw Chief nod. "Captain, what's our status?"

"The field teams have reported an all clear outside and are now fanning throughout the base looking for any remaining threats." Durn spoke quickly. "The outer perimeter teams have moved in to take their place."

"What about the eastern and central teams inside the base?" Chief's accent was getting thicker as he spoke.

"We have some losses, Sir, but most are either injured or unconscious." Durn paused and I thought I heard faint voices giving him updates. "Medics are rushing in to tend to all the wounded... for both sides."

"Good." Chief said with a hint of relief. "No one lower your guard, we're still under attack here."

I sighed and looked at David. He was still on full alert scanning both doorways intently. I moved over to him and took a peek down the door opposite the one we'd charged through. Nothing.

Finally, and quite suddenly, the sprinklers stopped which created an odd silence in the room. I heard Fier and Chief talking but I couldn't make out what they were saying.

David let out a small groan and I turned to look at him. He was studying his right forearm and I could see his sleeve was bright red.

"Damn it, you're hit!" My eyes boggled.

David shook his head. "It's not bad, just stings like a bitch. I've had worse."

"Bull, you'd better get that bandaged up. No bleeding to death, ok?"

His smile returned for a brief second. It was wiped off his face when a bullet soared right between our heads. "DOWN!" He yelled.

We ducked behind the same panel that had offered cover for the attackers we'd taken out only on the opposite side. Ether bolts flashed and flew over our heads at the attackers. The enemy assault ended and I heard feet scampering away. They were retreating.

Chief spoke between shots. "Fier, after them! Take two with you. The rest of us need to guard the main terminal!"

Fier ran without hesitation. "David, Sumir! With me!"

I wanted to go too but held my ground. This could be a trick to weaken the main station. I watched the three rush away through the wet, dark, smoky hallway after the fleeing fanatics.

"Hold your position, ladies and gentlemen." Chief said in a calm tone. "There's a large security force headed here to back us up. Hold tight."

I was almost about to let out a sigh of relief but before I could there was a high pitched, feral scream that filled the air. A woman with blonde hair practically flew into the center of the room. Her form moved so fast, it was mostly just a blur in my vision. I could only barely make out that she was armed with two curved blades.

She zipped up in front of Chief, quicker than any of us could react and swung the sharp edges up at the big man's chest, slashing clean through his body armor. The gear seemed to melt off him and Chief's big body fell to the floor.

The woman turned toward me. She had a triumphant, familiar look. Her face was one I'd been in love with for a few minutes once. Samantha Forrest.

I gritted my teeth and fired both weapons at her without hesitation. It seemed stupidly easy for her to move out of the way, avoiding the blasts. She whirled away and I lost track of her, desperately scanning the room.

One of the guards that had been with Chief collapsed to the floor, clutching his blood gushing throat. Forrest had soared in and sliced his neck in the blink of an eye.

"Huddle up, get together!" Someone, a woman, yelled.

It was as good a plan as any but I had no idea where everyone was. Rather than running out into the open I hunched down, aimed one weapon toward the ceiling and the other out in front of me.

Another scream filled the room, telling me someone else had been murdered. I couldn't take anymore. I wasn't going to hide and let my companions get hacked to bits. Screw this. I stood up and darted my eyes around the room.

A couple other guards were doing the same. I noticed Chief was sliding across the floor, inching closer to his dropped weapon.

A blinding fast foot came out of nowhere and knocked my weapon out of my right hand. The attack was followed by a hard fist that slammed into my left and sent the other weapon away. She was fast but I was still able to see the sharp points of her blades coming at me. Not that seeing them did any good. I was stumped with no idea where to move. My body tensed and prepared to die, pissed as all hell. The last thing on this effed up planet in this stupid life I was going to see would be Samantha Forrest's insane, hideous smile.

A split second later... I wasn't dead. The two blades were yanked out of her hands and tossed away. The woman was forcefully pulled to the ground.

After the shock of relief left my system I was surprised all over again to see August Cross straddling on top of Forrest. He had her pinned to the ground with his right hand firmly around her neck. She didn't budge.

I studied the Governor's face. It was red, angry and angry as hell with daggers for eyes and gritted teeth. I'd never seen a face so filled with rage before and that's saying a ton. His words were a deep, dark hiss. "It's over!"

The woman's eyes studied his face. "It's only over when you kill me, my love. Do it now, while you have the chance... and the will."

I watched Cross's chest heave up and down. I was no mind reader but I knew he was seriously thinking about doing it. Thinking about digging his fingers in deeper and squeezing the life out of her. The internal debate loomed for a time.

"Now!" Forrest yelled. Then, to my surprise, she laughed. Cross squeezed tighter, choking the laughter away.

Chief was standing over the two now, hunched over, arms straddling his chest and gasping for his own breath. Cross didn't look up as he jutted his open left hand out at the big man. "Gun!"

The Scot didn't hesitate and handed his weapon over.

Cross snatched it, thumbed the power setting, jabbed it against Forrest's stomach and fired.

He stood up and staggered away, letting out a series of grunts and bellows. I looked down on Forrest in disbelief. I didn't believe Cross had it in him to kill the woman and I was right. Her lungs were moving; she'd been heavily stunned.

Who could say if I was right to be partially disappointed? The woman should be killed. On the other hand, I was glad Cross restrained himself. That was his character, his nature. He wasn't a killer. Christ. I didn't know how it happened but I'd grown to have faith in the man. Faith that he was better than me, more principled. The better man wouldn't kill or harm a defenseless, beaten human. I would've.

"Sir. She needs to die!" Chief said. Well, it appeared the two of us had something in common.

"No." Cross said, turning around to face us. "We don't have the Orb. She knows where it is."

Fier, David and the other guard, Sumir returned from the hallway. "We got one of them, Sir. The other ran into a team of our soldiers and was knocked out. It looks like – Oh! Mr. Cross?" She spoke with sheer surprise.

"Is that *her*?" David asked looking down on Forrest's unconscious body.

I nodded. "Yea."

"Hmm," David shrugged, studying the sleeping woman. "I don't see the big deal."

"You didn't see her in action." I sighed and looked at Cross. "Or him."

Chief interrupted the conversation. "You two! Out of here. I don't even want you looking at her."

I furrowed my brow and regarded the man. Even with two, bleeding gashes on his chest he was still large and in charge. I wasn't sure what the big deal was but I didn't have the energy to argue.

"Durn! Report!" Chief roared. When he saw David and I hadn't moved yet, he marched over and forcefully shoved us away. "Go!"

We sauntered out of the room and passed several soldiers, detention officers and medics rushing around the base. Durn's voice filled my head again.

"The base is secure. The fires have been put out with minimal damage to operations. Security teams are posted throughout the base. The medical staff is attending the wounded."

"Good." Chief said, this time even more relaxed than after the last report.

I was hardly aware during our blind walk. It was long and far enough to reach the outside. We didn't speak and I didn't think. My adrenaline was exhausted and I was coming down hard. I yanked the helmet off my head and tossed it aside before plopping my ass on the cool ground.

My friend discarded his own helmet then ripped his sleeve off his right arm, examining his wound. "Just a graze. I told you. It's nothing."

I nodded and looked off into the distance. The smell of the forest mixed with the smoke from the fires created an odd ambience. Mostly though, it felt good to be outside and free from the threat of death.

David collapsed beside me. I saw him fumble around with something in his pocket and I'd have never guessed in a million years that he'd pull a cigarette out and light it up.

"What the hell?" I said. "I didn't know you smoked."

David chuckled. "Only after sex and war." He looked at me, raising an eyebrow. "Want one?"

"No thanks. Those things will kill you."

My friend smirked. "If it's not one thing…"

I laughed and rested a tired but sturdy hand on his shoulder, looking out into the woods. We made it out alive again. David and me, unstoppable.

# Chapter 18

Every inch of Eaglebase was thoroughly checked over before we were finally loaded back onto the transport for headquarters. David drove us home when we were cleared to leave. Good thing since I probably would've killed us both if I were behind the wheel. My nerves were shot and my body was beat up.

It was four in the morning by the time we reached our apartments. David and I stumbled off toward our own homes without a word. I hardly remember collapsing into bed and was out like a light.

Cross gave us the rest of the day off, thank goodness. We were told to remain on alert, though, in case any emergencies popped up. I doubted anything would happen. Something could go down, Forrest might have other minions scattered around, but I was too tired to care.

I slept in late, soundly until 1pm. The piddly nap I had before the battle the night before didn't help any. Kara's disturbing death and the alien cell had me tossing and turning the whole time. The past nine hours of sleep were just what the doctor ordered.

A buzz from my mobile phone finally pulled me awake. I wanted to ignore it but had to check if anything was wrong. I fumbled around for the device before checking the screen.

Wang Otaki had purchased a new suit at *Mr. Right's*, a clothing store in Tauros. So, he was back home…

Since I was up, I gave David a call. He sounded like a zombie when he answered, groaning more than speaking. I asked him if he'd heard of any signs of retaliation from Forrest's bunch and he told me he hadn't. Then he told me Cross reserved the entire space at Clovers for a private get together for the agents and some other security members. The meeting was to start around 8pm.

I yawned and nodded, not caring David couldn't see the gesture. After ending the call, I sluggishly got out of bed, exercised, showered and finally acknowledged the burning emptiness in my gut. After a large, healthy Cheeseburger and a pile of fries, I went back home and slept a few more hours. It was glorious.

After lounging around for a while, it was time to head out. The cool outside air had a clean, fresh smell to it and the night sky was full of stars. I felt good. I was rested and almost proud as I headed for the bar. My mind was clear and I could finally appreciate the fact that the psychopath, Forrest, was captured.

When I arrived there were a few guards standing outside the doors turning people away who weren't on Cross's list. The rejected guests grumbled, briefly about how unfair life was and I laughed. There were scores of other bars in the area. They'd just have to manage tonight.

I gave the guards, two men and a woman, my name and showed my ID, my real ID. They smiled and let me in. It was only five minutes after eight but the place was already packed. Almost all the tables had been cleared out so more people could fit in. Everyone stood around talking and drinking. I saw most of my fellow agents and some of the captains mixed with others that weren't familiar.

The Cup was there, sitting at their regular large booth, of course. That puppy faced, little man was there too and so was that loud, plump, lip-smacking guy who got mad if you said his name wrong. I couldn't remember his name so I made sure to not make eye contact with him.

I didn't know whether to gasp or laugh after seeing Chief. He was actually wearing civilian clothes; blue jeans and a tight, red polo shirt. The man looked even bigger outside the uniform but not quite as intimidating. He was also smiling which was just bizarre.

The mood of the place held an odd blend. Upbeat music played through the speakers and everyone enjoyed each other's company but there was a lingering sadness in the air. I could see it in people's faces; eyes were a little droopy and smiles weren't in full bloom. I knew it was remorse for those who'd died. We'd won, but there were always costs.

I cut through a cluster of people on my way to the bar and ordered a beer. The bartender, and owner of the place, whose name I also couldn't recall, recognized me and handed over a large glass filled with the house beer. I reached for my wallet and he put a hand out, palm first, stopping me.

"No charge, friend."

I gave the man a little toast-salute and started to turn around.

"Jason!" I was blindsided, nearly dropping my beer, when someone, a woman, wrapped her arms around me and squeezed. I pulled back to see who the abrasive person was only to see Fier Wren's cute little face beaming at me.

"Fier?" I asked, taking in her big, bright smile and watery eyes. "Watch yourself. You almost tackled -"

"Oh shut up! Give me a real hug, you fool!" She latched her arms around me again.

I squeezed back this time, surprising myself, enjoying the embrace. I'd never been much of a hugger but having Fier in my arms was amazing. If heaven existed, this was surely a small slice of it. I even went so far as to close my eyes for a few heartbeats, letting the woman's warmth and special power wash over me. Damn, so nice.

I opened my eyes and saw David standing behind her, smiling at me. I quickly broke off from Fier, backed up and then rubbed the back of my neck. Silly, but I was afraid he'd pick up on my feelings for her. I wasn't ready for that, I wasn't even sure how to handle the feelings myself. Quickly regaining my composure, I shifted my gaze back to Fier. "Ok. What was all *that* for?"

"For this morning, at the base, you ass!" She gave an admiring smile and a little swat on my shoulder. I didn't know what she was talking about and didn't care. All I wanted to do was grab her again and lay my lips on hers. I refrained, barely.

"What did I do?" I asked instead, gesturing toward David. "He was the hero. Did you see the way her plowed through those guys in that hallway? Or how he knocked out the team that had Chief pinned down?"

"Yes, I saw all that." Fier said, still smiling.

I could feel the muscles contort on my confused face. "Well then... What's the big deal?"

"Maybe she's just happy you're alive, Buddy." David said, happily.

Fier smiled at my friend then back at me. "Well yea, that and I watched the tape. I saw what you did at the beginning of the battle."

David laughed. "You saved us all."

Fier nodded vehemently. "Had you not acted, those bastards would have blown us to bits. How did you know?"

Oh yea, I'd forgotten. I thought back to the start of the fight and shrugged. "I saw they didn't have any weapons. I figured something was up. Simple."

"That," David began, "and you're just enough of a screw up to blatantly disobey orders and start shooting." He raised his own glass. "See, you're a hero. To the screw ups!"

I raised an eyebrow and chuckled. "Bah. I just didn't want to lose any limbs. Nothing heroic about that."

Fier smiled again. "You dope!" She hugged me again and kissed me on my cheek.

I was already in a strange emotional place and the female attention, especially from someone like Fier, was nearly overwhelming. That being said, I loved every second of it.

We pulled apart again and I worked on calming myself down, taking a huge pull on my beer. It was hard to know what to say. I wasn't a hero. I only did what anyone with half a brain would've done.

"Finish your beer. I'm buying the next round." David said, giving me a nice, friendly smack on my back.

I looked him in his eye. "They're free tonight."

"I know." He laughed.

Fier wasn't paying attention. She was busy glancing through the crowd. A quiet, somber hum escaped her.

"What's wrong?" David asked.

She held quiet and made me feel uncomfortable. I tried to play the upbeat optimist for a change and looked around the room. "Good turn out."

She shook her head. "Not good enough. I'm just seeing who's *not* here." Her shoulders slumped and she bit her lip. Swallowing hard, she made a dismissive gesture with her hand. "Never mind. Sorry. I'm not gonna be a downer."

Fier smiled but I could see the tears forming in her eyes. My god, the sad sight made my heart feel like it weighed a thousand pounds. I wanted to grab her, hold her, and tell her how impressed I was with her during the fight. I wanted to cheer her up and remind her that she'd saved a lot of us too. The crowd would've been even smaller without her strength and leadership. But I didn't, I chickened out.

She knew the dead a lot better than I did. I remembered how sad Sarah had been for Kara. Thinking of which… "Did you guys hear about Kara?" I asked. My head drooped a little.

"Yes." Fier said in a grim tone that matched mine. "More than you, I bet."

I looked into her sweet eyes. "I doubt it."

"Huh? What happened?" David asked, both confused and interested.

Before we could answer, a bunch of people started cheering and our attention was pulled to the opposite end of the bar. August Cross was there, standing on a table so he could be seen by everyone. He had a smile on his face and threw out a few quick waves.

Someone handed him a beer and he took a large gulp from it. The crowd cheered even louder and Cross burst into laughter. He passed the half empty glass to the nearest open hand, Chief's.

"Thank you." I could hear him say. The ambient noise level dropped after he spoke. "But too much of that gives me bad dreams." He looked out at everyone and I stared back. He surprised me again that morning. It was incredible how quickly he showed up out of nowhere and stopped the crazy whirlwind of death that was Samantha Forrest. He pinned her down with one arm and kept her from taking my head off. Amazing. I wasn't sure on the specifics, but it was obvious Cross had a lot more of those special powers than me.

"First off, I want to say thank you. You handled an incredibly serious threat this morning and for that we're all in each other's debt." Cross was beaming. He didn't seem to dislike public speaking tonight. "I know challenges will continue to arise along the way. There'll be forces trying to stop what we're doing. This was our first real obstacle and you performed wonderfully." He clapped his hands and the crowd joined him.

He nodded as the clapping quieted. "We've lost several friends, though. Friends from both sides of the fight." He paused and let out a little snort. "We need to remember that almost all of our foes in this morning's fight were our fellows. They have families and friends too." He straightened a little, balancing himself on the table top. "Most of us knew Captain Ashe. He fell defending the eastern entrance."

It felt like an ice cold hand suddenly slapped me across my face. I was no fan of Ashe but he seemed like an ok guy just doing his job. Shame.

"And," Cross went on, "Our friend, Agent Kara Childers died the night before in her cell."

Confused looks and puzzled murmurs passed through the group. My gaze shifted from Sarah, who had tears rolling down her cheeks, to Fier whose face was now strong and resolute, appearing like it was etched in stone, to David. My friend was looking back at me, eyes wide and mouth open.

Cross continued. "I'm sorry for those of you just now finding out. Our medical teams ran tests on her body and they found she'd been poisoned." He sighed. "Before they could find the specific reason for her death, the prisoners we collected from Eaglebase began dying one after another."

I shook my head. "What?" I said loudly.

"Put shortly," Cross continued, "It appears Forrest had all or most of her followers implanted with horrible devices that could be triggered to release a deadly substance into their blood. The prisoners from this morning died relatively quickly. Kara held on for a long time due to the strong hailiorum H count in her blood. Her body fought hard to heal itself."

I shook my head, feeling sick to my stomach. Part of the H count mystery was solved but that didn't matter right now. I thought of Kara convulsing and writhing in pain. That was Forrest's doing.

"The devices begin releasing their toxins if their timers aren't reset by whoever has the controls. In these cases, that person is most likely Samantha Forrest." Cross shook his head, his face was grim. "We found the one inside Kara had actually been detonated. The small amounts of toxin weren't enough so someone set the thing off, releasing too much poison for her body to fight."

I was both sad and pissed. So that's why Kara was in so much pain. Christ. Now I really wanted Forrest to die. What a effing monster.

I glanced at Fier and saw her studying my face. She could see the pain I was in and her eyes showed concern. No. No sympathy or charity for me. I didn't deserve it. I wasn't the one who died. Trying to look tough, I puffed out my chest and scowled.

She didn't buy it. Her right hand reached out to grab my left. She squeezed and I squeezed back. If I were a poet I'd describe how touching the gesture was. Instead I'll just say it was a perfect, beautiful blend of strength and tenderness.

"I'm sorry." Cross said. "This should be a happy night. We defended the base and defeated Forrest. I don't want to sound pessimistic but we all deserve and need to know the facts. Our tech teams determined that someone had to be close, inside our headquarters, to set off the device inside Kara. We'll find who was responsible."

My entire body slumped. Great. Another mystery.

Without thinking, I pulled my hand away from Fier and rested it on my hip. My eyes darted through the crowd. Maybe the traitor was mixed in with the group, here, right now.

"Anyways." The Governor continued. "Let's focus on the positives. As I'm sure most of you've noticed," Cross gestured the bar, "the drinks are free tonight. Rex and I have all your tabs covered."

There were a few cheers, none louder than that from old man Jack.

"Make sure you get home safe and take your time getting to work tomorrow." Cross hopped off the table but I could still hear him say "Have a great night!"

I wanted to rush up and thank the man for saving my life. I wanted to know how he took Forrest down so quickly. But he was already swarmed by people and I decided to let him be, one less distraction.

Fier turned to David and me. "You guys talk, I'll get us some drinks."

I nodded. "Ok."

David finished his glass. "I guess you didn't really have time to tell me about Kara, huh?"

"Not really." I shrugged. "And maybe I didn't really want to talk about it."

David nodded and rested a hand on my shoulder. "I hear ya. It's cool, just a shock, you know?"

"Too many shocks." I shook my head. "Kara died then I was blamed for it, put in a cell. Then the battle and you tearing around like a demon out of hell... How the eff did you learn to fight like that?"

"Training and natural talent I guess." David laughed. "I'm not that good. I did get hit, remember?" He showed me his right forearm; it had a small bandage over where the bullet had grazed his skin.

I rolled my eyes. "*Natural* talent. It's that hailiorum stuff. I don't know how natural all that is." I paused, getting my thoughts back on track. "Then you and Fier saying I'm some sort of hero."

"You are."

I sighed. "Yea right."

"Ok" David rubbed his chin. "Ready for another juicy little tidbit?"

"What? Something besides the fact that we may have a traitor in our midst?" I asked with an eye roll.

"Yea. Other than that." David's face showed that smartass smile I knew all too well.

I braced myself. "What?"

"I think Fier has the hots for you." David moved his eyebrows up and down in a 'hubba-hubba' kind of way.

"WHAT?!" I couldn't contain the surprise.

David put a finger to his lips. "Shh. I don't know for sure but it sure looks that way. I have a real knack for picking up on these sort of vibes."

"But," I shook my head, "but what about you?"

David straightened up. "What about me? It's her choice Yea, I like her but oh well, she's not the only woman on the island, you know."

I made a funny face. "Who cares, I don't care for her that way anyways."

David roared with laughter. "Bull! You must really think I'm a blind idiot, huh?" He laughed even louder.

Flustered, I nearly jumped out of my skin when Fier showed back up holding three pints of beer. I quickly grabbed one. "Thanks."

What was I going to do with this latest news? Did she really have feelings for me? Did I for her? Yes, I knew I did but how strong were they? I was horrible in relationships. Did I really want to start one up now amidst everything else going on? What would happen if and when things went sour? How could I work with an ex-lover who happened to be my commander? What if they went well? How could I function in life or death situations with someone I cared about in the middle of danger with me?

"You two are quiet." Fier observed. "Were you talking about me?"

David laughed. "Don't you wish?"

I laughed too, weakly. "I'm just thinking."

"There they are!" A happy voice called from behind me in a very proper English accent. I knew it was Mayor Krane before I saw him. The man made his way to us and joined our little circle. He wasn't alone. The little puppy faced man was by his side.

"I read a little of the recap from the battle report." Krane went on, his oval eyes were wide and his smile stretched from ear to ear. Boundless enthusiasm. "I wasn't the least bit surprised to read you three were instrumental in victory. IN-credible!"

I felt more than a little embarrassed. The Mayor's volume was attracting attention our way. I put a hand up in a 'calm down' gesture and shook my head. "All in a day's work."

"You see?" Krane addressed the little man. I swear he must've only been three and a half feet tall. "What did I tell you? Brave, capable and modest." He looked back at us then clamped a hand on my right shoulder and David's left. "My heroes!"

"I see." The puppy man spoke in a voice that was a bit deeper than I expected.

"How are you doing, Charlie?" Fier asked the small guy. He lifted his glass of beer, it looked gigantic in his little hand. "Excellent."

"Oh! I'm sorry." Krane boomed. "I haven't introduced you yet. Charles, I've told you all about Jason Sworn and David Holt." He looked down on the little man then back at us. "Jason, David, this is Charles Black. He's one of Mr. Cross's technology heads. He helped figure out how those dreadful poison devices worked."

I looked at Charles and raised an eyebrow. Instantly interested. "Really?"

"That, and Charlie is the fastest person I've ever met." Fier added. "You should see him run."

"Oh," Charles laughed. "It's nothing really. Just a mix of my hailiorum ancestry and the fact that I weigh around eighty pounds." The group laughed.

I wondered if he could move as fast as Forrest. The way she zipped around that morning seemed inhuman. Mostly though, hearing Fier's voice brought my mind back to the prospect of having a more intimate relationship with her. How the hell would that work out? Could it?

I took another large drink of my beer. "Screw it." I said under my breath. Of course, everyone heard me. I was rewarded with a collection of stares. I waved them off. "Forget it. I'm just thinking… thinking way too much."

That was it. I decided dwelling on any romance with Fier at this time was stupid. If things worked out, great. If not, oh well. I was tired of it. The whole thing could wait until recent events settled down and I could think clearly.

"So, I hear you two are new to Aswain but have already made names for yourselves." Charles said to David and me.

I shrugged. "I suppose so."

"Stop it, Jason!" Krane said. "You've done more in a short time than anyone I can recall. We'd love to get more people like you two. That would be spectacular."

He looked at Fier. "Captain, I hope you appreciate how talented these gentlemen are. They're very special and gifted hailiorea."

Fier chuckled. "Keep talking. Their heads will get too big for their thick skulls."

Krane seemed taken aback by Fier's jest. Charles giggled. She looked at us while speaking. "I'm joking. I'm proud of both of them." She paused. "They're some of the best people I've ever busted out of captivity." Her eyes locked with mine for a second before we both quickly looked away.

I growled on the inside. Ridiculous. We were acting like teenagers.

"Captivity?" The little man asked, curiously.

David scoffed. "Forget about it. It's personal."

I furrowed my brow and nodded. I didn't feel like going over the deep darkness inside me with the little guy or Krane either.

"Well," the Mayor boomed, "Perhaps someday we'll all be close enough to share such stories. Charles is a dear friend of mine and a gifted mind."

I looked him up and down. "Ok."

"Alright then." The Mayor seemed to realize he'd outstayed his welcome. "Drink up, have fun. I'm going to go catch up with some other friends. Come on, Charles."

The two marched off and I let out a sigh. "That guy is just endless energy."

"Yea, sorry I brought up the captivity thing." Fier said.

David rubbed her arm and patted her back. "Don't worry about it. Maybe I'm just overly sensitive about it. Not your fault."

"Same here, I guess." I said with a snort.

Fier nodded, still looking ashamed. "At any rate, I'll try to remember to keep my yap shut."

The three of us enjoyed a few more drinks together and time passed quickly. Fier talked a little about some friends that had died and gave a very generous recount of Ashe's past heroics. I also shared the story of Kara's last moments. We opened up to each other and connected on emotional levels. It felt alien for a bottled up person like me but it was the most enjoyable company I'd ever had. Before I knew it, it was well past midnight.

Fier gave David and me a hug goodnight and went to speak with a very drunk looking Chief before heading home. I told my friend I was heading home too and he told me he'd be sticking around a bit longer. He offered me the keys to our car which I quickly refused. I was far too drunk and still not comfortable driving.

I said goodbye and before I was out the door, David was meandering over toward a cluster of attractive young women. I chuckled, wondering how many cigarettes he'd be smoking in the near future.

The outside air was brisk, quickly chilling my ears and nose. I headed for the nearest light-rail station. The thing was usually pretty empty this time of night. Good.

"Mr. Sworn?"

I looked up and clenched my jaw when I recognized the old man. Pat Crow was huddled up under a thick coat and headed over to me. His bulging, wild eyes kept darting around, seeing things that weren't there.

"What do you want?" I hissed.

He swallowed. "I'm wondering about your progress. Have you found it?"

"Listen, you old bastard." I stepped up closer to the man and growled. Part of me wanted to punch him in his gut. "That damn thing nearly got me killed! I almost lost my job and could have been locked up or thrown out."

"You found it? Where is it?" He nearly squealed with excitement.

I huffed. "Are you even listening to me? I'm not helping you anymore. I'll get you your money back as soon as I have it on me. It's over!"

The old man nearly crumpled to the ground. "Oh." He shivered and I thought he was going to start crying. "I understand. I'm sorry, Mr. Sworn." He looked me in my eyes. His face was grave and defeated. "Keep the money. I don't need it."

I shook my head when Crow nearly jerked in fear.

"Oh God, it's him!" He called out, pointing at empty space. "The shadow man! Help me!"

I glanced around, there was nothing there. Crow was trembling now, frozen with fear. I grabbed him by his shoulders. "Go home old man, there's nothing here."

"Wait!" He straightened up. "It's gone!" He quickly turned to look at me and our noses almost touched. "Do you have it? It's the only thing that makes them go away!"

"What?"

I was about to ask another question when the pug faced puppy man, Charles zipped in out of nowhere. He'd been running if you can call it that, it was more like 'flashing' through the air. He stopped and looked at me quizzically.

"Agent Sworn?"

"Hey." I said, dazzled by the man's speed.

Crow pestered me. "Is it in your pocket? Please give it to me! I'll do anything!"

I turned to the crazy man. "I don't have it! Go now, before I take you in for questioning."

He backed up a few steps looking defeated again. "That wouldn't help me either." He quivered. "Goodnight, Mr. Sworn."

I watched the man walk off then regarded Charles. "Heading home?"

"Yes." He smiled. "My home is a quick sprint from here."

There was a sudden flash of light coming from across the street. At first I thought it was gunfire. I instinctively put myself between the flash and Charles. A glance later I could see someone standing outside a car with what looked like a camera.

Without turning I spoke to Charles. "Move along. I'm going to check this out."

"Looks like you have some fans, Agent Sworn. So long!"

I heard a strange whoosh and the little man was gone. I stormed over to the car and shouted when I was half way there. "Ok, what the hell are you doing?"

I curled my lip when I finally recognized the person. It was that woman, Otaki's Indian guard. "You!"

She closed her eyes. "Yes me. Is there a problem, ah, Agent Sworn is it? I thought the name was Waters."

"Just shut up about that. What are you doing taking pictures of me?"

"I wasn't." She said in a matter of fact way. "You just happened to be in the way."

I was an arm's length from her now. "Charles?"

"Correct. I'm checking up on something for my boss." She raised an eyebrow. "Last I heard, taking pictures isn't illegal."

I grumbled. "Why are you taking pictures of people in the middle of the night?"

She shook her head. "I don't have to tell you that. I'll just say Mr. Otaki will not be made a fool of." She climbed into her car and started it up. "The little man's hard to get a glimpse of. Thanks for the help. She winked and sped off."

I was left there, standing alone in the middle of the road feeling like an idiot.

# Chapter 19

The next day, Thursday, was uneventful. Fier stopped by my cubicle around noon and, since there was nothing else going on, decided to watch some of those information discs with David and me.

I had a hard time buying any of it even after everything I'd seen. We watched for a couple hours and I found myself shaking my head through most of it. The video confirmed that etherspring was in part generated from the actual energy or life-force of hailiorea descendants. It didn't go into extensive detail.

Later, it explained the original hailiorea were broken up into four groups: teachers, warriors, judges and healers. Each specialized in certain areas. The judges innately knew the truth, teachers brought ideas and clarity, warriors were the protectors and fighters and healers were doctors. I remembered Cross saying I was mostly a warrior. Big surprise.

The disc also talked about a race of evil beings called the osilea. They were supposedly demons of sorts which the original hailiorea battled fifteen hundred years ago. The video admitted all that could just be speculation and that research was ongoing.

I paid special attention to the part about people called the 'Controlled' and 'Controllers.' Apparently the Controllers were especially twisted, evil hailiorea who craved power far more than the average person. I immediately thought of Forrest and Morbal. The video said these Controllers were actually the Controlled. Strange. It was hypothesized that the Controlled were actually influenced by a dark force which may be remnants of Osilea.

The presentation jumped around a lot and was obviously a work in progress. After we'd had enough we grabbed a late lunch and then visited one of Prospous's city parks. The day was a sunny, seventy degrees and breezy, perfect. It was one of the most leisurely and relaxing afternoons I'd ever had.

David was still bursting with excitement over Forrest's capture and the marathon he had between the sheets the night before. It seemed whatever feelings he had for Fier were a distant memory. I still caught him rubbing his neck every now and then. I did the same.

The next day wasn't as relaxed. The morning started off calm but I was disturbed by a drastic, and I mean one hundred eighty degrees, change in David's mood. He became quiet, reserved and edgy. The change completely baffling me. I asked him what was wrong but he wouldn't say.

Around 11am my phone buzzed and I was alarmed to see Otaki was back in Prospous, spending time at a ritzy resort in the center of another city park. I pulled the latest information on the man and learned he'd been trying to set a meeting with Cross.

That was the last straw. I had to confront him. I remembered his guard, Nitya taking pictures after midnight. I remembered hearing that Kara's death was caused by someone in close proximity setting off the death device in her body. Otaki just happened to be in the base that night. Conveniently in a meeting which he requested be held there.

Then I remembered my headstrong blunder at *Club Aces*. Before I blindly went for Otaki I decided to play it safe and asked for permission.

Sarah Keen and John Durn were in charge that morning. I laid it all out, all my suspicions. It was obvious by their skeptical looks that the two doubted my suspicions but they let me go anyway, on one condition: I couldn't go alone.

David was free so I volunteered him. He didn't protest but didn't show any interest or excitement either. He only scowled and brooded the whole way to our car, plopped himself behind the wheel and started it up without a word.

I asked him again what was wrong and he only asked me for directions. Strange. I didn't like seeing my best friend, the most optimistic man I knew, in such a dark, mysterious place so suddenly. It didn't make any sense. But, he didn't want to talk about it so I respected his privacy and focused on Otaki.

We reached Green Arbor, an upscale retreat, and flashed our undercover badges, Waters and Stone, at the receptionist while asking where Otaki was. The young man nervously directed us to a gazebo in the middle of an open, green field.

I took the lead and stormed over to meet the developer. He wasn't alone, Nitya was absent but the man, Staal, I remembered, was there. So was Mayor Volkov which was unexpected but didn't matter.

Otaki saw us coming and gave a contemptuous look of disgust. He spoke after we stepped under the gazebo. "Oh lord, what do you want?"

I stared at Otaki, all but ignoring the others. "I have some questions for you."

"Don't use that tone with me, boy." The Asian man spat.

I growled, already annoyed. I didn't use any disrespectful tone… Whatever. "What are you doing here?"

"Having lunch." Otaki smirked.

My eyes narrowed. "Why do you want to see Cross?"

"That's personal business." He leisurely waved his right hand, dismissing me. "None of your concern."

I slammed my fist on the table. "Not anymore. I caught your servant taking pictures of a citizen in the middle of the night. You were seen at Club Aces. You were in our headquarters the night Agent Childers died. I know what you're up to."

"I don't have to tell you anything." He turned to the mayor. "Alexi, tell your pawn here to back off."

I cut my eyes over to Volkov. He shrugged. "Out of my league, Wang."

"You can answer my questions here or I can drag you back to base." I pressed both fists on the table and leaned toward him. "You're choice. Either way, you're going to talk."

"You're pestering is seriously beginning to annoy me, Waters... or is it Sworn?" Otaki's face was smug with pride having seen through my cover.

"That's your problem." I growled.

The man's eyes darted back at me, his long grey hair blew wildly in the breeze. "You don't have any grounds to take me anywhere or even question me for that matter."

"Wrong." I started for him but stopped when he closed his eyes, clenching them tight. The move caught me off guard.

Otaki drew in a deep breath and started humming. As the drone grew louder I felt the world start to spin. The ground under my feet seemed to become uneven. It was like gravity itself was shifting. I knew better.

"Stop, NOW!" It was hard to balance but I managed. His hailiorum talent wasn't going to stop me.

Otaki opened his eyes. "Fine." Sure enough, the Earth settled as quickly as it had acted up. He paused. "How do I know I can trust you, hmm? Your operation is swarming with spies and traitors."

Finally David spoke. "What?" It wasn't much but it was nice having backup.

I pressed. "Enough! Why do you want to see Cross?"

"Yes, traitors!" Otaki blurted. "But maybe you already know all about it. Are you with *them*?"

Having had enough, I reached out and grabbed the man by his expensive shirt, hoisting him out of his seat and over the table. "Talk!"

"Alright!" Otaki yelled.

Volkov interjected. "Calm yourself, Agent Sworn."

"I trust Volkov." Otaki began. "And now I trust Governor Cross again. I don't trust you! I need to tell him. It could doom me but I can't hold my tongue any longer."

I shook him. "Tell him what?"

"Sir!" Staal shouted. "Please, Sir. I beg just a moment of your time." He looked at me. "Sworn. I just need a moment with Mr. Otaki, please."

"Like hell!" I hissed at the bodyguard, staring into his small, bunched up face.

Otaki looked into my eyes and stopped squirming. "Release me and I'll tell you everything after a word with my associate." He nodded and his face lighted. "Please."

I dropped the man. He almost crashed to the ground but caught himself in time. I looked at Staal. "Two minutes. So help me, if you're not back here it'll be your ass."

Otaki straightened his clothes and snapped his fingers at Staal. "This had better be good, Jeremy."

The small guard's face white as a ghost. "Yes, Sir." He looked at me, nodded then followed after Otaki.

I watched them enter a small clubhouse not fifteen yards away. My gut fluttered with nervous uneasiness.

"What're they talking about?" David asked. He sounded as suspicious as I felt.

I didn't answer. Instead I started for the club house. It was a mistake letting them out of my sight. After only five steps, Staal bolted out of the small building. He wasn't as fast as Forrest or Charles but was still damn quick.

"Hey!" I yelled.

Without looking in my direction, Staal pulled out a pistol and shot at me. The thing was silenced but I could hear the bullet ripping through the air not far from my head. I dropped to the ground and called out. "David! Get him!"

By the time my friend had his weapon out; Staal was weaving through a group of startled guests. David couldn't risk taking a shot.

I cursed and pushed myself off the ground, rushing for the building. "Protect Volkov, call for help! I'm going for Otaki!"

I barged through the wooden door, nearly knocking it off its hinges. My eyes darted around, senses on full alert, unsure what to expect, weapon at the ready. A labored moan came from a room adjacent the small, empty lobby.

I moved, quickly yet cautiously inside. Otaki was there, laying and squirming in a pool of blood that appeared to be his own. I gritted my teeth and rushed out of the club house.

"ARE THERE ANY HEALERS HERE?" I hollered at the top of my lungs. "ANY HEALERS? HURRY!" I looked at David, he'd overturned the table and taken cover behind it with Volkov. "Call an ambulance! Otaki's been shot!" I rushed back to the man and knelt down.

His eyes rolled around in their sockets before finally managing to lock onto mine. He tried to speak. "I didn't know. I trusted that son of a -"

"Shh." I said, feeling helpless. Jesus, it was like Kara all over again. I couldn't take another person dying in my arms. "Calm down, breathe. Help is coming."

I looked at the hole in his stomach and grimaced. He was going to bleed to death. I'd seen it before.

Otaki lifted a bloody hand. I grabbed it and squeezed. "He's working for Forrest. He made me keep quiet. I'm a coward!"

I swallowed and tried to control my breathing. "Who? Who made you keep quiet? Staal? What is it?"

"No. Tell Cross… Tell…" Otaki drifted off. His eyes slowly closed. Blood dribbled out of the corner of his mouth. I could only watch.

David burst into the small room with a few others. "Jason! Move!"

I obeyed. The others huddled around the small man, already chanting and hovering their hands over the wound as soon as they were close enough.

I stood by David and watched. "Will he live?"

None of the three healers answered me.

-

Otaki's fate was still up in the air twenty-four hours later. It was Saturday and I had the day off so I visited him in the hospital. He was hooked up to series of machines being fed oxygen.

The doctors, some of Cross's very best, said they'd done all they could. The hailiorea healing may have only prolonged his life a little. Now it was all up to chance. He could recover, stay in his coma for an undetermined time or die any moment.

After Otaki was rushed to the hospital, David, Volkov and I headed to base to give our report. I told Chief, Cross and the three captains everything I knew about Staal and the missing Indian woman, Nitya Rai. They were both put on the highest watch list.

Before heading home for the weekend, Chief stopped me. He studied me for a long, uncomfortable moment before speaking. "I don't know what to think of you." He started. "You were a hero at Eaglebase but you always find trouble."

I gave him a thoughtful look, considering what he said. I didn't know how to respond.

That was it. Chief turned and strode away.

David drove us back to our apartments. He still wasn't talking and I thought I saw tears in his eyes at one point. I tried, one more time, to coax information from him. No good. He only snapped at me, telling me to buzz off in not so polite words.

Now I was sitting in my bland apartment, staring at the telescreen. It was showing some old movie about space aliens taking over people's minds. Before that it was a movie about a kid who was a musical genius or something. The clock mounted on one of my walls said it was almost three in the afternoon.

The whole time, my brain couldn't stop worrying and wondering about David. Eventually, enough was enough. I was determined to find out what was bothering him no matter what, even if I had to beat it out him. I slapped some sneakers on and marched over to the man's apartment.

He answered the door and let me in without much of a greeting. The guy looked horrible. His hair was a mess despite its shortness from our time at Morbal's. He hadn't shaved, his clothes were wrinkled and stained and he stunk.

The apartment didn't look any better. Beer cans littered the floor and dirty dishes covered several countertops and tables. The air in the place was stale and musty.

David collapsed onto his couch, staring blankly at his own TV. He'd been watching the same stupid movie I had on.

I sat down in the recliner next to the couch and huffed. "Ok, tell me what the eff's wrong. This is bull, I deserve better, damn it."

David groaned.

I stood, fuming, hands clenched into fists. "Stop! Talk to ME! WAKE UP!"

He quickly sat up and glared at me. "Fine! You want to know what's bothering me? Tearing me up inside? I've been a stupid, blind, ignorant piece of crap."

I looked at him like he'd proclaimed he invented the color red. "What the hell are you talking about?"

A mocking laugh escaped his mouth. "You were right, the whole effing time."

"About what? No more riddles! Spit it out!"

David looked at me. "Clear! Do you know how the stuff is made?"

"No effing idea!" It was hard to stop shouting.

My friend's eyes welled up and he shook his head. "It's made from the blood, skin, cells and negative energy sucked out from hailiorea."

I blinked. "What?"

"That's why those…" he struggled for the right word, "*bastards* took our blood and scraped the hell out of our skin after they tortured us." David gritted his teeth and snarled. "Morbal is nothing but a god damned drug dealer. He used us to make the crap and ship it out. It's how he's been funding himself and his little empire."

My mouth dropped open. "Whoa."

"And I, *I* helped sell the stuff. I used it, I vouched for it, defended it, told everyone how great it was." He was trembling now. "I contributed to our torture, our suffering. I'm a effing know nothing prick! GOD!" He roared, stood and stormed off toward his bedroom punching a hole in a nearby wall on the way.

I yelled after him. "It's not your fault. You didn't know."

I tried to put myself in David's position. Yea he'd messed up but I meant what I said. He didn't want to hurt anyone. Personally, I didn't see what the big deal was but it wasn't me who promoted the stuff. My friend had been a pretty heavy duty dealer for a long time. He always said it was harmless. Usually things like this rolled off his back. Not this time.

He came back into the living room in a white tee shirt and boxer shorts, holding a pair of jeans. "Not my fault? We're all responsible for our actions. I thought the crap came from a damned spider. That's only part of it." His voice fell. "God, I messed up."

I knew I couldn't fix this but was dumb enough to try anyway. "Look, it's done. You can't change what's happened. Now you know, let's move on."

David shoved a leg into his jeans. He looked at me, shaking his head. "You don't understand. All those people that suffered like we did. The torturing might've stopped if it weren't for me."

I almost found it comical that he thought he alone kept the drug alive, popular and in business. I wanted to tell him how stupid he was, but I didn't, not yet. "You know better than that." A pause. "How did you find all this out anyways?"

He was busy putting on his shoes now. "We found clear on a bunch of Forrest's followers. Fier told me all about the drug. I didn't believe her at first, then I looked the stuff up in our database. It's true. That's why Cross won't allow a grain of that stuff on the island. The crap is made from our fear, pain and hate. It's evil!"

"So this is why you've been pissed off the last two days?" I sighed and reached out for his shoulder. "Come on, let's go grab a beer or something."

"No!" He sprung to his feet. "I'm going to put an end to that junk right now!"

"Huh?"

David nodded. "There are trails leading back to the source from the traces we found. I'm going to find the dealers and wipe the effers out."

I raised an eyebrow. "Right now?"

"Right. Effing. NOW!" He grabbed his wallet and keys then looked at me. "Coming?"

Going to headquarters was the last thing I wanted to do but I didn't want to leave David alone. I nodded. "Sure."

David drove like a madman, swerving around cars and blowing through stop signs. He was in machine mode again only this time it was even more intense. He felt responsible and desperately wanted reprieve. Finding the dealers hiding on the island might help. Or it might not. I remembered all too well how I took revenge on my brother's killers. In the end all it caused was more pain.

We reached the base and headed down to our work stations. We passed the dreaded detention center on our way, sending chills up and down my spine. I nearly jumped out of my skin when the doors suddenly opened.

David and I stopped to look. Chief emerged and he gave us a startled look. "What the hell are you two doing here?"

David only stirred so I answered. "Some, uh, research."

Chief gave me a quizzical look. "Anything I should know about?"

"Not yet." David said shortly.

I looked at David and saw his face change from uptight and disturbed to fascinated and amazed. I followed his gaze and saw what, no who he was looking at. Samantha Forrest was coming through the doors behind Chief, shackled at her wrists and ankles, barefoot with shredded clothes and ratty hair. In spite of all that, she was still the sexiest creature I ever laid eyes on.

My mind wandered, fantasizing about the poor little slave girl. I licked my lips and prayed to whatever was listening that she'd be my slave girl. Then she'd turn the tide, overcome me, overpower me and make me her slave, forever. I wanted that so bad and my body reacted accordingly.

Chief slapped me across my face. "Sworn! Get a hold of yourself. Rub your damn neck!"

My neck was the last thing I wanted to rub.

"Holt!" Chief hollered. "Back off!"

I snapped out of the lusty daze and obeyed Chief while turning toward David. He was gone, head over heels in love and moving towards Forrest.

I lunged at my friend and pulled him away, forcefully massaging the back of his neck. "David! David, come on, snap out of it."

I heard Forrest purr lustfully. "Mmm, such beautiful men. Hi Jason. I missed you, sweetie. Can't you help me out here? I'll make it worth your while."

I looked deep into her emerald eyes. "Eff off, Bitch!"

David was slowly coming back to his wits and I continued to move him away from Forrest. He was still in a pretty thick haze.

"David!" Forrest called. "Come here, dear. You're the one for me."

Chief hauled off and punched the woman flush against the side of her head. She crashed to the floor, laughing.

I watched while still moving David away. Cross rushed up to Chief and Forrest from the detention wing. He looked at the woman and motioned a couple guards, speaking into a headset microphone. They were in full gear, helmets and all. "Get her up and let's get moving!" He looked at me, worry plainly clear on his tired face. "Are you two ok?"

I nodded and noticed how completely worn out Cross looked. "I think so." I gestured Forrest. "You go on ahead, don't worry about us."

The group moved on and we headed for our cubes. By the time we reached them, my friend's head seemed clear. He was back to his angry tormented self. I wondered what was worse, angry, guilt-ridden David or lust crazed David.

The man intensely worked his computer, tracking every place those who'd been found with the drug had visited. He jotted down names and notes with desperate ferocity, totally obsessed. I tried to help him check up on different places but he wasn't making things easy.

There were a lot names to check and David was behaving both erratic and unorganized. At one point I accidentally backtracked a couple men which he'd already looked into. He slammed his fist on the desktop and chewed my head off. "I already did them, you moron!"

I snorted, "Sorry, Dick."

David pushed me, not full force but enough to get my blood boiling. "If you're not going to help then get the hell out of here. You're only slowing me down!"

I couldn't take anymore and tried to convince him to go home and relax one more time. He ignored me, setting me off again. I told him I was going home and demanded the keys to our car. He handed them over without looking at me or saying goodbye.

Anger and defeat swelled in my gut as I left the base. I was also a nervous wreck driving home. It'd been years since I'd driven but I made it home without crashing.

The whole time I worried about David, doubting myself for leaving, feeling like I'd given up too easily. Still, he obviously didn't want me around and maybe focusing on his work would be like therapy for him.

After a long shower, plagued by an internal debate on whether I should go back or not, I planted myself back on my couch and eventually drifted to sleep.

# Chapter 20

I'd had lucid dreams a few times but this was different. I wasn't in control but I was still aware the world around me wasn't real. In the dream I was standing outside Forrest's cell, gazing at her perfect body. There were a couple men crumpled on the floor at my feet. They were either unconscious or dead, that wasn't clear. What was clear, somehow in my brain, was that I knew I was the one who'd put them in their place.

Forrest leaned against the far wall. Her wrists and ankles were shackled but she smiled. I only admired her, yearning to kneel before her. My brain played out fantasies of licking every inch of her skin.

She purred. "That's right, my love." Her voice was a song that made me tremble. I could hardly breathe. "I need you so bad." She moaned lustily.

I licked my lips, unable or unwilling to think of anything else. She was all that mattered. The whole world could burn in flames for all I cared so long as I could serve her, love her and give myself to her.

"Oh yes." She beckoned. "Come. I can give it all to you. Take me."

All other cares and concerns slipped away. I reached for the lock with excitement, burning with love, admiration and lust for the Queen trapped in her cell. Soon we'd be together.

"That's it." She winked. "Do it and I'll make it all go away. We'll be free. Free, Jason. Think of it."

I gripped the lock and started to pull. Soon. I knew there'd be no turning back after letting her out. She loved me and I was lost in her beauty.

"Open the door."

My vision blurred. It was hard to speak but I managed. "I love you."

"No you don't" said a voice that wasn't Forrest's. I ignored it. "NO... YOU... DON'T." The voice echoed.

I stared at Forrest's mouth. Her lips were soft, irresistible jewels. "Yes, Jason. Do it. For me."

I applied more force to the lock and could hear the restraints start to give way.

"Jason!" The voice, a different female voice called. "Look at me!"

It took every ounce of will to pull my eyes off my Mistress. I was more annoyed than curious. Who could be so inconsiderate to expect me to look away from the most beautiful sight in the world? I barely turned my head toward the neighboring cell.

It was Kara, bruised, bashed and bleeding. Her dark, sunken eyes bore holes into mine. I shivered. She shook her head. "No. Don't do it. Don't become like me."

I blinked.

"It's not too late." Kara said in a pleading voice. "Turn around and wake the eff up."

My voice quivered. "But," I shook my head, "we love each other."

"Turn away." Kara said as blood started gushing from her mouth. "Save yourself."

I looked back at the Mistress.

"What are you waiting for, my love?" Her emerald eyes glowed. "Hurry, before it's too late."

"I, I," I stuttered.

Kara screamed. "Wake up you stupid bastard!"

I pulled my hand back and felt my wits return. Anger quickly set in.

"Jason. Come here. Let me show you how much I care." She bit her lip and swiveled her perfect hips. "I'm ready."

I looked back at Kara who was now the shattered corpse I remembered, laying on the filthy, bloody floor. My head throbbed. I shook it. "No. No. I can't."

We stared into each other's eyes for a piece of time until Forrest pouted. "Shame. I guess you're not man enough."

I curled my lip and pounded on the thick glass. "Eff you! You've lost."

She shrugged. "You weren't my first choice anyways."

My eyes narrowed. "What?"

Forrest laughed. "That amazing specimen, that friend of yours." She nodded. "He's a lot better than you. Much more receptive. He'll do just fine."

I growled. "You stay away from him! I'll rip your god damned head off!"

"Oh I like that." She giggled. "So much passion and rage. How cute."

I reached for the lock again and pulled. The door opened. I wasn't going to worship her, I was going to shred her limb from limb. I stormed in, manic, and reached for her throat...

"Goodbye, Jason." Forrest's laugh rang in my ears.

I woke up and jumped off the couch. My legs were still asleep so I crashed to the floor, knocking my head on the small table between the couch and the telescreen. I cursed and crawled over to my phone. In a flash, it was dialing David's mobile.

It rang five times until his voicemail answered. I tried again and a third time, same thing each call. By now standing wasn't a problem. I dashed around my apartment, pulled on some jeans and shoes then grabbed my wallet, keys and pistol. I was out the door in seconds, racing for David's apartment.

The locked doors, one outside the building, the other to his home, were only a momentary setbacks. Each time, I stepped back, drew in a deep breath and kicked it with as much force as I had. The things each exploded.

"David!" I yelled, quickly scanning every room. The place was empty, looking exactly as it had when we'd left for base earlier in the day. I roared every curse I knew and headed out of the apartment.

"So, are you with *her*?" A slithery voice oozed from the dark. The speaker slowly stepped into the light.

I stopped dead in my tracks. Jeremy Staal's beady eyes were fixed on me. He had a gun in his right hand and it was aimed at my chest. I reached for my weapon while trying to move away but I was too slow. Staal fired and hit me in my gut. The blast blew me backward and I landed on my back.

The man didn't waste any time marching up to me. "I guess not." He aimed his weapon at my head.

A shadow moved in behind him and swung what looked like a baseball bat my attacker's head. It connected, knocking him to the floor.

I scrambled to my feet as best I could, punctured and bleeding, lunging for Staal. Somehow the would-be assassin was back up and barreling past the person who'd hit him and saved my life. He ran off.

I finally recognized the other man. Eric Rose. His blonde-white hair was hard to miss. The young man glanced at me before running off after Staal. He hollered back at me. "I told you I'd get that mother effer!"

I staggered after them, not even wanting to look at the wound in my belly. There was a good chance I'd bleed to death but it didn't matter. All I cared about was David.

Up ahead, I saw the silhouettes of two men wrestling. It was incredible Rose was able to catch up. One of the men finally overpowered the other. I got closer to see it was Staal who still stood.

By the time he acknowledged me I was on him, bellowing with hatred and grabbing him. Before he could even think of pointing his gun at me again, I picked him up and slammed his head through the front, driver's side window of a nearby car.

Staal's body went limp, half leaning inside the car from the waist up. I tugged on the back of his pants and whipped his body back. His head smacked hard against the concrete and didn't move afterward.

I didn't care if he was dead or not. Again, it didn't matter. I knew David was in serious trouble.

Eric was getting back to his feet. I called to him while heading for my car as rapidly as I could. "Don't be stupid! Call security!"

"HEY!" He called back. "Where are you going, you idiot? You're shot!"

I ignored him, focused on my mission. An icy wave flowed through me after I sat behind the steering wheel. It felt like the warmth of my body was slipping away. I ignored that too. David, I had to get to David.

I tore out of the parking lot and drove even more crazily than my friend had earlier that day. I made it to headquarters in what had to be record time.

The front parking lot looked normal so I rolled into the back. There was an unfamiliar van sitting near the back entrance that seemed out of place. It was running, smoking exhaust blew out from its tailpipe. I wanted to pull alongside it but my vision faded and I accidentally crashed into the thing.

My body rocked back and forth as the airbag went off, smacking me in my face. The car stopped moving so I stumbled out and nearly fell down.

"What the hell?" A woman's voice said from the back entrance. My blood curdled. I knew it was Forrest before I saw her. I started for her in a full rage, and then, then it felt like my heart was ripped out of my chest. David was walking beside the psychotic woman.

I couldn't move. I couldn't breathe. I saw his eyes when he passed through a trail of light coming from one of the many outside lamps. They were hallow, empty. They looked dead. I wished this was another dream. I almost prayed for it to be a dream. This couldn't be real, he couldn't be helping her.

He looked at me, and smiled. The son of a bitch smiled.

"Oh, it's you." Forrest laughed. "David, take care of him, please."

He strode up to me as the driver door of the van opened up and a man stepped out. The man was groaning with his head in his hands. The crash had rung his bell pretty good.

I stood there, nearly frozen in shock. "David?" I could only muster a whisper.

He moved within an arms width, reached out and pushed me. I stumbled backward until my back hit the undamaged side of the van and fell to a sitting position.

"David?" I said again. "What're you doing?"

Without a word, my friend reached into his pocket and pulled out his ether pistol. I could only sit there, bleeding, trapped in disbelief.

Before he could aim the gun at me there was a sudden, unnatural bend in the air. Some force pushed me harder against the van and David nearly lost his footing. I couldn't tell if I was hallucinating from the loss of blood but it looked like the light from the lamps actually swirled in the air. It was like a miniature black hole had suddenly sprung up out of nowhere.

The distortion disappeared as quickly as it arrived. In place of the weird shadowy pit was a man, dressed in black. I couldn't see his face since it was turned toward Forrest. His voice was icy cold. "They're coming, woman."

"My car's wrecked." Forrest shot back as she stepped up to the man.

He slapped her across her face and hissed. "Stupid, hailiorum mammal. You wouldn't get far with that anyways." He gestured David. "Call your pets if you want to keep them. We're leaving."

Forrest rubbed her cheek, barking at David and the driver. "Come!"

They obeyed, completely forgetting about me.

My voice quivered. "David... Don't go."

Either he didn't hear me or he didn't care. My friend glided over to Forrest's side, ignoring me. The strange man hummed words I didn't understand. Another swirl filled the air only this time I felt myself being pulled toward it.

The dark man, Forrest, the driver and David started to phase out of sight. Christ, they were vanishing! I managed a scream. "David! NO!"

He finally looked at me and smiled again. Then they were gone. I fell forward to the ground, landing on my face. New voices filled my ears just before darkness swallowed me.

-

I woke up and recognized I was in a hospital bed once again. Alarms sounded in my brain while as I quickly sat up. My body screamed with pain and my head felt like there was an entire percussion unit inside it. Damning it all to Hell, I didn't even waste time being thankful I was alive. I had to find David.

"You!" An unfamiliar voice said. "Just what do you think you're doing?"

I squinted at the loud person. She was old, even more prehistoric looking than the Golden Cup, and she was tall, well over six feet. She had dark skin, patchy gray hair and intense brown eyes. She laid her hands on me shoved me back into a lying position.

I grunted. "Get out of my way."

"That's the thanks I get for saving your life?" She scoffed, shaking her head. "Young fool, you're not ready, stay down or I'll strap you up!" She continued. "Hmph, crazy boy."

A perky laugh came from the other side of the room. "Don't bother, Sparks. He doesn't listen very well."

I labored to look at the other person. It was that young, happy, cheerleader like doctor... Chloe.

She smiled at me. "Hi, Jason. Glad to still have you amongst the living. You can thank Sparks for that."

"Thank me or don't thank me. Makes no difference." The old woman, Sparks said. "You just stay down."

I sighed. "Thanks. Now I have to go."

August Cross entered the room. "Where to, Jason?"

The man looked like I felt; beaten down, dead tired and completely drained of energy. His shoulders sagged and his normally bright eyes were droopy. He hadn't shaven and his natural smile was gone. His sorry look only made me angrier. I wanted to kick his sorry ass all up and down the hospital.

I curled my lip. "Where's David?"

Cross plopped down in a chair that was in the corner of the room. He sighed. "Sparks, Chloe." He took turns looking at each of them. "Thanks so much. Can we have a moment alone, please?"

The old black woman looked at me. "Ok. Just don't let him out of bed. The fool wants to go parading around already." They filed out of the room.

"Where's David?" I repeated with a raised voice.

"I don't know." Cross slumped even further. "With Sam I'm guessing."

That was it! I used every ounce of strength I had left to get to my feet so I could stare down at Cross. "Guessing?" My teeth clenched as I spoke. "Get off your ass and find him!"

Cross stood up and looked at me with pleading eyes. "Jason. He's shattered." His voice quivered and he bit his lip. "David is *gone*."

I howled, grabbed the man by his shirt with both hands and slammed him against the wall. "HE'S NOT GONE! If you would've killed her when you had the chance this wouldn't have happened!"

The Governor didn't fight back. He just looked into my eyes. His coolness forced my rage to subside. "Jason. If I could trade places with David I would but he made his choice. You have to let him go."

I released my grip. "Never. I can't." I stepped away, fighting for breath. I became aware I was only wearing a hospital gown. Eff it, I didn't have the time or energy to be embarrassed. I did, however, notice a heavy duty bandage around my stomach.

"We need to focus on Forrest, Jason." Cross spoke in a calm but disheartened voice. "She's the cause of this."

"How do we know David is shattered?" I said quickly, thinking aloud. "Maybe he's not totally gone yet."

Cross closed his eyes. "I saw the security videos. He killed," a pause, "murdered several people and injured others busting her out."

I only swallowed. It felt like my knees were going to give.

"And," he went on, "he knelt before her after releasing her from the cell. They embraced. When that happened, I could see her influence take full effect."

"What?" I tried to sound doubtful but failed.

"He's shattered." Cross sat back down and buried his face in his hands. "All that work, for nothing."

I studied the man. Part of me wanted to punch him and part of me felt sorry for him. I decided to spend what energy I had left constructively. "Then let's find her again."

Cross looked up at me. There was a hint of a flare in his teary eyes. He nodded. "We will."

"Where're my clothes?" I looked around the room and noticed another bed separated from mine. It was occupied by Wang Otaki. I blinked. "Has he woke up yet? He may know something."

"No."

I cursed then continued to search for my pants, shirt, underwear, shoes… anything.

"They're in the closet." Cross said in a robotic voice. "Sparks is going to kill me when she finds out you've been walking around."

I ignored him and made my way to a small closet against the far wall. There was a pile of the bloody rags I had on next to a fresh change of my own clothes. I turned to Cross with a confused look.

"Fier. She grabbed them for you. She's been by your side quite a bit."

I wasn't sure what to say about that so I just got dressed while Cross spoke. "Sparks is the best healer I've ever known. You would've died had it not been for her."

I looked at the Governor. "Where's Staal?"

"Was he the one that shot you?"

I nodded.

Cross grimaced. "He's gone. Eric Rose called in for a security unit but the man had vanished before they got there. Eric said he literally disappeared in a strange dark cloud."

I shook my head. "That's the same way David went. It's that dark man." I hissed. Amazingly, I could feel life coming back to my body. "Who the hell is he?"

"I have my guesses but I hope I'm wrong."

I pulled my shirt over my head and scoffed. "Ok, that tells me nothing."

"Sorry, Jason. I don't really know who or what he is."

I slid on my socks and shoes then stood up. I still felt like hell but it was nice being in real clothes. I shrugged. "What's our next move?"

Cross stood up and stepped close to me. "Listen, Jason. Our team is battered and short staffed. There's at least one traitor in our midst and I don't know who I can trust."

I studied his face, listening.

"We're going to give CT tests to everyone in security but in the meantime, I'm keeping the search for Forrest to a select few." He took in a deep breath. "You take it easy, rest, get your strength and watch after yourself."

I gave him an odd look.

Cross held quiet a few beats. "She came to you in your dreams didn't she?"

I knew the 'she' he referred to was Forrest. This was too private. "Ah, no."

The man grimaced and the color in his face faded. "Jason, do you know my strongest hailiorum gift?"

I shook my head.

"I'm primarily a descendant of truth. That means I can tell when others lie. It literally makes me sick to my stomach when people lie around me."

"Oh." I chewed on the information a bit. "I see. Yea, that makes sense, I guess."

Cross went on. "Do you know how the Cell Truth test works?"

"Basically." I was anxious to get out of the hospital. Cross was boring me. This may be interesting at another time but not now.

"Do you know why it works? What makes it work?" The Governor pressed.

I shook my head. "No, I don't. Cross I really need to -"

"I invented it using my own DNA." He let out a mild chuckle. "My blood, skin, hair, fingernails; they all work. When the device reacts to lies it's the small hint of my DNA that sets it off." His face showed a sad smile. He shook his head. "I never wanted to use my talent for anything like that, but it's helped make Aswain possible."

I tried to absorb what he told me but my mind was racing, thinking about my friend. Every second mattered.

He continued, "So I'll ask you to please not lie to me. Sam came to you in your dream."

"Yea."

Cross nodded. "She's interested in you which means she might make a move against you. Be careful. You could get hurt but her interests could lead us to her."

I tugged on my bottom lip, suddenly deep in thought. So I was possibly living bait. I could deal with that, anything to get closer to David.

"Call me if you find out anything, understood?"

I agreed. "Will do."

"Oh my Lord!" Sparks entered the room with Chloe behind her. "What on God's green Earth are you doing up? And dressed!" Her eyes bore into Cross's face. "I told you to watch him!"

Cross smiled. "He seems fine." I saw him wink at the old woman. "I'm not surprised though. You healed him. I can't believe he even needs the bandages."

"Oh, you're a big sweet talker, Mr. Cross but I'm not an angel. The man needs to rest!" She moved up to me and looked into my eyes. "The Boy's a shell of himself!"

I stepped back. "I'll be fine. I'm a quick healer."

"Quick healer?" Sparks exclaimed. Chloe giggled. "You were practically dead as a doornail not thirteen hours ago! Quick healer, my foot!"

Speaking of which. I looked at Cross. "What time is it?"

"Almost two o'clock."

Damn! Frantic all over again, I shook my head and raised my hands in an 'I have no time for this' manner. "I need to go."

"Go where?" Sparks asked.

Cross ignored her. "Calm, Jason. I'm on the case, trust me. You, take it easy."

I stepped out of the room with the Governor by my side. I talked while heading for the nearest exit. "I hope you're right. I hope she makes a move against me."

"Jason, you're the most resilient and determined man I've ever met." Cross said.

I made a dismissive sound with my lips. "Or the most stubborn and dumbest."

We were passing through the hospital lobby when a voice on a nearby telescreen caught my attention. I glared at it. "What did she say?"

"Once again, Jason Sworn, an upstanding member of our intelligence force was the hero who saved Mayor Krane during that awful attack." The woman reporter nodded at the camera.

There was a picture of my face in the upper left corner over her shoulder "News Six will have more on this exclusive story at five o'clock. Be sure to tune in."

I looked at Cross. He was dumbfounded. My life had just become a living nightmare. Who leaked the information?

Cross just looked at me. "I'll look into that too."

I swore a string of obscenities.

# Chapter 21

Seven cups of coffee over the next few hours helped transform me from an anxious mess into a jittery, angry one. My body hurt like hell from being shot. The healing helped save my life but it didn't do much for the pain.

It would've amazed me that I was up and about at all if I spared any consideration to think about it. Instead, I just felt guilty for leaving David alone. It was that guilt that drove me, now. It fueled the almost maddening, burning desire to find and save my friend.

With each cup I drank, I played over the last exchange we'd had. I remembered the zombie like slave Forrest turned him into. It nearly made me sick to my stomach. So much coffee didn't help either.

It was obvious I needed rest but no. I had to do something and sitting in my apartment wouldn't help David. Everything else fell by the wayside: Kara's death, Otaki's condition, Fier, my health; all secondary.

I meandered from coffee house to coffee house, hoping something would lead me to my friend. Maybe I'd get a call with some tips. No. Nothing. Just aches, pains, feelings of uselessness and coffee.

Not to say the time was boring, nor did I find any quiet time to sit and think. Rather than an outright physical attack against me, as Cross had feared, I was swarmed everywhere I went by people asking me if I was the hero who saved Krane. I lied every time. When the groups grew larger and more inquisitive, I moved on.

It was nearly 7pm and the Sun had set, allowing the chilly spring air to creep out from the shadows. While looking for yet another shop I wandered close to my apartment and decided on a quick shower.

The parking lot brought back memories of my fight with Staal. Everything was cleaned up. There weren't any signs of the car with the broken window where I'd shoved his head through. Moments later I was at my door. It wasn't locked. I must had forgotten to lock up in my mad scramble. I opened it and froze.

There were two bodies lying on the floor just inside the door, a man and a woman. My right hand reached for my weapon while my eyes scanned the dark apartment.

"Don't!" A woman's voice ordered from the darkness. "Hands up!"

I would've disobeyed but the light from the hallway was just enough to show Fier being held with a gun pressed against her temple. Son of a… I did as I was told, not wanting any harm to come to Fier.

"Good boy." The vaguely familiar voice said. "We've been waiting. About time you showed up."

"Who are you?" I spat.

"Down!" the voice yelled, frantically.

I was too confused to move. A beam of energy blasted from the hidden person's weapon and whizzed by my raised right arm. I could feel the heat of the ether bolt a split second before hearing a thump on the floor behind me. I turned. There was another man laid out, added to the pile.

While turned, my eyes caught a small blur blow past my door. It darted down the apartment building hallway. I couldn't tell if it was a man or woman but whatever it was, the form was gone in a flash.

"Damn it!" The woman said. She threw Fier to the ground. "It's him!"

When she stepped into the light I saw it was Otaki's guard, Nitya. She tried to rush past me to chase the speeding figure. No way, she wasn't getting away. As soon as the woman was in reach I wrapped my arm around her neck and yanked the gun out of her hand.

"Let go!" She struggled and squirmed.

"Like hell!" I turned my head slightly. "Fier! You ok?"

She was on her feet. "Yea, I'm alright."

"Turn on the light." I barked at her, kicking the door shut and then throwing Nitya on my couch. I aimed the weapon's barrel at her face and snarled. "Don't move."

The light was on and I saw the Indian woman smile. "I'm not your enemy, Sworn. I'm here because know I can trust you. I know where Forrest is."

I scoffed. "Bull."

"Jason," Fier began. "She's been telling me a lot. I think it's worth checking out."

I flashed a glance at her, she was dialing someone on her phone. My brow furrowed, confused by her calmness. She'd just had a gun pressed to her temple. "What? Who are you calling? What were you doing here, anyways?" I turned back to Nitya. "Where's your buddy, Staal? Where's David?"

Nitya gritted her teeth. "That traitorous son of a bitch isn't my buddy. Otaki's like a father to me, to both of us. Staal betrayed us."

"Damn it!" Fier exclaimed.

"What?" I asked, still focusing on Nitya.

"I can't get a hold of Cross." Fier slid her phone into her pocket, walked over to me and took the gun out of my hand. "I'll take that back, thank you."

As soon as she had her weapon back I pulled my own out and aimed it right back at Otaki's bodyguard. "Why are you trying to call Cross?"

"No time, I know who we can see." Fier spoke quickly. "My car's out front. Let's go." She gestured Nitya. "She's coming too."

"Going where? God damn it!" I was back in that all too familiar confused and pissed off place. "Who are these people on the floor?"

Fier swore and pulled her phone back out. "I need a security team at the Willow Apartments on Foust and Main, Jason Sworn's residence."

She went on with her call and I kicked Nitya's foot. "Who're they?"

The woman leaned back on the couch and actually managed to look relaxed. "They were your welcoming party. The first two showed up shortly after I did. Then the other's showed up just now."

I squinted.

Nitya shook her head and rolled her eyes. "They're hit men, get it? They were here to kill you."

"So let me get this straight." I smiled, sarcastically. "*You* saved me and then pressed your gun against her head?"

"Yes."

Fier put her phone away again. "Let's go. A team will be by to clean up this mess."

"Wait!" I put my arms out and looked at both women. "What the hell is going on? She was going to kill you!"

"You're an impulsive fool, Sworn." Nitya said in a nonchalant way. "And you're desperate to find your friend. It was the only way I could think of to keep you from shooting me on sight given the situation." He nodded toward Fier. "She agreed and helped me out."

I shook my head, about to ask follow up questions. There were so many other ways to go about telling me all this that didn't involve guns to peoples' heads. The whole thing didn't make sense. Fier stopped me before I started speaking.

"Done?" She asked. I looked at her, she was already half out the door. "Let's go!"

I followed without taking my eyes off Nitya.

-

We followed Fier to the front door of a rather large, expensive looking, perfectly maintained house. It was dark but lights from a small water fountain in the front yard showed how well landscaped and clean everything was. Large oak trees reached for the sky and the strategically placed hedges were well trimmed.

I could only wonder where the hell we were until Chief's large frame answered the door. He was wearing nothing but a pair of pajama pants, exposing his enormous upper body which showed a series of scars, the most recent of which came from Forrest's attack at the energy plant. He looked just as surprised to see us as I was to see him.

"What the hell are you doing here, Captain?" His eyes glazed over Nitya and me.

Fier snorted. "Sorry to bother you but it's urgent. I can't get a hold of Cross."

His eyes narrowed. "Come in." She breezed by him. Nitya didn't get through so easily. Chief acknowledged my drawn weapon. "Who are you?"

I answered. "This is Nitya Rai. Otaki's assistant. Staal's partner."

The big man's eyes blazed.

"*Ex*-partner." Nitya corrected with attitude. "Next time I see him I'll kill him."

Chief didn't budge an inch.

"Sir." Fier said. "She's with me. She has information on Forrest. You'd better hear her out."

The Scot folded his arms. "Oh, we will." He stepped aside, allowing us to enter. "Captain. Lead these two into my den and have a seat. I'll be right there."

"Over here." Fier beckoned. We followed and it was obvious she'd been in the intelligence head's home before.

What Chief casually called a den was bigger than my living room. I forced Nitya down on a large, leather couch while I took a seat in a matching chair across from her. The two were separated by an ornate glass table with various knickknacks resting on it. Fier sat down beside Nitya.

We didn't have to wait long. Chief bounded in the room and sat down in the open plush chair next to mine. He set a small device on the table and I instantly recognized the Cell Truth test.

"You." He shot at the Indian woman. "What's your name?"

"Nitya." She was already rolling up her right sleeve.

"Ok, *Nitya*. I'm not going to waste any time. Give me your arm." He bellowed.

I could only watch, fighting the uncomfortable feelings stirring in my gut. I knew the device served its purpose but the things always made me uncomfortable. Especially now that I knew a bit of August Cross's own cells were in it. Creepy.

Nitya, however, took it all in stride and actually looked pleased to have her arm prodded. Chief stuck in the needle and switched the device on. It let out a soft hum as it mixed the small, fraction of a teaspoon, amount of liquid with the woman's blood. A small ding later told us it was ready.

"Now, this will know if you're lying and you'll feel a sting you won't forget if you do." Chief said quickly.

I saw Nitya smirk. "I know. You're not my first." To her credit, the woman actually winked. Chief sighed.

"Where's David?" I blurted.

"Sworn!" Chief roared. "I'll ask the questions."

Nitya ignored the Scot. "I don't know. He's most likely with Forrest."

"Where is Forrest?" Chief pressed.

The Indian drew in a deep breath. "She's on Shard Isle, in Ravenfall."

Chief checked the test and nodded, approvingly. "How do you know that? What's she doing there?"

"Look." Nitya waved her left hand in the air and shook her head. "You suck at this. Just let me tell you what I know, ok?"

I nearly laughed at the look on Chief's face. He composed himself quickly. "Ok, go ahead. Not too fast though. I'm watching you."

Nitya chuckled. "First off, I'm helping you because Otaki wanted to help you. I also hate those bastards for what they did to him and they're after me so I really have no choice." She swallowed. "Otaki knows a lot more than I do, but he told me the Orb was headed for Shard Isle and that if Forrest escaped that's where she'd go."

"How did he know all this?" Fier asked.

Nitya looked at her. "He got mixed up with a bad crowd in Goldthorn where he was looking to start what would've been a very lucrative construction project. That dog-faced guy, Charles Black, approached him there. That little prick has been working with Forrest for a long time."

I heard Fier gasp and saw Chief's jaw clench.

"So that's why you were taking pictures of him that night?" I asked.

"Yes." She shrugged. "One of my gifts. I can track people a lot better with a fresh photograph. I don't know how it works, it just does. It's like a fresh scent to a bloodhound."

I raised my eyebrows and let out a sound that showed I was impressed. Damn it all to hell, I was beginning to like this woman.

"Ok, ok." Chief said in his usual annoyed tone. "So what did Black say or do to Otaki? How does this all fit together?"

"You know, you should only ask one question at time." Nitya said before continuing. "A few days before being hurt, Otaki told me Dogface threatened both him and Krane. My boss isn't a weak man and doesn't usually cave in to threats so whatever Black had over him must've been terrifying." She paused. "I suspect it's the same with Krane."

"Keep talking." Chief ordered while pulling out a mobile phone.

"Anyways, Otaki didn't know who to trust besides me and," she snorted, "Staal. So he stayed quiet, gathering clues as to what Dogface and his Mistress wanted. He said he'd been used to beat out the other builders competing for the Goldthorn job."

"Damn it!" Chief said.

I looked at him. "What?"

"I can't get a hold of Krane."

Nitya cleared her throat. "They probably got him too. He knows what Otaki knows."

Fier swore. "Ok, let's hurry this up."

I shook my head in agreement. "Right. We know Forrest is in Ravenfall. Let's get her." I left David's name out even though he was the one I cared most about.

"Wait!" Chief roared. I heard a shout from the other room telling him to quiet down and guessed it was Mrs. Chief. He lowered his voice. "You've been telling the truth so far but what does the construction deal have to do with anything?"

"Lots of builders were drooling over the land." Nitya said. "But Forrest wanted it too. She and Dogface made sure Otaki was in the mix to beat out the others. He's the best builder in the world, none of those amateurs can compare."

"But Otaki didn't get the contract." Chief said. "Mayor Burr from… Ravenfall…"

My heart skipped a beat and my mouth dropped open.

Nitya smiled. "I guess you boys do have some working brain cells in those thick skulls of yours."

"Mayor Burr?" Chief said.

Nitya licked her lips. "Forrest stayed with her for a while after she got into Aswain. Their plan was to have Otaki run off the competition then give up the job so Burr could snatch it."

"Why the eff didn't Otaki tell any of us?" I asked while standing up. I was ready to GO.

"Sit down, Sworn." Chief said coolly.

Nitya looked me in my eyes. "He didn't trust you."

"We're all in the same boat now." Chief said in a solemn voice. He swore. "...hard to know who to trust."

Fier spoke up. "This is as far as I've heard. Nitya, why would Forrest want Burr to get the Goldthorn assignment?"

The Indian woman was silent a few beats. "I don't know how accurate this is, but it all comes back to the Orb. Dogface helped create it. He always has that Soulphire on him. From what I've gathered, Forrest wants to use the Orb to spread her influence over the entire country."

Chief nodded. "We know about the Orb."

"Well, did you know that inanimate objects can serve as hub points for it to filter its power through?" Nitya asked with a raised eyebrow. "I've learned Forrest and some others work up some sort of spell on a large load of lumber in Burr's inventory. She wanted Burr to use that wood in her construction."

I looked down at the soft, fluffy white carpet under my feet and shook my head. This was almost too much.

"A permanent structure on the main island would make a great focal point where the Orb's power could filter through." Nitya went on. "It sounds crazy, but hey, *I* can track people, know what they're feeling, where they're going with a photograph so I think we can toss conventional logic out the effing window."

"That's it!" I was on my feet again. I'd heard enough. "Let's go! She's in Ravenfall. Let's get her."

Chief stood up too. "Sworn, don't let your feelings for David make you an even bigger fool. We need to plan. We need Cross."

I snarled and was about to reply but Fier beat me to it. "Where is he?"

"Resting." Chief said without taking his eyes off me. "He's exhausted after those intense sessions with Forrest. He should be up soon though."

"I can't wait for Cross!" I raised my voice and looked at Nitya. She was pulling the needle out of her arm. "Where *exactly* in Ravenfall is Forrest?"

She looked up at me. "The connection through my latest photo of Dogface is weakening but last I felt he was headed for Burr's house."

"That's where we're going." I stated with a nod.

Chief grabbed my arm. The strength of his grip nearly made me wince. "Like hell you are!"

"Sir!" Fier called. "Let him go. He's right. Time's short. We need to *move*."

Chief swore and let go of my arm seconds before I was about to start swinging fists at him. "Get out of here. I'm going to contact Cross and get ready. Meet us at headquarters."

"That's it, then? No more questions?" Nitya asked with a smart ass tone. "Aw, it was so nice chatting."

Chief rolled his eyes. "Get out of my house."

Nitya blew the big man a kiss and marched out. I was right on her heels and Fier was close behind. When we were outside the Indian woman fixed her large brown eyes on me. "I'm coming too. You're not leaving me behind."

I squinted, studying her, still skeptical as to her true intentions. "Fine. I'm not waiting, though. I'm going now."

Fier sprinted to her car. "Come on."

We ran after her. "Are you coming with us?" I asked.

She gave me a stern look. "You don't have authorization to use the rail. I do. *You're* coming with *me*."

# Chapter 22

The transport rail still astonished me, despite everything else going on. Not only were we moving at awesome speed toward Aswain's western coastline but it was also tearing through the short stretch of ocean leading to Shard Isle. I wondered how long it took to construct the tunnel underwater. It took us all the way to a small base in the northern part of Ravenfall.

Fier told us the entire rail system was one of the first things built on the islands. Cross put a lot of value on quick transportation from point A to B. I thanked whatever goodness there was in the world.

Back at headquarters, on our way to the train, we ran into John Durn. He had no intention of letting us go without Chief but a quick, little zap from Fier's ether pistol ended his protest. After he was knocked into la-la land, she took his weapon and handed it over to Nitya. It didn't feel right having her armed since I still didn't trust her but oh well.

We ran into a few guards at the base on Ravenfall who were surprised to see us. Fier flashed her badge and told them we were on a secret, urgent mission. It was the truth but she left out the juicy details.

The three of us hopped in an unmarked security car and headed for Mayor Burr's home. It was almost too easy but again, I was too frantic to care. All that mattered was that we were on our way to David.

By the time we reached the house, which was a giant wooden mansion, it was a little after nine o'clock. Fier parked the car a little ways out from the long, winding driveway that led up to the house's security gate.

A quick survey of the entrance showed two guards posted there. Fier initially wanted to talk with them and order them to let us by but I didn't think that was worth the time or risk. The two received the same treatment as Durn and were out in seconds. We pressed on.

There were several lights on in the house so we snuck around, peeking through every window, looking for activity. Nothing. We didn't see anyone inside so far.

I was pleased with how professionally Nitya moved. She'd obviously had practice in exercises like this. She was quiet, stayed low and kept out of the light like a pro.

Finally, after we made it to the backyard, we saw movement in what looked like a large entertainment room. My blood ran hot when I saw Forrest standing over Heather Burr. The Mayor looked like she'd been beaten and her wrists were bound. Then we saw Krane. He was sitting on a long couch, seemingly unharmed with his shoulders slumped and head down. He looked drugged.

Forrest wasn't alone. Puppy face, Charles Black was there as was Staal. Nitya's professionalism waned at the sight of the man. She was totally pissed and I had to physically grab her to calm her down.

Also in the room was that van driver from the last night and a fat, bald man I hadn't seen before. My heart sunk. There was no sign of David.

Fier gently touched my arm and pointed at a strange device resting on a table in the middle of the room. I wasn't sure, but I guessed it had to be the mysterious Orb.

Now that we were here, we had no idea what our next move should be. None of us had thought this far in advance.

My sails had lost their wind since I hadn't seen my friend. Maybe he was in another room somewhere…

Fier whispered. "It doesn't look like Burr's on Forrest's side. We need to get her and Krane out. And we need to get the Orb."

"I'm going to fry those two!" Nitya said with as much ferocious emotion as her lowered voice would allow.

"No!" Fier scolded. "We need to make sure the Mayors make it out alive. We'll take care of the others once those two are safe."

The whole time, I remained silent. My brain was a mess. Where the hell was David?

"Jason!" Fier urged.

I looked at her.

"Still with us?" She asked.

"Yea, sorry." I nodded.

"And how are we going to do that?" Nitya asked in regards to Fier's plan.

As fortune would have it, Forrest and her entourage suddenly exited the room, leaving Krane and Burr alone.

"Now!" Fier announced. We followed her to the back patio door. She gave it a pull and as luck would have it, the thing was unlocked.

We crept in as silently as a cool breeze.

"Simon!" Fier whispered, urgently.

The man whipped his head around and when he looked at us, I could see his eyes were red and filled with tears. "What are you doing here?"

"Shh!" Fier rushed over to Burr and examined her bindings. "Jason, get the Orb!" She ordered.

I went for it and spared a glance at Krane. He was holding something, something that looked like a pair of women's underwear. Startled, my brain flashed back to Kara and the way she stroked Forrest's stocking that day I was held captive…

"Wait!" I exclaimed.

Too late, before I could move Krane pulled out a weapon and fired it at me. It was another ether pistol and the blast merely grazed the left side of my chest. Even that was enough to knock me to the ground. I didn't go unconscious but I was unable to move, my body went into spasms.

Neither Nitya nor Fier could react in time to a dark blur that blasted in through the same patio door we'd used. Both women were on the floor and weaponless in seconds. The blur materialized into that damned dark man from the night before.

Forrest and her team rushed back into the room. She studied the three of us and smiled. "You see, now we have what we need."

"Shut your mouth, witch." The dark man hissed. "You knew nothing. Had we not been here to baby sit you, these fools would've escaped with the Orb."

We? I wondered who else the man was referring to.

"I helped, my Mistress!" Krane said gleefully. "Won't you love me again, now?"

Forrest gave the mayor an evil stare. "You're pathetic. I wish you would've died in that assassination attempt."

Krane fell back to his sitting position, looking sad and pathetic, a stark contrast to his normal happy, Elvin look. "But you wanted to kill Cross. I've always been loyal!"

The dark man slapped Krane. "Silence your pet! We can't stand hearing it talk."

My face wanted to make a confused expression but couldn't yet. He said 'we' again. I wondered what the hell he was talking about and assumed he was just crazy like the rest of them.

"Doctor, Elliot," Forrest motioned the two men standing near Puppy Face. "Put the would-be heroes on the couch."

Before I knew it, my limp body was tossed alongside Fier and Nitya on a couch across from Krane. I could feel my strength slowly returning but it didn't matter. The men had our weapons aimed at us and they were set to kill.

I knew we were screwed with nothing to lose so I roared. "WHERE'S DAVID?"

Forrest looked at me and let out an evil laugh. "David? I sent him home."

NO! I was able to shake my head in horror, hoping beyond hope she didn't mean what I thought she meant.

Another laugh. "The boy was payment to my partner, Maledro Morbal, for all the clear he supplied me. The good Doctor didn't like the idea of Cross stealing his property. Cross's attack set things in motion much sooner than they would've happened." She giggled. "So, as you can see, your freedom has led to the hasty fall of Aswain." Forrest raised her eyebrows. "You're his property too, but you won't be going anywhere."

I closed my eyes, fighting back the tears. I wanted to scream, maybe I did.

"Don't be sad, Sweetie." She spoke in a soft tone.

Fier barked in contrast. "Shut up, BITCH!"

Forrest gave her a devilish smile while she stroked the side of my face, continuing to speak in her smooth, sexy voice. "We needed the clear for the Olorus Orb. Charles here helped create it. The pain and suffering that makes the drug offers energy the Orb needs. It *feeds*."

I opened my eyes. My vision was clouded with tears but I could see the so called doctor smiling. He spoke "It also helped create that lovely device my Mistress instructed be put inside her followers."

"I helped too, fool." Puppy Face chimed in. "You'd have nothing without my invention!" He looked at Forrest. "My Mistress. I did it, you know that right? You love me most, don't you?"

Now Krane was on his feet, stamping up and down. "I was the one who triggered it in that agent Cross got his hands on. She would've cracked and told them everything had I not set it off!"

I couldn't breathe. Krane killed Kara. He was with Forrest the whole time. I looked at him. "You were the one who wanted the meeting in headquarters, not Otaki."

"That's right!" Krane looked at Forrest again. "See! That was my idea too!"

"Enough!" The dark man yelled. "We'll EAT the next creature that speaks on such insignificant matters."

Forrest turned to the dark man. "We have our sacrificial lambs now. Let's start the ceremony."

The dark man smiled. The gesture was one of the most heinous things I'd ever seen. He spoke in a cool voice. "Yes."

"Will we need to shred all three of them, or will just one suffice?" Forrest asked. She looked at us and licked her lips. "It'd be a pity to kill all of them. I could use more slaves and these three are so delicious. They'd serve me well, corralling any strays."

The dark man moved over to Forrest and punched her in her gut. She fell to the ground. I saw the others in the room, her slaves, wince. They looked like they wanted to attack, to defend their Mistress but were too afraid.

"We'll kill all of them." He said. "And your delusion of controlling this collection of hailiorea pigs is just that." The man spit on the floor, barely missing Forrest's face.

"What are you talking about?" She asked in a startled tone, standing back up.

The dark man let out a single chuckle. "You wasted your chance. The hub hasn't been set up on the mainland. The Orb's energy will be used instead to bring us fully into this world. We're tired of this pathetic form."

Forrest's face showed a mix of horror and rage. "That wasn't the arrangement and you know it! We even stepped up the timeline on Morbal's request!"

The man hissed. "Arrangement? You swore allegiance to US, hailiorum. *WE* are your master now. You don't have the energy to take on Cross, much less his little island."

"I do!"

An inhuman growl belched out from the dark man. "YOU DO NOT! You're weak, petty and insignificant! You're only use now is to activate the Orb. Shred these three and start the process in motion. Then watch as we rip this island apart!"

Forrest bowed her head. "It doesn't have to be this way, my Lord."

The man's eyes blazed. "Do it now and we'll let you live to rule the few, beaten down, sick, wasting scraps of *life* we leave behind. Fail us, and the flesh we're wearing won't be the only matter that gets ripped to pieces tonight!"

Not really following the pointless banter, I noticed I could move my entire body again. Not that it did much good. I was frozen with dread, given over to despair. David... back at Morbal's... Oh god. He'd be tortured mentally and physically, mutilated, worse than what happened to Mark. Why?

Fier started to squirm. Her mobility was coming back too. I glanced at her face. She looked brave, strong and determined. There was also something else when she looked at the dark man. A flame burned bright inside her. I could see it. She showed a resolution I could almost remember feeling myself.

I looked at the man. He wasn't a man. He was something else, something evil, something that HAD to be stopped. The same flame I sensed in Fier began to burn inside me too. He was the enemy. Something inside told me, this figure, which pretended to be a man, was the essence of everything corrupt and vile. I despised it. Passion bloomed in me. The god-damned blight of a thing needed to be stamped out!

Forrest finally caved. Her dreams of ruling Aswain died right there. She knew she was beaten and grudgingly headed over to Nitya, Fier and me.

Before she reached us, a blinding explosion of light blew through the patio door. The energy shattered the glass and destroyed half the wall adjacent to it. After the shock and debris settled, I saw figures standing in the freshly made hole. Chief was easy to recognize. Then I saw Durn's round form, two other men and in the middle, August Cross.

The explosion didn't even budge the dark man. He only stood and stared at the new comers. His voice cut the air, feeling like an icy claw. "Malerafi ect omolruus. Effing hailiorea."

He literally *flew* at them. A dark, wispy quilt fanned out from his arms and swallowed the group.

I heard them fighting but didn't watch. My attention was on the men who'd been aiming pistols at Fier, Nitya and me. They were on the floor, knocked down by the explosion, slowly getting back to their feet.

I jumped on the nearest body, the driver, Elliot, and let loose a series of blows to his head. By the time I eased up to search for the gun he'd had, his face was a bloody pulp. To my satisfaction, Fier and Nitya were up and fighting as well.

An ether blast surged past my ear. I whipped my head around to see it land square against Staal's chest. He was dead before he hit the floor. I picked up an abandoned ether pistol and glanced back for the source of the blast. Nitya's face wore a satisfactory look.

Fier had a weapon and was firing a barrage at Krane and Forrest who'd taken cover behind an overturned entertainment center. The Aswain captain defended Burr as best she could.

I was ready to fire my own weapon when a pair of hands grabbed my left leg and threw me through the air. My body crashed into a nearby wall. Black, armed with a wicked looking knife, charged me. The lethal weapon was aimed at the scar on my neck.

I swung my legs out and kicked the little man square in the jaw. The blow sent him reeling back. Now that he was off my back, I fired a few shots at Forrest.

We had her pinned and she knew it. Surprisingly, she grabbed Krane by his shirt and tossed him like a spear at Fier and Nitya. The collision knocked all three to the ground.

Forrest was on me before I could think, knocking the gun away and digging her nails into my throat.

I head butted her directly in her nose, shattering it. Blood splattered my face. After another good head bashing, I grabbed her by her shoulders and slammed her hard to the ground.

She wasn't near giving up. The woman was up on her feet nearly instantly. She kicked me in the groin.

The sickening pain only made me angrier. I kicked her back, flush against her ribs. She fell to the floor then I dropped a knee on her face. The sound of crunched bones fed my fury.

I planned to pick her up while she was down and break her neck but was interrupted when a chair slammed into the back of my head. I stumbled forward, tripped over Forrest and fell to the floor.

Puppy face was back up and on the offensive. His blade was coming at me again, ready to slice the life out of me. He drew closer until an ether blast lanced out and hit him in his head. The speedy, little inventor was no more.

I looked to see who'd made the shot. Fier.

While I was distracted, nearly getting killed, Forrest had gotten to her feet and charged Fier. She yanked the weapon out of the Captain's hand, turned the barrel on her and prepared to squeeze the trigger.

The young Captain was as quick as she was beautiful. She dropped and rolled to the side, away from the blasts.

I barreled into Forrest taking her to the ground with me. She snarled, pissed off and bloody as hell. We both got up quickly but she was a step ahead and landed a kick to my face. My body jerked backward. When I re-aligned myself, Forrest was rushing out of the room with the Orb in her hands.

Fier and I chased after her, running through the chaotic war going on in the room. Durn and one of the others with Cross were sprawled out on the floor. Chief was holding the dark man by his arms and the Governor was punching him in his thin, sharp, dark eyed face.

I wanted to help them but I wanted to help Fier more. Besides, Forrest had the Orb. The two were faster than me so I followed a trail of overturned furniture that led to the front door.

Outside, the two women were wrestling. I bounded for the Mistress, bear hugged her and threw her to the ground. As I did so, an explosion went off inside the house. The blast wave knocked Fier to the ground. She landed hard on her head and stopped moving.

Forrest stood and started hobbling away. I gave chase but before I could reach her, a set of vice like hands grabbed me by my waist, lifted me into the air and slammed me down. I landed on my left shoulder and heard an odd 'pop.'

I looked up to see the dark man's black eyes beaming down on me. I cursed and tried to scramble away. He had me, game over. To my surprise, though, the man stepped over me, his gaze was fixed on Forrest.

"Start the Orb. This *thing* will serve as sacrifice." I thought he was referring to me but I quickly realized the man was regarding Forrest's slave, the doctor. One of the slave's eyes was swollen shut but he smiled, raising his arms in the air. "Use me! I love you!"

I looked at Forrest and was surprised to see tears in her eyes. "Come here!"

In the time it took me to struggle to get to my knees, Forrest had set the Orb down on the grass in front of her. Her pawn was standing over it with a psychotic smile on his fat, dumb face. The woman put one hand on his head and the other over his heart then spoke words I didn't understand.

I could only watch as a strange glow surrounded Forrest's hands and the doctor started to scream. The bloodcurdling was intense but brief. The man's lifeless body collapsed and so did Forrest. She placed her still illuminated hands on the Orb and the thing pulsed, sucking in the light.

"NOW!" The dark man yelled.

Forrest picked up the Orb, pointed it at her master then spoke in the strange language again. Nothing happened.

I grunted and stood up, shooting a quick glance over at Fier. To my relief, she was working on getting herself up. I turned back to the dark man who was smiling.

"Did it work?" Forrest asked.

The man didn't speak. He slowly moved up to Forrest, reached out his left hand and brushed her bloody cheek. "Oh yes. But we need more. The Orb is still filtering."

The woman closed her eyes and nodded. "Sworn will do. Let's take him."

She turned to me but the dark man's hand grabbed her arm. "No. He's not good enough. He hasn't given himself to us yet. You have."

Horror flooded Forrest's face. "WHAT?"

I saw the dark man's face change, his eyes sunk into his skull and his hair withered away. His right arm looked like it had melted, turning into a thin, sharp spear. He drove the pointy lance straight through Forrest's throat. The woman gurgled for a moment then fell silent. Her lifeless body was tossed to the ground and the dark man turned to Fier and me.

I should've been terrified, I should've turned and ran. This creature was powerful beyond anything I'd fought before. Instead, I felt alive. A strange surge of rightness grew in my chest, in my heart. This *thing* was the enemy.

I stood my ground and puffed out my chest. The pain in my left shoulder wasn't bothering me anymore but I knew I couldn't use the arm. Fier stepped up beside me.

She uttered one sick, revolting word, filled with as much disgust as I felt. "Osilea."

I nodded.

The thing continued to change, no longer resembling anything human. Its clothes had flaked away and its skin turned into thick, black scales. Both arms were now sharp tipped spears and another appendage sprung up from its back. Most revolting of all were the mouths began to open up all over its body and face. They were filled with lethal sets of teeth.

I'd had enough. My tone was even, calm and focused. "Fier. My shoulder is out. Can you put it back in?"

There was no question or hesitation from the woman. She grabbed my left wrist and placed her free hand behind my shoulder. A sharp tug later and I could use my arm again. I didn't know how I knew she could fix me but I didn't care. The instant I was whole again, I rushed the monster.

When I was close enough I kicked the thing square in its chest. It flew backward, fell to the ground, rolled and hopped back up. It bounded for me and swung its arms. I ducked under the first but the second hit me hard in my chest sending me sailing through the air.

Fier picked up a large rock and crushed it over the thing's head. It roared and kicked her in the stomach. She fell back.

I was getting up for another attack when I heard voices call from behind me. I turned. Chief was holding Krane, Cross was holding Durn, and Nitya was standing beside one of the other men who was carrying Burr.

Cross's eyes were locked on the creature. They almost glowed with intensity. His chest heaved. "Jason, stay down."

Both he and Chief dropped the men they were carrying and aimed their weapons at the thing. They fired, both hitting it dead on. The monster hardly even stumbled.

A voice seemed to ooze from the creature's body. "Not complete yet. Soon."

Cross and Chief fired again and again. The ether blasts did little, if anything. I was done staying on the sidelines and rushed the thing. This time I laid a series of punches, careful to dodge the maze of snapping mouths. The beast stumbled back a bit but didn't fall. It only continued to change.

While it was backing up, Fier rammed her body into its back, pushing it toward me. I punched it has hard as I could in what used to be its head. Unfortunately, all the blows did was rip through the thin flesh covering my own knuckles.

Chief entered the fray, bellowing a primal roar. He picked the monster up and crashed it to the ground. Bolstered by the man's action, we all began kicking it.

Still, the damn thing didn't seem to mind one bit. Our attacks seemed useless. It finally rolled in a circle and took out our legs.

I scurried away from the creature and heard Chief scream. When I looked, the dark thing was on top of him, hacking and slashing.

Cross whizzed up and grabbed both spear arms. He pulled the demon off Chief and threw it a good distance away. Rather than wait, the Governor charged. I saw he was armed with a blade of his own. I rushed to help.

Nitya and the other guard only stood and watched, unsure what to do to help. Hell, I didn't know what to do either but I wasn't going to stand by while the thing changed and ripped us to pieces.

Cross was slashing his weapon while ducking and weaving under the beast's attacks. His quick movements were dazzling.

I rounded behind the creature and grabbed hold of two of its three spears, giving Cross an opening. "Do it!" I yelled.

Instead, I was shocked to see Cross run the edge of the blade over his own left palm. Blood oozed from the slice.

"What're you doing?" I cried.

The beast struggled and I was losing my grip, slipping on the collective blood and gore. The Governor smirked and planted his bloody palm flat on one of the snapping mouths.

With a quick, sudden shake, the creature threw me off its arms and I was on the ground again. It bound backward, away from Cross, seemingly frightened. The dozens of mouths instantly closed up and vanished. Now the beast was nothing more than a nightmarish, scale covered blob with two legs and three thrashing tentacle like spears.

"Our blood!" Cross shouted. "It can kill it!" He charged the demon. It kicked him flat in his chest and sent him flying backward, the blade fell from his hand.

Finally, Nitya and the other guard charged. Fier wrapped her arms around the creature's legs, trying to bring it down and Chief was slowly getting up.

I picked up Cross's blade, threw myself on top of the thing and drove the edge down into where its head had been. I carved out a large chuck of the asphalt like skin until it bucked me off like a tossed bull rider. It also thrashed its limbs and sent Fier back.

Nitya had picked up one of the abandoned ether guns and shot the thing over and over. Stupid. The beams didn't do anything.

"Move!" Cross roared, grabbing the creature, somehow able to overpower the demon which had tossed me aside like a rag doll. He forced it down to its knees then managed to turn its own spears in on itself. The lethal tips dug into its scales and dark blood poured out from the holes. Fier had gotten back up and was busy tugging back the third spear which was aimed for Cross's head.

I helped just in time. As soon as I had a good grip on the spear, the monster backed up and tripped the Captain, causing her to lose her hold.

The thing bellowed and pulled its spears out of its own wounded body, flinging Cross in the process. It bounded after him, pulling me along, and slammed both tentacles against the sides of the Governor's head. His body collapsed.

Now I was alone with the creature. Nitya and the guard tried to help but the man was knocked upside his head and the Indian woman was stabbed through her shoulder, then tossed aside.

It moved to make the killing blow on Cross. Every ounce of my being surged. I screamed and tugged with all my might, just barely able to yank the savage creature away from the Governor, saving his life. It lunged at me and shoved me onto my back. I kicked the thing's knees, knocking it to the ground then leapt to my feet.

Now I was standing over the creature but its spears were still ready to strike. Cross regained his wits and hurled himself at the thing, grabbing up two of the tentacles in his arms. The third struck at me, I moved just in time to keep from getting killed and caught it under my right arm.

I could feel the power of the monster as it whipped me around with ease. I held on. Cross growled and closed his eyes, straining. Unbelievably, he managed to snap one of the tentacles in half.

The demon jumped up and turned its full attention on Cross. I still held on. The remaining, intact spear the Governor had been holding slithered free and was now driving for the man's throat.

I reached for it and missed, still holding the third spear back. Blood gushed from the open wounds on the creature's head and chest. I gritted my teeth and pulled the point of the spear toward my own neck, right at my scar. The tip easily tore through the tissue and I winced, feeling my own, warm blood race out. Throwing the spear aside I climbed the monster's back and planted my wound right over the gaping hole on top of its head. My blood drained into the thing's gaping wound and it went wild.

It started spinning around like a hurricane, whirling and whirling. Cross and I were launched away and the creature fell to the ground in full out spasms.

"Now!" Cross shouted. "All of us!"

He ran to the convulsing monster and we followed. "Bleed into it! Hurry!" Cross followed my lead and sliced his other hand with one of the spears, then shoved them both inside the holes on its chest. Everyone followed suit, Nitya, Fier, Chief, the guard; each took their turn as the creature started to actually dissolve away.

Moments later, as if it had never existed, the Osilea was gone and we all sat around panting and bleeding. We'd made it up to Burr's porch and examined each other. Chief was the worst off of the living but seemed ok. He even gave me a salute and shook my hand.

"I was wrong about you, Sworn." He nodded with as much respect as his beaten body could show. "You're a true warrior."

I shook his hand back and let the feelings of victory surge through me. We had the Orb, Forrest was dead, Fier was ok and things seemed in order. Even though it was horrible news, at least I knew where to find David.

Above all, I felt incredible from killing the creature. It made me feel like I could accomplish great things, overcome any obstacle. I *could* and *would* find David. I wouldn't lose him like I lost my brother. I'd find him and save him. I helped destroy an Osilea, I could do anything.

A scream came from inside the house. I turned to see Forrest's driver aiming a gun at my face. Quicker than the mad man could pull the trigger, Cross had my would-be killer's head in his hands. With incredible speed and ease, the Governor of Aswain snapped his neck. He let go and the body crumpled to the floor.

Cross sighed and looked at me. "Unfortunate." He grimaced. "But I think that makes us even."

I locked eyes with Fier and we just stared at each other.

# Chapter 23

"I'll have another coffee." I told the young waitress when she asked if I wanted anything. She nodded and headed off. I watched her go and told myself to enjoy this next cup. The food and drink in Tehlasrin couldn't compare and there was no way to tell how long I'd be gone.

Things settled pretty well in the five days following Forrest's death. Her remaining followers were rounded up and placed under deep psych evaluations. Every single guard on Aswain's security force took the CT test. After the checks, trust quickly returned.

Most of us were given a few days off to relax and mend any wounds we might have. I spent some time with the Cup who were all concerned for David. They talked a lot about the Osilea, amazed some of their theories on the creatures had been confirmed true. The monsters were indeed evil beings which the hailiorea were meant to hunt and destroy.

Harry, the gruff, silent Cup member, pulled me aside from the rest of the group and expressed the importance of our fight. "It's a true battle between good and evil." He told me. "The forces behind the atrocities in the GU are swayed by the dark. *We're* the ones charged with resisting them."

Krane was removed from office and I still found it hard to believe he'd been in league with Forrest for weeks before I even arrived on Aswain. I later found out Forrest had her eye on David and me from day one. He confessed Morbal had told her all about us. He was also the one who told the press that I was the one who saved him. Bastard. Forrest wanted me dead after resisting her and she figured I'd be an easy target if everyone knew who I was, including those whose friends or relatives died during the attack on Krane.

Fier and I spent a lot of time together and I stopped denying my feelings for her. Even when I'd rub the back of my neck I still had butterflies in my stomach every time she smiled or flirted with me. She was also sick about David but didn't believe he could be saved.

She, Chief, Cross, Durn and Nitya all recovered from the fight with the osilea and Forrest's group. The Indian woman was now a proud member of the intelligence team. Cross offered her the position in his hasty, trust of character way and she accepted since Otaki, who'd survived, had retired.

My own body was nearly back to normal. My head, unfortunately, wasn't. I couldn't rest knowing my friend was locked back in that god damned asylum. Cross checked with some of his contacts and confirmed David was indeed back at Morbal's rehabilitation center. I only asked the Governor once for help and the man sadly told me there wasn't any hope.

I didn't hold anything against Cross. He'd earned my respect and I knew he truly believed what he said. Besides, he had a lot of bigger things to worry about. Where I was concerned about David, he was responsible for Aswain and issues around the world. He told the intelligence team that the GU was in upheaval and becoming more unpredictable with each day. The Union could even attack at any moment. He needed to fortify the island, the last free nation in the world, as best he could. Yea, full plate there.

So, I decided to take matters in to my own hands. I knew it was reckless and doing so often ended badly but I didn't see any alternatives. I had to try. As prepared as ever, I was still disturbed by some of the methods I needed to resort to. I had to do things I wasn't at all proud of.

First, I needed money. The quickest way I could think of was to steal the Soulphire from the intelligence vault and sell it to Crow. The man paid me the fifty thousand gems he promised. Once he had the jewel he became a completely normal person, no longer plagued by 'ghosts.' So, the orb was still secure but, without the missing piece, it was useless.

Second, and far worse, I had to steal Fier's list of resistance contacts in Tehlasrin. She and I had gone out the night before and she had too much to drink so I walked her home. Once there, she told me how much she cared for me. David had been right. I laid her down in her bed and she gave me a passionate kiss before passing out.

I searched her home and soon found the contact list. I left a note trying to explain things but I doubted it would do any good or that I'd convey any of my intentions or feelings well. The woman would feel angry and betrayed. I felt like a worthless pig. Fier is an incredible woman and I admired her. Hell, I loved her. Yea…

Still, I didn't see any other way. I was going to save David and I needed to know who I could trust in the forsaken Union.

I also sent a letter to Cross which included my badge. I didn't feel worthy of keeping it. Aswain was heaven. People were free and able to actually *live*. They could take their lives and make them better. They could prosper. I loved everything the island nation stood for.

So there I sat, at the Sadgport docks lobby, ready to leave it all behind, bound for Morbal's asylum. I had money to bribe guards, a list of people to contact for help, two ether pistols and a bolstered resolve after destroying that osilea. Not much, really, but it would have to do.

For what they were worth, I also had my hailiorum gifts. I still didn't know much about them, what they could do or even where they came from, but I hoped they'd help save my friend.

The waitress set my coffee down. "Anything else?"

I didn't speak so she moved on. A confident smirk popped up on my face and I muttered to myself, "I'm coming, buddy. Hold on."

My brother would be proud.

# About the Author

This is the second completed novel by Adam Austin and the first in the Hailiorea series. He nearly always has other works of fiction in progress and currently lives outside Phoenix, Arizona. Aside from writing, Adam's interests are in music, film, outdoor activities, history and captivating fiction. More than anything, he enjoys spending time with his family both at home and around the country.